# THE HEROES

# THE HEROES

LEGEND OF THE SPEAR SAINT
BOOK THREE

A. T. Valentine

Podium

*For my family*

Published in 2026 by Podium Publishing
Los Angeles, California

Cover design by Narendra B Adi



ISBN: 979-8-89539-399-4

Library of Congress Control Number: 2026939484

www.podiumentertainment.com

Podium

# THE HEROES

## CHAPTER ONE

# Steps to Recovery

The spear's shaft met the edge of a sword in a cascade of sparks, both weapons spared from damage only by virtue of their quality and the thick mana coating them.

Rowan took several hurried steps back in response, trying to stay well out of range of his sparring partner's retaliatory strikes. The spear demanded he keep his enemies at a relative distance.

In spite of that, he needn't have bothered, really. His partner's follow-up strikes steadily grew slow and sluggish. Their initial ferocious power trickled away into nearly nothing, despite the swordsman's best efforts to keep supplying mana to his strikes.

The man was beyond flagging already, so Rowan chose to end things with a blisteringly quick jab and swipe of his weapon.

The jab struck precisely against the sword's blade, parrying it aside and opening the man's defense. A step and swipe then introduced the shaft of his spear to the man's head. He promptly folded with a startled yelp.

"You ass! You know how much that hurt?" Blake hissed, one hand pressed gingerly against the side of his head while he squinted blearily up at Rowan.

In response, Rowan grinned and offered him his hand. "Not my fault that you don't know when to stop. If I need to keep reminding you with little boops every once in a while, I'll do it. Better me than some monster or demon out in the field."

"*Little?*" Blake looked away and grumbled. The Radiant Hero looked tired and resigned, even more than his weary body suggested. "Like I'll be making it out of this town anytime soon . . ."

For just a moment, Rowan had no clue how to respond. The anguish and worry in his best friend's voice was enough to give him pause. Of course, he promptly rallied and bopped Blake again, making it a point to poke the sore spot on the other hero's forehead.

Ignoring the pained hissing, Rowan dragged Blake toward one of the benches. "Stop that. I keep telling you, you're gonna be fine."

Rowan stuck to that prognosis, no matter how bitter, tired, angry, or frustrated Blake became. And he seemed to be rotating through those emotions every hour, at least.

It wasn't like Blake ever took those emotions out on others. Even Rowan, insistent as he was on keeping him company, was spared from any emotional outbursts. Somehow that was worse for the hero, though.

Instead of lashing out or arguing or doing *anything* at all, Blake insisted on bearing all the emotional turmoil squarely on his own shoulders.

The loss of his class due to a corruption attempt by a demon? His fault. The loss of his army, who were nearly slaughtered to the last soul? His fault. The fact that he was surrounded by three women, one of whom was set on upsetting every sentient creature within a thousand-mile radius? His fault.

To be fair, *some* of that might have even been true. The loss of his army and his garbled status window were direct results of his recklessness. If he hadn't insisted on charging ahead in an attempt to eliminate all threats before his party could get stronger, he wouldn't be in that mess.

Unfortunately, Rowan could somewhat understand his motivation.

Being summoned to a different world wasn't exactly easy on a person's psyche. Rowan himself had struggled, singled out due to a bad Heart Card and an even more problematic divine patron. It wasn't every day that a *former* patron god of a kingdom claimed a hero, after all.

He was even forced to rely on a singular patron in the form of a frontier baron, sent away to that faraway frontier, and then pushed into defending a small village from a large demonic horde.

Rather importantly, however, Rowan wasn't forced to do all that in total isolation. He had Olivia with him—who had rapidly grown into more than just a friend—and the sincere support of Baron Kayden Sutton, limited as it was.

Blake didn't really have that.

The king himself had chosen to take the hero in, but the more Rowan heard about the reality of his best friend's circumstances, the less ideal they sounded.

Blake was lauded as a hero. A savior. The chosen of Goddess Sarina herself. For most, the status might go to their heads, overwhelming the responsibilities that came with the corresponding power. For Blake? It just forced him into a corner. His frustratingly self-sacrificing personality constantly drove him to try and live up to people's hopes and dreams and the responsibilities of being *the* hero.

So, when each of the heroes were eventually sent to the front line to engage in combat against the demon, it wasn't exactly *surprising* that he'd acted the way he did.

At least he wasn't acting like Kayla. Rowan shuddered, thinking about his other friend and fellow hero. She seemed to take to politicking like she was born for it, but Rowan was far more unnerved by the way she always showed up just a little late.

Just a convenient step away from preventing things from getting out of hand.

She had saved his life from the final boss of the monster horde and dispatched the ugly thing threatening the village of Felton's Mill. But she only acted after far too many lives were lost, a crucial officer in the baron's army was out of commission, and Rowan himself was about to die. She looked unbothered by it all, floating on high.

Likewise, she only showed up to Blake's rescue after Rowan had done all the work and passed out with his fellow hero, trying to take them into her own custody.

Rowan was more than a little glad she'd been foiled there. Or allowed herself to be foiled.

This way he could at least cling to the notion that she wasn't purely malicious and that some of his friend's former personality was still present.

"I still don't understand why you insist on these daily practice sessions," Blake grunted, collapsing onto the bench bonelessly and throwing his head against the wall it was built into with a dull thud. Rowan winced a little, and Blake winced a lot.

"Because you're getting better, dumbass," Rowan grumbled, plopping himself down next to him and reaching for one of the pitchers of blessedly cool water the serving staff had laid out for them. He filled two glasses, then pushed one into Blake's hands. "And I mean that in all sorts of ways. Now, drink."

"You know, it's not good to chug down water immediately after an intense workout. Especially cold water," the Radiant Hero complained, but did as he was told.

Rowan couldn't help but roll his eyes. "That's only true when you *don't* have a magical physique and healing powers. I'm sure whatever issues the water would have caused are irrelevant to you now."

He meant it, too. Already, the mana slowly seeping into Blake's body was visibly improving the hero's complexion. Rowan could literally watch his cheeks, flushed with exertion and slicked by sweat, return to normal.

It was all thanks to the card Rowan could share with the other hero thanks to his latest class, [Spear of Unity]. Designating someone as his [Knight] allowed them to access a duplicate card from his own deck. His Epic-tier regeneration card was doing wonders for Blake and he felt good about his choice, regardless of the man's current status.

Unfortunately, while it was able to treat a part of Blake's injuries and keep him in relatively good physical condition, the card could do frustratingly little for the metaphysical wounds. Being nearly crippled with corruption and then having said corruption violently purged through a spear to the chest had done more than just fracture Blake's class and set him back in levels. The other hero's stats weren't even showing up properly, and a weakness had gripped his body unlike anything that conventional healing could fix.

And people had tried.

Olivia, with all her amazing alchemy skills, had failed. The few healing-oriented mercenaries found in the city of Rest's Remorse were likewise helpless. Even an inspection by the baroness, Olivia's mother and Kayden's wife, Camilla Sutton, failed to produce any meaningful results.

As far as she could tell, Blake's body was working just fine.

The first clue they got was when they forced Tamara, the resident exiled mage of the kingdom, to take a look at him. According to the woman, Blake's mana was on the fritz, rampaging through his body and refusing to properly settle.

At least Rowan's card seemed to be doing something for Blake's state. Even when he was perfectly healed up physically, the card kept drawing on mana, and he *was* seeing a slow improvement to his condition.

Being active and sparring at least a little also seemed to supercharge the process, pushing Blake to relative health even faster, which is why Rowan was regularly tormenting him in spite of his protests. He definitely, definitely wasn't thoroughly enjoying teasing his friend.

Blake seemed to have a few things to say on the subject. "You're impossible and I hate you," he grumbled, even if he did so with a slight smile.

Rowan immediately clutched at his chest, pretending to slump against the other hero. "Your words have slain me where I stand. Very well, then. Abandon me in favor of your harem . . . I mean, party. I totally meant to say *party.*"

Rowan knew he'd won that particular exchange when Blake flinched and gave him a look of total betrayal.

"Don't say that. Never say that."

"It's not my fault they're acting like they're all married to you already and have complete authority over your autonomy and how you should spend your time," Rowan said, his bitterness only slightly faked.

There was a princess he desperately wanted to hurt just a little. You know, in the name of equality, and all that.

Before Rowan could convince himself that *stopping* himself from punching such an annoying person in the face just because she was a woman would be misogynistic, sexist, and generally not the right decision, Blake interrupted his thoughts.

"I don't know what you're thinking about, but stop it. I don't need a mind-reading skill to know it isn't anything productive."

"I'll just say this much, my friend: I genuinely do not know how you live with them."

"They're not that bad."

"Around *you.*"

And it was true, much to Rowan's eternal frustration. All three of the women, the princess and two daughters of high nobility, were on their very best behavior around Blake. For the former that still meant being unbearably bossy, but she did it in a far more subdued and classy way.

Catch her away from Blake? Well, as Rowan had learned firsthand, she'd insult you, demand you surrender authority over your army, and then order you never to approach your own best friend ever again. Naturally, he ignored her, but that seemed to only incite her anger further, making her even less bearable to be around.

"Speaking of women . . ." Blake trailed off, and Rowan followed the direction he was looking to see what he meant.

Immediately, his eyes caught the way light played over the forest-green tresses of Olivia Sutton, turning them an odd shade of greenish silver and copper. The sight took his breath away for a second, and the way her green eyes sparkled with amusement in Rowan's direction didn't help.

Naturally, he ignored the noises of disgust coming from his best friend as he blitzed across the training ground in a second, sweeping the alchemist off her feet and spinning her around before pulling her in for a kiss to silence her giggles.

"Hey, you," he whispered quietly, entirely incapable of hiding the giddy happiness that filled his voice.

"Hey yourself. You know, didn't we go over doing this when you're all sweaty from exercising?" Olivia teased, but locked her arms around Rowan's neck and ran her fingers playfully through his hair all the same.

"Like Blake's good enough to make me sweat," Rowan taunted just loud enough for the other hero to overhear.

"I resent the accuracy of that comment!" Blake shot back from across the training ground, the smile that played across his features reassuring Rowan that he wasn't actually upset.

Naturally, Rowan once more ignored him. "Why do I have a feeling you didn't just come to steal kisses and hang out, though?"

"Stealing kisses? *Me?*" Olivia scoffed, then sighed. "Unfortunately, you're right. Mother needs to speak with you—she's waiting for us in her study. You should take your friend along, too."

Olivia wasn't rude to Blake, or confrontational, or anything similar. She did, however, seem keen on keeping a certain distance from him for some reason.

Rowan had noted it but ignored it at first, until he finally couldn't help but ask her directly what was happening there.

The answer surprised him as much as it made sense, and it rang in his ears every time he thought back to that moment.

*"Listen, I don't hate the man. If anything, I value the fact that he's your friend. But I don't think I can really be friendly with him as long as he's actively traveling and associating himself with a Treagon. It's bad enough that we're hosting her."*

Rowan understood. He really did. He'd never pushed for all that many details, but the Sutton house weren't always barons. They used to be dukes. At least they were until they lost their standing to the Treagon family more or less overnight.

The baron never budged on the subject when Rowan tried to subtly or directly inquire about how such a thing could happen. He was, however, more than happy to discuss how treacherous and untrustworthy Treagons were.

From the very moment Olivia and her mother realized one Mirabella Treagon was now in their midst, they'd both done their level best to entirely ignore her existence. Funnily enough, the woman in question more or less followed their lead herself.

Out of the three spoiled brats following Blake around, she was the best behaved. It was like she didn't even exist within the walls of the mayor's manor.

Be that as it was, Rowan did his best to jolt himself back to the present. If the baroness was looking for not just him but Blake, too, then it was unwise that they should tarry.

So, with much reluctance, he separated himself from his favorite alchemist.

"Oi, on your feet, lazybones. We need to have a chat with Olivia's mother," Rowan called back, making Blake groan and look at him with all the petulance of a child told that they can't have another five minutes in bed. To his credit, though, he did stand up on slightly wobbly legs with no further complaint.

"You know what I need to do?" Blake griped as he limped his way across the training ground, falling in step with the other two as they adjusted their pace to his. "I need to hire a mage to float me everywhere. Goddess, am I jealous of that class."

Blake scowled a little, and Rowan wondered if he, like him, was reminded of their likely former friend at the admission.

"Yeah, well, it's not like you have space to complain. You can make solid constructs out of light and pull all sorts of other nonsense with your Heart Card. I can only ever work on stabbing things better."

It was a gross oversimplification, of course, and Rowan had to admit that he'd been offered several choices to branch out into magic over his various tier evolutions. Unfortunately, any childish desire to wield cosmic forces fell to the wayside in the face of practicality and choices that *wouldn't* mess up his entire build.

Even then, there was plenty he enjoyed about his class, and more as time went on. There was so much to be gained through increasing spear mastery, subtle mana manipulation, and more. And that wasn't even mentioning the possibilities his latest class evolution offered.

If he could just get around to designating more [Knights], he could get bonus stats, passive experience gain, and a steady path to greater power. Just the stats alone, like a few more points in perception, wisdom, or intelligence, would be amazingly beneficial. The ability to better sense his mana, to grow it, and manipulate it better, would be huge.

That was a pretty big and frustrating *if*, though.

Finding people worthy of knighting was proving to be profoundly frustrating, and everyone seemed to have an opinion of their own on what would constitute a perfect [Knight]—from their stat spreads to their current tier to vetting their loyalty, dedication, and character.

Further complicating things was the fact that he could only designate a replacement after a year if he was ever forced to strip someone of their status as a [Knight] as well as the limited slots he had available.

"Jealous, Rowan?" Blake taunted softly and bumped into his friend's shoulder, a smile taking the edge off the words as he winked.

Rowan was thoroughly amused that Olivia stiffened, her hand briefly squeezing down on his own a little tighter than necessary.

"Yes, actually. I can do wild things to hurt something, but actual, honest-to-goodness magic? Bleh. Not that it would work with my stats, of course. I *know* that. Still doesn't stop me from resenting you a little. Especially since you have so many stats in wisdom you can actually get creative."

"Yeah. All my wisdom stats." It was Blake's turn to wince, and Rowan briefly regretted his comment. He firmed his heart, though. It wasn't like they could endlessly dance around the subject without ever bringing it up.

"Anyway, I was thinking—"

Rowan never did get the chance to share his splendid idea, because the figure of the baroness practically teleported in front of them. All of them flinched back, her sudden presence and the slap of the slightest bit of her aura more than enough to startle them.

Even though he was at the Epic tier himself, there was an edge to the baroness's aura that Rowan had nothing but healthy respect for.

"There you are. I thought I was clear that this was a matter of some urgency," Camilla snapped, her eyes briefly flickering over to Blake before dismissing his presence.

"You said to meet you in your study. We're on our way there, Mother. You didn't say I needed to hurry," Olivia groused, but quickly shut her mouth when her mother leveled an unimpressed look her way.

"Just . . . follow." Camilla sounded as tense as she did upset, in a way Rowan had come to associate with dealing with annoyances too important or too powerful to just make disappear.

"What's going on? It's not the kingdom, right? We came back only recently, and the number of Epics we killed this time around should be enough to keep the local monsters in check for quite a while," Rowan ventured, trying to get a sense of what they were about to be dealing with.

Unfortunately, the baroness grimaced and nodded her head. "A messenger arrived quite suddenly at our gates. They're not accompanied by an honor guard, but they did present the official writ of royal authority. They want you and your party present, for some reason."

The way she looked at her daughter suggested that she wanted her as far from the messenger as possible. Still, Rowan liked to imagine he saw a tiny bit of worry when she looked at him.

"And, of course, there's no other explanation or warning he saw fit to offer?" Olivia gritted out, trying to crush Rowan's fingers in a fit of rage. It was a good thing his strength did reinforce his body a little, and his alchemist was so averse to investing in body stats.

"*She.* And, obviously," the baroness replied in a clipped tone of voice. "Now, I want you to do as we practiced. No obvious shows of emotion. No weakness."

Rowan wanted to sigh, but he did as commanded. He briefly relaxed his facial muscles, letting them slip into an expression of indifference marred only by the slightest smile. Then he locked them in that position, straightening his posture as he went.

The whole exercise was frustrating at the best of times, let alone when he wanted to brain the king's messenger with his spear.

Still, the baroness had been putting his party through rigorous social training just for such occasions.

Olivia, naturally, needed no such training. She fell into the role easily and naturally, like it was second nature. The trouble with Rowan's favorite alchemist wasn't that she hadn't received etiquette lessons.

It was that she typically chose to ignore them.

Surprisingly, even Blake followed their example. The other hero was, all of a sudden, the perfect study in royal posture. The fact that he could pull that off still didn't surprise Rowan as much as the fact that the baroness had spoken so openly in Blake's presence, though.

It seemed that, even if she disliked the man, Camilla was willing to take Rowan's word for it that he was at least somewhat trustworthy.

Then their unfortunately short journey was over, and they were stepping into the atrium of the mansion, where guests or important figures were supposed to be greeted.

Except, instead of a whole array of servants on both sides, the space contained a much more interesting cast of characters.

Representing the manor and the mayor's seat was Henry, Rowan's chamberlain—as odd as it was for him to still have one. Rowan's party members, the wolfkin twins Milena and Marcus, stood by his side like bodyguards.

On the opposite side was a woman wrapped in a traveling cloak.

She was surprisingly young, by Rowan's estimation, around her early twenties. Her clothing, what little of it he could see under the cloak, was made out of rich and vibrant fabric. Unfortunately, most of it was flecked with mud, and the entire lower half of her cloak seemed caked in it.

Whatever message she bore, it was important enough to make her rush all the way from the kingdom to the frontier.

Of course, things couldn't possibly end there. It wasn't enough for them to have to deal with a messenger from the king. So to even things out, standing between the two sides like she was the star of the show, was Princess Amanda.

Behind her, the other two members of Blake's party stood, though they looked uncertain and hesitant at best.

That didn't stop the princess from shooting Rowan the smuggest look possible.

"I apologize for forcing you to wait," Rowan started them off, stopping a respectful distance away and forming the final point of the social square they found themselves stuck in. "I was training with my fellow hero, and we hadn't received prior notice of your impending arrival."

All that was a polite way of saying, "What the hell are you doing here, lady?" but the woman just smiled and waved his excuse away.

"It is no matter. My arrival is rather sudden, I know. However, His Majesty felt that delaying this matter would be unbecoming."

"We are ready to serve at His Majesty's leisure, of course," Rowan said, lying through his teeth.

Judging by the smug look of victory on the princess's face, it was very likely that they might need to kill the messenger and then check if Blake was okay with them offing one of his party members.

*At least it wouldn't be that hard to do it, seeing as she's basically just a healer.* That was the only comforting thought Rowan could manage. Rebellion would not exactly be the best solution to whatever problem the king was about to throw their way, but it was one he was surprisingly willing to commit to.

The messenger took that as her cue, extracting a rather large roll of ceremonial parchment. Frankly, Rowan wanted to sigh. Most of the kingdom used paper, an innovation made possible by one of the previous heroes.

That the kingdom's officials insisted on parchment was a matter of tradition, and while it did add to the atmosphere, it all felt a little contrived. The grandiose way the messenger spoke didn't really help, either.

"In the name of His Majesty, I am here to proclaim the following edict:

"Rowan Clairfont, the summoned hero and champion of the kingdom, for his part in the most efficient rescue of Hero Blake and his party, is declared a marquis of the kingdom. He is to be granted as his fief Rest's Remorse, which is hereby declared a city, and surrounding lands up to the kingdom's existing borders. He may establish up to three lesser settlements within these lands and may lay claim to the subsidy relevant to his rank annually whether it be in terms of coinage or in cards.

"Olivia Sutton, member of his party, is granted the title of viscountess and granted the right to establish an additional city within the confines of her ancestral lands as an existing noble. She may lay claim to the subsidy relevant to her rank annually whether it be in terms of coinage or in cards.

"The twins Marcus and Milena of the hero's party are hereby recognized as honorary nobles of the kingdom attached to the holdings of Rowan Clairfont, granting them the right to establish one minor settlement each that falls under their autonomy and outside the authority of the local marquis. They may also lay claim to the subsidy relevant to their rank annually whether it be in terms of coinage or in cards.

"You have the thanks and friendship of the royal family, and we wish you the very best in your future endeavors."

CHAPTER TWO

# Of Kings and In-Laws

Surprisingly, or perhaps not surprisingly at all, it wasn't Rowan who spoke first. He was stun-locked and missed the opportunity.

"What? Father is making him a noble?" the princess shrieked. She sounded downright horrible and looked just as betrayed. Like she had been just told that people were getting ready for her execution and she needed to attend at her earliest convenience.

"Correct, Princess Amanda." The messenger turned toward the insufferable woman, and Rowan didn't miss the slight smile she wore. Or the fact that she was addressing the princess by name.

"He can't do that! That's not—" She cut herself off. Her face grew frighteningly blank before the fires of anger made their reappearance. "I sent a missive with my request to my father days ago."

That was news to Rowan. Very unwelcome, *very* unpleasant news.

Oh, he had no delusions that he could keep the princess under lock and key, but he would have liked to know she was contacting the king while under his roof. He sent his chamberlain an ugly look, which the man weathered without so much as a shift in expression.

That was the downside of establishing yourself as a benevolent figure, Rowan supposed.

Then the fact that he was officially a marquis hit him.

Up to that point, his authority came from the fact that he was a hero and the local mayor. It wasn't an inconsiderable amount of authority, but he was definitely not an official noble in any capacity.

He wasn't trained on how to act like a noble. He wasn't even trained on how to act as a minor local lord yet.

Before he could start hyperventilating, though, Rowan steeled himself to continue to function. "I thank you for your good tidings, and the well-wishes of our king." He actually managed to sound polite and earnest. "Would you care to join us for a meal? My chamberlain will prepare a room for you to rest."

"Ah, that will not be necessary. I will be continuing my journey immediately. I still need to make my way to Hero Kayla's current location posthaste."

Rowan didn't shout in joy or breathe a huge sigh of relief, and he was inordinately proud of himself for that. Of course, what the messenger was actually saying caught up to him rather promptly. "Hero Kayla? Is she receiving a similar missive?"

"Unfortunately, no." The woman did look regretful, at least to Rowan's eyes. "There is a minor matter of the neighboring kingdom's activity along that particular border. It is nothing to worry about, I assure you. The defenses of our kingdom are still as solid as ever."

Rowan highly doubted that, considering all the recent nonsense he'd been through, including but not limited to the demon wave that had broken through Rest's Remorse itself and flooded into the baron's lands.

It was difficult enough dealing with the demons, and now it sounded like they needed to potentially worry about sabotage from supposed allies, too.

"Of course. His Majesty's grace will continue to protect us," Rowan said, throwing every polite combo of words he could think of at the messenger in the hopes that she'd leave even a little bit faster.

There was a bit of a snag when the messenger realized that she hadn't turned over a very elaborate wooden box, but that at least was easily rectified after the baroness noticed. It contained signet rings meant to denote the freshly risen nobles' new statuses, as well as serve as seals. Without that catch, things would have been far more complicated than they already were.

Thankfully, Blake used the opportunity while they were seeing the royal messenger off and sorting that out to slip away himself. When they reentered the atrium, he and his party were long gone. A good thing, too, considering the way the baroness had gone still and stared down the princess after her outburst.

"Walk with me," the baroness demanded coldly. There was little the hero party could do but comply.

Surprisingly, Henry, too, elected to join them, trailing behind at a respectable distance. Rowan sort of hated the fact that he could properly gauge and evaluate said distance now.

"They made us all into nobles." Rowan stated the obvious just as they reached Camilla's study, earning a slight glare from her as she opened the door and almost stomped her way to her designated seat.

"Yes, they did. More importantly, they made my daughter a viscount," the woman growled, making a tent of her fingers in front of her.

Rowan hesitated, eyes flitting between mother and daughter. Olivia had a deeply conflicted look on her face, one Rowan didn't like at all. "Isn't that supposed to be a good thing? It's a step closer to your previous title."

"It would be . . . if Olivia was the designated heir of the barony." The baroness sighed in a rare moment of open weakness. "However, that would be her older brother. The same brother who is currently stuck *studying* in the capital." The bitterness was palpable.

Rowan didn't know what to say to that. There had been oblique mentions of a sibling in the past, but Olivia had never actually discussed the man with him. Point of fact, she typically kept away from any topics concerning her family and their history.

Obviously, there was something he was missing, but he didn't even try to pretend he understood all the intricacies of the noble scheming.

He opted for honesty. "Explain it to me like I'm six, please."

Olivia chortled, but it was a sound more tired than amused. "It means that my parents need to either transfer the right of succession over to me from my older brother, or eventually put him into the awkward position of a baron having a viscount on their land as an attached noble house."

"Which is an issue because . . . ?"

"Because that's a recipe for disaster. It's a bit convoluted. I need to marry eventually, and that would give my husband's family the opportunity to meddle. Granted, the same issue crops up if my parents designate me as the heir. My brother has an official, long-standing engagement to prevent such nonsense, but the king himself could designate a suitable suitor for me and cause all sorts of trouble because I don't have one."

Rowan stiffened at that, eyes growing almost unnaturally wide. "He can just order you to marry someone?"

Olivia looked distinctly discomforted, but eventually nodded. "Yes. If an important noble fails to find the right spouse or enter into an engagement with a prospective spouse of good breeding by their age of majority, the royal family has the right to step in for the sake of preserving an important bloodline of the kingdom."

Rowan felt mounting horror at the news, indecision and doubt warring inside him. The twins, too, seemed to have a couple of things to say on the subject.

"Wait, does that technically apply to us, too, now?" Milena immediately asked, looking, if anything, even more panicked. "We were just made into nobility, too, right?"

"Technically, yes, it does. However, you are not from a long-standing noble family, and your designation as nobility fall under the scope of the frontier as Rowan's attached noble houses. Things are a bit different out here. In fact, the special dispensations for frontier lords are the primary reason there's never been a noble house with territory solely within the frontier."

"I have special rights as a frontier noble?" Rowan latched on to that, trying to follow any train of logic that would take him away from how worried and pained Olivia looked.

"Correct. You have far more freedom and far fewer obligations to the crown. It is understood that as a frontier lord bordering the demonic wastes, you cannot receive the normal support the kingdom would typically offer. Likewise, demands and expectations placed on you would differ."

"So, we're safe?" Marcus asked just to confirm, even if he was already exchanging relieved glances with his sister.

The baroness sighed, glancing her at her daughter. "Yes, *you* are safe. This is why every noble house has at least minor holdings within the kingdom proper. It allows the king to maintain more direct control and exert more influence. The crown must have failed to procure a territory quickly enough if they're resorting to this."

"Why make us nobility at all? Why now?" Rowan asked, somewhat disgusted with himself at the fact that a part of him was starting to regret ever setting out to rescue Blake.

"Your achievements are starting to pile up, and popular hero or not, the public will be interested in tracking your progress. You should've received an honorary title a long time ago. Now? The crown was forced to recognize your efforts after saving the hero adopted by the king."

That, more than anything, was a slap to Rowan's face so profound he actually reeled back. "Adopted?"

"Yes. Were you not aware of the fact that he was accepted as part of the royal family? That automatically makes him a part of the king's own household and necessitates an appropriate reward for rescuing him. Besides, saving the other members of his party requires similar compensation, too."

There was a lull in the conversation. A tense moment of silence as everyone stopped to process everything that had been said.

Rowan's eyes, of course, drifted back to Olivia.

He knew her well enough to recognize all the signs of *profound* distress. The way her hands shook ever so slightly, in spite of all the hours she'd spent training herself to keep them steady in her lab. The way her lips quivered. The way her eyes darted around as she desperately looked for a solution. Even the deepening pallor of her skin was something he could easily track.

He'd certainly spent far too much time sneaking glances at her face to miss such a change in her complexion.

The problem was, Rowan was terrified. There was a fear, a seed of doubt, that refused to shrivel up and die within his chest.

He more than cared about her. He loved her, without a single doubt. He wanted to spend—well, not *all* of his time with her; that would quickly grow overwhelming for them both—but at least most of it. So, what was there to hesitate about? Why wait?

Deep down, he knew he had one single trepidation. A tiny, insecure part of him wasn't completely sure he would turn down an offer to return home.

There was genuine joy, wonder, and a surprising amount of happiness in his new life. But there was also plenty of pain, uncertainty, and inconvenience.

His Heart Card and his sheer desire to prevent himself from collapsing into an inconsolable puddle on the ground did much to keep Rowan's mind together. Plenty still chafed at him.

The horrible conditions when he was out on expeditions. The level and lack of technological development that made long-distance travel a chore, not to mention anything like modern entertainment options. The tasty, yet admittedly odd food that was just a little off from what he expected.

And, of course, all the trauma, fear, pain, and guilt. Couldn't forget that.

So, what would really happen if he came face-to-face with the choice between staying with his newfound friends—or even family—and going back to the world of convenience, coziness, and low expectations?

Could he really guarantee that he wouldn't crack?

And was that enough to justify seeing that expression on his favorite alchemist's face?

In that moment, Rowan decided that it wasn't. He didn't bother thinking any more. He just stepped forward and enveloped her in a hug.

It was the cowardly part of him that justified cradling her head against his shoulder as touching and thoughtful. If it let him avoid eye contact? Well, that was a nice little side benefit.

"Olivia, will you please marry me?" He didn't apologize for the missing ring, the lack of explicit parental approval, and whatever thousand and one other local traditions he was likely trampling all over. He didn't rightly care about those.

Apparently, neither did she. "Yes, you absolute dummy," she sobbed out, and then she was kissing him and crying and Rowan didn't even mind all the tears making the experience taste decidedly awkward. He was far too happy and relieved to care.

He'd asked the question, and now all the decisions were behind him. More importantly, she'd said yes.

The happy couple and the twins both missed the happy little smile on the baroness's face.

It was only an embarrassing amount of time later that Rowan actually paused to think about the legality and official recognition of his proposal.

By that point, both of them were properly seated in front of Olivia's mother, and the twins and Henry had been ushered out of the room under the guise of "dealing with family affairs." So, Rowan moved to immediately clarify the issue.

"I don't mean to undermine my proposal, but . . . is it actually valid? Do we need the approval of the crown or anything?"

"How can you be both so competent and so hopeless at the same time?" Camilla's response to the proposal came only after she had internally collected herself. "Are you sure you want this one, daughter?"

"I couldn't be more sure," Olivia was quick to reassure her, with only a mild glare.

"Very well. Rowan, the answer to your question is that as nobility, one of you being a high noble at that, you need to submit your engagement request to the royal family. If the king deems the engagement to be valid and unproblematic, then you would be made an officially engaged couple, to be married at your convenience."

"Somehow, that sounds like the perfect opportunity for the royal family to block marriages they don't like," Rowan hissed. "What even constitutes a 'problematic' engagement?"

"Actually, it's not that bad. They can delay and they can cause trouble, but they can't say no without a very good reason. For example, the lineage of the houses is carefully considered to avoid any potential dangers of incestuous relationships. If there are no problems of that nature or similar, an engagement is almost always approved," Olivia reassured him with a light smile, in a much better mood now.

"*Almost always* still implies they can get away with denying a marriage if they really want to."

"Hardly." Camilla took over again, leaning back in her chair in a much more relaxed posture now that the twins were gone. "Feuds, coercion, and the like are the other reasons a marriage might be turned down. Not that it's an issue in this particular scenario. You don't need to worry about royal approval."

"Yep!" Olivia was practically bouncing in her seat, and Rowan found her cheer infectious. "I am marrying into your family because you have the higher rank title. So, the frontier laws apply. Out here, the highest-ranking local noble has the right to approve marriages. There are no dukes out here, so that would be you!"

Rowan wanted to cackle evilly, but contented himself with a smile. "So, I need to ask myself if I'm okay with my own marriage? Hmm, I don't know . . ."

Olivia rolled her eyes and poked him in the side, provoking laughter. It really did feel like a huge rock had been lifted off his chest.

"The best part is, because I'm marrying into a marquis family now, I can leave my own title to my brother," Olivia said smugly, which Rowan found adorable. He failed to hold himself back from lifting her hand and pressing a kiss to her fingers.

He found the way she blushed even more appealing.

"I'll get to drafting the relevant documents right away." The baroness approved and was highly motivated, much to Rowan's relief. He was perfectly content with leaving those parts of his duties up to her still.

He didn't like the glint of promise in her eyes that she *would* be teaching him all about his newfound status and the requisite skills to live up to it, though.

That did leave him with an opportunity to have a bit of fun. "Thank you, Mother," he quipped, a smile growing on his face as Camilla flinched and then looked at him with wide, startled eyes.

Eyes that promptly narrowed at him dangerously, as a smirk to match his grin emerged.

"You are welcome, *son.* Of course, you are aware that your brand-new fiancée's father, who was not informed of this engagement prior to it forming, is set to arrive in two days' time, correct?"

Rowan swallowed thickly, and thoughts of levity and happiness fled him like wildlife before an apex predator.

He had, in fact, forgotten.

Rowan nervously toyed with his new signet ring, eyes set on the horizon. By all accounts, the ring should have reassured him.

He was a marquis, waiting to meet a baron.

Naturally, it was his other newly obtained ring that was making it hard to relax.

He and Olivia had made a personal visit to the most skilled local blacksmith, and Rowan had to admit that the man managed to work a wonder at record speeds.

Their rings were crafted out of the bluish-green tint of mythril silver, with flecks and swirls of precious stones naturally included in the design. It was as though the smith had managed to melt the sapphires and emeralds used in the making of the rings, incorporating them far better in the design.

Perhaps he *had* done that.

Whatever the case was, they were left with a pair of rings that were as beautiful as they were spotlessly smooth. Considering the fact that they would be taking them into active war zones, that was an extremely important quality to insist on.

Rowan had a predominantly green ring sitting pretty on his finger, while Olivia's hand was graced by its blue counterpart.

The rings were perfect, and the generous rewards Rowan handed over to the smith were, in his opinion, more than justified. No matter the disapproving looks he got from the baroness when he handed over one of the few Heart Cards he had.

That still didn't shield him from having to greet his new father-in-law.

When the visiting procession came into view, Rowan's breath hitched in his throat. They'd been warned a couple of hours ago by a forward scout, true, but that had only exacerbated the sense of expectation Rowan was struggling with.

The baron had graciously accepted him into his home, and Rowan had then effectively proceeded to snatch away the man's daughter.

Olivia, of course, had no compunctions or fears. She was already excitedly waving at the emerging silhouettes of her father and his men on horses, and all but vibrating in place in her eagerness to greet him.

Funnily enough, the baroness was barely doing better. Long years of etiquette training and impeccable decorum were likely the only things keeping her from bolting ahead to meet them.

In a way, Rowan understood. If he was separated from Olivia for as long as the baroness was forced to spent time away from her husband, he'd likely feel the way she did, too.

Then the figures came into proper focus, and Rowan forgot all about his worries for a time.

"Bron!" Olivia's gasp clued the hero in the second she spotted the officer herself, and then the only thing stopping *her* from running ahead was her hand in his.

Right there at the front, riding practically side by side with the baron, was Bron. Rowan didn't hesitate to fully engage his perception, pushing at what its meager number could allow him to do.

The man wasn't fully healed. Not nearly. Rowan could make out the bandages perfectly well, and they still covered his limbs like mummy wrappings. Bron's face, however, seemed fully recovered. Even his hair had grown out a little, reminding Rowan once more of his own unruly mess.

Rowan didn't even bother trying to hide the fond smile that played over his features. Olivia looked so happy in that moment, so relieved, that he wanted to hug her. Giving in to the impulse, he did. Then he felt the freezing pressure of an aura, even with how far out the baron still was for a moment.

That brought the jitters right back, and they didn't fade again until the man was finally in front of them, immediately getting swamped in hugs by his wife and daughter the second he was off his horse.

Bron needed assistance getting off his own, but as soon as he was stumbling on his feet, he was patting the hero's shoulder with a grin.

"Well, look at you! Don't you look way more impressive than you were back at Felton's Mill? I even hear you've finally been made a noble, eh?" Then the man scanned Rowan's fingers for the signet ring and found something else entirely. "An engagement ring? Didn't hear about that one."

Rowan would later swear that he could pinpoint the exact millisecond Bron's words reached the baron and the moment the man processed them fully.

The weight of his attention was a fully physical thing.

"It seems we need to talk, boy," Olivia's father ground out, and Rowan eyed the horse he'd so recently vacated with contemplation.

Surely he could snatch the animal and make a run for it, right?

Rowan had expected shouting. Maybe some menacing intimidation or even a plain attempt at politely discouraging Rowan's interest in his daughter.

What he did *not* expect was for the baron to trade a few quiet words with Bron, snatch Rowan up, and go in search of Blake. Now, with two startled heroes more or less literally in hand, he led them to what could only be described as controlled chaos.

In other words, a rough-and-tumble celebration organized on the spot.

Several hours and plenty of thoroughly confusing conversations later, most of them centered on how to split his time between his duties and his wife, and the baron's advice was rapidly turning into slurred nonsense.

"You need to follow your friend's example better, son," the baron rumbled. His cheeks flushed before he flinched at the term he'd unconsciously used, and then glared like it was Rowan's fault that he had said the words.

"He never was good at parties. Or drinking. Or drinking parties," Blake slurred, slumping sideways in his seat. If he hadn't been seated next to the wall, Rowan was pretty sure he'd be on the floor by that point.

"Well, we'll have to remedy that, ey?" Bron shouted merrily, raising his own glass and downing it. Again. For what seemed like the thousandth time that night.

Rowan had no clue what the actual alcohol content of the spirits they were drinking was, but his bet was on high. Which made the fact that Bron wasn't even flushed yet all the more confusing.

Rowan was relatively fine, too, but that was only by virtue of his regeneration card. It *really* didn't like when he had alcohol in his system, and it was working double time to purge him of it. Thankfully, against all biological processes, that didn't just dump ludicrous amounts of liquids into his bladder.

Less thankfully, Rowan could actually *see* plumes of purged chemicals rising from his skin, not to mention smell them. He positively reeked of medical-grade rubbing alcohol.

"Of course," Rowan answered reluctantly, lifting his glass so it could be refilled once more by the enthusiastic officer. "*Why* are you trying to poison me again?"

"Poison you? We're just celebrating your good fortune!" Bron insisted, downing yet another cup of alcohol with relish.

Rowan just grimaced, followed suit, then promptly broke into coughs. That was even stronger than what Bron had forced on him before, and there was absolutely no chance he was enjoying even a hint of the taste the drink supposedly had.

Presumably it was some kind of expensive whiskey or some such, just like the rest of the bottles they'd raided from the manor's cellars. Rowan would really have preferred wine if he was forced to drink at all, but that didn't seem to be in the cards.

Outside their window, the sounds of laughter, arguments, and not a few fights rang out. The mayor's army and the troops that had accompanied the baron were making merry as well.

If someone had told him a man who had nearly died, incapable even of breathing without pain, would provoke a citywide party, Rowan would have readily chided them for their overactive imagination.

As it was, he could only stare at Bron with astonishment. Less than a day after the baron's arrival, he was already showing a whole new side of his personality to Rowan. Now he knew why Olivia liked him so much.

"Listen here, boy," the baron suddenly rumbled, face even redder than it was mere moments before. "I like you. You are . . . respectable. However, you better protect my daughter with your life. If you're going to drag her into nonsense, at least make sure she doesn't end up hurt, okay? I failed at that. I let my family get involved. Don't let them do that to you, too."

The baron broke into ramblings, eyes drifting slowly shut, as Rowan watched in astonishment. He'd originally expected the man to be confrontational, if not outright deny the legitimacy of their engagement. Instead, he'd asked his daughter if she was happy, and then legitimately congratulated them. It was one of the more confusing moments in Rowan's life.

Seeing his father-in-law slump over into the lap of his comatose best friend was something Rowan would carry with him for years.

"How are you not passed out already?" Rowan directed the question at the lieutenant, who was happily polishing off an entirely new bottle of drink.

"Because I know my limits, and because drinking an elixir that you really shouldn't be able to survive tends to do all sorts of wacky things to your body."

Rowan jabbed his finger at the passed-out baron accusingly. "*He's* Epic. You're *not*."

At that, finally, a sly smile quirked Bron's lips. "He's also the one that's had three bottles of liquor clearly marked out as something to be consumed only by Epic tiers and above."

Rowan stared, then chuckled, then laughed. By the time he was finally brushing happy tears out of his eyes, he had already managed to finagle Blake's arm over his shoulder.

"I'll put Hero Blake to rest first. I can't get your lord standing with my arms full already," Rowan complained.

"Only if you come back to keep me company."

Rowan snorted, thoroughly amused. "Fine."

Stumbling his way over to Blake's quarters, where he handed him off to the trio of grumpy, upset women, and then over to where Kayden was staying close to his own room, Rowan even meant to keep that promise.

Of course, when Olivia opened the door to his room and dragged him in for a kiss, all thoughts of doing so evaporated.

CHAPTER THREE

# To Name a Knight

Rowan didn't have a particularly high vitality score. He did, however, have an amazing regeneration card and the good sense not to drink himself into a stupor.

So it was that out of the group of people who stumbled their way onto the training grounds the next morning, Rowan was the only one blessedly free of any headaches, nausea, or other signs of indulging in excess. They had all agreed to meet there the night before, but none of them anticipated that just standing up straight would be so difficult.

Even Olivia had woken up wincing and glaring at the world, though she had swiftly remedied all that with a couple of choice potions. That meant that she was chipper and smiling when her parents dragged themselves over to her like zombies.

"Yes, Mom, Dad?" Olivia quipped like butter wouldn't melt in her mouth, her grin a thing of utmost smugness.

"Give up the potions, you brat," the baroness hissed, clearly refusing to play any of the games her daughter was up to. "Don't forget who approved your engagement while your father was away."

That seemed to do the trick, or Olivia just wasn't willing to torment her parents. She quickly doled out a pair of potions to each of them. After they threw back the oddly colorful concoctions, the effect on the baron couple was immediate. Stiffness left their shoulders, their postures improved, and even the bags under their eyes were partially erased.

Once more, Rowan was reminded of just how amazing his favorite alchemist actually was.

"These are the potential [Knights] you have for me, then?" Rowan muttered while the duo finished gathering themselves, eyes sweeping over the five people shuffling away from the family scene.

They were obviously suffering from the effects of last night, too, but Rowan didn't really care about that much. What was far more important to him was the apparent age of the knight hopefuls. Not a single one of them looked like they were a day older than fourteen.

And in a world where people often physically matured more quickly due to the presence of the system, that wasn't exactly promising.

"The best that I could find," the baron confirmed with unquestionable pride. "They all have an excellent Heart Card that will take them far. Not necessarily a *high-ranking* Heart Card, but the point stands."

"And how old are these potential recruits of mine?" Rowan couldn't help the question.

"They're from the newest batch, obviously, so they're all around thirteen," the baron admitted easily and without even a hint of guilt, even if the words made Rowan flinch.

That felt . . . young. Granted, people in this new world of Rowan's considered their children partial adults from the moment they awakened the system around age twelve, but that didn't mean he shared the sentiment.

In fact, in many ways, he felt that the treatment of children was odd.

They weren't expected to marry at that age. Mercifully enough, that was reserved for late teens or early twenties. Instead, they were, if they chose to pick up a combat class, expected to readily charge at the nearest available monsters within their tier.

The only obstacles preventing more child soldiers were the long training times and the absolute chore that leveling up was. Most soldiers in the frontier army were fifteen or sixteen, unless they were a real combat prodigy. However, his blessing made things a bit morally gray. Granting children access to a powerful card was practically *begging* them to act recklessly.

On top of all that, any [Knights] Rowan acquired would naturally be folded into his army, and that wasn't the safest place to be.

In spite of those facts, he remained silent. He didn't ask the potential recruits why they'd chosen to follow the baron all the way out to the frontier and risk their lives, either. Instead, he focused on the resolve in their eyes that shone through even with how dazed and wrung out some of them seemed.

"Fine," the Stalwart Hero sighed, more than a little resigned. "Let's see what they can do."

Two spears met with a loud clack, but while one got pushed aside and driven into the ground, the other proceeded to travel along its intended trajectory and met the tender forehead of a girl with yet another thump.

A sword rose up toward Rowan's back with power born of desperation, but he twirled out of the way with laughable ease. His perception lent him more than enough awareness to be aware of the strike from the start, to the point where he didn't even need his boosted dexterity stat.

Of course, he swept out the wooden spear he was using for the bout and applied just enough strength to clobber the final knight prospect into near unconsciousness in retaliation.

"Stay down, if you've had enough." Rowan's voice was cold and cutting, more than enough to signal his thorough lack of amusement with their pathetic attempts to prove themselves. Or that was the attitude he was trying to project, at least. On the inside, he was cringing, stuck between trying to test them and wanting them to willingly flunk out.

After all, to an outside observer, Rowan was abusing a group of young teens. Rowan's sensibilities agreed with the sentiment wholeheartedly.

Unfortunately, what he needed wasn't an amazing card or the right kind of background. Those things were likely to help the recruits along, of course, but ultimately, they weren't that important. What he *did* need was the grit and determination to keep going.

He needed the sort of recruit who would keep pushing when their limbs were almost torn off in the hopes of getting out of combat alive. And he so very desperately wanted them to stay alive if he did take them on as his [Knights].

Three of the recruits showed that resolve.

A red-haired spear wielder, a rarity that had Rowan raising his eyebrow questioningly at the baron; a plucky young swordsman; and a shield-hammer-combo–wielding brute of a man. Well, boy, but with his stature and size, Rowan *really* had trouble associating the knight prospect with a thirteen-year-old.

Those three were still struggling. Still trying to stand and crawl back into some semblance of a stance to continue fighting. That was in spite of the way Rowan had dismantled them, especially the shield wielder. The boy's left arm, the one he used to lug his shield around, was broken. The fingers of his right hand were in only marginally better state, but you could spot the swelling and redness with ease.

The spear wielder's forehead was red, weeping a bit of blood, and looked like it had the beginnings of horns growing out of it. She insisted on trying to meet his strikes each and every time with flashy overhead blocks. So, Rowan kept beating on her in hopes she would learn. Today was clearly not the day that would happen, though.

The swordsman was the worst off out of the trio.

His left leg dangled behind him, his left arm was stained with blood where Rowan ran it through to stop him from wielding both hands for his strikes, he had multiple lacerations along his right shoulder, and the bump on the back of his head, coupled with the way he stumbled with unfocused eyes, hinted at a concussion.

*Gods dammit, I'm going to have to accept them at this point, aren't I?* Rowan took a deep breath, then let it out in one frustrated gust.

He really didn't want to.

"That's enough," Rowan snapped, irritated at himself, the baron, and the world he'd been thrown into in general. The kids froze, trying to focus on him through bleary eyes as he stomped off in Olivia's direction.

He threw the practice spear aside, a frown thoroughly dominating his features. It faltered a little when Olivia closed the distance between them and enveloped him in a hug, but even that wasn't quite enough.

"How are you feeling?" she asked quietly, eyes rowing over his face in search of an answer she failed to readily find with how closed-off his expression had grown toward the end of sparring.

"Like I just beat up a bunch of children, who I now feel obligated to accept into an army that's going to be trying to commit a very elaborate suicide in the future."

Olivia winced but didn't really have a good answer to that. Instead, she pulled out one of her potions and proffered it to him. He recognized it immediately as a very mild healing and stamina potion blend. "Want a pick-me-up?"

"No, thanks, love," Rowan mumbled, for once entirely indifferent to the presence of her parents as he leaned down to press a kiss to her forehead. "I'm just in a bad mood. Save the potions for *them*. Speaking of, could you heal them up for me, please?"

"Of course," Olivia answered with a smile and one final hug, before she quickly headed in the direction of the suffering knight hopefuls.

Rowan wanted to continue his stomping tantrum all the way up to his quarters, but he had an obligation to stick around and talk to the kids. So he waited, giving the baron a chance to strike.

"Well? What do you think about your prospective recruits?" Kayden asked conversationally, though he did keep a careful eye on the way Rowan scowled at him.

"They are . . . fine," the hero snapped, then paused and tried to moderate his response. A deep breath and a moment to let the tension bleed out of his shoulders did enough to let him at least maintain civility. "They show promise. I hate how young they are."

Both of the statements were true.

Frankly, the swordsman and the spear user were almost as good as Rowan was, in terms of pure skill. Now, that might seem like a boast on Rowan's part, or failure on theirs, considering the fact that the hero had only been fighting for a couple months at best.

That was, however, a gross underestimation of the effects of his tier-ups.

Nearly every class Rowan picked came with a direct upgrade to his base ability to wield a spear. All of them made it easier to use his weapon and master it, pushing the spear to the farthest reaches of its potential.

Now, Rowan wasn't exactly there yet. Not by a mile. However, he did have the solid foundation hammered into him by the baron and his otherworldly arrival benefits. He'd taken that, and then improved it through a whole lot of encounters with monsters.

Live combat was a great teacher by necessity, and he'd even had the chance to spy on some of the other spear users, their training, and the way they fought. Most of what he saw didn't apply to him. After all, those spearmen tended to fight in formations, under strictly controlled and organized maneuvers. But that wasn't to say they *didn't* have a trick or two to teach him still.

So, while Rowan was by no means a master of the spear, he was very solidly an advanced wielder of it, thanks to all the system nonsense.

The fact that the kids were almost there as well? It was impressive.

Even the two Rowan had handily laid out to the point where they took their lot in life and passed out were similarly promising. They just didn't have the grit needed to punish themselves in a silly attempt to throw away their lives faster.

"Will you be accepting them?" the baron pushed again, eyes briefly going to the trio Olivia was doing her best to patch up.

They were quickly getting better, seeing as the potions of an Epic-ranked alchemist were some of the very best you could ever get your hands on.

Rowan's first instinct was to say no, just because he wanted to. "Yes," he growled instead. "Yes, I will. The three of them, at least. The other two just won't cut it out in the wastes. I refuse to feed them to monsters."

Rowan thought that he saw a brief flash of some emotion in the baron's eyes. Understanding, perhaps? Or pity? It didn't matter, because it vanished as quickly as it appeared. "That is reasonable. I'm happy to know you at least found the other three to your liking."

*Liking* was a very strong word, but Rowan wasn't about to continue acting like a petulant teen forever. "Thank you for all your effort. I'm going to talk to them and see if they actually want to join up now that they understand the risks and suffering a bit better. Just . . . if you look for more candidates . . ."

"Yes?"

The tug-of-war between his gratitude that the man cared and was trying warred with Rowan's innate disgust over the whole thing. "Just . . . I'd prefer it if they were . . . a bit older, perhaps?"

"That would be difficult, lad. Not many good prospects around that aren't already beholden to one lord or another. You need either a solid foundation or the best possible high-tier you can find. Most people who are still stuck at Common are stuck there for a reason."

Rowan disagreed with that, with his own army being a great example of people who just needed one opportunity to advance their station in life, but he wasn't about to fight with his fiancée's father over the subject just yet.

One day, when all the major threats were gone and he could sit down and do something about all the rampant discrimination? Sure. But not before then.

"All I'm asking is that you try," Rowan insisted again and waited for the baron to nod before turning to observe his future knights again.

The trio was finally more or less in shambling shape, so Olivia led them in his direction. Thinking about just how he wanted to handle the encounter, Rowan decided to keep things simple.

"Can you maybe take care of those two?" he asked the baron couple and, at their nod, moved on. He offered Olivia his hand. She took it with a smile, and Rowan turned toward his mansion.

It still felt weird to refer to the structure as such. In Rowan's mind, it was the *mayor's* mansion for the longest time. It may have belonged to him by virtue of the king's say-so and the previous owner's death, but it still didn't feel quite real.

It didn't feel like he *deserved* it.

But, for better or for worse, Rowan had lost a lot of that compunction after returning with Blake in tow. He'd risked his life, bled and fought, and protected the town. Well, city now, he supposed. If that didn't make him worthy of laying claim to a single fancy home, what did?

Rowan *was* still doing his best to ignore the fact that he'd inherited all the servants that came with it, though.

A small, somewhat petty part of Rowan did find amusement in the way the trio lumbered behind the couple like zombies. The healing potions did a thoroughly amazing job of healing up their injuries, but the effect they had on stamina was minimal.

So, he treated his stroll to the kitchen, and then to one of the upstairs meeting rooms, like one final part of their test.

None of them failed.

So it was that the Stalwart Hero found himself seated across from three young teenagers in a comfortably luxurious room in his mansion amusedly ignoring the way they eyed the basket full of finger foods.

Rowan cleared his throat. "First, I need you to know I am genuinely impressed with the way you handled yourselves. It is *not* easy to keep pushing past your breaking point like that, and that you did speaks volumes of your dedication, grit, and bravery."

They perked up at that, shooting each other small smiles. Rowan wasn't sure if they knew one another well, but even if they were near-complete strangers, a sense of camaraderie seemed to have grown between them due to his test.

"Having said that, I want to have a chat with you all before I officially make you [Knights]. First, do any of you actually know what that means?"

For a few moments, no one spoke, before the oddly muscled boy finally found his voice. "Um, it has something to do with your class, my lord? Baron Kayden told us you are looking for eight people to join you, but . . . isn't that more than a party? Don't you have your own party already, too?"

He seemed deathly afraid of even speaking out so much, so Rowan offered the boy a reassuring smile and a nod. "Excellent questions. Yes, I do. And yes, it is. You see, my class is somewhat unique, from what I've been told. I have the ability to designate eight [Knights] and share certain benefits with them."

Rowan stopped there, curious whether any of them would be brave enough to venture any further questions on their own. The spear user finally did, though her voice broke the first time she attempted to speak. When she finally managed, it was mouselike and hesitant. "What kind of benefits?"

"Another good question. Well, for me, I get a percentage of the stats my [Knights] have, and even get a share of some of their experience gain. Don't worry, I don't steal the stats or anything. Actually, I'm not sure if experience is siphoned away or just shared—still need to test that out."

"And the [Knights]?" she asked again, this time far more sure of herself. His praise was working as intended.

Rowan leaned forward with a smile at the question. "The [Knights] get to pick one of the cards I have in my deck. When they do, they get a copy of that card to use as they wish, and it doesn't count against their own deck. For the record, I have Epic-tier cards in there."

The effect was as immediate as it was predictable. The flash of desire, bordering on greed, flared up in each and every one of them.

Rowan could understand perfectly.

All of them were barely awakened. Level one, each and every one of them. The baron had apparently kept them as such, declining to let them level up until they were either accepted into the hero's service or turned down in order to maximize the benefits Rowan would get.

Naturally, that meant that the trio was far, far away from even making it to Uncommon. Their cards, likewise, were confined to the Common tier, or if they were particularly lucky, they had one or two Uncommon cards from their inheritance.

Even if their families somehow had an Epic card lying around, they would have to make it all the way up to Rare before they could ever equip them in their decks. That's how the rules of the system were: One tier higher than your own was all that you could equip.

So, to hear that he could make it possible for them to wield an Epic-tier card from the very start? One that didn't even take up a slot in their decks? Yeah, that had more than a little appeal.

In fact, Rare- or even Epic-tier individuals would likely feel tempted as well. A whole additional card, at the tier where cards were rare and getting a useful one even more difficult? If Rowan's regeneration card was common knowledge, he could easily see powerhouses applying to "assist" him with his duties to the frontier at the cost of giving them access to a [Knight] slot.

Granted, none of them knew that Rowan was capable of feeling the emotions of everyone he designated as a [Knight], but then again, that was a secret he wasn't about to share with anyone but his closest allies.

"What kind of cards do you have?" the swordsman asked hungrily before flushing when all eyes turned on him. "Um, lord, sir?"

The way he tacked on the attempt at politeness gave Rowan a good-natured chuckle. He didn't rush to assure him it was okay to be casual. Unfortunately, the last few months in his new world had taught him better.

"To answer the unasked question, yes, I have a damage-oriented combat card. It's Rare, but it's powerful. No, not all of you can use it properly. Only she could." He motioned at the spear user, who grinned like she'd won the lottery. "I also don't recommend you pick that card if you do decide to join as my [Knights]."

"Why not, my lord? It's an Epic-tier card, right? That means nothing could stop me from getting up the tiers!" The girl was practically bouncing in her seat, eyes sparkling in her eyes.

Rowan really hated to be the bearer of bad news.

"My build is a bit . . . unusual. The card is powerful, yes, way more powerful than people typically associate with spear cards." Wasn't that an understatement? "But it would also outright kill you if you're not careful when using it. It draws on your mana, life force, blood, and even flesh to fuel its might. You're more likely to turn into a desiccated corpse than win if you use it."

Rowan tried to break the news gently, but all three of them paled and immediately shot him odd looks. Probably because he was not a desiccated corpse.

"What I do recommend you pick is my regeneration card. It's at the Epic rank, too, and it saved my life way more times than I can even count." Rowan shuddered a little, incapable of keeping bad memories at bay entirely.

He needed the assistance of his Heart Card and its ability to make emotions feel like distant inconveniences to deal with the worst of his traumas at first. Now, Olivia's cuddles mostly kept nightmares at bay.

In spite of that . . .

The memories flashed through him like daggers. Teeth digging into his skin, his eyeballs popping like grapes. Corrosive blood sweeping over his body, threatening to eat it away until it was nothing but a rapidly melting skeleton. Fire and concussive force playing havoc with his body until there was no discernible difference between his skin and his leather armor that had fused together.

Rowan shuddered.

Without that particular card that had started off a not-so-humble Rare tier won from a demon, Rowan would probably look more like Frankenstein's monster than a human. He really didn't fancy the thought of being little more than a mound of scar tissue.

Predictably, the thought of the card appealed most to the shield and hammer user, who leaned forward eagerly. "A regeneration card, my lord?"

Rowan was more than happy to move on from his traumas, and so launched into an explanation immediately.

"Correct. It can restore your body fully back to a pristine state and even has some effect on soul injuries, according to what we've been able to observe. It also has the nice added benefit of improving stamina. You'll never be forced to stop fighting until you're somehow put down or your enemies are dead if you use it right."

He *did* neglect to mention that most of his own staying power was owed to **Gluttonous Banquet**, a card that let him gorge on food well past his normal capacity and store away the energy it produced for future use. He could, in fact, store thirty times more energy than his body could naturally manage.

This synergized perfectly with both his regeneration card, which dipped into that energy pool, and his suicidal attack card, which drained his body of all it could offer.

Altogether, he could hit much harder than he should, and if his defenses were paper-thin, well, he could come back from some serious punishment.

In fact, Rowan wasn't exactly sure he *could* die until all his energy was exhausted.

"Now, I could do something reckless like cut off my own arm to show you just how the card works, but I don't want to ruin the upholstery with my blood, and my lovely fiancée here would probably kill me if I did something that stupid. So, you'll have to trust me when I say nothing short of complete bodily destruction will be able to kill you if you pick that card."

Rowan planned to provide his [Knights] with a card that could keep them in the fight longer. He did, after all, have both the Rare- and Uncommon-tier versions of the **Gluttonous Banquet** at one point or another. Getting more of those wasn't impossible.

"Before all that, however . . ." Rowan paused, letting his eyes drift over the kids sitting across from him. Hope. Worry. Intrigue. Desire. So many emotions warred on their faces. "I'd like to get to know you a bit better. Why sign up for this? Kayden did not tell you about the benefits, obviously. So, why decide to come here just so you can become one of my [Knights]?"

Rowan wasn't going to turn them away just because they failed to provide a good answer to the question. Still, he felt compelled to know. If their motivations and personal ambitions would be better served elsewhere, he was going to do his very best to get them there.

The Stalwart Hero made himself comfortable, ready to push until he had all the details he wanted.

## CHAPTER FOUR

# Personal Flaws

Rowan's eyes swept over the trio of [Knight] hopefuls, curious to see if he would need to encourage them to speak or if they'd gather the courage on their own. Interestingly enough, it was the spear wielder who chose to speak out.

"My name is Fia. Just Fia. My family isn't wealthy or anything like that—I was just lucky. I got an Uncommon Heart Card, one that makes any spear-based combat card stronger. I thought they'd turn me away because, well, you know, spear. But then the baron ended up bringing me here."

Rowan smiled wryly, looking at the girl with more than a little pity. If he had caught a ton of criticism for being a hero forced to wield a "weak" weapon like a spear that didn't have high-end attacking card options, she must have been in an even worse position.

After all, [Spearman] was typically considered a class best suited for large groups, not solo powerhouses. The class went in the direction of quite a few good team combat–based upgrades. Then again, the more Rowan learned about the system, the more he came to suspect that the established upgrade path for the spear class was more a result of people's attitude about the spear than the other way around.

Both Olivia and her mother mentioned having to create or rediscover classes on your own. If no one was interested in the spear because it was weak, couldn't that also mean that it just needed a larger or more talented pool of people to help develop it?

Regardless, Rowan didn't allow himself to become too swept up in the theorizing and focused again on the conversation at hand. "So, when you heard about the opportunity to work with a hero that uses a spear himself, you said yes?"

The girl nodded with a light blush and refused to meet his eyes. "Yeah. I mean . . . If anyone can help me become at least somewhat competent with the class, it's you."

She wasn't entirely wrong, but Rowan wasn't sure if he should encourage her. As he'd told them already, his combat style was more than a little problematic. Still, having heard all about her motivation . . . "Fine, then. Pick the regeneration card, got it? Can't help you if you don't."

Rowan focused on his newest card, and it eagerly provided its power. Just like that, the girl gave a startled wince as a system window popped up in front of her, providing her with the option to accept her designation as a [Knight] and select her preferred copied card.

"Thank you! Thank you so much! I'll make sure you don't regret this!" she squeaked out, then devoted herself to finalizing the process.

Rowan turned his attention to the shield and hammer–wielding boy. "What about you? What's your story?"

Put on the spot, the boy looked like he'd rather avoid the topic for as long as he could. Eventually, though, he did speak up.

"I'm . . . I'm not entirely human," he admitted, gesturing at his body. Rowan had actually been wondering, to be fair. In spite of supposedly being thirteen years old, the guy looked like he could snap the hero in half.

"That's fine. It doesn't bother me. You do know that I have two wolfkin in my party? They're more reliable than almost anyone I've met," Rowan ventured, trying to reassure the boy before he bolted for the door because he looked about ready to do that. "How about you share your name with us?"

The boy flushed, looking mortified that he'd forgotten. "Greg. My name's Greg. My ma named me. My dad's . . . not around. He was a halfling, too. Troll. People don't really like that combination, and he was way more obviously a mixed blood. We had to move from our previous home, but then he left so we could live in peace. I . . . I want to find him, someday. It's not his fault. None of it's his fault."

Greg said that, but Rowan noticed the way he'd hunched his shoulders, the way he tried to squeeze himself into the groaning sofa under him. While the boy didn't resent his father, Rowan strongly suspected he resented *himself*.

Though, that did leave one question that needed to be asked. "Trolls have excellent natural regeneration. Did you happen to inherit that?"

The boy looked relieved that his family history would not be discussed anymore, but he didn't seem much happier to talk about his natural gifts. "Yes. I can keep regenerating, but, well, it puts a strain on my body. I'll eventually pass out when I don't have the energy to keep healing."

Rowan hummed, impressed with the selection of recruits the baron had found for him, in spite of how their age made him feel. "What about your Heart Card? The baron mentioned all of you have good card synergy."

"Mine lets me absorb part of any damage I take and temporarily store it as a charge, then unleash it when I attack. It's Rare tier, too, so it's pretty decent," the boy stated proudly, hope slipping back into his expression.

Apparently, healing until utter exhaustion wasn't something Greg was proud of, simply because it came as part of his lineage. Rowan wanted to scoff. He would have killed to have such an ability naturally, especially back when he first arrived in this new and terrifying world.

"That's pretty great, I'll admit. I value your ability to heal yourself more. You clearly picked some kind of defender class, right? That will be invaluable for you. Anyway, I suggest you pick my **Gluttonous Banquet** card—it'll serve you well."

Rowan sent the boy an offer of knighthood, too, and then turned to the final applicant, who smiled at him wanly.

"I don't really have a sad backstory, I'm afraid," the boy started, in a joking tone that almost covered up the nervousness lurking underneath. "My name is Desmond Baker, and my father is one of the baron's officers. I've been taught to use a sword my whole life, and I think I'm good at it."

Rowan nodded along, then prodded the boy for more information. "And your Heart Card?"

The swordsman paused and tried to hide a wince before continuing. "Rare tier. I can, well . . . If I keep attacking, it lets me keep hitting harder and harder. The catch is, I can't stop chaining hits without penalty. If I take longer than two seconds, the effect drops. And . . ."

"And?" Rowan didn't like the way the young man didn't want to continue his explanation.

"And I can't really control it well. The strength of the blows continues to grow, but my ability to deal with the recoil or even wield that strength doesn't grow in concert with it. If I keep it up too long, my arms snap."

Rowan leaned back into his seat. "Pick the regeneration card," he ordered, then sent the last of his newly acquired knights an invite, too.

He really didn't know what else to say. The baron had, whether he planned on it or not, played him. Each of the trio was, in one way or another, *flawed.* Each of them could be made so much more powerful with Rowan's help.

The spearman needed his advice and help to get her class off the ground and deal actual damage. The defender needed his **Gluttonous Banquet** if he wanted to last longer in battle and properly leverage his lineage. Meanwhile, the swordsman needed his regeneration card if he wanted to survive his own Heart Card.

Briefly, Rowan wondered what was wrong with the other two he'd decided not to accept before discarding the thought. No second-guessing here. Each of the three in front of him was going to *need* grit and determination if they wanted to grow more powerful. Getting hurt was going to be an inevitability in their futures, not something that could be avoided.

No matter how potentially promising the other two were, if they were going to fold at the first step, Rowan wasn't going to go back on his decision.

Rowan felt the exact moment each of the three finalized their decisions. There was an odd jolt that traveled through his body, and then he was *aware* of them.

Fia was a bundle of anxiety and expectation, hope blooming freely in her chest to the point Rowan had to fight back his own smile.

Greg was still wound tight with shame and doubt. It felt like he was waiting for the other shoe to drop every second now. He *expected* the knighthood to be canceled, and to be asked to leave.

Finally, Desmond was pure anticipation and relief. Likely, Rowan guessed, because of finally having a way to deal with the injuries his Heart Card could so easily inflict on its user.

Be that as it was, the hero was thoroughly drained from all the interactions, in spite of a newfound strength blooming within his body. "That will be all for now. You three can head off to the barracks. Look for Clarke when you're there. He'll help you settle in."

The trio recognized the dismissal for what it was and, with a few final words of thanks, filed out the door. Belatedly, once they were already out of sight, Rowan realized he hadn't actually told them *where* to find the barracks.

*Oh well, that should be an interesting experience all on its own for them,* Roan thought before he was thoroughly distracted by his favorite alchemist plopping herself onto his lap.

"Well, what do you think of them now that you're done getting to know them a bit better?" she teased, laying her head on his chest and looking up at him with a small smile.

He took a second to wrap his arms around her and get a bit more comfortable before replying. "I really don't like how young they are. Past that, though . . . yeah, they have potential. I mean, their Heart Cards really *are* good for them. Even I don't have a straight damage boost Heart Card like Fia."

And didn't that feel annoying to admit? Sure, he was deeply thankful for what his Heart Card could do for his mental health. However, **Keen Spear** definitely left a lot to be desired in a whole variety of ways, and Rowan couldn't help but wonder what he could have done with a more damage-focused card.

Could he have moved away from his near-suicidal battle style? Maybe he could even have contributed to the fight against the very first Epic he encountered, rather than be stuck watching as Kayla obliterated it.

His self-doubt was abruptly ended when Olivia twisted in his arms and pulled herself up to kiss him. For a few blissful seconds, there were absolutely no thoughts in his head at all.

"I understand why you feel that way," she finally whispered when they parted, a gentle look in her eyes. "But there's very little we can do about that. They need to fight. To grow. If they really wanted to pursue whatever ambitions or dreams they have, they would have ended up in similar situations regardless."

The hero groaned and laid his head on her shoulder, pulling her closer. "I know. I know. I really don't like this world sometimes. Then again, you're in it, so . . ."

She giggled and wound her fingers into his hair, pulling him back so she could kiss him again. "Aren't you sweet! Guess I need to remind you why this world can be nice."

As reluctant as he was to run away from Olivia's kisses, Rowan did do so eventually. There was plenty to do, after all. Classes with her mother, training with the soldiers, prep work for future expeditions. On and on the task list went, so he headed toward the training grounds and she split off back to her lab.

For all her grousing over not getting to spend more time with him, Olivia did love spending time with her experiments. Especially lately, considering the fact that she hadn't yet managed to do much with the new, exotic materials they'd recently acquired.

She still had the flesh of a draconic creature, as well as the blood and some materials collected from several of the Epics they killed while rescuing Blake. They hadn't managed to take as much as they would have liked in their reckless escape from the scene, but something was better than nothing.

So, Rowan's favorite alchemist had more than enough tasks of her own.

Meanwhile, Rowan was no longer able to ignore the feeling of strength, no matter how subtle, that had taken root in his chest.

For the first time in a very long time, Rowan took a thorough look at his status.

**Rowan Clairfont**
**Level 63 Spear of Unity**
**Mana: 65/65**
**EXP: 900,000/3,000,0000**
**STR: 68* (+3)**
**VIT: 15 (+3)**
**DEX: 68* (+3)**
**PER: 23 (+3)**
**INT: 13 (+3)**
**WIS: 14 (+3)**

**Deck (6/6):**
**[Heart] Keen Spear (Epic, Passive)**
**[Class] Knight Designation (Epic, Passive)**
**[Class] Reaping Spear (Rare, Active)**
**[Class] Blood Siphon (Uncommon, Passive)**
**Natural Renewal (Epic, Active)**
**Gluttonous Banquet (Epic, Passive)**

**Blessings:**
**Awakened Blessing of the Stalwart Hero**

**Bound Weapons:**
**Spear of the Blood Well**

The first thing that stood out was the fact that he finally, *finally* had more mana to play around with. And he would have gladly invested more in his intelligence stat if he had any points to spare at all.

The second thing that demanded his attention was the confirmation of what he feared, and one of the main reasons why he'd avoided pulling up his entire status recently: Blake wasn't giving Rowan the extra stats that he should have gotten from designating the hero as a [Knight].

Particularly annoying was the fact that he should have gotten at least eight or so stats in both his strength and wisdom, the two stats that [Holy Paladin] prioritized.

Still, even with all that, Rowan couldn't deny that he was starting to feel excited. Already, just from designating level-one [Knights], he got an extra three points in every stat. That was an equivalent to stats he could gain from *nine* levels.

*I really need to hurry up and find more knight candidates. Even if they're not particularly exceptional, the stats alone will help me immensely.* To say that Rowan wasn't tempted to just venture into the barracks and start making [Knights] would have been a lie.

The only thing that stopped him was knowing that such reckless behavior would be a waste. If he could pick out or train competent fighters and then give them an extra card from his own deck, they'd be far more useful in the long run than any immediate boost to his own stats.

Rowan was so caught up in his thoughts, and so used to venturing to the training grounds set aside for his use, that he was barely aware of his surroundings. Only when he finally set foot inside the walled-off section of the manor grounds did he realize there was already someone there.

Desperate shouts of frustration filled the air as Blake drove a practice sword into a training dummy again and again. Frustration burned in his eyes, and his face was fixed in such a rictus of discontent that Rowan was tempted to back off and leave.

It was only their friendship and the tears streaming down Blake's cheeks that kept him rooted in place, silently watching as the other hero finally faltered, sword slipping from cramping fingers, and collapsed to his knees.

To say that Rowan was caught up in indecision would have been an understatement. The desire to help his friend warred bitterly in his chest with the knowledge that he likely didn't want to be in such a state.

Thankfully, Blake took the pressure of making a choice from him.

"I know you're there." Blake's voice was practically a whisper, barely loud enough to reach Rowan. "Saw you on my way down. You might as well stay."

Bitterness. That was the main emotion that tinged the statement. That, and an unhealthy dose of self-loathing. Rowan ventured closer, approaching the way he would a wounded animal. Of course, he scolded himself for that just moments later, then plopped himself into the dirt right next to his friend.

A glance at said friend's hands revealed that they were raw and bloody. Rowan had no clue how long he'd been out there, but he was apparently proficient at tormenting himself. At least his borrowed regeneration card was already working hard to fix the problem.

"What happened?" Rowan asked. It was a simple question, but encompassed so many others he'd rather have asked.

When he spoke again, Blake's voice was remarkably calm. "I saw you. With those kids. [Knight] hopefuls, right? Did any of them pass?"

"Three. The other two gave up too quickly. Can't take them out there if they're going to quit on me the first time something tries to put them in the ground," Rowan answered without much thinking, then had to fight down a cringe when he realized how it might come across.

The other hero gave a bitter laugh. "Yeah, that checks out. Hey, Rowan? Do you think I'm weak?"

"Where's that coming from now?"

"I saw you testing them. I didn't stick around until the end, but they were *good.* You might not have been taking them very seriously, but they did push you. I saw that, so don't bother denying it. Do I ever do the same, when we train together?"

They'd only started very recently. It took several days for the other hero to even regain enough mobility to be able to start. However, Rowan hesitated to answer his actual question.

The truth of the matter was that the answer was a resounding no. Blake wasn't utterly horrible or anything like that. But he fought like a beginner. His attacks were sluggish, his skill nothing to write home about, and the less said about the quality of his stances the better.

It was like someone had put Blake through a couple of swordsmanship classes, until he was able to copy how most of the moves should look, and then called it quits.

"That bad, huh?" Blake ventured when the silence stretched. "Yeah, you don't need to say anything, I guess. I know you've been trying to help me fix that, you're not exactly known for your subtlety."

"I don't know a whole lot about using a sword," Rowan said lamely, trying to use it as an excuse for his lack of comment. It was true, too. He had no clue how to help his friend without bringing in an expert. All he could do was fight and let him figure things out on his own.

Blake scoffed, then leaned back on arms that were still trembling from his exertion. "Yeah, no. Stop that. I just suck. You know I suck. I know I suck. We all know I suck. Guess that's why I got my ass handed to me so badly."

Rowan wanted to protest. To point out that, from what the other hero had mentioned, he could use blessings, miracles, and other priest spells that he relied heavily on in combat. But then, wasn't his class supposed to be focused around weapons combat and supported by those spells?

Rowan didn't know a whole lot about paladins, but he was pretty sure of at least that much.

"We can train together. If, well . . . if you don't mind, I can ask the baron to help. Or maybe Bron. Or any one of my sword wielding officers. Better the first two, really. They know a whole lot about the sword, but the latter can keep things quiet if you prefer that."

"You really think they'd train me? I mean, I drank with Baron Sutton yesterday, but that was more down to your engagement than anything else. Congratulations again, by the way."

"Thanks." For at least a moment, a smile spread across Rowan's face. Every time he was reminded of his new premarital status, a warmth blossomed in his chest. It was just slightly blunted by their current conversation. "And yes, I think they will, if we ask."

"Even though Mirabella's family stole their lands and title?"

Rowan hadn't expected that question. His head whipped to the side so fast he could swear there was a crack in his neck that made his regeneration card kick in. "What?"

Blake laughed, even if it was a bleak, humorless sound. "Again, Rowan, I'm not blind. I asked her when I noticed all the tension. I know she comes from the Treagon family, but she's really not like that, I promise."

Rowan had a guess that there was already history between the two. He released a weary sigh, then let himself fall back fully. When he thumped onto the ground, Blake joined him a second later.

"I know I probably shouldn't get wrapped up in all the politics and dislike her myself, but it's kind of difficult when both my in-laws and my fiancée feel so strongly on the subject. I do promise they'll stay civil. And yes, I think Kayden would train you even with all the drama."

What Rowan failed to mention was that Kayden Sutton was far more likely to dislike Blake due to his patron goddess. As one of the very few followers of Aristaeus left among the noble ranks, the literal chosen one of the light goddess was likely to rub him the wrong way.

Still, Rowan was pretty sure the man wouldn't say no. He was set on protecting the kingdom first and foremost. An incompetent hero could not properly assist with that task.

"Well, if my opinion counts for anything, I don't blame you for that. Just, please try?" Blake asked. "She's probably my favorite member of my party. Never tried to marry me, doesn't get crazy overprotective, she's just . . . there. And helpful."

Rowan felt the need to groan. He'd already known that the woman was Blake's favorite. Knowing his friend, even with how dense he typically pretended to be on the subject, Rowan suspected he was actually tempted to start a relationship with the Treagon.

That's what the last few days of observation told him, at least.

"I'll try. For you. Now, no avoiding the subject anymore. What happened here?"

It took several long moments for Blake to respond. When he did, he just sounded tired. "I'm not sure I can do this, Rowan. My swordsmanship is a mess. My magic's barely there and I can do nothing with it. Even my connection with my goddess is cloudy and weak, at best. My stats, too. They're not working."

"So, what exactly are you trying to say?" Rowan asked, his heart hammering away in his chest. He really didn't like the way Blake was talking. He sounded far too resigned.

"Maybe I should go back to the capital. Maybe they can, I don't know, fix me? Or if they can't, maybe I can join the church fully. I don't think I'd do so badly as a priest. Or maybe I should just go out into the frontier and see what happens."

He said it like a joke, but the amount of self-loathing imbued in those last words let Rowan know exactly what his best friend was hoping for.

In less than a second, Rowan was on his side and looming over the other hero, a scowl etched on his features. "No. You're not going to say shit like that again. You'll feel helpless and you'll hate it, sure, but if you suggest you want to commit suicide one more time I'll—!"

He cut himself off, his stomach roiling as he fought down the anger and fear. The pained expression on Blake's face broke his heart, but served as a great reminder that blowing up at him wasn't going to fix a single thing.

So, Rowan pushed his depressingly low intelligence and wisdom stats as far as they could go. *How can I fix this?* Such a simple question, with seemingly a simple solution that was immediately apparent: Blake felt useless and weak. All he had to do was make it so Blake wasn't useless or weak.

Of course, that *would* demand a bit of a gamble.

"You know what, Blake? That's actually a great idea." Rowan lied through his teeth, fear hammering away inside him. "Why not go out into the wastes? In fact, we're going tomorrow. Together. I'd rather you didn't bring your party along, but I'll understand if you do."

"Rowan?" Blake asked uncertainly, but the Stalwart Hero was already walking away, thoughts tumbling through his mind.

Blake's stats weren't working. His class was all scrambled, and his level was lower than it was supposed to be. In fact, even his deck was locked away behind errors and whatever system nonsense happened when the corruption that had taken root in the hero was violently removed.

Removed by Rowan's spear going through Blake's chest.

The Stalwart Hero shook away the guilt, nausea, and disgust with his own weakness. He'd done what he had to. The alternative was letting his best friend become a corrupted demonic creature, or even a true demon outright.

Besides, there was one thing they could focus on, one thing that was giving him hope: Blake still had an experience bar.

So, what would happen if they filled it?

Would it jostle his stats into action? Would it give him back a fraction of his former strength? What if they got him all the way back to Epic?

It wasn't going to be simple, necessarily, but with the hero blessing's experience boosts, it wasn't exactly an unreachable goal, not with Rowan's entire party at Epic now.

The only trouble was, he didn't want to dangle that hope in front of Blake. If they tried and they failed, something told Rowan that his best friend would be utterly crushed.

And the Stalwart Hero wasn't sure he could pull him back from that particular cliff.

## CHAPTER FIVE

# Resolve

Rowan would forever deny the accusations that the two of them sneaked out of the city. Or that it happened just a single day after his decision to do something about his best friend's depression.

But for all his denials, it didn't change the fact that it was more or less true.

Rowan had organized several parties of experienced soldiers to accompany them. Likewise, convincing his party members to play along was a simple affair. But trying to reason with the three overprotective women Blake had following him around?

That wasn't something Rowan was willing to tackle without very good incentive.

No, it was much easier to kidnap Blake right out of his room. Besides, it was kind of funny when Rowan entered the room, bundled him up in the covers, and just carried him out. The other hero looked amused rather than upset, and bringing a smile to Blake's face was nice, however briefly.

Getting him into gear was a little more embarrassing, seeing as Blake was forced to shimmy out of his pajamas in front of a whole group of onlookers, but he gamely got through that, too.

Blake only put up a minor fight when Rowan tried to offer him a sword, but Rowan managed to talk sense into him eventually. He was not going to let his best friend fight with only a light construct, which would disappear the moment he ran out of mana.

"You do, of course, realize what's going to happen when they realize their hero has vanished during the night, right?" Olivia quipped, pressing herself close to Rowan's side as they made their way out of the city.

"Well, it probably won't be pretty," the hero readily admitted, but the self-satisfied smirk more than attested to the fact that he didn't care. "Do you think they'll actually come hunt us down in the wastes, though?"

Olivia laughed, and Blake scoffed. "They're probably going to be asleep when we get back. Was it really necessary to get up this early?"

"It's not *that* bad," Rowan defended himself, eyeing the sky.

True, the sun was only starting to peek over the horizon. Still, if they ventured into the wastes early, they could return well before nightfall. That was a rather big priority for Rowan, all told. In spite of getting relatively used to it, he did prefer his own bed to sleeping in a tent.

Cuddling up with Olivia was a whole lot easier that way.

"You're the boss," Blake said.

There was a sort of peace about Blake that confused Rowan. Just the day before, the man was a mess. Enough of a mess, in fact, to prompt Rowan's insistence on the excursion. Now? He seemed far more at ease with himself, even if there was an odd stiffness to his movement.

"You good?"

"Yes, why?" Blake looked legitimately confused by the question.

"It's nothing, sorry for pushing," Rowan mumbled, deciding to drop the subject for the time being. They did have an entire day ahead of them, after all.

When they were well within the wastes and with scouts sent ahead to find something for them to fight, Rowan turned toward Blake and his newer, less experienced knights. Blake gave him a small smile, but the three looked more than a little worried about their surroundings.

"Now then. All three of you have decent skill with your chosen weapons. Good work. What you need now is leveling experience, so that's what we're out here for. Welcome to the wastes." Rowan paused, taking the chance to gauge their reactions. In spite of the fear he felt from them, they seemed to be determined to make the most of the outing, if their expressions were anything to go by. He could work with that. "Since most enemies out here are at least at the Uncommon tier, you'll be working with Hero Blake. He's currently weakened due to an injury, but he's still more than skilled enough to cover you and let you show off what you know. You can't really party up with him, since he has his own party already, but—"

"Actually, they can," Blake cut in, causing Rowan to shoot him a confused expression. "I temporarily disbanded my previous party. They were using the party link to track me down whenever I needed a moment to myself, so . . ."

"Ah. Well, that's lucky then, I suppose. Turns out, you lot are going to be leveling up even faster than I expected," Rowan said.

Rowan watched as Greg, the party's defender and current party leader, sent an invite to the hero with eyes so wide they were threatening to pop out. There was definitely some hero worship going on there, literal and metaphorical, that Rowan found kind of cute.

Still, he needed to move things along.

"Here's the advice I can give you: Whatever kind of combatant you want to be, put your all into it. I'm not a swordsman or guardian, so I cannot comment there. However, Fia, I want you to commit fully to each and every attack you made. You have party members. Trust them to cover you from damage."

She nodded seriously, while Greg paled at the responsibility that suddenly landed in his lap.

Rowan wasn't entirely convinced it was the best possible choice for the girl to follow in his footsteps. Still, with her Heart Card, she needed to get a more aggressive class if she wanted to make good use of her advantages. So, the least he could do was get her started down the right path.

"By the way, I don't want any of you trying to play hero—yes, I'm talking to you, too, Blake. Do not get all self-sacrificial to block each other from damage, or try to get in the killing blow as quickly as you can. You have excellent regeneration, each and every one of you. Plus, my party's here, too. You'll all live, so just focus on your jobs and doing them well!"

Rowan got a round of nods from the younger trio and a solid pout from Blake. Rowan was just about to let his worry get in the ways of things and lecture them some more when the scouts returned.

"My lord, we've discovered a group of Uncommon monsters just to the east of here. There are three, all around starting levels for the tier, and they're those weird lizard things we ran into when building the fake monster stampede. Should I lead the recruits there?"

Dale, as always, was a picture-perfect example of dedication and efficiency. It drew a smile to Rowan's face to see him again. With all the chaos happening recently and with the hero party hitting the Epic tier, there really wasn't much excuse to venture out into the field personally again.

Of course, Rowan had authorized the request for the level-grinding expeditions to continue. At that point, there wasn't really a soldier in his army that was still stuck at Uncommon. As far as the hero was concerned, a mere three recruits didn't count.

"Go on, then. We'll be right behind you. Knights, I want you on his tail. Engage as soon as you spot the enemy."

Having given his orders, Rowan watched the group surge after the scout. Dale was slowing down his pace to allow everyone to keep up. Out of all the soldiers under Rowan, the hero was fairly certain the man had one of the highest levels.

"I don't want any of you jumping in to save them at the first sign of trouble." Rowan addressed the three parties of soldiers who were still hanging around them, the fourth one they'd brought along being the scouts.

"Not even me?" Marcus ventured uncertainly, brow furrowed. "You know, I can easily keep them one hundred percent safe."

"I know, that's the problem. I want to see how they do against opponents when faced by actual monsters. Besides . . . I really need Blake to get his act together. He's not really okay at the moment. Trust me, he needs this. Besides, they do have my **Natural Renewal**."

"True. Well, okay, if you think that's best."

Rowan really wasn't sure of anything, but he had to try *something*. If he left things alone, he'd probably regret it for the rest of his days.

He refused to share that with the rest of the party, though. Instead, he rushed after the rapidly fading silhouettes of the knight party.

Ironically, they almost overtook them.

The speed at which mere Common-tier classes could move was far below Epic tiers. For Olivia and Milena, even if they never invested a single point in their physical stats, there was a certain quality to their mana and bodies from being at the Epic tier. That meant they could personally witness the very first clash between the newly formed party and their opponents.

The monsters were vaguely humanoid lizards that nonetheless preferred to move around on all fours. Rowan hadn't fought them personally, but he knew they didn't use any particularly special or tricky cards from reading reports.

The worst they could do would be to maul the four a little, but they were overall safe. His regeneration card prevented wound infection, and Greg was protected by his natural toughness as a troll halfling, too.

For a moment, just a split second, really, Rowan saw Blake hesitate. It was right before the battle. Rowan saw himself, back when he first arrived in the world, reflected in Blake then. The Radiant Hero could no longer tap into most of his strength. Would that be enough to rob him of his courage, too?

Blake rid Rowan of that fear when he charged forward with a cry. It wasn't a particularly brave or intimidating cry, but it was definitely filled with enough frustration and anger to make the lizard creatures flinch.

His first strike was a critical hit, too. The sword took on an iridescent sheen as Blake channeled his mana into it, using his Heart Card to hone the edges of the sword with light constructs far sharper than most natural metals.

All that meant the sword parted flesh like water, and be it arms or the creature's torso, they were all neatly sheared through.

The entire top of the lizard creature listed, then collapsed back in a spray of blood.

The show was, unfortunately, a little much for the inexperienced recruits. All three of them froze up, and that ended up costing Blake.

The leftover lizards leaped at him, claws first. Which was when he complemented his amazing opening with a critical fumble.

Blake stood there and glared, preparing his sword for a swing. His body flared with light, and while that was enough to briefly stop the claws and fangs of the first lizard, the addition of the second one was enough to both stagger the hero and break through his defenses.

He only managed to get out a strangled *ack* before he was on his back and the monsters were chewing through his limbs.

The gory sight of their ally going down jerked the other three into motion.

Greg swung his hammer around and brought it down on the nearest lizard's head without thinking, dazing the creature and denting its skull, but also drawing a scream from Blake when the attack pushed the creature's teeth deeper into his flesh.

Fia, meanwhile, followed Rowan's instructions to the letter. With a manic look in her eyes, she squared her shoulder and charged the other lizard. She was aiming straight for its face, which Rowan figured could go either very well or very badly, but the monster turned to hiss at her.

In other words, it shifted and opened its mouth at exactly the worst moment possible.

Her spear met the back of its throat, and then the young spearwoman *lifted* the monster off Blake, muscles pumping with all her strength before she slammed everything down and speared it to the ground.

It thrashed and struggled, but it took mere seconds before life bled out of it.

That left their intrepid swordsman, who paused midcharge at the sight of his teammate taking out a monster on her own before rounding on the other lizard and desperately trying to get a stab in where the creature was now writhing on the ground and getting hammered again and again by Greg.

It lay on the ground a minute later, with plenty of shallow cuts and looking a lot like tenderized meat.

Honestly, Rowan had no clue what to say. No, that wasn't entirely right. He had *several* choice words he wanted to say.

"What were you thinking, freezing up and trying to tank those monsters like that?" scolded Rowan, inspecting Blake for leftover scratches, bruises, and other marks of combat.

His regeneration card still wasn't working at full capacity for the other hero, but with the assistance of one of Olivia's healing potions, Blake was right as rain in minimal time. Really, Rowan was just fussing over him because he was a big idiot who ate attacks to the face willingly.

"Um, that I could defend myself using my Heart Card?" Blake ventured, a hesitant smile on his face. Somehow, the other hero looked happy with the way things had worked out, in spite of being used as a chew toy.

It infuriated Rowan, and he really hoped that his glare showed that properly.

"You, too, Greg. Check to see if you *should* start swinging wildly before you do it. And while we're at it, try to make it possible for your allies to fight alongside you. You almost brained Desmond several times."

"Sorry, boss. I mean, my lord," the part-troll mumbled sheepishly, rubbing his head.

Rowan didn't have time for that. "Desmond, I know you wanted to contribute. And you'll have a chance to do it, trust me. However, that doesn't mean you should try to butt in on this big lug here making mincemeat out of a monster. He was clearly in a panic and not paying attention. Pick your battles more carefully."

He turned toward the final member of the group, who sent him a hesitant smile and wave. "My turn?" Fia asked. Rowan's lips threatened to twitch into a smile, but he smothered his amusement.

"Yes. Your turn." Rowan paused for a dramatic moment, before finally letting that smile show. "Good job. Lucky shot, don't get me wrong. But still. You committed, you succeeded, and you held on until the damn thing stopped twitching. It's all I could ask of you."

"Thank you, my lord!" She beamed, then shot a look of superiority at her teammates. Well, at Greg and Desmond, at least.

A blush rose on her face when Blake shot her a happy grin. Rowan really wanted to scoff and brain him just a little with his nice metal spear. Blake had enough trouble at home without accidentally winning over Rowan's newest recruit.

"Okay, the lot of you are just fine now. Well, Blake has shredded armor, but he'll live. Might remind you not to just eat enemy damage in the future." Rowan took the chance to glare menacingly again. Blake once more returned a radiant smile. "Get ready to move out. Scouts found another group."

And they did. Dale had slipped away to rendezvous with his party while Rowan and Olivia took care of the aftermath and the twins looked on in amusement. He'd shown back up before they were even done with a few whispers of other discovered monster groups.

Rowan was tempted to lead them straight toward the poisoned mushroom monsters the man told him were farther east, but decided that kind of test could wait awhile. Instead, he told the scout to take them toward more of the lizard things.

With how numerous they were now, Rowan was pretty sure they had been displaced en masse into the territory near his city by either the dinosaur Epic that had tried to make its way to Rest's Remorse or by the massive battle waged to rescue Blake.

Either way, they were convenient opponents for the knights. As far as he could tell, the only really troublesome card they had was one that allowed them to make their teeth and claws extra sharp. That was how they so easily tore through Blake's borrowed armor set.

For just a moment, Rowan wished they'd taken along Blake's own set of armor.

While Blake didn't have a particularly good sword—it wasn't even bound like Rowan's own spear was—his armor *was* superb. It had easily seen him through the earlier monster siege and didn't even have a scratch as far Rowan saw.

That was also exactly why he didn't want Blake to have it while they were trying to get him back to Epic. It was far too much of a crutch. If he'd had it, he *could* have made it through the fight unblemished.

*But what happens the first time he fights something that doesn't care about armor? Like, oh, I don't know, a Legendary demon*? Rowan thought, genuinely upset and worried. *Whoever trained Blake to fight like that needs to be shot. Or run through with several spears, rather.*

Rowan was ready to volunteer his services there.

Before they could reach the next group of monsters, he wanted to make sure his fellow hero understood exactly what was on the line. "Blake?"

"Hmm?" Blake turned, shooting him one of his frustratingly charming signature smiles.

"If you just stand there and let a monster savage you, I'll help you fulfill your masochistic tendencies instead. I'm going to carry you back to the city stuck on my spear like a kebab," Rowan said, menacingly enough that his friend actually paled.

"You wouldn't, right? Right?"

Rowan said nothing. He just stared.

It wasn't like Blake could call his bluff when he actually meant every word he said. He'd either learn, or Rowan would *force* him to.

"O-okay! I get it! I promise!"

"Good."

Blake did, as he said, get it. Unfortunately, that didn't mean that he was suddenly and magically graced with the right mentality and muscle memory.

He froze up and hesitated. Overall, he was a big doofus that worried Rowan to no end. Rowan ended up spending at least half of the trip oscillating between panic and a desire for violence. If there was one thing Blake was good for, though, it was following through on his word.

Not even once did he try to consciously tank the attacks of the monsters. He tried to dodge or force a distance. As battles went by, he was even getting better at playing keep-away, much to Rowan's relief.

So, he improved from battle to battle. Killing lizards, battling poisonous mushroom treants, crippling weird glowing spiders—it all helped hone Blake's instincts.

In fact, seeing how quickly he was improving, Rowan was baffled at how he'd ended up with such a sloppy fighting style to begin with. He'd always known Blake to be highly athletic. So if Rowan had managed to learn how to fight, logic dictated that Blake should have been more than fine as well.

The answer was as obvious as it was sickening: sabotage. Someone had made sure that a hero *adopted by the king* himself was a subpar fighter at best. Someone had led him to overly rely on his greater stats, cards, and blessing to claim his victories.

The only question was who. Was it his party who wanted him gone? A rival of the king who somehow weaseled himself into a position of trust and authority within the court? Or was it the worst possible option—the king himself?

Rowan simply didn't know.

And as he watched Blake fight, he resolved not to care overmuch, either, until they got strong enough to do something about it together.

To finish out the day, Rowan asked the scouts to find one final group of lizards for his knights to battle. This time, there were four lizards in the group, and Rowan could not have been more proud of the way they handled themselves.

To start things off, Greg released a loud shout of rage that had all four of the enemies perking up. With his tower shield at the front and firmly planted between himself and violence, the defender met their charge.

Meanwhile, Fia and Desmond fanned out around him, Fia using her spear on Greg's left and the swordsman using his great sword on the right.

They responded perfectly to the lizards' attempts to slip past the shield, harrying them to remain behind the barrier while Greg enthusiastically brained any of the monsters that tried to scamper over his shield.

And then there was Blake, rushing in from the side with his sword blazing.

No matter what Rowan said, the hero refused to see reason and properly stick behind the shield bearer, but at least this time he didn't embarrass himself.

His sword slid through limbs with expert ease, aiming to disable, cripple, and generally deal unpleasant injuries rather than trying to end things in one glorious attack right at the start.

A part of Rowan was a bit upset at how quickly the other hero had gotten more proficient with his blade. His attacks didn't belong to any particular style, true. They weren't exactly graceful, either. Forced to fight for his life without any security or big battle-ending moves, Blake had adopted a butcher's efficiency with his chosen deathly implement.

Each strike had no pointless frills and was aimed right where the hero needed it to go. His sword sliced, stabbed, and even parried claws or fangs at times. The latter might have been a good way for a swordsman to quickly destroy their own weapon under different circumstances, but Blake's light manipulation and construct conjuring were just as overpowered as the first time Rowan saw them. Worse, really, since he'd had considerable time to practice since then, and it was the one thing he really had put effort into in the past.

His light kept the sword razor-sharp, unblemished, and looking like he'd only just accepted it from the armorer, who had withdrawn it from the fresh equipment supply just that morning.

Of course, Blake was still hardly perfect. He was eventually forced to fall back after dicing up two of the lizards when the others tried to get him from the sides, seeing him as an easier target than the shield.

However, he kept his wits about him, properly falling back while keeping his enemies at bay with shallow, quick strikes, and did more than enough to distract them until the other knights could strike.

Strike they did.

Fia's admirable ferocity shown at the start of the day only burned brighter as it continued. With a silent thrust that was backed by her full strength and the weight of her body, she drove her weapon into a lizard's throat. From there, Rowan got to watch a repeat of her first fight.

Desmond, meanwhile, was far more in his element than he was in the morning. Hours of beating down Uncommon creatures gave him level after level, and that was doing plenty to bolster his courage. Unhampered by the doubt and fear of total inexperience, he was starting to show promise.

He fell upon the monsters and damn near took his chosen target's head off with a merciless swing of his great sword. In the end, the lizards were cleaned up without so much as a scratch.

Only Greg was left looking dissatisfied by the battle, glancing between his shield and his hammer speculatively.

"Marcus?" Rowan quietly caught the wolfkin's attention, then pointed in the direction of the part-troll boy. "Could you maybe do something about him?"

Marcus looked confused for a second before understanding flooded his features. With a determined nod, he marched off toward the boy and with a few hushed words took him aside. Frankly, Rowan knew Greg was in the right hands.

Marcus put everything, heart, soul, and stat points, into defending his party. If there was anyone who could properly explain the importance of a tank to a party's long-term survival and success, it was him.

Frankly, Rowan was pretty sure that Blake's presence was the only reason Greg wasn't being showered in compliments and thanks. With the hero—a fighter determined to risk his life in the dumbest ways—added into the mix, Greg hadn't had a real opportunity to shine yet.

On that subject, Rowan marched closer to the celebrating trio. "You know, I really wish you'd just start fighting with a bit more caution," he grumbled in Blake's direction. "You are setting a bad example for them."

The puzzlement on Blake's face clearly said he had no idea what Rowan was accusing him of.

"Not everyone runs around with solid light constructs, top-quality enchanted armor, and a whole party dedicated to keeping them alive, Blake."

"Oh. Well, um, I'll work on it?" Blake did look sheepish, but Rowan sincerely doubted he'd take his words to heart.

In Blake's head, the whole thing was simple: If he risked his hide by charging in, other people were safer. Ergo, it was an amazing thing and he'd keep doing it.

"Don't lie to my face, you ass."

Before Blake could come up with an excuse, they were interrupted by Dale's return. The scout didn't look worried, but he was definitely approaching them quickly enough to get Rowan's attention.

"My lord, there's another group of these lizard monsters not far from here. They're led by a Rare tier, which is noticeably bigger and stronger than the rest. We think it only tiered up recently, given the small size of the group."

They'd come across similar groups throughout the day, and Rowan had insisted they avoid them for the time being. Blake's frustration might be clear on his face since he needed experience, but it wasn't something Rowan was willing to risk just yet.

"How many are there?"

"Just four, the Rare tier included."

Rowan blinked. That really was a low number. All the rest had at least twenty Uncommon lizards following them around. "Okay, lead us around them. We're done for the day, anyway."

"Wait." It was, of course, Blake's voice that cut in. Rowan sighed, knowing exactly what was about to come out of his mouth. "I want to fight it. There's only three others, right? You guys can take those on your own?"

Predictably, the rest of Blake's temporary party nodded quickly.

That left the Stalwart Hero staring directly into Blake's eyes, wondering what to do. He almost startled at what he saw there.

Resolve. Quite unlike anything he'd seen from Blake in the last few days. It shone through, loud and clear, reminding Rowan of the Blake he'd always known.

As such, there was really only one thing Rowan could say. "Fine. But if you somehow get yourself killed, don't come crying to *me*."

The knight party broke into excited chatter, and Rowan couldn't entirely resist a smile. Perhaps the outing would be good for his old friend after all.

## CHAPTER SIX

# Struggle

Rowan had been caught up in worry, fear, and more than a little doubt ever since Blake's awakening. That's why it was such a relief to see a real smile on the man's face. Not the smile that he put on when he knew Rowan was looking, since he'd long ago grown adept at spotting those, but a sincere, genuine smile of *hope*.

When those first experience points started trickling in, when he realized that there was a way for him to potentially regain strength, Rowan's chest swelled with happiness for his friend.

To see him marching forward, determined to face down an enemy at his own tier despite his weakness? Rowan might have been acting all grumpy, but truth be told, there were few things he'd rather see than that.

However, there was a trace of underlying worry about what could happen when Blake faced down his foe in true, one-on-one combat. Which was why Rowan subtly slowed down his steps, letting the excited and nervous knights put just slightly more distance between them and his own party.

Olivia noticed immediately, of course, seeing as they were walking hand in hand, but she just sent him a sly smile and played along.

Milena and Marcus took a bit longer to catch on, but no one could make the claim that the twins were slow on the uptake.

"What's wrong?" Marcus asked, his eyes shooting between Rowan and Blake. "Want to call this off after all? It *might* be a bit much."

"No, no." Rowan took a deep breath and then tried to release all his worries with it. "I don't want to hold him back. Not now. Not when he's finally starting to believe that he can get back on his feet. Just . . . keep an eye on things, yeah? You can react a whole lot faster to such things than I can."

"Got it. I'll be ready to use my aura if need be. Still, you really think this is a good idea? What if he, you know, gets hurt? Badly?"

Rowan ignored the question for the moment, because he honestly didn't know. He didn't want to outright say it, but Rowan could understand Marcus's worry.

Throughout the day, they'd gotten to see what the kingdom's darling hero was really made of, and none of Rowan's party members were particularly impressed. Milena, in particular, had stopped paying much attention to the fight long ago.

Now she was still stuck with her nose in a thick book with a rather suspicious cover, one that Rowan was absolutely sure was made of some kind of leather or, dare he say it—*skin.*

"What?" Milena noticed the way he was looking at her and curled her lips in a literally fanged grin. "Your mother-in-law got this grimoire for me. Neat, isn't it? I'm going to be so much more useful when I master some of the rituals in here."

"I thought you chose to follow your particular advancement path because you knew rituals and such that you could use already?" Rowan asked. He was most definitely not changing the subject just because he didn't want to face the fact that his best friend might be in danger. It was completely down to his fascination with the [Shaman] class, of course.

Milena's smile dimmed a little and she turned back to her book, but she did answer. "I didn't have many, exactly. Sure, I could make temporary familiar bonds like I did in Felton's Mill, and I can summon ancestral spirits, and I do have a couple other rituals, but . . . Well, when we left our home, we didn't take much with us. We couldn't."

Rowan shot Marcus a look, and the other twin filled in for the unasked question. "It would have been stealing. Some of the scrolls that [Shamans] use are unique. We couldn't exactly rob our own clan of important artifacts. The shield and staff were made for us, and the rituals my sister knows are relatively common."

That didn't sound like the whole truth, not really. Rowan seriously doubted that a ritual that summoned the souls of one's ancestors was common, but he wasn't willing to press.

"Anyway, what you should be worrying about aren't my rituals," Milena said. "Let me repeat Marcus's question: Is your friend going to make it?"

The question sent another stab of doubt through Rowan chest.

The facts of the matter remained. Blake *was* practically crippled, and most of his stats' effects were sealed off, leaving him with a physique barely on par with a strong Uncommon tier. His mana was impacted, too, losing some of its, for lack of better words, weight and volume. His cards were also an issue none of them knew how to solve yet. And while he *was* coming along nicely with his sword skills, they still weren't great.

In spite of that . . .

"Yes. Yes, he will. He can do this." Rowan chose to believe in his friend and reassure his party. It wasn't something he could pin down and define properly. However, that look in Blake's eyes? Well, he couldn't exactly ignore *that*.

It didn't take them long after their little chat to draw close to the group led by the Rare tier.

The creatures, according to the scouts, were hunting and scavenging for food. Before Dale left the group to inform them of their presence, the lizards had managed to bring down a couple other forest denizens, too.

As such, when they finally cautiously drew close, the group of four were caught up in stuffing their faces with meat from wolflike monsters.

This gave Blake and his temporary party a chance to strategize a little, which they were taking full advantage of in quiet whispers.

"I'm going to charge straight at the leader, but if I get surrounded, I don't think I'll be able to handle them all." Blake seemed pained to make that particular admission, but Rowan just saw it as progress. If he could stop being stubborn and trying to handle everything himself, his friend might just survive the coming battles after a hopeful recovery.

"I can try and taunt all of them?" Greg offered, then quickly rushed to explain when the rest of his party shot him disbelieving looks. "I don't want to deal with the Rare, I know I can't, but my taunt's unlikely to affect it anyway."

"That sounds like a great idea, then," Fia quipped with a grin. "That will draw all the Uncommon lizards to us, and our intrepid leader can handle the Rare on his own. Sound good?"

Blake looked like he was about to protest her nickname for him, but he eventually smiled and nodded his head. "Sounds good. Besides, that lets us keep our plan nice and simple. If we try for something complicated, we'll just mess it all up. Trust me."

From where Rowan was standing and listening in, he had to fight the urge to chuckle. That particular comment sounded like it came from experience.

With that done, the group finally straightened and, with what was starting to resemble familiarity, charged forward.

That sent an odd twinge through Rowan's chest.

Was it cruel of him, to force them to team up like that, knowing that the trio would not be able to continue fighting with Blake? He was watching in real time as the other hero won them over with his sincerity and natural charisma.

When it was time for them to part, and the time would come much sooner than anyone would like, would they be able to work smoothly with Blake's replacement?

The battle started with Greg's roar echoing through the wastes, and Rowan tore himself away from his downward spiral.

The lizard monsters startled from their meal, immediately whirling around to face the intruders. There was no hesitation as they went on the offensive, but there was a cruel gleam of something resembling intelligence in their eyes.

While the Rare tier squared up and started charging straight for the appearing humans, the other three lizard monsters dispersed, going for a flanking maneuver that would let them take advantage of their leader's superior presence on the battlefield.

Of course, that was when Greg took advantage of his card effect and three of the lizards stiffened before pivoting and heading straight for them.

Surprisingly, this was enough to actually give their leader pause, and in a show of definite cognitive improvement, the thing let loose a string of hisses at its subordinates.

When said hisses were ignored, rage lit up in its eyes, but whatever revenge or punishment it had planned were interrupted by Blake's advance. With a shout of his own, the hero's sword lit up and slashed toward the monster with surprising speed.

For once, however, Blake's speed failed him.

The hero's eyes widened as the lizard leaned away from the strike, its feet firmly planted even as the top half of its body jerked out of the way, tipping so far back a low-level human would not have been able to copy the move.

At the same time the lizard surged forward, its own claws shone menacingly as it took frantic swipes. Some of them landed on Blake's arm while one caught him right across the chest, and the hero stumbled back with a low hiss of pain.

The aura of light and the hero's armor might as well not have been there at all. The monster hadn't even aimed at particularly tattered sections of the hero's protections. Its claws simply sank right through the treated leather.

For a second, just a second, Rowan felt strongly tempted to ask Marcus to intervene. Then Blake's face was crumpled in a scowl, and the hero started to fight with a ferocity he'd lacked before.

His sword left trails of light in the air as he slashed again and again. This time, he didn't aim for the monster's chest or even head—his strikes were focused on its limbs, preventing the Rare tier from taking free potshots when the hero missed.

And he did keep missing.

Blake's new strategy was to keep the lizard on the back foot, but that was all that it achieved. As Rowan watched, it quickly dawned on him exactly why the reptilian monster's movements seemed so familiar to him.

It was like he was watching himself fight, back when he still heavily relied on the **Feline Physique** card. Rowan highly doubted it was the exact card the lizard was using, but even if it was adapted to its own reptilian body, the effects were similar. The lizard's ability to dodge and control even the minuscule movements of its own body was honed to a fine edge.

The question was, what would Blake do about that?

The hero in question was already starting to pant. His exhaustion still wasn't bad enough to prevent him from fighting effectively, but it was definitely starting to slow him down a little. Enough, in fact, that the lizard's own attacks were starting to get through.

Shallow cuts were opened all along Blake's forearms, only to seal over and stop bleeding in a matter of seconds. The reptile noticed this, too, because its hisses grew from something resembling amused to angry and agitated.

Obviously, its strategy of slowly bleeding Blake to death wasn't going to succeed easily, though Rowan privately thought it might still work out if it persisted.

Blake's regeneration still came at a cost, after all. Even if such minuscule wounds could be mostly healed by the card's draw on ambient mana, there was a limit to such things. A very small amount of the hero's own energy was still getting consumed.

Paired with his use of attacks and attempts to defend himself? Blake definitely had less stamina in this particular battle than the lizard did.

Apparently, Blake understood that just as well.

With a sudden hardening of his features, Blake drew back. He created a false opening and hoped to counterattack, but his opponent chose to pause as well instead of immediately pursuing. As they stared at each other, the two enemies took the opportunity to catch their breath.

And then, with a sudden glow that covered his entire body, Blake was moving again.

Blake raised his sword high, then brought it down with a two-handed brute swing that had Rowan wincing. The sword sang as it cut through the air, moving faster than Blake had managed since his awakening.

It still wasn't fast enough.

Blake was trying to cleave the lizard monster right through its left shoulder in an awkward blow, yet the creature easily twisted around the sword and surged forward.

Its eyes were glowing with malicious glee, claws stretched out and on a direct path to disembowel Blake. As the sharp implements started to break through his skin, the hero didn't even flinch. If anything, the smile on his face was downright vicious.

Flexing his arms, the hero changed the trajectory of his sword just so. The attack shifted and sailed through flesh and bone easily, slicing off the lizard's left leg at the hip.

Of course, the hero didn't come out of the exchange unscathed.

The monster's claws swiped over his stomach, and Rowan had to fight down his rising panic as he fully expected Blake's entrails to come tumbling out. Except that didn't happen, much to the confusion of both Rowan and the lizard.

Confusion that Blake immediately punished with another blow that caught the monster in its side. It very nearly spilled the monster's own guts across the jungle floor, but it managed to pull back without dragging the sword with it.

It might have managed to lessen the severity of the hero's blow, but the monster lost its balance in the process, tumbling to the ground—its lack of limb preventing it from landing properly. Blake was there a second later, following up with another angry swing of his sword.

The monster tried to redirect the blow with its right forearm, but the hero's sword simply cleaved through that limb, too, sending it off high into the air.

From there, what followed was the work of a butcher.

Blake's anger and the adrenaline of battle made him bring his sword down again and again until the lizard was little more than a pile of mutilated flesh. Rowan wanted to step in, yet didn't.

There were tears glistening in the other hero's eyes, and Rowan was pretty sure that the adrenaline was only part of the equation of what was happening. He'd deal with that eventually, but for just then he directed his attention fully to his other [Knights].

The kids had done just as well as Blake. Better, really.

From the very start of their battle, they were calm and in control.

Greg engaged his skill and then turned himself into the immobile fortress he was getting so good at pretending to be. His level of expertise was drastically different than when they had set out that morning.

He no longer needed to brace his shield fully on the ground. With lower monster numbers, he kept the shield outstretched, and each motion or twist of the weapon battered an enemy away. It was a lovely augmentation to his angry hammer blows when the lizards dared to try and sneak past him.

Fia was performing well, too. Rowan had taken the chance after their last battle to ask if she would like to try a slightly different style next time she fought, just to see how she liked it.

She didn't seem to enjoy this kind of battling all that much, but she was flawlessly harassing one of the lizards with numerous light jabs of her spear. Rowan didn't want to admit it, but that was the kind of stance that he could only pull off when he's finally reached the Uncommon tier.

Meanwhile, the last of the trio looked a bit underwhelming in comparison, at least if you just judged them on the flashiness of their attacks.

Desmond's weapon of choice was a great sword, and he was doing an admirable job of keeping Greg's other flank secured. The boy no longer went all out, trying to claim his own glory in battle. Instead, when the lizard he had his eyes on finally ventured too far and got bonked, he surged forward and performed a textbook downward swing. Metal met limb, and the metal won.

From there, the swordsman was masterfully quick to dismantle the monster, all from the safety of his position behind a defender.

Fia's foe went down to a finely placed strike that skewered the monster through its eye, and the final lizard died shortly after a shield bash threw it to the ground. Before it could recover or dodge to the side, Greg took a step forward and brought the shield down without mercy.

The move reminded Rowan of a guillotine, especially since it had the exact same effect on the monster.

That left them with a clearing full of dead creatures, three panting knights, and a hero who was hobbling toward the ground with a pained yet victorious smile. Naturally, Rowan immediately chose to meet Blake halfway.

"Amazing work," Rowan muttered, eyes roving over the other hero's body and cataloging the fading injuries. "How did you stop that blow to your stomach? I swear that thing's hand was halfway *inside* of you at one point."

"I—I didn't," Blake admitted with a wince. Then, at Rowan's disbelieving look, he gripped the front of his armor and pulled it up.

An long, angry red line was revealed. It was no longer bleeding, but now that Rowan knew what to look for, he immediately spotted the suspiciously dark stains that stretched all across the lower half of Blake's body.

"What the hell? Sit down, you idiot!" Rowan shouted immediately, using one hand to force his friend to do just that as he motioned to Olivia to come closer. "You know you don't have my card running at full strength yet. What were you *thinking*?"

"I was thinking that if I embarrassed myself further, you might just decide to put an end to the fight and kill the thing yourself." Blake was clearly not regretting any of this, given that he was *still* smiling. Rowan really wanted to slap that smile right off his face, but the thought of hurting him any more stopped him.

Then Olivia appeared, and Rowan's rapidly rising blood pressure calmed a little as she forced several potions down Blake's gullet.

For once, the alchemist looked just as confused and worried as Rowan was. "How are your insides not outsides right now?" she demanded, still fussing over the hero yet clearly unsure how else to help.

Rowan was wondering the same thing himself, at least until he spotted the faint glow around Blake's wound. "Wait. You're using your light constructs to keep your wound shut, aren't you?"

The smile Blake shot him was dazzling. "Yeah! I never thought about using them this way before! Honestly, this was *great.* I need you to find me another Rare monster, because this fight was so much more useful than all the others, and . . ."

The hero finally trailed off, noticing something on Rowan's face that was enough to give him pause. Good thing, too, because Rowan was just about ready to sock him in the face, consequences be damned.

In silence, the trio watched the wounds littering Blake's body slowly close and fade away like they'd never even been there, including even the blow that would have disemboweled anyone else.

In that silence, Rowan stewed.

A part of him knew he was being ridiculous. He had admittedly done much worse, to the point where Olivia had wanted to kill him herself a couple times. Trying to crawl his way *into* a draconic demon with caustic blood? Yes, not the smartest of moves. He wasn't really the best person to be scolding Blake, and he knew it.

Still, at the time, there were things he put his trust in. His regeneration card, for one, and, most importantly, Olivia and the twins.

The fact of the matter was, Rowan was one hundred percent certain that Blake would have tried to pull off that nonsense whether there was someone backing him up or not, and that's what set him off.

Rowan bent down, grabbed the other hero under his shoulder, and started dragging him away. "Can you please give us just a couple of minutes, love?" He tried to keep his voice even and relatively chipper as he tugged, but he could tell he'd failed just by the look Olivia shot him.

It was fine, he'd talk to her later and explain.

Thankfully, none of the others made a fuss of things. His soldiers would not overstep, and the twins, while concerned, were busy praising the trio of recruits and offering them advice.

Marcus was particularly taken by Greg, and Rowan was pretty sure he considered the boy his apprentice at that point.

"Where are we going?" Blake asked quietly, the smile slipping a tad now that they were drawing away from the others.

"We need to talk. Well, I need to talk. You need to listen," the Stalwart Hero growled, a part of him hoping Blake would try to contradict him.

Infuriatingly, he didn't. His only answer was a quiet *okay.*

When they were finally far enough away to avoid the ears of someone with a high perception stat, Rowan stopped and turned to face his friend. For a long few moments, they just started at each other.

Then the Stalwart Hero gnashed his teeth and pulled his hand back, ready to throw a punch. Blake's didn't even waver.

Rowan spun around, burying his hand in a tree.

The loud noise of impact and the shower of splinters startled him for a second. Caught up in his anger, the hero had completely disregarded the effects of his stats, and a shudder of fear at just what might have happened if he had struck Blake flickered through him.

"Why are you doing this shit again?" Rowan asked quietly, back still turned. "We talked about this. Fuck, you promised you were done with it. You fucking promised, Blake, long before we ended up here! You promised that you'd—"

Of all the things he'd expected his friend to do or say, Rowan didn't expect Blake to hug him. It was awkward and more than a little hesitant, but it did do the job of shutting him up.

"I'm not, okay? I'm not," Blake whispered, quickly drawing away and raising his hands when Rowan turned around to glare at him.

"The hell are you saying you're not? Doing *that* to yourself just to kill a Rare-tier monster?" Rowan demanded and crossed his arms over his chest to stop himself from lashing out again.

He wasn't typically violent. Even with all his rage, he couldn't bring himself to hurt Blake in the end. But if the other hero kept pushing him, Rowan really didn't know what would happen.

"Oh, come off it." This time, some of Blake's own anger showed. "I didn't do a single thing you haven't already, and you can't tell me otherwise. I talked to Marcus and Milena, you know? I've heard all about what you've done with this regeneration card."

"It's not working at full strength! What if it couldn't heal you quickly enough to keep you on your feet? What then?"

"Then you would have jumped in and helped me. Don't pretend you wouldn't have. I noticed the way you were looking at me. I was never in any danger, especially since Olivia is such a good alchemist. Or were you lying when you were bragging about her?"

"I wasn't lying! And still! We could have been too late. If it got you and obliterated your brain or whatever, that's game over! No retries!"

"That's why I was protecting my head, you idiot! I didn't let it chew on my face, did I? I just let it get me in the stomach, that's all! I killed it right after!"

"Yes, and you almost—"

The whispers had become shouts by now, and Rowan knew they should stop. He knew what could happen in the wastes if you crossed certain lines. In spite of that, when a beast crashed through the trees behind him with a roar, he was still startled.

That didn't stop him from answering its anger with his own, a scream of frustration leaving him.

The monster was a bear, or at least one of the creatures that resembled one. It was also rather sizable, and on its hind legs, it stood well above Rowan's own height.

That didn't help it when he buried his spear in its leg and obliterated it, sending the creature pitching forward. It also didn't help when he buried his fist in its stomach, showing the bear *away* from him and sending it crashing into a nearby tree.

It also didn't help when the angry hero descended on it, spear flashing and carving through limbs until the monster was reduced to a whimpering pile of fur that was barely clinging onto life.

"Well, what are you waiting for?" Rowan snapped, looking back at a sheepish Blake, who didn't look sure whether he should stay or bolt. "Going to finish it off or what?"

"Urgh, this reminds of the way I leveled up the first time," the other hero grumbled, affecting levity as he strolled up to the bear.

"Yes, well, it's Rare. Probably higher-level Rare. I'm not wasting it just for you to feel better right now," Rowan hissed, prompting Blake to roll his eyes.

In spite of that, the other hero did as he was told and stabbed his sword into the monster's heart. For a moment he looked startled, then a smile actually swept over his features.

"What now?" Killing the monster had helped, so Rowan's voice was halfway to civil once more.

"I leveled up," Blake said.

## CHAPTER SEVEN

# Chasing Light

There was a lot of grumbling, complaining, and even a little bit of cursing, but Rowan managed to drag Blake away from the scene of the slaughter and back to the main group.

Only for a little while, though.

Olivia was the first to notice them and walked up with a questioning glance pointed toward the trees that the two heroes had left.

"Can we make camp?" Rowan's voice was caught between a growl and a plea.

She took one more glance at the tree line before turning her attention back to the now-bloody Rowan and Blake. "Fine. But you're telling me everything once we get back to the city."

The parting kiss Olivia gave Rowan loosened the final bit of ice and anger that had been gripping his heart.

When he dragged Blake away from the rest of the group for the second time, Rowan was far more gentle. He also didn't forget to ask the scouts to fan out around them and keep any monsters from bothering them if they got loud again.

That may have limited their ability to monitor nearby threats and left the main camp with less forewarning, but be it the first signs of arrogance or perhaps even simple confidence in his party's abilities, Rowan wasn't worried about his army.

Some ten minutes of stomping and a short encounter with a monster that seriously overestimated itself later, Blake and Rowan were once more alone.

This time, they weren't in a clearing, and there wasn't even a particularly notable landmark around. All that surrounded them were the trees, the gentle sound of leaves crinkling in the wind, and a nice little spot made of gnarled roots where they could sit.

Rowan collapsed on the spot first and threw his head back, letting it thud against the tree's hard bark. Blake hesitated, but ultimately did the same.

"So . . . you leveled up, huh?" Rowan ventured, all of a sudden reluctant to delve straight into the subject he'd dragged him out to tackle.

"Yeah! Felt amazing, really. Level fifty-seven! I swear I can even feel some of my stats returning if I really focus." The grin threatened to sprain Blake's cheek muscles if he kept it up much longer. Blake had *hope*.

At that admission, Rowan briefly brought up his own status. His eye twitched when he saw the erratic behavior of his stat screen. The pluses next to his stats would glitch and go up, then quickly revert back to normal.

Blake blabbered on. "And one of my cards! It's not really back, yet, but if I push just right, I can get some of its effects."

"Huh," Rowan grunted. "What does it do?"

"Body reinforcement, but active. It gives way more of a boost than a passive card might, but it draws on your mana pool. So, you know, trade-offs."

"Huh, if it's useful enough for you to use it, I'm guessing it's pretty great. Epic tier, right?" Rowan asked.

"Nah. It's just Rare." The look of pure shock Rowan shot him made Blake guffaw. "What? Did you think they'd just stuff me full of Epic-tier cards?"

Rowan scratched his cheek awkwardly and looked away. "Kind of, yeah."

"I mean, they did help me upgrade all my class cards to Epic, so there's *that*. I even got another Epic card on top of that myself. But yeah, apparently letting me get some cards myself was meant to 'build character' or whatever." Blake snorted, and even Rowan smiled.

"Probably cheaped out at the last second."

"Probably."

A silence stretched, and this time it felt a tiny bit more comfortable than before. Just talking and joking like they used to put Rowan at ease.

Of course, he knew better than most that just because Blake was willing to do all that didn't mean the problem he was afraid of wasn't lurking around the first corner.

"Hey, Blake, remember when we met?" Rowan asked, nostalgia and a healthy dose of regret slipping into his voice.

Blake snorted, but Rowan could hear the smile in his voice. "Yeah. The pitiful introvert, lurking at the edge of the class after moving, too awkward to talk to anybody."

"Oh please," Rowan scoffed, unable to keep the annoyance entirely out of his voice. "Not my fault most of them were looking at me like I was about to beat them up and steal their lunch money. At their age, too!"

"Well, you were always kind of tall and blocky, weren't you? Real miracle you managed to snag yourself a fiancée before I did."

"Yeah, well, vision of beauty, why haven't you proposed to your Treagon yet or whatever? Wait, stop changing the subject! Remember how we became friends?"

"I'm not just going to ask a girl who probably doesn't even want to be around me to marry me, Rowan," Blake said. "And yeah, I remember, what's your point?"

"Blake . . . She doesn't act like someone who doesn't want to be around you. Anyway, I'll never forget that day, either, even if what you did was . . . most definitely not smart."

Rowan could perfectly recall the day, as he'd said. He'd been a horribly awkward transfer student. Blake was the plucky center of the class. And the idiots that cornered him in the bathroom? Well, they *were* idiots, convinced Rowan was some kind of standoffish rogue planning their downfall or whatever.

He never did get to the bottom of what kind of class hierarchy he'd threatened with his appearance.

All that mattered was that he had been cornered by four surprisingly buff guys, and he wasn't skilled at or predisposed to violence. They'd tried to take advantage of that, and if Blake hadn't intervened, Rowan would have limped away sporting more than a few bruises and fractures.

As it was, Blake was the one with the bruises, but the idiots were definitely the ones who ended up with fractures. Never before that day had Rowan seen someone so utterly enraged over what they perceived was blatant injustice.

It was only later that he learned that was Blake's default response to that kind of situation: If possible, assist, then *strongly* discourage perpetrators from ever trying that kind of nonsense again.

It was more than a personal belief in justice or some such. It was a *compulsion.*

"I get that you're trying to draw parallels here, but there aren't any, Rowan. I beat up some bullies and got a little hurt, but I don't regret it. Likewise, it's not like I risked my life to kill that lizard, either. Some pain and blood, sure, I risked those. But not death."

"And how long before you start slipping again? How long before you try and pull shit like walking up to an *actual, armed gang* and trying to get them to leave the people they're beating half to death alone, huh? Or, I don't know, how long before you charge into the wastes without a plan again?" Rowan asked.

At that, finally, Blake froze and shut up, posture tense and lips pressed tightly together. "I was just trying to help."

"That's the *problem*!" Rowan shouted, then caught himself and bit his lip until he tasted blood. More calmly, he continued, "Blake, this is the stuff we forced you into *therapy* over. You're not invincible, not even now. You can't just run around trying to hero everyone's lives into perfection."

"Isn't it our job? Isn't that what we're supposed to do? What we were summoned for?"

"No, we were summoned to kill the demon king when he shows up. And yes, we need to kill the Legendary-tier demons before then, but not at the cost of your life."

"And what if we're too late? What if we take too long and things get *worse*?" Blake was whispering again, and Rowan could easily recognize the way he'd turned in on himself, eyes slightly glossy.

"Tell me, did you do the exercise we came up with? Did you calm down, assess the pros and cons? Weigh what you want to do versus other potential solutions? Just give yourself time to think *before* doing something reckless?"

The silence was telling, as was the morose *no* that broke it.

"And would you do the same thing now, with everything that's happened?" The question was somewhat cruel. Rowan just hoped it would drive the point home.

"So many people died because of me, Rowan," Blake confessed, drawing his legs up to his chest and pressing his head against his knees. When his voice came out again, it was muffled. "*So many.* I knew them, you know? The officers, a lot of the soldiers, too. And now they're dead. Because of me."

The only reason Blake didn't know them all by name, Rowan was betting, was because he hadn't gotten to spend much time with them. Blake was *heroic* like that.

Rowan was trying, and failing, to get to know most of his soldiers. Some deep part of him was yelling that he would be the one to lead them to their deaths. He didn't need their faces haunting him in his sleep alongside all the other night terrors that struck whenever Olivia wasn't with him.

With a heavy heart, and feeling like a manipulative asshole, Rowan twisted the knife. "And what if your party members died? Actually, how would they feel if *you* died? You can't pull suicidal shit like that anymore, Blake. You just can't."

Rowan ignored the sobs that slowly picked up and hit his head against the tree again. The pain wasn't much, but it kept his head clear, and it felt like a tiny bit of self-flagellation. He let go of the spear a little.

For the first time in a long while, he sincerely missed Kayla. Everything about her. The good, the bad, and the ugly. He'd probably welcome even her new self.

Their relationship was complicated, to say the least. Whereas Blake had adopted him relatively late, Kayla had been with him from childhood. Both of them were messed up in their own ways. Somehow, they'd kept each other together.

Rowan really should have known that things would fall apart the second they were taken out of their familiar, comfy reality and thrust into a whole new world.

"Just do better, please?" Rowan asked quietly and threw his arm around Blake's shoulders, ignoring the way they were shaking.

Blake wasn't suicidal.

Blake didn't reach for self-harm.

He wasn't even stupid.

The problem with Blake, as his therapist eventually told Rowan and Kayla, was that he saw no inherent value in *himself.* His childhood, messed up as it was, had left him convinced that there was something he needed to constantly make up for. To atone for.

So, jumping off a bridge if it meant *potentially* saving someone from drowning? Sure, sign him up! It was an extremely messed-up and dangerous attitude even in a relatively safe world. Out in the demonic wastes? Rowan didn't regret what he was doing for a second.

It hurt him. He wanted to stop. But he didn't regret it.

It wasn't like Kayla was conveniently around to fill in for him.

The thought of the individual in question sent his thoughts spiraling in a different direction.

Kayla. The ever perfect. Ever ready to jump down the throat of anyone who doubted her. A faultless mirror for Blake, with completely opposite needs and desires. If Blake wanted to help people, Kayla wanted attention and control.

All of it. So her life could never spiral into a nightmare again.

In a way, Rowan trusted her implicitly with Blake's well-being exactly for that very reason. According to the drunk ramblings of the woman herself, she adored him. Wanted him all for herself. When she was at her lowest, he was always there to help.

No matter that he came to school with more bruises than she did.

"Fuck. When did it all go to hell, dammit?" Rowan hissed, thumping his head against the tree again.

He didn't expect an answer. He got one anyway. "When we showed up here, I guess?" Blake's voice trembled with both a sob and a laugh.

Rowan wasn't quite so sure. Maybe it was the third or the thirteenth time Blake and Kayla broke up over his recklessness before inevitably getting back together? The queen bee and her loyal knight, stuck like glue all the way up to college.

He wasn't foolish enough to say that out loud.

"Well, it certainly seems to have helped bring out your bad side," he said instead, fully expecting the shove he got in return for the comment.

"Oh really, mister perfect hero? What about you, then? What deeply messed-up side of you did this place bring out?" Blake quipped.

Rowan decided to indulge Blake's blatant attempt to direct attention away from his issues. "There were no 'messed-up' parts of me for this world to bring out, Blake. I do, however, now have a myriad of traumas and mental scarring that's unlikely to heal."

He'd meant to say it jokingly. It came out more bitter than anything.

It took Blake another few moments before he asked his next question, and it wasn't anything Rowan expected. "Are you planning to leave, if—I mean, when we win? Are you going to return back home?"

"I thought we touched upon this discussion before? Well, to answer your question . . . no, I don't think I will. I mean, I have a fiancée now. I'm actually starting to like this world, at least when it doesn't suck as hard as it currently does. Besides, I *was* made a noble. *Someone's* gotta take care of Rest's Remorse."

"That someone doesn't have to be you."

"Well, what about you, smarty-pants? When we kill the demon king and you get the choice, are you going back to the life we used to have?"

It said a lot that Blake didn't answer for long, quiet minutes. When he finally did, he just sounded tired. "I don't know. If you asked me just a couple weeks ago, I'd have said no. Now . . ."

"Now, everything sucks, and you just want it all to be over with?"

"More or less, yeah. My system is still messed up, but I guess we're fixing that. My party members are all up in arms, I got my entire army killed, and I can't even feel the presence of my goddess properly anymore. It's so weak now. I can't hear her voice or feel her guidance. It's just gone."

Selfishly, Rowan considered hindering Blake's attempts to recover his class if that meant his connection to the goddess of light would remain severed. He didn't press the subject, though. "So, does that mean you're leaning toward going back after all?"

"We'll see, I guess. Once everything's done. Or, at least, once this stretch of my journey's done. Hells unholy, do I wish I'd just listened to my goddess and stayed in the capital longer. I could have actually done something useful instead of ending up like this."

"You mentioned that before. What does she actually want you to do that's so important?" Rowan managed to ask the question casually, without any fidgeting. He was inordinately proud of that achievement.

"There are heretics in the capital. I don't know how my goddess found out about them, but we intercepted a couple of their couriers and even busted some of their meetings. They're always too quick for me to properly pin down, though. They have powerful classes on their side."

Rowan shot him a disbelieving look. If there was someone capable of standing up to a nearly fully realized hero, then he imagined the king would be up in arms over it, too, rather than sending away one of his best trump cards. "Really?"

Blake's cheeks flushed, and Rowan could swear he spotted shame in his expression as his friend ducked his head, breaking their eye contact.

"Well, they're either strong, or, um, I was weak? I mean, I know my Heart Card is good. And they guided me through the tiers to the class the king wanted me to have, so there's no way my prep was inferior to the heathens'. Still . . . seeing you, and your party, it kind of feels like I wasn't doing all that well?"

Rowan thought back to watching Blake fight. His assumption was that Blake's stats and cards, not to mention class, let him perform more than a little better in combat. Still, if that *was* the extent of his skill, then the Stalwart Hero really couldn't say much to make his friend feel better.

"Well, when we get you all fixed up, we can have some practice bouts. Just, who taught you to just stand there and take all the punishment? Because let me tell you, they need to be fired. It's like they gave you basic combat training on how to swing a sword and then shipped you off to level."

Blake once again ducked his face out of view, making Rowan's eyes narrow dangerously. "Um, well, they kind of did do that. I mean, it's on me. Isn't it? That I couldn't figure things out on my own from there?"

With gritted teeth, Rowan spoke. "No, Blake, it's not on you. I've had what certainly *felt* like months of training. I know it wasn't, but Kayden almost literally hammered the basics into me. How to move. How to breathe. Handling all the spear stances. That's not something you can just *pick up* on your own!"

Maybe Rowan was wrong, and all that was something people expected heroes to just know. Still, the baron's attitude and approach to his training suggested otherwise. And if that was the case, then why was Blake's training so badly fumbled?

Even Rowan was treated better!

"Maybe they were in a hurry," Blake supplied, even if his voice was plaintive and clearly dubious of his own suggestion.

It was a minor miracle, really, to know that Rowan's constant complaints about the king were finally starting to chip away at Blake's natural predisposition to trust people no matter the circumstances.

"There's something there, Blake. I mean, and I do hate to bring this up, but Kayla left you with a warning, didn't she? What exactly did she tell you when you last saw her?"

"I'm not sure. I—I wasn't really listening properly. She said something about some kind of scheme. About how I needed to be more careful, and that I shouldn't trust Harold, the king. Maybe I should have listened to her a bit better, but she was acting off since our arrival. I could barely recognize her."

Rowan did his best to rack his brains, thinking back to before their arrival to their new world. Were Blake and Kayla going steady, or were they in one of their off periods? He wanted to curse when he realized they'd broken up again just a couple of days before it all went down.

Typically, they would have been back together by the end of the week, and then Rowan wouldn't have to worry about them for months. Clearly, the timing of their abduction was highly inconvenient.

"You can't remember anything else? Nothing at all?"

"No, sorry. My goddess wanted me to continue leveling up and hunting for the heretics, so I didn't really pay attention to much else."

The admission was another strike against Sarina's agenda, whatever it was. Really, the more Rowan learned about the goddess, the more he became convinced she needed to be replaced yesterday. Her spot in the pantheon was better off in someone else's hands.

"Dammit, Blake, when the hero chosen by the *goddess of secrets* tried to tell you something, no matter how you feel on the subject, *you listen.* You can overanalyze whether it's a trap or whatever later, but first, you listen."

"I get it, I get it! I'll do better."

"I sure hope so." Rowan filled those words with as much grouchiness and sarcasm as he could fit.

Overall, though, Rowan was satisfied with how the conversation had gone. If he could just keep Blake from doing stupidly reckless things in the future, he'd count himself a winner. Even if his friend was chronically incapable of distrusting suspicious individuals.

As such, Rowan forced himself back to his feet, twinging a little when the stiffness brought on by their awkward sitting position made itself known to his muscles. To his relief, it didn't even take a full second for his regeneration card to kick in, and then the pain melted away.

"Want to head back? The others are probably waiting for us, and it is getting pretty late, all told," Rowan offered, signaling that he was willing to drop all the uncomfortable subjects for the time being.

He expected his friend to jump on the opportunity. Blake always hated when Rowan or Kayla pulled one of their interventions, but this time, he actually shook his head no.

"Actually, I was hoping you'd help me test something," Blake admitted as he stood up. "It's true that I haven't been using my Heart Card all that well. I always kept to the basics of conjuring weapons and armor with it, but it occurred to me today that I don't have to use it only for that."

Rowan scoffed. Of course, he wasn't saying no because he wanted to talk more. At least he couldn't fault his fellow hero for what he was trying to do. Frankly, anything that would help him stay safer was a win in Rowan's book.

"What did you have in mind? Want to test some kind of a new shield or something?" One could hope, and Rowan certainly was doing that.

"No. I actually want you to block a couple of my strikes, then I'll tell you before I test out my theory and you can tell me if it worked?"

"Typical that you're already planning out new attacks. I told you that you need to stop being so reckless in battle. I did tell you that, didn't I? That constant charging in won't cut it?"

"Yes, Rowan, you told me. Now, are you going to help me or not?"

Instead of a verbal reply, Rowan took up his position opposite Blake, making the best of the space they had between the thickly clustered trees.

The other hero took a deep, centering breath, drew his sword, and attacked. Just like before, it wasn't anything to write home about.

With Blake's level-up, the attacks came more quickly and carried more power behind every swing, but that was it. Rowan was still easily keeping ahead of the assault, each strike blocked in almost lazy motions thanks to his dexterity and strength.

Blake gave up after about a minute of relentless strikes, jumped lightly on the balls of his feet, then nodded. Rowan took that as the signal and squared up a bit more tightly, actually paying attention.

If Blake did somehow pull off some ludicrously powerful attack, then Rowan wasn't going to let himself get run through just because he was getting cocky.

As it turned out, that was a good thing.

Blake's entire body lit up as his mana wound around his limbs and torso. The only part of him that wasn't covered was his head, a fact that Rowan immediately took note of. If this were a real battle, that's where he'd aim first.

Then Blake was moving, and it was unlike anything the hero had done before.

Rowan's eyes widened a fraction when he realized that the speed of the attack now almost approached something that could threaten him when he wasn't fully committed.

Thanks to his previous caution, he didn't let the strike slip past his guard. Likewise, that was the only reason his spear wasn't launched out of his grip.

The strike was powerful in a way none of Blake's previous attacks were. It carried far more strength than the hero was supposed to be capable of bringing to bear, to the point where the entire length of Rowan's spear quivered with a sonorous sound of echoing metal.

Blake's face was lit up in pure glee, and then the hero's limbs blurred once more, striking again and again. Slowly, Rowan's own lips turned up in a smile, then he broke out into laughter.

They were sparring. Actually sparring, rather than Rowan taking time out of his day to indulge or look after his recovering friend. His happiness was such that he tapped into his stats more fully, pushing back at Blake's progress to see how well his new trick would hold up.

Thankfully, the trick held up wonderfully. Blake even managed to push himself a tiny bit more, speeding up his strikes and upping their ferocity.

Of course, that's when weapons clashed, rang out, and Blake's elbow *snapped.*

Rowan had to quickly abort his own retaliatory strike, and only managed due to his recent bump in perception and dexterity thanks to all the recruits leveling up some and investing their stats.

"What was that? How did you manage to break your own arm?" Rowan demanded immediately, stabbing his spear into the ground and reaching out to inspect the limb.

Blake, meanwhile, was staring at it like it had betrayed him. "It's nothing. *Really.* I promise. I kind of twisted it too far? I guess I should admit that I wasn't exactly using my body stats to manage all that."

Rowan wasn't sure what to make of the admission. So, his answer was simple. "Explain."

"It's my Heart Card. I mean, if I can manipulate light and create all this armor, then why can I sort of force my body to move the way I want? It's a bit like I was piloting myself inside a robot suit. I mean, my Heart Card feels like a perfect extension of myself, you know? It's so *easy* to use it."

Rowan did not, in fact, know what that was like. His Heart Card was passive in nature, but *that* was neither here nor there.

"Then how did you get hurt?"

"I twisted my arm awkwardly, as I said. It couldn't quite stretch the way I wanted it to, but my light armor didn't care, and . . ." Blake motioned clumsily at the hand Rowan was already helping him secure in a fixed position.

He didn't have a sling handy, but he could find plenty of dried-up vines, even if most of them were covered in thorns.

Rowan's feelings were dancing somewhere between fondness and exasperation. In spite of that, he couldn't quite stop himself from smiling in tandem with his friend. His happiness was practically radiating off him in waves.

"Just be more careful, okay? Still, I have to say I'm proud of you. That's amazing! I wonder what it will let you do in tandem with your stats once they're recovered."

"I know, right? Still! This means I'm no longer useless. You can let me fight Rare-tier enemies without hovering, and maybe we can even go after an Epic!"

Rowan's heart twinged at the way Blake once again discarded his own value so casually, and he wasn't quite sure he'd be willing to let him tag along on an Epic hunt just yet, but the outlook of Blake's recovery was looking brighter and brighter by the day.

And that, at least, was a good thing.

## CHAPTER EIGHT

# Tense Dealings

The way back was a slow, sauntering affair, mostly because Rowan refused to push anyone harder than was necessary.

Besides, no one *really* cared about their glacial progress toward the city. The radiance of Blake's mood was infectious. Even Olivia, predisposed toward disliking the man, couldn't keep a smile off her face.

Granted, with how she kept sneaking glances at Rowan, that was mostly down to the fact that Rowan was also sporting a smile. Rowan still counted that as a win. So long as there was some kind of connection between her and Blake, however indirect, Rowan was pretty sure he could finally get the two to become reliable allies, if not good friends.

A link, so to say, between his old life and his new reality.

He didn't want to be forced to choose between them. Partially because he knew exactly what his answer was going to be. The truth of the matter was that Olivia would win ten times out of ten if it really came down to it, even if that made him feel more than just a little conflicted at times.

There was something to be said about that. About choosing a future he so badly desired over a past he sometimes feared wouldn't be enough to keep a friendship alive. A fear that started gnawing at Rowan every time his old friend started invoking the name of his goddess.

Still, he'd be damned if he wasn't going to do his very best to keep both of them in his life. He just needed to make sure that no frustrating nobles or gods could sink their claws too deeply into Blake. And he could do that—if his friend let him offer up the help he needed.

For the time being, Rowan had to focus on a much simpler task: getting them back to the city as quietly as he could manage.

There was no real way to hide the passage of six entire parties, especially when they contained so many important figures, but that didn't mean he needed to cause enough of a fuss that even Blake's party members would catch wind of it immediately.

The good news was that their way back wasn't mired by the annoyance of dealing with monsters that gave little to no experience. The scouts did their jobs perfectly, allowing the tired knights to avoid any more combat encounters that could quickly grow tricky in their current states. Rowan or one of his party members could always step in and assist them, of course, but he was trying to teach them a valuable lesson here.

They needed to be able to take care of themselves out in the field.

So, with hopes of getting to rest soon, they charted their way through the wastes and then slipped into Rest's Remorse.

Rowan was feeling pretty proud of himself when they slipped into the manor's back entrance, especially since they'd managed to avoid the vast bulk of the crowds traveling the newly minted city so they could get home before the rapidly approaching twilight.

He asked one of the scouts who had grown up in Rest's Remorse to lead them through the back alleys typically familiar only to the locals, and had even dispersed most of their entourage, leaving only one party of soldiers to accompany them.

It wasn't like the threat of assassins was particularly notable after they had already cleaned house. He was even feeling proud of how few servants they encountered on their way to the main staircase that would let them access the higher floors.

Rowan's pride didn't last. Almost as soon as they reached the staircase, they were met by a trio of glowering women who had posted up right there in the middle of the hall, prominently blocking their way up.

"Where have you been? Bed's empty! No note! You could have been abducted! We were out of our minds with worry and do you care?" the princess shouted, advancing with intent and menace. "You could have died! You could have been—"

She cut off abruptly midsniffle, finger poking into Blake's chest, as though realizing, for the very first time, that she had an audience.

Rowan couldn't resist. "Please, do continue," he said politely, motioning for her to do just that with a beatific smile.

Of course, the only thing that did was make her switch targets. "And you! I know you had something to do with this. I knew you were a bad influence on our hero from day one, but I really didn't think you'd go as far as to encourage such stupid recklessness."

Rowan strongly suspected she would have advanced on him, too. Fortunately, his brave alchemist stepped right in her path, imposing herself between him and the crazed princess.

Amanda glowered in response, but Olivia's only response was an unimpressed sniff. Something seemed to pass between them, an unsaid acknowledgment or something similar born of an odd level of familiarity, before the princess actually backed off.

"We are leaving. I am not going to stay here a minute longer if it means having to trust your life with this *rabble*." She bit out the word so angrily Rowan actually winced a little, and even Blake frowned.

For a moment, Rowan thought he might admonish her, but then she whirled around and grabbed his hand, trying to drag him away.

Much to the princess's shock, the hero didn't budge.

"We're not leaving, Amanda. And *you* are not putting my life in anyone's hands. *I am.* I know Rowan, and I trust him. He's already helped me make a significant step forward, or have you not noticed? I can access more of my stats now, and even my deck is starting to recover."

A whole host of emotions fluttered across the princess's features, most of them positive. Most notable among them were happiness and relief, but there was something ugly lurking there, too. She composed herself remarkably quickly.

"So, we owe your *friend* a favor for helping you kick-start your recovery," the princess said. Rowan really thought she didn't have to say the word with such distaste. "Very well. I will make sure we pay him back. However, that doesn't mean we should stay here. I keep telling you this, but it really is unwise for us."

"No, Amanda. Just no. I like it here. It's not even just because of Rowan. I've met his party and some of Rowan's recruits, too, and I enjoyed spending time with them. I want to stay here for the duration of my recovery. Maybe longer, too. It will be easier to organize a joint expedition if I do that."

Blake's refusal to comply was apparently shocking enough to temporarily paralyze the princess. Right after, however, Rowan saw the way she sent them calculating looks. He recognized that look, that of a person wondering just how far they could push.

She was also obviously unhappy that their little spat had an audience. Unfortunately for her, Rowan wouldn't bow out and leave Blake alone. Something told him she was pretty confident that she could bully him into acquiescence if Rowan did that.

At least if he could secure a solid promise from Blake to stay, he could trust in his tendency to prioritize promises over all else.

"Blake, we need to return to our town. We need to show people there that you're okay, and that we're setting up another expedition to try again. We can't just stay here," the princess said. This time her voice was calmer, cajoling.

It still didn't work.

A brief flicker of pain did radiate out of their bond, the bond that Rowan had done his best to suppress and ignore for the duration of their outing, but Blake didn't back down. "That sort of thing can be arranged using missives. It's not just that I don't want to go back right now, Amanda. I *can't*."

That admission, more than anything, seemed to jolt the princess out of her insistence. It was as he watched the pain and hurt slip into her guarded expression that Rowan was finally forced to acknowledge a simple fact.

She cared.

She actually, genuinely cared.

Now, he wasn't exactly willing to bet on how long the princess had been nursing feelings toward the hero she was accompanying. Perhaps, at the start, she'd approached him with less-than-sincere intentions. But somewhere along the line, Blake's natural charisma and genuinely good nature must have won her over. Rowan had seen that kind of thing happen plenty of times before, but he had no clue what to do about it then and there.

His eyes flickered instead over to the other two women.

The de Vort woman wasn't easy to read. She had mostly chosen to follow the princess's lead for the duration that Rowan had known them. However, there *was* something in her eyes. Even if Rowan couldn't call it love, it was, at the very least, fondness.

The Treagon, of course, did not need to be mentioned. The woman was quiet and withdrawn, but her care for the hero in her party was more than apparent. She looked stricken now, like she wished she could reassure him.

Rowan wanted to groan loudly and walk away from the scene. It was a harem situation after all, and he was stuck watching Blake play it out.

"Very well," the princess said at long last, taking a literal and metaphorical step back. "Perhaps we can stay for a little while longer. However, I would like to request a formal meeting with the noble of this domain."

Her eyes snapped onto Rowan, then slid down to Olivia, daring her to say no.

"That can be arranged," Rowan's alchemist quipped, and he had to fight really hard not to feel like he was just betrayed. "Would you like to meet tomorrow morning? Perhaps *first thing* in the morning? It wouldn't do to delay."

Rowan could hear the smirk in Olivia's voice, and he couldn't deny that he loved the way the princess stiffened before reluctantly agreeing. After living under the same roof as the stuck-up royal for so long, there was no way Olivia was unaware of the fact that she didn't like waking up early.

That was the clue he needed to realize that the game was very much on.

"In that case, I believe it is best that we retire for the night. Would you not agree as well, Blake?" The princess switched her attention back to the hero, and this time, he could do little but nod.

With one last glance at Rowan and a hesitant smile, Blake was practically dragged up the stairs. Something told Rowan that it was unlikely that he'd get to sleep in his bed alone that night, even if the Stalwart Hero had no real clue how his friend felt on the subject.

It was definitely not his former relationship with Kayla that was holding him back.

The two were a lot of things. Friends, lovers, more, and all in between. But Rowan never could figure out if they had actual, sincere romantic feelings for each other. There was far too much codependency and obsession tied up in that relationship for it to ever truly be healthy.

*Then again, the irony and hypocrisy are not lost on me.* Rowan chuckled—be it at his thoughts or at what he'd watched play out, he didn't know.

He understood very well that his feelings for Olivia were definitely several levels above regular affection and somewhere in the ballpark of

"I need her to sleep and function." However, she wasn't just a coping mechanism for him.

Rowan had made sure to take a long, hard look at his feelings. The warmth brought to him from a mere mention of her name or a stray thought in her direction was sincere. He loved her. He well and truly did. If he also happened to *need* her, well, it was a happy coincidence that they got along so well.

"Do you think there's going to be trouble?" Rowan asked his fiancée, stepping forward to entwine his fingers with hers.

"Oh, I know there will be. You can't deal with royalty without them causing some kind of a fuss, after all. We'll just have to be ready for whatever nonsense she throws our way tomorrow. Unless, of course, you want to kick them all out? We *could* do that."

"I thought you were starting to like Blake?" Rowan questioned, and there was no accusation in his voice. He was genuinely curious about what his fiancée thought about his best friend.

"I say this with the utmost reluctance, but yes. He's not as bad as I feared that he would be. He hasn't done anything egregious so far, and he does earnestly consider you a friend. So, for now, that's enough. I would still kick him out, though, because that would solve all our current problems neatly."

In other words, she didn't like Blake enough to let him continue inconveniencing her family. Rowan could work with that.

"Thank you for putting up with them for me," he mumbled against her hair as he leaned down to kiss the top of her head.

The flush on her cheeks brought a smile to his lips.

"Stop teasing me! Let's just get something to eat and then finally head to bed. I'm not going to tackle her royal pain in the ass without enough sleep."

Naturally, Rowan had absolutely nothing against that plan.

The next day found the Stalwart Hero sitting across from Blake and his party in one of the rooms in his fancy manor dedicated to such meetings.

On his left sat the baroness in all her scowling glory, her husband on the other side of her. On his right sat Olivia, and if anyone noticed that they were holding hands under the table, they didn't see fit to point it out.

Everyone was tense, including the three daughters of nobility who flanked Blake. But the hero himself was absent-minded. Rowan tried and failed to decipher the odd look on his friend's face.

"You wanted to have a meeting. Well, we are here. You can speak your piece." Olivia's opening statement was not particularly polite or friendly, but with only the two groups in the room, she apparently didn't feel the need to act differently.

The princess took a sharp breath and fought back whatever her first reply was, much to Rowan's shock. "We would like to ask for an official alliance. Hostilities benefit none of us, and so I propose we pool our resources together, at least until the threat of demons has been eliminated."

Olivia didn't immediately scoff or say no. Instead, her eyes slowly swept over the group arrayed in front of her, carefully gauging each of their reactions.

The Treagon looked worried but also content, the de Vort looked disinterested in the discussion, keeping her eyes on Blake, and the princess was, well, the princess.

"Would you please elaborate on this *we*? Do you mean to imply that you speak in the name of our king, or do you freely represent your hero's party?"

Here, for the first time in a while, Rowan got to see a smug grin on the princess's face. He didn't really miss it. "As of yesterday, all three of us are engaged to the hero. The engagements are both valid and binding, and we will strive to finalize our marriage as soon as we are able."

Immediately, Rowan's undivided attention was on Blake, left eye twitching as some of his exasperation showed on his face.

He really wanted to strangle his friend.

For his part, Blake flushed and looked away from everyone, but Rowan in particular. He also didn't speak up to deny the princess's claims, which only made her smug grin grow. The other two women looked more than satisfied with the arrangement as well, if the way the Treagon was now cozying up to the hero was any indication.

"Congratulations, then," Olivia offered, sounding like she wanted to say anything but. "You did not, however, clarify who you are representing in this meeting."

The princess flushed, and that same old petulance shone true for a moment. She must have prepared herself for the barbs, because she actually managed to hold herself back once more.

"I represent Hero Blake and his fiancées, as well as the town of Gilbert's Folly, which is currently under Hero Blake's command." The speech sounded officious and precise, much like Olivia's own tone.

There was a subtle difference, though. Whereas Olivia spoke confidently and with force, clearly in her element despite preferring a lab to the negotiating table, the princess lacked that assurance. She was making up for it with fire, but it was still an unavoidable fact that she came across as stiff and inexperienced at best.

"I see. And what can you offer to this proposed alliance?" Olivia asked.

That had even Rowan eyeing her hesitantly. The princess obviously hadn't expected the question, either, if the sudden sputtering and darting eyes were anything to judge by.

"I, well, that is . . . A hero! Of course, having the guaranteed assistance of a second hero is invaluable under these circumstances. And, I think—no, I'm certain that our town can field a second army, larger than the army you have here, to accompany us into the wastes." The princess's confidence began to crumble.

"Having a second hero around would be nice, yes. But only if he can actually use his powers. Need I remind you that it's *us* helping him level up to Epic again? Assistance in battle against demons is, therefore, already implied."

Another score for Olivia, and another sputtering session for the princess. At that point, Rowan was starting to realize that something odd was happening.

Sure, the princess was a brat, and he genuinely didn't like her. However, her behavior went past that. If he didn't know better, Rowan would think that she'd never been coached on dealing with other nobles for a single day in her life.

Blake had apparently had enough of watching his brand-new fiancée flounder, too, because he leaned forward and rested his elbows on the table. "Listen, I know Amanda's been pretty rude, but I think what she's been trying to say is pretty simple: I'll do *whatever* I can to help. We will, I mean. I mean that."

Olivia eyed him with a measure of exasperation, even if Rowan could tell she was fighting not to smile. "Oh really? *Whatever* you can, hmm? Does that mean we can expect you to support us with cards? How about additional funds and supplies? We could use some building materials, for example."

"I mean, I'm pretty sure we have some extra funds? I didn't really look at our finances much when I took over the town, but the mayor seemed to be on top of things?"

It was Rowan's turn to jump into the conversation with considerable exasperation. "Wait, what mayor? Your town has a mayor?"

"Yes? He's in charge of the town. Don't you have one?" Blake asked. Rowan really didn't think his friend needed to look *that* baffled.

"*No*, I don't," Rowan gritted out, leaning back in his seat. "He got eaten by monsters before I ever showed up. How are you still in charge, then?"

"Because I'm a duke?"

"You're a *duke*?"

The two just stared at each other, both flabbergasted, before Olivia loudly cleared her throat. "Yes, yes, Hero Blake has, due to his adoption into the royal family, officially been declared a duke of the kingdom. There was some rumbling from the temple to make him a grand duke, but it didn't work out."

"Obviously." The princess jumped in this time with a dainty snort. "To claim *that* title, you need to be of royal blood. Or to be married to a member of the royal bloodline and have a designated heir born from that union. Maybe Blake will get the title now."

Rowan did a double take so quickly his neck was starting to hurt. "You're pregnant?"

"No! Why would you *ask* me that? Obviously I'm not pregnant! We're not even married yet!"

"But you said you'd need a designated heir to—"

"Rowan," Olivia cut him off, and she didn't sound very happy. "Could you please stop cutting in? I'm trying to negotiate with the princess."

Rowan stopped, letting his shoulders droop. "I get it. And I get that it's important. But can't we get to the demands already? We know we'll say yes, they know they'll say yes, so do we *need* this bit in the middle?"

The baron was fighting laughter and losing, if his chuckles were to judge his inner battle by. The baroness was trying to glare at him over her daughter's head, but the way her lips were twitching was betraying her feelings on the subject, too.

Olivia was upset with him, though, but then again Rowan was pretty sure that was because he wasn't "properly taking care of his interests," as she told him she'd do before the meeting.

"Okay, that's it. The two of you, out. We don't need two offworlders throwing in comments they don't understand. *We'll* take care of this, and we'll let you know what we hash out in the end. You two go hit each other with sticks or something."

Rowan knew he was being scolded, but couldn't help the grin regardless. So, he stole a quick kiss from his adorable fiancée and then hurried away from her grumbling about dignity to snatch Blake out of his chair.

Before they could change their mind and call them back, the two heroes fled from their fiancées.

While he was more than happy to leave all the politicking to Olivia, there were a couple of things Rowan wanted to clarify himself.

That's why the very first thing he did after putting some distance between them and the negotiations room was press Blake against the wall with his hand on the other hero's chest.

"Okay, Blake, what the *hell*?" Rowan rightfully demanded, forcing his friend to maintain eye contact as he glared.

"Um, lovely weather we're having?"

"Forget about the weather! What in the world happened yesterday? I leave you chipper about your success after having that depressing talk with you, and now I find out that you're *engaged*? Did they blackmail you into this? Emotionally, I mean. Or literally, I guess, if they somehow found dirt on you . . ."

Blake slumped a little, forcing Rowan to put in more effort into holding him against the wall. "Look, like the two of us did, me and my party . . . talked. There was a bunch of stuff I didn't know, okay? Stuff about their families and them that I didn't think to ask before."

"Stuff like why Kayla was convinced the king is scheming about something?"

Blake briefly looked reluctant to answer, but eventually relented under his glare. "Yes, stuff like that. Look, I'm *still* not sure about Kayla, but . . . there *might* be something. Amanda clammed up when I asked her about it, so I didn't get anything out of her."

"And so you decided to marry her? Are you now certifiably insane?"

"No, I'm not. Might not have gotten that little tidbit of information out of her, but I did learn about a ton of other things."

"Like what? What would possibly convince you to marry all three of them when you were waffling on whether you even liked the Treagon?"

"She's not going to be a Treagon for long, so please stop with the hate already."

"Answer the question, Blake."

"Fine," Rowan's best friend huffed, then shifted away from his hold and headed down the hallway. "Did you know they raised them to eventually accompany a hero? All three of them? And that they're not the only ones?"

"What are you even talking about?"

"My party members, obviously. According to them, girls and boys are picked out from among high nobility when hero summoning is near, and then groomed into 'ideal' party members. I don't need to explain exactly what they prepare them for, do I? Two sets of girls, two sets of guys."

That briefly made Rowan falter, the ridiculousness of what he was hearing making him lose his footing in spite of his high dexterity. He recovered instantaneously, but it didn't stop his mind from spinning away instead.

"But . . . they never tried that kind of thing with me, though?"

"Nor did they try with Kayla, apparently. Nine people, raised to pander to heroes and then discarded. Well, not discarded. Sold off to interested nobles as spouses, if Amanda's to be believed. No use wasting perfectly good trading goods."

The anger in Blake's voice was visceral, and if he had the heads of high noble families in reach, Rowan was pretty sure they'd all end up dead.

"I . . . I wish I could say I'm all that shocked, but they did treat us as like goods at an auction, Blake."

"I know that! I know that. What was I supposed to do, though? Tell them I don't want them? That they'd follow me around for a while then go home so they can be shipped off to some strangers? They said they, um, they said they fell in love with me. I—I believe them. So, I said yes."

For several long moments, neither of them spoke. Rowan eventually sighed and continued, "That's messed up. Everything about that is messed up."

"Yeah, tell me about it. At least I finally talked them into trying for an alliance with you, though. That'll help. Right? Can never have enough reliable allies." The attempt at levity didn't really work, but it did make Rowan think.

Apparently, nobility were all about utility. And they did need allies within the city willing to support and accompany them out into the wastes. Just as importantly, *he* needed [Knights].

If most nobles really were as mercenary as he was now starting to think they were, well, maybe there was one resource he could exploit within easy reach.

CHAPTER NINE

# Negotiating With Terrorists

The next day was tense. If there was one thing to be thankful for, it was the fact that Blake's party members were, for once, actually cooperating.

This meant that Rowan could send them off into the wastes with his [Knights] and some soldiers for accompaniment with minimal worry.

Granted, he still worried a little.

A part of him expected the princess to kick up a fuss and do something stupid in an attempt to establish herself more firmly, but he couldn't dedicate his existence to babysitting a bunch of grown-ass adults who should know better.

There were more important things to do. One of which needed Camilla's approval. And so, Rowan found himself in the baroness's study. It was a rare occasion that Olivia didn't accompany him there, but his favorite alchemist was missing from the occasion.

Even with all the explosions that still accompanied Olivia's alchemical tinkering, Rowan still felt that he was in a worse-off position than she was.

"You want to do *what*?" The baroness's voice wasn't cold. It was glacial. It was Fimbulwinter sweeping across the world to announce the beginning of Ragnarok, and Epic tier or not, Rowan almost quailed under her mighty gaze.

Almost.

"I would like to approach your least favorite Epic-tier mage and try to recruit her as one of my [Knights] in anticipation of our campaign to track down and then eliminate Legendary-tier demons," Rowan said.

His train of thought was simple: If he laid out all the facts, then maybe the baroness would approach the discussion with the calm rationale of civilized discourse.

"You will not be taking that snake into your service, or so help me every god and goddess out there, I'll stab you in the back myself. At least that way you'll know it's coming, and I'm sure your card and my daughter can patch you up!"

Rowan winced. *Maybe that was hoping for just a little too much.* The hero took a deep breath and geared himself up to try again.

"I know it's a bad idea." Rowan saw the baroness open her mouth and quickly jumped to continue before she could say something scathing. "But! Just hear me out, okay? I swear it's not nearly as bad or as stupid as it sounds."

"Oh. Sure. Go ahead. I'm *certain* that your idea of giving that woman access to an additional Epic-tier card, especially one that seems to naturally draw in ambient mana, is *completely* logical and won't come back to haunt us," the baroness snapped, leaning back in her chair.

Rowan took a deep breath. "I told you, my party and the Mercenary King how my new class works. *However*, Tamara chose to skip that meeting. I might not have said a thing if she did attend, but she didn't. And none of the aforementioned individuals are likely to share info with her, right?"

The baroness eyed him for a long moment, before finally nodding reluctantly. "Right."

"Well, then, she doesn't know. Obviously, the stat benefits and experience sharing are something I'll tell her about. With what we now know about those, she won't have a reason to object, anyway. So, do you think she's likely to accept if she doesn't know I'll be able to feel her emotions?"

The baroness processed that, nibbling on her lower lip in a way that was eerily reminiscent of her daughter. At long last, however, a slow smile swept over her features. "Yes, I do think she might say yes. Especially if she believes it'll make you more inclined to trust her."

"Exactly. And if I have direct insight into what she's feeling and keep her relatively close, we'll at least have some warning before she inevitably betrays us. Besides, I need those stats. If I have more mana and the ability to use it better, I genuinely think I'll be much better off."

There were a few things Rowan wasn't saying, of course. For example, he wasn't entirely convinced Tamara would betray them. She seemed selfish and opportunistic. But if Rowan's side was winning, he really saw no reason why she might turn on them.

Clearly, though, the way he'd couched his argument was enough to please the baroness. Camilla's smile grew more as she asked her final question. "And you can cancel your [Knight] designation in the future, correct?"

"Correct."

"Excellent. Then, let's discuss the details of this arrangement."

Rowan sighed and let his shoulders slump just a smidgen. The hardest part was done. Now, he just needed to actually deal with Tamara herself.

Rowan had, upon his arrival in Rest's Remorse, attended a gathering meant for its most influential mercenaries and local figures. It was held in one of the town's nicer neighborhoods, and it was also the first and last time he'd rubbed shoulders with the local elite.

Since then, he'd been much more interested in his soldiers and regular citizens than whatever the rich elites were doing. Especially since they were remarkably unhelpful by every possible metric.

They hadn't deigned to assist the town when it needed to be defended against the monster horde that ruined entire sections of it. They hadn't offered up funds to repair said sections of town. And when Rowan took over? Their streak of neglect continued.

In fact, some of them even chose to flee when the suspicions of a new monster wave lead by an Epic demon spread through town. After all, the baroness could only stop the less affluent commoners from running.

The merchants with particularly heavy purses and whatever nobility the town had? There was little she could do when they had plenty of illegal ways to circumvent any notices or even laws she enacted.

This meant that as Rowan journeyed through the wealthier part of his city, he saw an odd juxtaposition of well-appointed homes that were either at the peak of maintenance or looked like they were on the verge of falling into total disrepair.

Sections of neighborhoods that were still clearly lived in stood directly across from neighborhoods and homes that had obviously been abandoned in a hurry.

Some enterprising individuals from less wealthy parts of town had clearly learned about the situation, too. Many of the abandoned homes had pieces of furniture, decorations, and more strewn across lawns where the looters chose to discard them. Whether it were out of anger or due to their minuscule value, Rowan couldn't tell. The windows and doors hung on for dear life, but the buildings' insides had been gutted like fish and left for all to see.

And deep within this depressing city district stood a building that was doing its level best to pretend it was a mage tower.

The building was oddly blocky and reminded Rowan of something vaguely like an apartment building. It was definitely taller than all of its neighbors, yet didn't stretch as high as the hero had been assured true mage towers did.

Apparently, there were laws about that sort of thing.

No building other than those owned by or registered under the mage association could surpass a certain height. Magic was, according to Olivia, a substance that had a tendency to swirl up toward the sky. The higher you got, the more turbulent and more abundant mana got.

You could, of course, also go in the opposite direction and dig deep to where subterranean deposits of mana slept, but most of those were crystallized or difficult to rouse and put into motion.

Humanity and most mortal species were therefore stuck in the awkward middle of the sandwich: the part where mana existed but didn't tend to pool or gather naturally.

Mage towers were the first answer to this conundrum. They were a way for mages to reach toward the heavens and claim what they saw as rightfully theirs. In turn, everyone else was held to the height limit, and the days of upward expansion in cities were halted.

Tamara's home was doing its best to push these limits to their breaking point.

Rowan was pretty sure you'd need ridiculously precise tools, or perhaps a spell, to prove that she hadn't crossed the line and was, in fact, at the very edge of it.

Likewise, the tower was much better appointed than its neighbors. There were reliefs carved in its faces, twisting statues of various monsters, and even luxurious tapestries depicting battles and various fantastical forms of magecraft. It was like time and weather were irrelevant in the face of the magical might Tamara was trying to claim as her own. And at the Epic tier, she might even be actually capable of fielding some of the force she was so badly trying to project.

Unfortunately for Rowan, he hadn't been allowed to venture out to the tower on his own. Both the baroness and his fiancée had put a quick veto on that idea. Instead, he was accompanied by an entirely excessive number of fifty soldiers, each of them dressed in the finest gear they could field.

Neither the baroness nor her daughter was there to accompany him, either—that was something *he'd* insisted on.

Camilla was still sparse on the details of just why she hated Tamara, but the feeling was clearly mutual. Olivia, meanwhile, was tainted by association. If there was even the slightest chance to make things easier by leaving them behind, Rowan was willing to try.

So when Rowan finally stood before the doors of the pseudotower, he motioned for his lead escort to knock on them.

Dale stepped forward and lifted the massive door knocker attached to the wings of doors pretending to be gates. He briefly grunted under the strain of lifting the thing, and when he let go, it produced a hollow boom that echoed loudly throughout the structure.

A few seconds later, the doors swung outward, forcing the scout to scramble back and revealing a lush carpet that stretched all the way to a set of spiraling stairs and a ceiling that were much more luxurious than Rowan had expected.

"Welcome, welcome. Please come in, Lord Clairfont," Tamara greeted him, sweeping forward in a dress that was even less practical than her usual attire.

Clearly the woman was going all out that day, because the abomination of silk and fur was trying to smother her in its softness. No normal human could possibly manage walking in something *that* tight.

Rowan was suddenly extra glad he'd insisted Olivia stay behind, because he was pretty sure his fiancée would take particular exception to him going anywhere near a woman dressed that way.

"Thank you for your hospitality, and for greeting us so quickly on such short notice." Rowan gave a shallow bow, one for which he'd been excessively coached. The exact angle, the position of his arms, his legs, and even the way he moved his head, had been drilled into him.

He was convinced that because of his stats and cards, he'd mastered the move within the first fifteen minutes. But Camilla and Olivia had insisted he keep practicing for another hour afterward. Even now, he couldn't feel the slightest difference between that first moment the movement clicked and the last bow the mother-daughter duo made him give before deeming him ready. He was pretty sure they were just having fun tormenting him for leaving them behind.

Be that as it were, Tamara looked delighted to receive his greeting.

"Think nothing of it, my lord. It is my honor to swiftly present myself at your leisure." The words were, as it so often happened with the woman, laced with a dangerous and suggestive undertone that Rowan ignored.

It was all pageantry and nonsense anyway.

He'd sent his notice that he intended to visit the woman the day before, right after discussing the matter with the baroness. Likewise, if it turned out that she *hadn't* been tracking his progress through the city using either magic or mundane scouts, Rowan was willing to cut off both of his hands.

Several times, even.

As plastic as the whole affair was, Rowan still couldn't deny that the show Tamara was putting on was impressive.

Her students were strewn about the massive space that *shouldn't* have fit within the tower, acting industrious while they handled all sorts of tools and scrolls.

Everything had the soft, ethereal glow of mana—even the most unassuming items.

Plenty of different scholarly implements and scrolls were floating, some even zipping around the room when one student or another summoned them with a mere beckon of their hands.

It was here that deep envy gripped Rowan once again.

Magic. The very essence of what dreams are made of, and something he had spent an inordinate amount of time daydreaming about as a kid.

If he could just master such a mystical force, then perhaps the experience of being stolen from his home and forced into a battle that wasn't originally his would have been worth it.

Instead, Rowan was stuck wielding a long, pointy stick.

Tamara must have noticed his hungry expression because she sent him a sly grin. Mercifully, she stayed silent as they left his soldiers by the doors and took the spiral staircase that hugged the wall all the way to the top.

There, the staircase ended in a doorway, and beyond that yet another set of stairs. At the top of *those*, however, was yet another floor.

This one may have looked much comfier and more lived-in, but it was equally fantastical nonetheless.

Floating couches, tables, and more dotted the vast open space. The ceiling was at least as tall as the previous floor. Another spiral staircase swept up the walls, but this time, said walls were covered in various doors rather than bookshelves.

Rowan spotted one of the students emerging from one of the doors, offering a glimpse of a sizable, comfortable room that looked like their personal quarters.

"I hope you don't mind a bit more walking, my lord," Tamara demurred, and Rowan elected to simply nod, not trusting himself not to say something stupid as he admired the interior of the mage tower.

Once more up the stairs they went, all the way up to the top.

This time, though, the stairs led straight up to a trapdoor rather than dipping into a wall, giving Rowan a close-up view of the opaque, glittering material of the ceiling. There was something odd about it, but he only realized what it was when Tamara pushed the trapdoor open and they stepped into the space beyond.

The floor was made entirely out of one-way glass.

Beneath them stretched the space dedicated to the rest, mingling, and relaxation of Tamara's students. She had the perfect view to observe them at her leisure.

Rowan instantly wondered how many of them knew just how much of their privacy was in the hands of the mage. More importantly, if she felt so comfortable making such a blatant show of force and influence, did freedom even exist within her tower?

It wasn't exactly a stretch of the imagination that she had more than one scrying spell or ward installed, giving her a glimpse into whatever aspect of her students' lives she pleased. Rowan had to fight down a shudder.

It wouldn't do to show blatant disgust with his host's personality even before pitching his proposal to her.

"So, what can I do for the illustrious new noble of the kingdom?" Tamara purred, making her way daintily toward a massive desk, which was almost buried under a pile of papers and arcane implements Rowan could make neither heads nor tails of, and taking a seat.

In fact, that was the general theme of the space: controlled chaos composed of things Rowan couldn't understand.

In one corner, a potion setup that reminded the hero of Olivia's own bubbled away. In another, books fluttered through the air, snapping at each other like hungry birds. To the side were jewelry tools and magnifying lenses of every size, shape, and thickness.

The things went on and on, and the various doors that dotted the walls of the room only added to its mystique. After all, if that's what Tamara left out in the open, what did the mage see fit to hide?

Rowan tore his attention from everything that surrounded him with some effort and took a seat in front of her desk before finally focusing on the woman.

"I have a suggestion I'd like to make. Tell me, how much do you know about my Epic-tier class? Did you happen to hear anything about it at all?" Rowan asked.

The question was as much a test as it was an opening for their discussion, and Tamara did very little to offer up actionable intel.

"Not much, I'm afraid. Really, I must admit that your soldiers and servants are surprisingly loyal. All my attempts to dig deeper into what class you earned when I helped you hunt down that Epic were met with failure," Tamara said.

An admission of weakness, a hint at her influence, and a reminder of the favor she did for him all rolled into one. She was good, Rowan would readily admit, but that didn't mean he had to play her game at all.

"The class I got is called [Spear of Unity], and it's a little odd. Honestly, it's not the ideal scenario. I wanted something more versatile with high damage potential, but I wasn't offered a class that worked unless they also came with serious strings attached."

Was he giving away too much information too quickly? Perhaps, but that would hopefully set her at ease and butter her up a little before he got to the core of what he was offering.

"Oho? Why, I am terribly flattered that you would be sharing details of your class so readily with me. Is there a problem with your class that I might be able to assist you with, then?" She leaned forward eagerly, running her tongue over her lips as she did so.

Rowan leaned back in his ridiculously comfy seat and fought off the urge to curse. Of course mages got all the most premium furniture on top of all their cosmic powers. The damn thing was probably enchanted to be extra comfortable.

He was feeling more relaxed than ever, in spite of his attempts to keep his mind sharp. Everything in that room seemed designed to distract and draw the eye.

"You could say that. You see, my class gives me eight slots for [Knights] I can pick. It gives me access to some of their experience and stats. I've already tested it out. I don't steal from people either, I just get a percentage based on what they earn and the stats they have. Guess the system just brings it all into existence, I don't know."

Tamara looked intrigued, but not overly engaged just yet. "And I suppose you would like me to take up one of those [Knight] slots? I can understand why. The stats of an Epic tier such as myself *would* be a significant boon no matter the percentage you'd get."

Rowan ignored the implied question of just how large of a fraction he'd get. He *was* there to negotiate and prove his sincerity, but if he was *that* open with all his personal information, he was sure to draw suspicion instead.

"Exactly. I'm not happy to admit it, but I couldn't invest nearly as much into my mana pool as I'd like while leveling up. That's left me with a very nice foundation for my boosted stats, of course, but I'd love to shore up some of my weaknesses. It's not like there's nothing in it for the [Knights] I choose."

"I would love to hear more about that, of course," Tamara led on, leaning even farther forward. At that point, her chest was pressed against her desk suggestively, and the twinkle in her eye said she knew it.

Like every self-respecting engaged man would, Rowan kept his eyes firmly on the woman's face.

"Any [Knight] I choose gets direct access to my card deck, and they can pick out one card from it. They then get a copy of that card that doesn't count against their own deck limit. I haven't tested yet what happens if I remove or upgrade any of my cards, but I really don't think the system would make my [Knights] dependent on my whim. There are probably safeguards in place."

"Hmm, you would be surprised. There are plenty of classes that are rather ruthless to any subordinates the class designates through them." Tamara drew back a little, like the suggestion of potential issues was enough to give her pause. In spite of that, there was little the woman could do to conceal the glint of greed that was now shining in her eyes.

She was a disgraced former noble cast out by both her family and the Mage Association. She didn't have the kind of support most mages got to enjoy, and she definitely didn't have a pool of inherited cards to draw on.

That meant that each and every card in her deck was something she'd *earned*. And for an independent class? Even for one as well established as her? Epic cards were the epitome of power and luxury. Rowan was willing to bet she didn't have more than two.

And that was counting her newly minted class card.

"Well, I suppose we'll find out. Really, though, this isn't a monarch class or anything in that vein. For the most part, the class description and its effects all point toward a more equal relationship between peers, rather than between a master and subordinate."

"So, with one of your cards on the line, you would like to offer me a position as one of your [Knights]?" It was a question, and Tamara didn't pretend it wasn't.

Instead, her eyes bored into his, searching for lies, traps, and anything else that might hint to his true intentions. "Correct," Rowan said slowly. "I need to fill those slots before I'm forced to march against *legends*. I can't spend months carefully vetting all the potential candidates. Besides, I'd like to think I can trust you."

That, finally, earned him a beaming smile and got the woman to lean forward in interest again, but she didn't give him an answer immediately. "You know, I really thought I'd be having a different conversation with you when you finally visited my tower."

"How so?"

"Well, you see, [Spearman] isn't typically a very prestigious and impressive class. Plenty of people would resent it. And while such choices are typically set in stone . . . well, for a skilled mage, few things are *truly* impossible."

Rowan's breath hitched in his throat, and he hated the way Tamara's eyes smugly fixed on his own. "You mean . . . ?"

"It *is* possible, with the right rituals, to change your class. Not much can be done about your Heart Card, of course. Still, a mage is an incredibly versatile class. You could have made it work. Of course, I acknowledge now that sacrificing your current path would be far too much of a waste to consider that."

Rowan fought down the turmoil and the traces of desire. He wanted his magic, but he tried to focus on what was important. On what the woman across from him was implying.

"You mean you would like to take me up on my offer, then?" Rowan managed to keep his voice from breaking or trembling, which was a massive win in his books.

"Correct. I'd love to take advantage of such a unique opportunity. I daresay I suspect what a couple of your cards are, and if I'm right, then I definitely won't regret my decision."

"Very well, then. If you truly feel that way, I'd be more than happy to accept you as one of my [Knights]." With that, Rowan sent the invitation and watched as the woman's eyes lit up in delight.

Out of everyone he'd chosen as one of his [Knights], she was the one who made her selection the fastest.

The second she did, a rush of power thundered into Rowan's veins.

Slowly at first, then all at once, a fundamental shift came over his mana. It became purer, more potent, like a whole new dimension was added to his intelligence and wisdom stats.

That's when it finally hit him.

What he was getting was a percentage of a person's stats, of course. However, that also covered stats that were improved, boosted by their class choice, and honed to a razor's edge.

A force of mana unlike anything he'd felt before built up within him in seconds, and his composure was sorely tested as he fought the urge to grin like a lunatic and test his mana pool then and there.

He still couldn't fight down a smile, of course, but he'd take whatever wins he could get.

"This was, as I'd suspected, *definitely* worth it," Tamara admitted happily, taking the hero aback by the sincerity of her words. "Now, if my hunch is correct, you're not here solely to discuss your class and this wonderful exchange of ours?"

Rowan grinned fully now. The happiness over his improved stats, as well as the surety of the emotions he could feel drifting in from the mage, mingling into a sense of newfound confidence.

"You're right. As I mentioned, we'll need to tackle the Legendary demons soon, and on that front, we could definitely use your help."

Tamara matched his grin. "Let's hear what you have to say."

## CHAPTER TEN

# Heart to Heart

Rowan oscillated between disbelief, mild dread, and utter elation as he left the mage tower. Things had gone unexpectedly well with Tamara, and the novel feeling of mana swirling around in his chest was evidence of that.

He had so much more of the energy to work with all of a sudden, it was sort of ridiculous. The sensation wasn't necessarily unpleasant, but it was *almost* overwhelming. Newfound power aside, he had other things to consider. Most notably, the feelings he was now interpreting from the shifty old mage.

There was nothing alarming, but the smug bite of her satisfaction was more than a little discomforting. Rowan also felt more than just a little vindication from her, which was not an emotion he'd expected to feel.

There was *something* there. Something he wasn't fully understanding, even though he now had a literal direct line to the woman's innermost feelings.

Rowan was so distracted by his musings as he entered his manor that he nearly walked straight into the princess. She was waiting for him with a stormy expression on her face.

"Ah, I apologize," Rowan said, already dreading whatever their interaction would lead to. "I assume you are waiting for Blake, right? He's probably not going to be back for a couple more hours."

That was an understatement, but Rowan didn't care. If the woman chose to haunt the halls waiting for her fiancé to return, it wasn't his problem.

As he went to go past her, however, she made her determination clear. She was waiting to bother *him*.

"I'm not waiting for Blake. I'm still happy to spend time with him—even with his ridiculous insistence on sticking with that party you introduced him to—but the reason I stayed is because we need to talk."

Rowan's first impulse was to make a hasty excuse and make a run for it. That's also what his second and third impulses were. Unfortunately, after looking the princess in the eye, he got the feeling it wouldn't work.

She looked oddly composed and determined. Her usual arrogance and empty bluster were gone, and the only thing left reflected in her eyes was a steely sort of spirit that he'd never associated with her before.

"Fine. Let's talk." He was annoyed at being cornered, but there was really nothing he could say.

They walked in tense silence to a small, nearly forgotten library. It was one of the manor's designated meeting rooms, which supposedly made it safer than the rest of the house, even if he still didn't understand why.

As they sat down at opposite sides of the table, he watched as her resolve began to crumble.

"I'm listening." Rowan's voice was the perfect blend of bored and obnoxious. As he was hoping, it made her sit up straight in her chair.

It still took her a couple of moments to get the words out.

"Blake trusts you, for some reason," she opened, her tone tinged with more than a little bitterness, "and I have come to accept that. This means that we need to . . . work together."

Rowan's first instinct was to taunt her again. He chose to be better than that, just for Blake. "I'm . . . glad that we can move past our issues. It would make Blake miserable if we continued fighting."

"Yes, quite."

Another silence. Rowan sighed, rubbing his forehead. "Can I just ask why? Why do you hate me so much? Any why did you really want to talk?"

"I mean, you were supposed to be . . ." The princess took a deep, steadying breath. "You weren't supposed to do better than Blake."

"You mean, you were upset that when we finally met, I *wasn't* some useless sap who couldn't even reach Blake's feet?"

"No! Yes! I mean, Blake shouldn't have needed your help to begin with! That wasn't the plan at all." She slumped over in her chair, and a bad feeling took root in Rowan's stomach.

"The plan?" The pit in Rowan's stomach steadily grew more uncomfortable. He had a feeling that this was related to the king's scheming. "Amanda? What plan?"

She winced and looked away. "Blake was supposed to be the competent one. He was supposed to be the one to kill the demon king. To rally the people to him. You weren't even supposed to be here!"

"Why, Amanda? Why is it so bad that I'm not failing? Is it because of my patron god?" Rowan pitched his voice lower, keeping it gentle.

"The kingdom isn't in a good spot right now . . ." Amanda admitted, still refusing to meet his eyes. "A lot of the original nobility is upset, and the peasants aren't exactly happy, either. This wasn't a good time for the demons to reappear. It's like—like someone is plotting against us. The king thinks so, at least."

*"The king." Not Father, or Dad, or whatever. The king.* Rowan found the wording very interesting.

"Are you saying the king thought *I* had something to do with it? Why?"

"Not you in particular. However, it's suspicious that you appeared *right* when the people could be roused into a rebellion with the right leader put in front of them. Most of the lower classes still worship Aristaeus."

"And so he wanted me out of the picture, or at least as weak as possible."

"That's right."

Rowan eyed the woman again. He would have thought that the admission would make her feel better, or at least less nervous. Instead, she looked even more on edge than before.

"Is that *all* you wanted to talk about? Nothing else? Because I'm really not upset. I mean, I'm not happy, don't get me wrong. But I kind of knew that the king wasn't happy with me already. Hard to miss that when he forced us to fight to the death on day one, in the name of the prophecy."

If anything, his attempt to reassure her made her look even more miserable. Rowan noticed her eyes and the way she was gnawing on her lower lip.

"The prophecy . . . it wasn't real."

"What?" Rowan was stunned.

"The prophecy wasn't real. There was no prophecy."

"You mean to tell me he just forced us to fight for—what? His entertainment?" Rowan's voice had gone decidedly dangerous, which he realized a moment later when she looked ready to bolt for the door. "Wait! Sorry, just—I need a moment."

Rowan focused on breathing, eyes closed. He rubbed his temples. He could practically feel his heartbeat through his eyelids. Slowly, his hands unclenched, but he didn't even know when he'd closed them around his chair's armrests.

He winced a little when he saw the damage his fingers had done, the perfect impression of his hand impressed into the sturdy wood. If he'd squeezed any harder, he would have shattered the chair.

"Okay, okay. Now, *why* would your father do that?" Rowan asked.

"Heroes are dangerous," the princess stated quietly, still not looking him in the eye.

Considering the fact that his expression was probably the manifestation of anger, Rowan didn't blame her.

"Dangerous? You steal us from our world and force us to fight your battle, and *we* are dangerous?" Rowan half yelled.

"It's . . . it's a pretty well-documented thing, actually. Heroes often turn on the kingdoms that summoned them, and things are bad enough as they are. We need the heroes, yes, but that doesn't mean we have to like them. Or get along with them."

"So you mean to tell me that you don't actually love Blake?"

"No!" the princess roared, eyes blazing as she finally faced Rowan properly. "I do! He's the best thing that's happened to me in my whole life! He could have been cruel, or violent, or neglectful, but he's not and I want to help him and you're not helping with that and—"

She clamped her mouth shut suddenly, looking pale again. *At least she didn't break eye contact this time*, Rowan thought.

"How am I not helping, Amanda? And you don't have to look at me like I'm going to strike you down for your impunity. I'm not exactly a saint, but I'm not going to hurt you, either. I don't think I've ever been violent toward you," Rowan said.

He didn't tack on a *yet*, both because he didn't want to threaten her and also because he was starting to believe that she did care about Blake.

"You haven't been," the princess admitted. "And you're trying to help Blake. It's just . . . you don't understand. *He's* supposed to be out there, winning. *He's* supposed to have an army. Not you. Why do you have an army?"

She was starting to sound like a broken record, and Rowan was becoming more and more confident that there was something she wasn't telling him.

"Why is it bad that I have an army? And why is it so important that Blake be the one to have an army?"

"Because . . . because that's what the king wanted. He wanted Blake to prove he was the chosen of Sarina. To prove that the kingdom chose right. Your success is giving the rebels ammunition."

Rebels. That was the very first time she brought them up explicitly, and Rowan could see the moment she realized it, too. The flush of her cheeks, the panic in her eyes. Something told him the rebels weren't supposed to be common knowledge.

"I promise you, I have nothing to do with rebels. Neither I nor my fiancée's family, for that matter. I'm just trying to do my job. I'm going to stop demons from killing a whole lot of people and help Blake recover. I really don't think that's unreasonable." Rowan watched as the princess bit her lip again, and he was struck by how childish she looked. She looked more like a chastised kid than the princess of a kingdom.

"Is this why you tried to commandeer my army so many times? Why you tried to get them under Blake's command?" Rowan asked.

"Yes." Her voice was quiet, resigned. "He needs to rebuild his army and start making achievements soon." To Rowan's ears, she sounded desperate.

He leaned back, hand tapping away at the table as he contemplated things. She *was* desperate. Far too desperate for a princess who was simply upset about the state of her kingdom.

In fact, Rowan strongly suspected this whole situation wasn't about the kingdom at all. She'd always framed those parts of their conversations as her father's demands and expectations. She'd never once stated that she cared about that.

The only thing she seemed to care about was Blake.

"So . . . there's something you're not telling me. I get that the king might be disappointed. I guess I even understand why he was upset to see three heroes instead of two. However, you still need us to kill the demon king. Why the hostility? Why are you so worried about Blake? He needs to recover before he can be useful."

The princess froze, her eyes shining with panic and briefly flitting toward the doors. "I . . ." She trailed off, breathing more heavily. If Rowan didn't know better, he would have thought she was about to have a panic attack.

He leaned forward, and this time his voice came out lower as he tried to sound soothing. "Please, help me understand. You *know* I care about Blake. What's happening here?"

"I can't tell you," she whimpered, eyes wide and panicked. "I can't. I want to, but I *can't*. I just—I need you to help him get better soon. I need him to show the kingdom that he can still fight. *Please.*"

"Okay, I promise. I promise. Calm down, now." Rowan rushed to reassure her, noticing the edge he'd driven her to. He felt more than a little flustered himself. He'd never been good at reassurance or any kind of moral support.

The princess nodded. "I'll do everything I can to help Blake. Everything. I don't care what I have to do, but I'll keep him safe. I love him. I want him to stay with us. We're supposed to get through this and have a family. *Be happy.* I just want us to be safe."

There was just one problem with it all.

If she was so desperate to help Blake, why was she pushing him straight toward the demonic wastes before he'd even earned his class back? If she was so desperate to get him out there and racking up achievements, then there could only be a single reason for it.

She was convinced he'd be in more danger if he stayed in Rest's Remorse and did nothing.

That, more than anything, was enough to send a shiver of fear down Rowan's spine.

Calming a frightened princess was an involved affair, and Rowan eventually resolved things by dumping her in the kitchen. She was surrounded by plenty of desserts and a couple of servants to fuss over her.

The woman still looked shell-shocked and more than a little traumatized. She was nibbling on a cookie when Rowan finally made his escape.

He had intended to head straight to Olivia's lab so they could discuss things together, but Henry tracked him down before he could. The man looked as poised as ever, but there was a hurried quality to him that almost threatened to break that composure.

"Lord Rowan, sir. You have a guest waiting for you. I directed him to your study, but you might want to see him at your earliest convenience, sir," the chamberlain said.

Reluctantly, Rowan changed course. "Who is it that can make you so flustered, Henry?"

"The Mercenary King, sir."

*Well*, Rowan thought, *that would do it.*

Rowan found his guest waiting patiently, sipping on a dainty cup of tea that looked ridiculous in his massive hands.

The moment Rowan opened the doors of his study, the Mercenary King zeroed in on him with uncanny focus.

There was an intensity to the man that Rowan had seen once before.

Typically, the Mercenary King was stoic, withdrawn. Rowan had had the privilege of seeing his relaxed, jolly side while they were marching, but there was none of that here. Rowan had last seen this level of laser focus moments before the man led Rowan's army in a charge against the monsters.

"Lucius, to what do I owe the pleasure?" Rowan hoped that invoking his name instead of his title would make the man relax. But if anything, the man looked even more focused.

"I come to you with a request, and to discuss our future cooperation. I've given this a lot of thought and I believe that I've found the best way forward for us both." The Mercenary King put the tiny teacup down carefully, then crossed his arms across his chest as he watched Rowan take his seat across from him, brow furrowing briefly at the cold, weirdly formal tone.

"I'm listening. I promise I'll do whatever I can to help. We've fought together, and I know that you didn't need to help us. That means a lot more to me than I can put into words." Rowan meant it, too—but he did reflect the same frigid tone right back.

"I'm glad to hear you say that, Lord Rowan. In that case, I want you to make me one of your [Knights]."

Rowan's world flipped upside down for the second time that day.

One of the few people aware of the full extent of his class and its effects was asking him to use that same class on him.

Rowan opened his mouth to ask questions, then thought better of it.

Lucius looked, for lack of a better word, determined. He knew what he was asking for. And if he'd decided it was still worth all the hassle? Rowan would not deny him. It wasn't like the proposition was all bad.

"I accept. Whatever you need, you'll have it," Rowan said solemnly, then sent the invite.

The man cracked a small smile, relief and something else warring on his face. "Thank you, lad. Let me take a closer look at this."

It only took Lucius a couple of moments to make his way through the menu that would make him a [Knight]. When he did, Rowan gasped.

A wall of energy slammed into him, almost making Rowan double over as his body creaked and shook. A sense of vitality, solidity, and resilience washed over every inch of his flesh. It almost felt like his body had ballooned outward, only to condense back down to its previous size at a much higher density.

There was a secondary change to his mind and mana pool, too. Both grew a little, but it was the speed at which his mind made connections and the speed of his mana regeneration that were really boosted.

*Vitality and wisdom, then.* Rowan found the main stats of the man known as the Mercenary King surprising, but he wasn't about to complain.

He may have gotten the evolution of the mind stats from Tamara already, but the boost to his vitality was going to be invaluable.

Already, he could feel that his body could hold a ton more energy. In response, **Gluttonous Banquet**'s own limits surged upward, letting him save up even more energy for future use.

Of course, his soaring mood was somewhat dampened when the link between him and Lucius was finally complete and the Mercenary King's emotions slammed into his own.

Vindication, relief, quiet self-satisfaction. These positive emotions, mostly caused by Rowan accepting the man as his [Knight], were by far eclipsed by what lurked underneath. Anguish. Worry. Regret. Disgust. A gaping chasm of helplessness. And all of it seemed to have something to do with Rowan.

The hero could tell that much, clear as day. His eyes fixed on the Mercenary King's, and he could feel the man willing him to *understand.*

There was something deeply, bitterly wrong. Lucius knew full well of Rowan's ability to peek at his [Knights'] emotions, and the man was doing his very best to encourage him to do just that.

"What were you hoping to discuss? Our future campaign to put down those Legendary demons, perhaps?" Rowan exuded casualness and amusement.

The hero knew that they should be safe. The manor was home to more than a few Epic-tier individuals. The baroness herself had an assassin-based class and could recognize intruders with plenty of advance notice. In spite of that, the sheer turmoil Lucius was feeling immediately put the hero on edge.

"Yes, exactly. I know that you'll have to venture out sometime soon, Lord Rowan. The job ahead of you won't be easy. In light of that, I'd like to offer up my own mercenaries as backup. If you'll have us, we'll join you so we can put an end to this demonic threat." The contrast between what the mercenary king felt and what he said was horrifying.

Rowan swallowed, taking a few moments to parse his way through the Mercenary King's emotions.

"Ah, I didn't expect that. I hope you know I mean no disrespect, but I was under the impression that you couldn't move without royal approval. The situation with Blake was, as I understood it, an exception. One made possible by the royal request to assist the hero in question quickly."

"These are trying times, lad. Of course, we can't always move only on the king's say-so."

Rowan felt each emotion like different ingredients in a dish. The bitter twist of a lie. The regret over its necessity. Then, heady satisfaction.

"I understand. I appreciate it, truly. Having you there to assist us will be a major boon, since I know that you'll help keep us safe. Your abilities will be invaluable for anything we plan to do. On that note, do you have any suggestions on the way we should approach hunting down the demons?"

"You can leave your back to me. If you hand over command of your army, I'll keep any lower-level threats from intervening in your battle against the enemy leaders. It'll keep you fresh and ready to face foes to assure your victory."

Bitterness, again. A sour taste, along with a pinch of horror.

"That does sound good. However, I would like to remind you that my party won't be alone. We'll have Blake and his party with us as well. Are you sure you want to leave us to deal with the leaders of the demonic army while you take care of everything else on your own?" Rowan tested the man.

A swelling wave of disgust. Of anger and supreme annoyance. All of it tinged by vicious self-satisfaction. "Yes, of course. I know how close you and Hero Blake are, so it doesn't surprise me to hear you'll be fighting side by side. Regardless, I'd still like to do my part."

"Of course. We'll be happy to have you. Your speed boosts alone will be invaluable. I see no issues with placing my soldiers in your hands, so I'm looking forward to what else you can do with them."

Amusement, now, and a curl of relief.

"Thank you for your trust, Lord Rowan. I look forward to seeing the demonic forces shattered. I'm confident that you'll be facing the demon king in no time, so we can bring this crisis to a close as quickly as possible."

Annoyance, disbelief, resignation.

"Thank you for your sincere trust in my abilities. I'm sure that my new Epic-tier class will allow us to make it through this unscathed. After all, I've finally caught up to my peers. That has to count for something, right?" A plastic smile slowly crept up Rowan's face, stopping just before his eyes.

Lucius answered in kind, a swirl of pride and worry coming through their bond. "Then I'll leave you to continue making preparations. I believe it won't take much longer for you to be ready to rout the demons, then?"

"Correct. We need several more weeks, but that will pass in no time. I'm sure you'll be impressed by all the progress we've made by then."

"Of course. If you'll excuse me, my lord?" The mercenary king gestured at the door, and Rowan readily nodded.

"Go ahead. Contact me at any time if you need assistance to prepare. Potions are something I can assure you we can provide, at the very least. At superlative quality, too. My fiancée has been hard at work so even the weakest of our soldiers have the best chances of survival possible."

That, at least, wasn't doublespeak. Olivia had devoted a stunning amount of time and effort to making the most of her Epic alchemist class. While it was highly geared toward combat, it still let her surpass her past accomplishments.

"Thank you, I will keep that in mind." The Mercenary King nodded, and then he was finally gone.

Rowan immediately collapsed in his chair, a tired sigh escaping his lips as he placed his hands on his face. If his chat with the princess wasn't enough, then Lucius's visit was the final nail in the coffin.

The kingdom of Rhys was not their friend.

He'd known, or at least suspected that for a very long time. The question that gnawed at him was the why of it all.

Why be hostile to your own summoned heroes from the start? Why try to sabotage the people who are supposed to help you protect your kingdom? Why make a potential enemy where you could have had a valuable ally?

Rowan didn't know, but he resolved to find out.

Once the demon king was dead, King Harold was next in his crosshairs. And he really didn't care what Blake's princess had to say about that.

## CHAPTER ELEVEN

# For a Future

Rowan paced back and forth in the library. Organizing a meeting in a hurry had been surprisingly tricky, especially considering the fact that he needed to get his full party, Olivia's parents, and Blake in one room. *I guess the stress was going to catch up to me at some point—might as well be now.*

The baron couple had been busy ever since the engagement celebration, catching up and working on improving the state of Rest's Remorse. Doubly so, now that the engagement meant that their daughter would eventually be directly in charge of the city.

Rowan's pacing continued above, and Blake's sword swings were being practiced below. Sweat dripped down his forehead into his eyes, and he was forced to pause. The kingdom's chosen was using every waking moment he had to grow, to get back to where he used to be. He managed to claw his way back up to level fifty-nine before eradicating the local Rare population.

In order to find more prey, Blake would have to spend the night outside the city walls, but both Blake's party and his gaggle of fiancées were still leery of letting him do that.

In response, the fallen hero spent his time strengthening Rowan's fledgling [Knights], intent on staying sharp and building a backup party beyond his harem.

Rowan was, overall, amused. But also somewhat worried that Blake might have effectively stolen his newest recruits.

The combination of complications he'd unearthed meant that he had to force a meeting regardless of people's busy schedules. He managed to gather everyone a couple of minutes later, but people were shooting him ugly looks at their schedules being disrupted, unaware of the severity of the situation.

"I know all of you have plenty of things to do, so I'll keep this brief. Yesterday, I met with Tamara, Lucius, and Amanda. The things I've learned talking to the latter two are somewhat . . . troubling."

The room exploded with stunned silence. Blake's eyes narrowed at Rowan's admission that he'd had words with his fiancée, and the mention of Tamara was enough to warrant a particularly icy look from the baroness.

"What did you learn, exactly?" Blake demanded, prompting Rowan to launch into the story.

It took a while to cover the nuances, especially his chat with the Mercenary King. "So, overall, I'm afraid that we're stuck. I have no clue what orders Lucius got, but they're obviously not benevolent if he felt the need to warn us in such a roundabout way."

"Whatever it is, they're planning to pull it off during your venture into the wastes. It isn't as if you're going in blind," Kayden supplied, looking the calmest out of everyone in the room. Camilla looked shocked and worried, but her husband showed quiet resolve. There was something in his eyes Rowan couldn't pin down, something between pride and resignation that made him vaguely suspicious.

"Knowing when it will happen still doesn't help us stop it," a wolfkin quipped. Marcus had his arms crossed over his chest and his fur was all puffed up. Hearing the news that the king might be working against them had rattled him, but he clearly wasn't cowering.

"True, but we can make educated guesses. We know they need us to fight the Legendary demons. So, why? If they want those gone, why are they so eager to end us before we kill the demon king?" Milena rumbled with a vicious look in her eyes.

Rowan shot a questioning look at the baron, but the man was silent now. Lips pressed into a tight line. It was Camilla who spoke up next.

"There are plenty of stories about heroes, most of which end with the death of the demon king and the heroes' return to their world. But when the heroes decide to stay? Occasionally, it ends *quite* badly for the local nobility." She hesitated, eyes flitting between the two heroes. "What story is the king thinking of that's frightening him so much? Without that, it doesn't make any sense. Why be afraid of people you chose to summon?"

"Technically, gods summon heroes. The chosen kingdom just helps facilitate the process," Olivia chimed in, grinning mischievously even when her mother shot another glare her way.

Thankfully, her interruption eased the stifling atmosphere of the room considerably.

"Olivia, behave. There are too many stories to be sure. There are some stories that paint heroes who stay as paragons who start prosperous kingdoms and go on to be the best of kings. There are just as many, however, about heroes who proceed to act like tyrants and monsters. Heroes with a maligned sense of justice that ends up driving the world into war."

Rowan panned over to Blake, only to find his fellow hero shooting the same look back at him. Rowan was really loath to admit it, but he could easily see the way such a thing might happen. And while he'd like to say he wasn't tempted to try and change things, it would be a lie.

The way lower classes were treated here made him want to act out. And Blake? Well, Rowan strongly suspected that there wasn't much his friend wouldn't do if his goddess asked him nicely. That was still something the Stalwart Hero needed to confront him about.

"So, that's it? The king is worried that we'll destroy his kingdom afterward?" Rowan asked bitterly once he managed to get out of his staring contest with Blake. "Couldn't he stop us easily enough? The kingdom must have enough Epic tiers to form a small army."

The baroness shrugged, visibly uncomfortable. "The king may be powerful, and he does have a strong following, yes, but you overestimate how many nobles would willingly fight for him. Besides, if the stories are to be believed, heroes become much more powerful when they finally strike down the demon king."

"More powerful how? Do our blessings get boosted somehow?" Blake asked eagerly, eyes lighting up in expectation.

"All I can tell you is that it happens, and that it's intrinsically linked to heroes. The details of the process are a closely guarded secret. I'm not sure anyone knows, past the royal family, of course."

"Of course," Rowan echoed, stealing another glance at Kayden.

The baron's face was carefully blank, and though he maintained eye contact when he caught Rowan looking, the hero got a strong feeling he'd prefer not to.

The Stalwart Hero felt frustration bubbling up. Time after time he found himself talking to people who were supposed to be his allies. And time after time, they refused to tell him the whole truth.

The most painful part of the whole affair was that he strongly suspected that they actually *couldn't.* The princess had used very precise wording. And he'd never seen the baron with quite that look on his face before.

Thinking back to all the discussions they'd had, the man always skipped over certain topics. Certain topics that mostly had to do with hero cards and why they were so appealing. For the time being, Rowan decided to shelve his suspicions in favor of practical matters.

"Whatever the king is scheming, I think it's safe to assume we'll face a knife to the back while we're fighting the Legendary demons. This means that we need to worry about the demons and the scheming both. Any suggestion on how to deal with that?"

"Power," the baron immediately spat out, the word coming out with both distaste and stubborn insistence. "We need you all to be as powerful as you possibly can be. This means no more wasting experience, cards, and training time. I admire what you're trying to do, but this is not the time."

Rowan wanted to object, but couldn't. "What do you suggest, then? It's not like we can benefit much from hunting down Uncommons and Rares. Well, other than Blake—no offense, buddy."

"None taken."

The baron ignored the byplay. "Sure, you can't benefit from killing them directly. Your [Knights] can help, but you need to increase your overall strength. In this case, it means working on your decks. You can't tell me you all have a perfect spread of Epic cards."

He eyed them all like he was daring them to countermand him, but none of them did.

"Getting enough cards to pull something like that off is going to be tough," Rowan said hesitantly, thinking about his own cards. He still had an Uncommon in his deck, after all, even if **Blood Siphon** was a pretty solid card.

"Not if you pool all your resources. Think like a duke. If you order all your troops to sally out and collect cards for you, think about how many they can collect in a day. If each soldier contributes five Uncommon cards a day, you'll meet your needs soon enough."

Rowan twitched. He genuinely hated the idea of sending his men into combat and then demanding their hard-earned trophies just so he could empower himself. A part of him wanted to insist on earning everything himself.

"Do *not* give me that look, young man." Surprisingly enough, it was Olivia's mother who snapped at Rowan. "You made a commitment to keep my daughter safe. Now, you're going to honor it. With everything in your power, keep both of you safe. You might see it as a grievous injustice, but there is practical merit to that tradition here. You must gather power to protect your people, too."

There was a tense moment of silence while everyone waited for Rowan's answer. Even Blake's eyes were fixed on him, though Rowan couldn't figure out what his friend was thinking. "Fine," he spat out at long last, sagging at the agreement. "But I wish I disagreed."

Rowan understood the underlying logic. He understood why Olivia's parents were pushing for that particular course of action. Still, he felt like he'd fundamentally failed the people who put trust in him. His shoulders sank. *That means I'm failing myself, too.*

"It's okay. We've got plenty of time to buff everyone up to Epic once all the demons are dead if that's what you want," Olivia offered with a sad smile, squeezing his hand underneath the table.

That did make him feel better.

"I'll stop pouting, don't worry. I recognize that it's . . . immature, I guess. I just wanted to do things differently. Is that really so bad?" He might have been talking to Olivia, but Rowan really asked the question to the room at large.

"It's not. But even back home, similar rules are respected by all. You need a strong leader to protect everyone and give them a chance to grow," Milena supplied softly, surprising Rowan.

"I'm with you on making everyone stronger—you know that, dude," Blake chimed in with a genuine smile on his face. "But I don't think you're letting them down, Rowan. Hells, I know for a fact your soldiers all love you. It's kinda weird, to be honest. You were never this popular back home." He winked.

Rowan rolled his eyes at the good-natured teasing, but another surge of optimism coursed through him. If he looked at it like he was asking for help, maybe it wasn't the worst thing in the world. Everyone needed a hand occasionally, right?

"Fine, fine, I'll do it. I'll organize an assembly and pass out the orders. Is there anything else we can do to prepare? What about you guys?" He addressed his party members, unable to deny his curiosity. "Do you need something special to make your new classes work better?"

They still hadn't sat down and properly discussed their new classes, much to the hero's chagrin. Even Olivia had weaseled her way out of telling him what she got, though he could tell it was because his frustration amused her.

Milena pulled at her fur a bit while she considered things, but still answered first. "Afraid not. Well, I obviously need scrap cards so I can upgrade my deck's rarity, but otherwise, I'm set. I got [Elder Shaman] years earlier than I thought I would. Really, I should blame you for throwing off my schedule." Milena's smile was light and teasing, making Rowan grin.

"I'm similarly set. My class was . . . a bit of a surprise, honestly. Didn't think I'd get something so unique," the other half of the twin set said, then surprised Rowan when a system window came up in front of him.

**[Bulwark of Salvation]**
**You are the saving grace, the life-sparing shield,**
**the final bastion between your allies and death.**
**Hold fast.**
**By selecting the [Bulwark of Salvation] class you will gain the ability to prevent, redirect, and delay damage dealt to you and your allies.**

**Additional beneficial effects:**
**A grand boost to the effectiveness of your vitality and wisdom stats.**
**A massive boost to all your resistances, including resistances to esoteric effects.**
**You can trigger a five-second window of time where all damage taken by you and your allies will be delayed and stored instead. You can hold on to this damage for ten seconds before it is all dealt to you or an ally of choice.**
**If your wisdom and vitality stats' total is twice that of your enemy, you can shift all stored damage to them when in direct contact with them. Weapons and armor are treated as an extension of your body in this instance.**

**Class Penalties:**
**A grand decrease to your damage output.**

**Attached card: Salvation's Blessing (Epic, Active)**

"That's . . . impressive, especially damage onto an enemy," Rowan remarked, eyes going back to the description of shifting damage to an enemy again and again. With it, as long as he had some relatively weak monsters within reach, it was unlikely that Marcus would ever go down.

"It's impressive, sure, but you need to read the descriptions a bit more closely. I can only hold one charge at a time. Even if the damage from it doesn't trigger, I can't sponge more hits until I offload the current charge. I can still get obliterated."

Marcus was aiming to be humble, but there was a gleam in his eyes that told Rowan he was more than a little proud of his class.

He'd also chosen to share freely, something his sister hadn't done. Rowan could only assume it was because her own class came straight from their clan and was likely considered sensitive in some shape or form. He didn't begrudge her for keeping the details to herself, regardless.

"And you, you little gremlin?" Rowan snarked jokingly, looking down at his favorite alchemist. "Are you going to finally tell me exactly what class you got, or are you going to keep teasing me?"

She gave him a Cheshire grin, and Rowan almost resolved himself to waiting longer before another system window popped up in his notifications. His eyebrows climbed higher the farther he read.

**[Alchemist of Entropy]**
**The world is your playground. Dissolve or enrich it as you please.**
**By picking the [Alchemist of Entropy] class, you get to tap into the Law of [Entropy], imposing it on the world or a dy reversing its effects.**
**Warning: This class deals with a fundamental law.**

**Additional beneficial effects:**
**A grand boost to the effectiveness of your intelligence and wisdom stats.**
**A grand boost to the growth of your mana pool.**

**Your mana bears the flavor of [Entropy].**
**You can leverage [Entropy] in your alchemical pursuits, dissolving certain traits of your ingredients or condensing others.**

**Class Penalties:**
**They Are Watching.**
**BEWARE OF WIELDING FORCES YOU CANNOT COMPREHEND, CHILD.**

**Attached card: Entropy's Embrace (Epic, Active)**

"Olivia, dear, you never get to tell me to stop being reckless ever again." Rowan somehow managed to say that without gritting his teeth or sounding upset.

"Whatever do you mean? I did nothing wrong." Olivia's expression of perfect innocence was not working as intended, but Rowan found it difficult to feel upset. He'd done his fair share of stupid things, after all.

Unfortunately for Olivia, she'd apparently neglected to let her parents know about her class prior to the meeting as well. And, judging by the way the baroness was choking on her own spit and staring at her daughter with bulging eyes, she wasn't happy.

Even her father looked pained, though the way he was staring at her spoke more of resignation than of any real anger.

"Can I ask why, of all things, you chose to pick a class like *this*, daughter? You know as well as I do that plenty of [Alchemist] classes are monitored if not outright forbidden by the temples."

"I did it because I refuse to be a burden, and because I refuse to be weak. With this class, I can match any one of you," Olivia declared, steel in her voice.

Rowan didn't doubt what she was saying for even a second. He wasn't entirely sure what the class entailed, but it certainly looked like it would have plenty of application in direct combat. Whatever else might happen due to her choices, Olivia was unlikely to feel vulnerable again.

"Just . . . let me know what I can do to help you improve your cards, okay?" Rowan offered, and got a dazzling smile in return. "I'll even refrain from ribbing you about all your complaining—but only if you decide to be less reckless than me," he added, and the smile was replaced by a scowl.

"You can be such an ass," Olivia grumbled, but Rowan felt like he was the winner when she gave him a small smile anyway.

"Yes, yes, touching emotional moment aside, we need to finish up here. Anything else we need to plan for? We've got our Epic-tier classes, and we'll be working on getting our decks up to the same tier, too. Can we do anything else?" Marcus got the group back on track.

"Well . . ." a very meek Blake sheepishly said, "I'd like some help, if that's okay? I need to go deeper. Rares are pretty much gone from the area, and I'm not getting nearly enough experience to get back to Epic any time soon. Maybe a small hunting trip?"

"I can help with that, if you'd like," Rowan offered immediately. His mind went back to the conversation he'd had with the princess.

"*We* can help. I'll come with. I need to experiment a bit with my new class anyway," Olivia joined in immediately, wrapping her arms around Rowan a bit more tightly. He shot her an apologetic smile in turn, only for her to roll her eyes at him.

"I could use an outing, too. I haven't played around much with my new ability to shift damage to an enemy. It's not a good idea to test that kind of thing when the situation is dire," Marcus offered as well. All eyes fell on his sister.

Milena huffed and threw up her hands in exasperation. "What? Don't look at me like that! I'm all for solidarity and all that, but I need to study, unlike the rest of you. Rituals don't perform themselves, you know? I'll be staying, thank you very much. You lot have fun."

"Do you think your party will want to tag along, too, Blake?" Rowan ventured hesitantly, making his fellow hero sigh.

"Almost definitely. I'll ask them to stay this time around, though. Maybe they'll accept if I ask them to hang out with your knightly trio?"

"I swear, they follow you around like lost puppies. I tried to make an elite party of [Knights], and you snatched it right out from under me," Rowan complained, but his joking tone made it fairly obvious that he wasn't actually upset.

"Well, maybe you should take better care of your subordinates, man!" Blake shot back with a cocky smirk.

Rowan just huffed. "Maybe." *Or maybe I should just keep them away from ridiculously charismatic heroes instead.* "Okay, well, if that's all for today, let's get to it. I'll get my troops together and pass on my orders, then we'll head out tomorrow to wrap up Blake's recovery."

There was a wave of general assent, and then people started streaming out of the room. Rowan stayed seated, though, with Olivia still attached to him.

With the meeting done, he suddenly felt tired and worried. It felt like the final moments of peace before a storm were slipping out between his fingers.

"It's going to be okay, you know?" Olivia said quietly, scooting her chair closer and plopping her chin on his shoulder. "We'll be ready, and whatever the demons and kingdom throw our way, we'll be fine."

"I really want to believe that. I do. It's just . . . I'm worried. I just want to stay here, with you," Rowan admitted, guilt and dread swamping him. "But I don't want any more of my soldiers to die, either."

He knew full well that plenty of resources and struggle had gone into his journey already. People had paid the ultimate price on his behalf, at his command. To falter now and choose to hide would be spitting directly on their memory. Even then, the temptation remained.

Olivia sighed and brushed her hands through his hair before firmly forcing him to face her. The kisses that followed didn't solve all of Rowan's problems, but they definitely made them feel more distant and bearable.

Rowan's summons had gone out, the soldiers had mustered, and now the full array of his troops stood before him. A bit over five hundred souls, each and every one sworn to him. Each and every one willing to march at his order, to glory or to death. The sun was still low in the sky, but it was high enough that its golden light crept over the walls.

He took advantage of the officers doing final inspections of their troops to delay the moment when he'd have to start his speech. He was usually queasy before making large troop announcements like this, but knowing how sharp the thorns were on the path ahead, Rowan tasted bile in his mouth and swallowed it down as stealthily as he could.

Finally, the last uniform was straightened, the last piece of armor forcefully polished, and the last warning about sloppiness and military etiquette given out.

Which meant it was time for him to open his mouth.

"Thank you for gathering here so quickly. You still have your normal duties to attend to, so I will be brief," Rowan opened, sweeping his eyes over the arrayed troops.

He knew all of them at this point, if not by name then by features. It was hard to force himself to commit their faces to memory when it was so much easier to pretend they were a faceless mass afraid of death. It would be much easier to send a nameless grunt to their death than it would be to send a soldier named John who'd married his childhood friend only the week before.

That wouldn't be fair to any of them. He would remember who they were, future pain be damned.

"I'm here today to inform you that we're almost ready. The time to charge into the wastes is nearing, and we *will* bring the demons to heel. We *will* kill the leaders of their armies, Legendary tier or not. And we *will* bring triumph over demon kind. We *will* have another peace again. That I promise you."

Rowan felt pathetic, making that particular promise. It was hard to stand tall when he feared he'd have to ask them to take up arms against fellow humans immediately after.

He still meant every word.

"To do this, however, we need to finish our preparation. For this reason, I give you the following orders: I need you to go out into the wastes in force and cull as many monsters as you can. Bring back their cards so that we can guarantee our victory against demons. I promise you, we will not fail your hard work and effort. The cards you collect will be invaluable for the task we have been entrusted with."

He expected to hear jeering, not cheering. He thought he'd see unhappy faces, at the very least. Instead, the Stalwart Hero's heart broke a little when he saw the proud smiles and determined expressions. *Are they actually happy about this?*

Their lord, their hero, had given them a task.

His army would do their best to fulfill it.

"Thank you once again for your service. Thank you for your loyalty. I couldn't ask for a better army. Even if the king were to offer me his royal guard to replace you, I'd choose you over them in a heartbeat." Rowan's speech concluded, sincerity ringing in his every word. He bowed.

A ripple spread through his army before they returned the gesture. Rowan only barely kept the smile on his face as he walked right through their ranks, exchanging greetings and comments.

Olivia was right by his side, a steadying presence in the whirlwind that was his mind.

*Why don't they resent me?*

"You did amazing out there," his fiancée whispered once they were in the manor, away from all the orders and the weight of expectations.

"Did I?" Rowan asked.

"You did. You realize they wouldn't so readily follow any of the previous mayors in Rest's Remorse, right? Whether you want to acknowledge it or not, you've improved their lives, Rowan."

That, at last, brought a smile to the hero's lips. Perhaps it felt a bit hollow, to improve someone's life and then ask them to risk it all.

They had a war to win and a future to fight for. Rowan swore he would do whatever he could to bring them all back.

## CHAPTER TWELVE

# Mending Light

It felt fitting to venture out of the city with a smaller group.

The baroness would typically insist on having at least two parties of soldiers following along, but this time Rowan had been able to dissuade her. Bringing up the fact that the men would be best put to work hunting down more cards was what did the trick.

As such, it was only Blake's party, Rowan, Olivia, and Marcus who made their way deeper into the wastes.

Somewhere along the line, Rowan realized that he'd lost his fear of the place.

Where once he might have felt on edge, now the embrace of the wild, twisted jungle felt just as welcoming as the walls of Rowan's manor. When paperwork was involved? The wastes actually won the popularity contest.

Even then, Rowan felt that the main source of entertainment on that particular trip was Blake's party members.

The three women looked so resigned yet determined that Rowan actually felt like giggling. It didn't help that they dressed almost like they were planning to walk into some high-class gathering instead of heading into combat. All of them wore dresses that were just shy of completely impractical.

"You know, I really wonder what's going to happen to your harem if we need to run or something," Rowan mumbled to Blake, keeping his voice faux quiet.

Judging by the way said harem stiffened and shot him glares, they definitely heard him.

Looking at the self-satisfied smile on Rowan's face, Blake could do little other than sigh.

"Can you please not poke fun at them? I'd like it if you got along. At the very least, try to stay civil? I know snark comes naturally to you, but please?" He was complaining, but then again, only Rowan was in the right position to see Blake's smile.

"Sure, sure, I can do that, just for you . . . for now."

"Of course." Blake rolled his eyes. "I can't ask for more than that, I suppose."

"No, you really can't, not after the stuff you and Kayla pulled at that Christmas party!" The look in Rowan's eyes turned decidedly malicious when he noticed that he suddenly had the undivided attention of Blake's ladies.

Blake had gone pale and unnaturally still, something that the women also picked up on.

"Now, what's this about a . . . Christmas? Party?" Jacqueline, the member of the trio Rowan knew least about, asked with a blinding smile and more than a little vindictiveness.

"Another day, I think," Rowan laughed, relishing the way his friend's face had gone completely red.

Maybe they were heading into a demon-infested landscape riddled with monsters in order to claw back Blake's full strength.

In that moment, though?

Rowan was relaxed and happy, surrounded by friends and a trio of acquaintances he might just be able to learn to like, too. And for the Stalwart Hero? Well, that was enough to improve his day.

Their progress was swift, but they still encountered their fair share of opposition. And, every time, Blake insisted on stepping in himself to take care of whatever threat got in their way.

Frankly, Rowan was impressed.

The last time he saw his fellow hero fight, Blake was still awkward, trying to scrounge together something approaching an actual combat style.

Blake hadn't exactly reached the peak of mortal swordsmanship while Rowan wasn't looking. He had, however, put together an absolutely vicious style that fit him oddly well, even if one wouldn't think him capable of fighting with such savagery at first glance.

Blake's style was all about maiming and permanently damaging his opponents if they somehow managed to survive an encounter with him.

At the same time, there was an odd, almost artificial quality to Blake's movements that made it even harder to anticipate his strikes and face him in direct battle.

As Rowan watched the other hero take apart a bear-type monster, he seriously wondered how he'd fare against his friend in one-on-one combat if they competed in pure skill.

Blake would dash forward, leave a shallow wound on the monster, and then immediately zoom back like a marionette with its string yanked. This would enrage the Rare-tier monster, and it would swing and claw with wild abandon.

The way Blake contorted around those strikes made Rowan wince, but his fellow hero found an opening to jerk his sword up with such force that it nearly cut fully through one of the bear's meaty paws. All that done from a position where he should have had zero leverage to deal a blow that powerful.

From there, Blake slipped right behind the monster, spinning around the kick it tried for by collapsing forward onto all fours, and once again lashed out.

A spray of blood and the bear's screams of pain announced its collapse onto its right side, both its front and back legs utterly savaged and incapable of supporting its weight.

After that? Well, that didn't count as combat. It was a simple execution.

In spite of that, Blake didn't rush in like he might have done in the past. He calmly and methodically disabled every limb that tried to reach for him until he'd made a full circle around the monster and once more stood in front of it.

His sword fell one final time, and the bear's cries petered out.

Rowan didn't even resist his urge to clap, shooting his best friend a dazzling grin when he turned around to give him a look that was asking whether the congratulations were sincere or mocking.

"I can't believe how much better you are now!" Rowan gushed, walking forward to thump Blake on the back.

The other hero winced and stumbled forward, awkwardly shaking himself off. "Thanks. Do you need to try to break my back, though? 'Cause I mean, ow. Be a little more gentle, please."

Rowan rolled his eyes, entirely unamused. "Oh, come on, I barely even touched you!"

Surprisingly enough, the look he received in return was very nearly scathing. "Rowan, I'm genuinely telling you to stop trying to break my back. This is, like, the third time."

Rowan opened his mouth to tell Blake that he hadn't even engaged his strength, then stopped.

His strength was no longer what it used to be. A bit of thinking and pulling up his status screen showed him that almost half his knights had chosen that particular stat as their main source of strength, and the knight trio was coming along very nicely, already well into their early Rare-tier levels.

The revelation startled him, making Rowan spin toward Olivia immediately. "Wait, with the way my strength's been growing, I never hurt you, did I?" The very prospect of that had made his face grow pale.

"Oh, sure, get all concerned about hurting your fiancée by accident. Your best friend? Who cares if you've been doing domestic violence to *him*," Blake commented from behind.

Olivia chuckled and stepped forward, landing a quick peck on his lips. "Don't be silly, Rowan, you'd never hurt me. You've always been exceedingly gentle with me. Well . . . almost always."

Her smile was a taunting, wicked thing, and it made Rowan flush so hard even his neck colored red.

"I feel a story there," Blake purred, plopping an elbow on top of Rowan's shoulder and making the Stalwart Hero stumble. "Want to share?"

"Want to explain what you and Kayla were doing that one time you told me to visit then didn't answer the door?" Rowan quipped right back, which did the expected job of getting Blake to back right off. His expression looked pained enough to almost make Rowan regret the comment, especially when he spied the reactions of his harem trio. Almost.

"Your fiancée is off-limits when it comes to jokes. I got it. Locked and loaded. Don't need to teach me that lesson twice. I'll behave!"

Rowan took the moment to eye his best friend, then grinned. "Good. Keep it that way. Now, shall we continue on our merry way?"

"Let's."

As they proceeded deeper into the jungle, the trio of women descended upon Blake like vultures ready to pick apart a fresh carcass, and Rowan contentedly fell back to walk with his own party members.

"Well, what do you think?" Rowan asked, sweeping their surroundings carefully in search of any ambushes or suddenly emerging predators.

Being out and about on their own was refreshing, but he was seriously starting to regret not bringing a scout along.

"He's good. Not the best we've seen, obviously, but he's definitely good. Gotta say, whatever he's doing to move like that, it freaks me out." Marcus shuddered lightly at the admission, shooting the other hero a quick glance. "It kind of reminds me of the way some demons move, really."

"True. Still, you can't deny that it's effective," Olivia chimed in with a reassuring smile sent in Rowan's direction. "Really, you don't need to worry about him anymore. We'll help him find an Epic, level him up the final time, and then head back home. Sure, we might need to camp out, but that's not too bad."

Rowan worried away at his lower lip before he finally decided to bite the bullet. "Yeah . . . about that. How are we going to find an Epic tier out here without any scouts?"

Olivia blinked at him in confusion, then broke into laughter so loud it drew the attention of Blake's party before she waved them off. "I'm sorry, you just looked so adorably worried and confused, I couldn't help it!"

"Well, it's not my fault! Or, well, it is. I just wasn't thinking. Do we need to turn back? It'll be a bit awkward, but better than wandering out here for days."

"No, Rowan, we don't need to turn back," Olivia said with fond exasperation, smile still upon her lips. "I can find an Epic for us, no problem. Well . . . actually, you can probably do it, too, now that I think of it."

"I'm not a scout, though. That said, neither are you. How exactly do you propose we do what you're suggesting, love?"

The little term of endearment earned him another smile, but it didn't distract his favorite alchemist. "Epic-tier monsters have an aura, just like humans do. Now, it won't be particularly powerful, but it's there. Here's the question, though: What *is* an aura?"

Rowan didn't need to think particularly hard on that question. "It's mana, isn't it? Tiering up makes a person's mana stronger and heavier, for lack of a better term. And when an Epic tier actively expels their mana, it has a significant effect on anyone in their vicinity who doesn't have the same level of mana or incredible willpower."

"Correct! Now, here's a hint why most monsters have a lackluster aura. They don't really understand how to properly use it. Their aura is mostly bound to their flesh, and it takes a lot of time, practice, and effort for them to learn how to project it."

"That's . . . fascinating, but I still don't get where you're going with this," Rowan admitted, furrowing his brow. "How will that help us find an Epic-tier monster?"

"Well, even if *most of it* is bound to their bodies, monsters constantly leak a certain amount of aura. And, as we just ascertained, aura is mana. So, all we need to do is look for areas around us that have denser pockets of mana."

"You can do that?" Rowan found the suggestion thoroughly impressive and couldn't stop that from showing in his voice if he tried.

"Of course I can, silly. I'm a class that uses a ton of mana manipulation and sensing. Now, typically, you need to commit to a class that boosts the quality of your intelligence, or maybe wisdom, in order to really master the process. However, with your nonsense class, you got the benefits of such a class through your [Knight]." She was grumbling when she mentioned that, making Rowan smile helplessly. Olivia really didn't like how he'd chosen Tamara as one of his knights. She understood. She supported it, even, when the logic was explained. She just didn't like it.

"So, um, what do I need to do to start on the whole sensing thing, then?" he asked, trying to hurry her along past the awkward part of the conversation.

She shot him a half-hearted glare, but she acquiesced to the change in subject nonetheless. "Well, for starters, you need to learn how to disperse your mana around you without letting it slip your control. If you just let it go, then you'll use up your mana pool in no time. You need to keep it a part of yourself."

Over the next few hours, as they headed deeper and deeper into the wastes, Rowan struggled and failed to do what Olivia described. Rowan was fairly sure that she wasn't giving him excessively vague explanations just for the fun of it or to get back at him.

At first, he was even having trouble just expelling mana from his body in a controlled manner. Such attempts resulted in something that resembled offensive blasts of mana rather than anything else. Apparently, his relatively high amount of mana for a physical class was getting in the way there.

Mages would typically start on such exercises when they were just starting out, and they'd need to keep them up in order to maintain precise control of their mana as their pool grew.

According to Olivia's comparison, he was trying to do an exercise people usually tackled with the lightest possible training sword while wielding a large, heavy, two-handed broadsword.

Graceful and refined control this did not make.

Eventually, though, just before they decided to call it a day, he did manage to softly disperse his mana into his surroundings and maintain that level of output.

The problem then became the fact that he was leaking mana like a sieve, rather than successfully hanging on to it in any way, shape, or form.

"I don't get it," Rowan snarled in frustration, wanting so badly to hurl his mana away from himself *on purpose*. Unfortunately, it was doing a good job running away from him all on its own. "It just stops being a part of me the second I release it. I don't think my class can do this stuff, love."

Olivia was looking at him with exquisite amusement on her face. "Rowan, this isn't some advanced technique that only mages and mana-wielding classes can do. It's a *basic exercise*. Trust me, you can do it."

"You say that, but I haven't managed to do it *once*!"

"And do you think that's because it's impossible, or are you just trying to do it wrong?" his fiancée demanded, making Rowan's rage deflate right on the spot.

"It's because I'm doing it wrong," he mumbled, not at all petulantly.

"Okay, here, let me try and guide you through it. Give me your hands."

Rowan scooted forward in their hastily erected tent, until their knees were touching where they sat with their legs folded. Olivia took his hands in hers gently, and then Rowan gasped when he felt *something* brush across his skin. The sensation repeated itself, reminding him of a gentle breeze tickling his skin.

"Feel that? It's my mana. When you keep your connection to your mana, you can sense it, control it, and shape it. It's what lets mages and a lot of other direct mana users shape spells, rituals, and the like. We don't need you to be able to do any controlling or shaping right now. You just need to sense your mana."

"But, it vanishes immediately. Completely and utterly," Rowan said quietly, almost like he was afraid of talking too loudly and scaring off the sensation of Olivia's mana playing over his skin.

It felt warm, soft, and just a little nippy. He liked it.

"Just focus, silly. Actually, the process of sensing your mana and keeping your connection to it needs to be mastered almost simultaneously. If you can't sense it, you can't hang on to it. And if you can't hang on to it, it stops being your mana, so you can't really feel it anymore."

"How am I feeling *your* mana right now, then?" Rowan asked, still luxuriating in the sensation Olivia's mana was giving him.

"Your mana is a part of you. It's one of the reasons higher tiers are so much tougher than lower ones. The mana passively reinforces your body, including your skin. So, when I run my own mana over you, it's coming in direct contact with your own reserves. If you ever drain yourself fully dry, it will become impossible to sense mana, too."

Rowan didn't particularly like the implications of that, but if he was ever forced to such a brink, then he was probably on the verge of losing whatever fight he was in.

Instead of complaining about things he couldn't change, he focused on getting this one thing down. Slowly, still letting Olivia keep hold of his hands, he made a tiny improvement.

From the sensation of just letting mana rush out of him, he transitioned to the feeling of mana slipping through his fingers. It felt like, the harder he fought to hold on to the mysterious substance, the harder it was to actually leverage it.

He went to bed that night feeling frustrated, but like he was making actual, noticeable progress toward earning a new and useful skill for the first time in a while.

The next day, Blake was ready and raring to go. While Rowan had eventually succumbed to very comfortable sleep and woken up feeling refreshed, he wouldn't be surprised to hear that Blake hadn't caught a single wink at all.

"So, I take it you're excited to track down an Epic and finally get back to the tier yourself?" Rowan asked jokingly, only to be hit by the most dazzling smile he'd seen from his friend in recent history.

"Yes! Goddess, I can't tell you how horrible it feels to be so far behind everyone else. I mean, your entire new extended family is at the Epic tier! Our parties are at the Epic tier! Those mercenaries are at it, too! It feels like I've been standing in one place for the longest time."

"You realize that's not true, right? You've made amazing progress. In fact, if you fought the you from a couple weeks ago, back when you *were* at Epic, I bet you'd have a chance to win." Rowan wasn't even joking.

"Yes, yes, I know I'm doing better and all that," Blake said dismissively, literally waving the argument away. "But I'm not at Epic, right? And heroes *need* to be at Epic to be useful."

"Then what was I until a couple weeks ago, hmm? An ornament to make my party look nicer?" Rowan quipped, mostly managing to keep any bitterness out of his voice.

At that, Blake's eyes got huge. "I didn't mean it like that! Really! I mean, I was just saying, that's what *I'm* like, not—" He broke out into stuttering before he finally noticed the smug smile on Rowan's face. "Oh, you ass!"

He couldn't help it—Rowan broke into laughter as he dodged away from Blake's retaliatory swipe. "Sorry, not sorry! Stop acting like the Epic tier is something commonplace, though. It's not. I've got a full army and none of them are at the Epic tier yet. Besides, you'll probably get there today."

That alone was enough to restore Blake's smile, and the man went right back to being annoyingly chipper. Rowan, meanwhile, fell back to his place by Olivia's side.

"Ready to continue practicing?" Olivia asked.

"I am. Still, do you mind helping Blake find his Epic? I'll obviously keep working away at it, but I want to quickly help him get back to that stupid tier. I think it'll do wonders for his sense of self-worth. Not that he should need it."

"You know . . . Blake and his party are really not what I expected them to be," Olivia admitted with a thoughtful look on her face.

"What were you expecting, then?"

She didn't answer that question, but she did shout out to Blake. "Blake? If you want to find an Epic, I'd head that way." Rowan's favorite alchemist pointed, and off they went.

Rowan wasn't one hundred percent sure about Olivia's directions. However, as they drew ever close to whatever monster Olivia was tracking, he did think he was starting to get flashes of insight into the mana around him.

The entire wastes were tinged by mana. Something slithering, slimy, and malignant, hiding within every plant, every bush, and even the soil itself. It made him want to recoil, but it did do much to solidify his sense of his own mana in his mind.

That's why, a mere hour and a bit after they set off, Rowan finally managed to hold on to his mana. And he really wanted to punch something at just how foolish it was to attempt such a thing in the literal sense.

Instead, he found that the trick was to sort of expand his sense of self, extending it past his own skin and becoming something vaguely defined to his own senses.

That, of course, made him realize he'd done such things before, even if instinctively and with no idea what was happening. Several times before, he'd gotten impressions of demons and particularly powerful foes using mana.

Now, he knew exactly how to force those impressions whenever he liked. Sort of.

Regardless, as they finally drew close to the Epic's stomping ground, he was more than satisfied enough with his progress to shelve further experimentation.

And he was definitely certain they were drawing close.

The ground and trees were pockmarked by scratches and craters, and the jungle looked worn-out and worse for wear compared to its usual stark beauty.

"It's a big one, whatever it is," Marcus supplied, putting his hand against one of the scratch marks. It dwarfed his palm, making it apparent that they weren't about to fight a teddy bear.

"Well, I mean, how bad could it be?" Rowan quipped, feeling more than a little certain of their victory.

Even with just the three members of his party, he was willing to give taking down the Epic a shot. After all, they'd scythed through the Epics that had besieged Blake, easily taking them down.

In spite of his own casualness, Rowan felt Marcus's aura slip over him, preparing them to face anything that the Epic might throw at them.

"Rowan's right! This is going to be easy with all of us here, you'll see." Blake supported his friend with a smile, sword already in hand and a smile on his lips.

The princess, for once, didn't share his enthusiasm. "I don't know. I think we should still—Urgh!"

The woman was cut off when one of the trees they were just passing by *moved*, bringing two massive claws down on top of the princess and the de Vort. The attack was as vicious as it was sudden, and the massive shock wave it released threw enough dirt in the air to stagger everyone.

Rowan cursed but kept his footing thanks to his high dexterity. The rest weren't so lucky. Only Marcus and Blake managed to remain standing, too, and all three of them rushed at the monster at the same time.

It was only when Rowan was practically on top of it that he could finally see what was attacking them. A massive, monstrous chameleon with claws that ended in wickedly sharp, long points and a tail that was cutting through the air to the accompaniment of whip cracks.

Rowan roared, mana and vitality spiraling around his spear as he readied a strike. Right before he committed, a flash of newfound strength filled him as Mirabella Treagon staggered to her knees, erupting into light that bolstered her allies.

Blake was closer to the creature, so when their attacks landed, they hit at nearly the same time. Blake's cut into the wrinkly scales and failed to penetrate past a couple of inches.

Rowan's dug deep into the base of one of the creature's legs, and the following explosion tore out the limb entirely.

In spite of that, the monster was still able to lash out, its tail hitting the Stalwart Hero right in the middle of his chest and launching him into and through the nearby trees before it brought down its front paws again, this time leveraging both to turn Blake into a pancake.

Blake cried out in pain, but when the monster pulled back, he wasn't a mere smear on the ground. Instead, Marcus's face paled further, even as he finally drew close enough to lash out with his mace.

The weapon landed lightly, almost like it was wielded by someone with barely enough strength to lift it. Then the chameleon monster rocked back, bones squealing and snapping as it partially slumped against the tree it still clung to.

With a sputter and curse, the princess dug herself out of what was a nearly two-foot-deep hole, a corona of light forming above her as it washed over her allies, melting away fatigue. Jacqueline took action, panes of force forming up around each of the humans that would stop the blows of monsters while letting their own through.

Despite that, there was little need for them to act. The monster was whimpering, struggling to even lift its limbs again. A fact that Blake was more than willing to take advantage of.

With a vicious shout of his own, the hero launched himself into the air, bringing his sword as high as it would go before driving it down into the monster's skull.

For a moment, Rowan feared it would still not be enough. Then the monster's skull sagged, its shattered state failing to let it withstand the damage, and the killing blow was dealt.

Even then, for several long, tense moments, the chameleon squirmed on top of Blake's sword like a particularly large worm caught on the tip of a fishhook.

And then it stilled, and the clearing was washed away in a surge of light that erupted out of Blake.

CHAPTER THIRTEEN

# The Legendary Expedition

The manor was a swarm of activity, servants and soldiers bustling about every corner in a united front, all working toward making everything *perfect* for the moment of departure.

In the midst of all that, Rowan found himself with little to do but wait.

No one was going to let him contribute to putting together bundles of equipment for the soldiers, most of all the servants. They were likely to have aneurysms if the marquis himself were to pick up supplies to polish and maintain armor and weapons.

Perhaps it wasn't that there was little to do, but that his main task was more than a little nerve-racking.

Rowan took a deep breath, looked down, and hesitated.

It wasn't hard to understand why.

Having claimed a whole lot of resources just to progress his own deck, Rowan had a very nice set of cards ready to go.

**Spear of Malaise (Rare, Active) × 3**
**Cursed Blade of Sundering (Rare, Active) × 3**
**Bloodwhisper Spear (Rare, Passive) × 3**

And, of course, the final piece of the puzzle:

**[Class] Reaping Spear (Rare, Active)**

With a final deep breath in and a quick bit of praying to Lady Luck, Rowan hit the fuse button on his interface.

A purple light erupted forth, so wobbly that Rowan was convinced the fusion would fail. Yet, as seconds crawled by, it slowly began to stabilize and relief surged through him.

Eventually, a card dropped down in front of him in all its new glory.

**[Class] The Grim Spear (Epic, Active)**
**Empower your spear with mana that deals devastating injuries. Death, rot, and corruption mana will infest every wound dealt under the effect of this card, and each wound will resist healing and regeneration effects.**

Rowan let his breath out, and a grim smile stretched across his lips as he imagined just how difficult that particular card was going to be to deal with.

Most people following the path of the spear had cards with low offensive potential. However, Rowan was pretty certain that even an underwhelming offensive class could make its mark with a card like that.

Rowan sent the card back to his deck and directed his attention to the next upgrade he had lined up. This one, he was far less sure of.

**[Class] Blood Siphon (Uncommon, Passive)**
**Each wound your spear inflicts will provoke severe bleeding, draining your foes of their life essence. The bleeding effects grow in proportion to the damage dealt.**

The card was as simple as it was useful, and it had served him well. However, he didn't really get many good options to merge it with. He had enough cards for a total of three attempts. And a single failure would outright destroy the card.

Although Rowan only had three attempts, he had five different card combos that he could use in crafting the fusion and enough cards to try any combination he pleased.

**Blood Crest (Uncommon, Passive)**
**Collect the blood you spill in special crests that can be drained for a boost to your healing.**

**Bracken Blood (Uncommon, Passive)**
**Each wound you inflict has a chance to infect your opponent's bloodstream with a rot-aligned poison.**

**Carving Strike (Uncommon, Active)**
**Each wound you inflict is widened, causing more severe blood loss and injuries.**

**Flesh-Seeker Spear (Uncommon, Passive)**
**Your spear sinks into flesh easily and hungrily, inflicting deeper and more severe injuries.**

**Blood-Churn Spear (Uncommon, Active)**
**Apply mana to your spear so that every blow you inflict on your enemies speeds up the circulation of their blood, resulting in more severe blood loss.**

He could pick two cards and fill out all the slots with them, or try to mix in a bit of every card in hopes of a stronger end result.

Unfortunately, the warnings he'd received were very clear on one subject: If he introduced more than four different types of cards to the fusion, including the class card itself, it was all but guaranteed to fail.

*Three cards it is.*

Picking an active card while trying to upgrade a passive would be risky, but Rowan eventually made his choice. **Carving Strike**, **Flesh-Seeker Spear**, and **Blood-Churn Spear** would be the ingredients that went into his new Rare card.

Rowan closed his eyes and finalized his choice.

*What? This doesn't feel right at all.*

The system worked so subtly that he was typically entirely unaware of what went into the process of card fusion. This time, however, Rowan could *feel* the flood of mana that surged out of his body and sank into the melting cards. It just didn't sit right somehow.

The light that surrounded them fluctuated and shook, shuddering on the very verge of explosion. Rowan knew that very second that his attempt to fuse the cards would fail.

He'd reached too far, and the cards were refusing to play nice.

And yet, in the middle of that floating sphere, he felt something. A presence that was so muted, such a small part of his deck, that he didn't even get any real feedback from it. A simple, quiet card that did its job, and did it well.

Without even meaning to, Rowan used every last bit of advice Olivia had given him on their outing to reclaim the mana the system had taken from him. As he did, his awareness of his class card surged.

It relished in blood; it yearned to spill it; it yearned to *grow*.

So, Rowan fed it every scrap of mana he had to let it do just that. And all throughout the process, he urged his mana to calm, to coalesce, to forcefully seize the cards that were fighting the process of getting ground down and integrated into his own.

He imagined all the different ways they could strengthen and contribute to the fusion, and **Blood Siphon** *listened*.

The cards reached out, too. One by one, bolstered by their unified strength, their individual cries harmonized into one. The fusion devoured every scrap of power it needed to succeed.

Rowan slowly opened his eyes, unsure of what he was seeing. A blue hue came into focus as a card drifted in front of him, gently laying itself to rest on something . . . fluffy? He wiped the bleariness from his eyes, and the blood he saw on his hands shook him completely out of his delirium. It seemed that in his efforts to merge the cards, he'd passed out onto the carpet, blood dripping from his nose. He must have fallen right out of his chair.

"We're not doing that again, okay?" Rowan groaned to no one in particular as he pulled himself to his feet, staggering and shaking like a newborn calf.

In spite of that, he couldn't help but feel that the results were worth it.

**[Class] Scarlet Flood (Rare, Passive)**
**Every wound you inflict is much deeper and wider than it should be and will severely drain your enemies of their life blood. The cursed nature of your strikes ensures continual bleeding, the severity of which is directly proportional to the amount of damage dealt.**

Rowan loved it, especially loved the *severely* part. The system didn't mess around, so for something to get flagged with those words, it had to be impressive.

Of course, that left him with another jump he needed to make.

"I swear, if the process goes as poorly as it did this time, I'm letting it fail. I really don't think I can stop an Epic-tier fusion from blowing up in my face," Rowan grumbled as he awkwardly wiped blood from his nose, but the pulse of *understanding* he got from the card he'd yet to banish back to his deck made him pause.

Exploring the mystical bond he seemed to have with his deck, Rowan blinked in both surprise and confusion.

More than any other card he possessed, more than even the Epic tiers, **Scarlet Flood** felt both *aware* and like *a true part of him*. The conflict between the two traits should have sent his mind reeling, yet he understood and accepted it as par for the course.

It felt like a part of him, as if some deep, primordial part of his core personality had come awake and now dwelled within his chest. Unfortunately, it wasn't a good discovery. That piece of Rowan had an urge to stab things to death and then watch them bleed out. Rowan grimaced, pushing down his discomfort.

"I'm really gonna need a therapist when this is all settled."

Rowan's card selection for upgrading **Scarlet Flood** to Epic was better, and he didn't need to struggle nearly as much to come up with a final list. If anything, he was impatient for this mana to refill out of an abundance of caution.

At long last, though, the moment was there.

**Do you want to fuse [Class] Scarlet Flood (Rare, Passive)**
**with the following cards:**
**Aura of Devouring (Common, Passive) × 3**
**Draining Assault (Common, Active) × 2**
**Bloodhound Spear (Common, Passive) × 4**
**Y/N**

The thrum of power, of sheer *potential*, threatened to make Rowan lose his seat again. He felt the card suck him in, and he witnessed as it hunted each of its future constituents down with ruthless efficiency.

If there was ever any doubt that the fusion would succeed, it disappeared within moments of triggering it.

When the slaughter was over and his new card hovered in front of him, Rowan felt a faint amount of awe.

**[Class] Scarlet Envy (Epic, Passive)**
**Your blows are the heralds of a scarlet flood. You thirst for the power trapped within the blood of your victim, and you can now claim it. When your weapon causes a wound, you can channel your mana into increasing the severity of their blood loss.**

Rowan had noticed a curious tendency as the tiers of his class and cards continued to climb. Both the verbosity of his cards' description as well as their vagueness grew right alongside their power.

His Heart Card's description was vague from the start, and the Epic-tier classes all had more spiritual and mystical allusions than they did actual useful information. There was enough detail to make a solid selection, but beyond that, he was left with a lot of guesswork.

In spite of that, he knew *exactly* how his new card was supposed to work. The second it coalesced and became part of his deck, his awareness exploded beyond the confines of his body.

He was aware of the servants hurrying down the hall outside his room. He could sense the twins in their rooms, bent over their own decks. He could even, spiraling down the connection with his knights, sense them, too.

Rowan could do all this because he could *feel* the blood coursing through their bodies.

He knew that the second his spear left a nick on their skin, he could coax the blood out, draw it to him, and devour it until it empowered *him* instead.

Rowan let out a shuddering breath and banished the card to his deck. He swiped his eyes over the collection of cards he now owned and felt a tiny bit worried.

He did, after all, own two cards with direct allusions to deadly sins.

**Deck (6/6):**
**[Heart] Keen Spear (Epic, Passive)**
**[Class] Knight Designation (Epic, Passive)**
**[Class] The Grim Spear (Epic, Active)**
**[Class] Scarlet Envy (Epic, Passive)**
**Natural Renewal (Epic, Active)**
**Gluttonous Banquet (Epic, Passive)**

"Are we the baddies?" Rowan chuckled, whispering the words under his breath as he scanned the list again and again.

If he was being fully honest with himself, it didn't bother him all that much. He was perfectly willing to leave the blatant heroics to his best friend. *He* wanted to do only one job, and the purpose he was summoned for would finally be complete.

Then he'd have a whole life to live at his leisure—provided he put a stop to whatever plotting was going on in the kingdom, of course.

Rowan found Blake exactly where he expected: in the training yard.

The grim determination and hurry to reclaim his power had left Blake's features, leaving behind a dazzling smile and a surety that reinforced every motion of his body.

The trio of [Knights] Rowan expected to find were there, too. They'd been all but adopted by the other hero, and Rowan couldn't find it in himself to be upset when Blake was finally making sincere friends in their new world.

The person Rowan *wasn't* expecting to find there, however, was Bron.

"You're doing so well now, Mister Hero!" the baron's officer taunted as he smoothly glided out of the way of Blake's sword, flicking his own just so to make Blake's weapon ring and almost jump out of his hands. "But you need to do better."

"It's not my fault that you're so slippery!" Blake quipped right back, easily recovering the stability of his stance and going right back to his attempt at skewering the spry older man.

A part of Rowan felt amused. Another part of him wanted to slap both of them upside the head and send Bron back inside and to a bed, where he belonged.

He'd yet to recover from his use of Olivia's potion. His limbs were covered in bandages as tight as a mummy's, and Rowan knew for a fact that even light activity hurt him. The potion had burned both his skin and muscles away. And while the skin had recovered fairly quickly, the muscles had only just recently grown back before their arrival at Rest's Remorse.

Yet there he was, sparring with Blake and taunting the hero like a man half his age. Some days, Rowan felt like he was trying to herd a bunch of cats.

He followed the walls of the workout space all the way around until he reached the benches where Blake's party members sat and watched. "What is going on here, exactly?"

"What does it look like?" The de Vort snorted daintily and rolled her eyes. Rowan would have been upset if his limited interactions with the woman hadn't taught him that she treated more or less anyone with that same level of disdain.

It made her relationship dynamic with Blake interesting. Especially when Rowan had caught them kissing in an empty meeting room.

"Well, it looks like Blake is trying to skewer a half-cooked man who should be resting, and whom I consider a dear friend. Or am I missing something?" Rowan snarked right back, earning a small smile.

"No, you're right. Though Shorty here's got them covered, so don't you worry." She plopped her hand down on the head of the Treagon scion, who was, in fact, much shorter than her own considerable height.

It was then that Rowan finally noticed the subtle blue sheen that covered the bodies of the people sparring, both Bron and Rowan as well as the [Knights]. Granted, the latter were mostly swinging their weapons absentmindedly while watching the other two spar. Rowan resolved to scold them later.

"And whose idea was this from the start? Bron should really be resting, that stubborn old fool," Rowan said.

"Bron's, actually. Even before the trip, he tracked down Blake while he was training to restore his class. He's been helping him with swordsmanship ever since."

As Rowan examined his best friend a little closer, he was starting to see it. There was a trace of the style that the baron's troops seemed to favor. It wasn't quite matching up to anything coherent enough to be called a school of swordsmanship, but it was there.

*I'm going to have to thank Bron later.*

The two finally wound down their practice, with Bron scoring one final point against Blake. Blake hadn't managed to touch the officer even a single time.

Of course, while Bron was likely pushing himself more than he should have been, Blake was holding back. With his return to Epic tier, the chances of Bron winning a fight against the other hero were low, even if the baron's officer was back to peak form.

Rowan was still caught between disbelief and mild envy over Blake's new class.

**[Flawless Beacon of Radiance]**
**You have reforged your light so that it may shine upon all and guide them to a better tomorrow.**
**You have earned a fragmented portfolio of [Freedom].**
**You have earned a fragmented portfolio of [Radiance].**

That was all that Blake had shared about his new class, other than that most of its other effects were similar to what he had before. In spite of that, the mention of portfolios made Rowan pay attention.

He still didn't know exactly what those entailed. However, every mention he'd heard of them came in the context of the divine. It was also important to note that the description of Blake's class no longer explicitly mentioned Sarina.

The bond between the hero and the goddess was not gone.

The second Blake got his new class, Rowan felt a connection bloom between his friend and something inhuman, something completely alien. It radiated energy directly into Blake's soul, almost threatening to sever the link Rowan's class had wrought.

But the link held.

Rowan endured as he felt the alien's feelings slipping through, nudges and impressions that the goddess was sending Blake's way. The Stalwart Hero had worked long and hard to properly isolate himself from the emotions of his [Knights]. Yet, the goddess's attention threatened to burn right through his effort.

Even when he was doing his best to block it all out, he could feel her lurking. The only fix to the issue seemed to be distance, seeing as it muted all impressions he got from his [Knights] until they were nearly entirely gone when he ventured far enough from them.

Blake, of course, was ecstatic. The return of his goddess had as much to do with his good mood as his ascension back to Epic.

In spite of that, Rowan was glad to feel a thread of doubt and suspicion inside his friend's heart. He was willing to embrace his goddess, even trust her, but all the revelations about the king and the hostility of their new world had finally put him on guard.

Frankly, that was all that Rowan could really hope for. Blake wasn't someone who would just break away from the goddess on Rowan's suspicion, no matter how much the Stalwart Hero suspected the gods of scheming *something*.

If the goddess did try to get him to do something egregious, Blake might hesitate now and think for himself.

"Rowan! When did you get here?" Blake's voice tore him away from brooding, making Rowan genuinely smile.

"Oh, he's been chatting with your ladies for a while now. I understand that you prefer to focus on your training, but you really should work on your awareness, too, lad," Bron mocked softly, even as he quickly made his way over to a bench.

The old officer sat down and the blue glow vanished. The baron's officer practically collapsed, as his vigor seemed to leave him all at once.

"You know, I'm extremely grateful that you're helping Blake. I really am. But are you telling me that you won't pass out if I poke you right now?" Rowan teased, quickly making his way over to Bron.

Surprisingly, Blake was looking at the man with pity but didn't make a single move to help. Bron waved away a potion when Rowan pulled one out of his pouch.

"Those won't help me much, lad. You know this. I'm going to have to heal slow and steady, like all the regular folk get to do. No fancy healing for me."

"We haven't had a chance to chat much. The baron mentioned trying, and failing, to help you heal," Rowan ventured, taking a seat next to Bron. Blake joined them a moment later, sitting on the other side of the officer.

"Aye. He really did try his best. Nothing works, though, and neither of us wanted to make a trip to one of the bigger temples to see if they could do something, either. Honestly, the closest anyone's gotten to helping me is the lady here." He motioned to the Treagon, some conflict obvious in his voice.

The girl flushed and looked away, muttering something about doing her part to help Blake train.

"Thank you for toughing it out for me. Really. I . . . haven't had many people do that sort of thing for me," Blake admitted quietly, toying with his sword and checking over its blade as he did.

Rowan felt embarrassment and genuine, bone-deep affection for the officer coming from the bond he had with his best friend. Rowan didn't doubt for a second that if Bron just asked, Blake would rush headlong into stupid amounts of danger.

"Don't mention it, lad. I was curious about what a friend of Rowan's would be like. I have to say, you didn't disappoint. You have a genuinely good heart. I hope you manage to keep it. Now, Rowan, walk with me? I'd like to have a quick chat before you run away into the wastes again."

Rowan rolled his eyes and grumbled, but he complied. Bron didn't put up too much of a fight when he insisted on helping the officer make his way back into the manor, a tremble in his limbs betraying the exhaustion and weakness he felt.

"You know, I really do think he's all right," Bron began the moment they were out of earshot, shooting Rowan a smile. "Didn't know what to make of him, at first, but he really *is* the knight-in-shining-armor stereotype. He's not just pretending."

"He's not," Rowan said softly, patting the officer on the back. "Blake's good people. Just a little . . . self-destructive."

"Noticed that, too." There was silence for several moments as they just focused on reaching their goal. "I want to ask you for a favor, lad," Bron said at long last, voice serious enough for Rowan to pause and look him in the eye.

"Just say it, old man."

The old man scoffed, shaking his head. "Young'uns these days. Anyway, I'd like you to make me your [Knight]."

Of all the things Rowan had expected the man to say, that wasn't one of them. "You do know what that entails, right? All the details?"

"Yes. The baron explained it to me."

"And you know that it's unlikely to actually help you?"

"Yes. The potion effect isn't gone. Any healing and regeneration effects I could get from your card wouldn't work."

"Then why?"

"Because, Rowan, I don't think you're making the best possible use of your class." Bron's voice was earnest and dire.

"Explain."

"Has anyone tried to claim the card your class gave you? Or did they just immediately snatch up whatever card could help them fight better, or survive?"

That did the job of silencing the hero. Technically, there was nothing in his class or card description hinting that people couldn't pick his **Knight**

**Designation** card and get some [Knights] of their own. However, Rowan was reluctant to experiment.

Not only would the person making that choice have to take the risk of giving up an actually useful Epic card in favor of one that might not even work, but the hero had no idea of what would happen if the card *did* work and he was eventually forced to cancel his [Knight] designation for whatever reason.

Would the whole string of [Knights] collapse outright? Would the links remain? There was far too much vagueness to the whole thing to risk it.

"I don't think refusing to take risks is a bad approach to system mechanics you don't fully understand, Bron."

"True. But you have a person willing to experiment right here. I can't benefit from your other cards until I recover, and that might take . . . years, at least. If this works out, I can get some experience myself, and who knows? More stats might speed up my recovery."

"I don't know . . ."

"What do you have to lose? I'm pretty high up the Rare ranks, so the stats you get won't be bad. Besides, I think you'll get a . . . pleasant surprise, if you do pick me," the man promised with a crooked grin, refusing to elaborate any more.

"Fine," Rowan agreed just as they made it back into the manor and sent his invitation. And Bron accepted, betting his future and dreams on a chance.

As he did, and the bond formed, a fire bloomed inside the Stalwart Hero's chest. "Oh, you ass!"

Rowan gritted his teeth in pain as the system ruthlessly modified his body. By the time the process was over, Rowan was covered in sweat, and Bron was the one holding *him* up. The baron's officer wore a shit-eating grin, mirth shining in his eyes.

"Doesn't feel great, does it?"

"I'm going to punch you the second I feel better. Also . . . thank you," the hero added quietly, a smile tugging at his own lips as he spared a glance at his status.

The preparations were finally done. The soldiers were armed, outfitted, and ready. The two hero parties were as well prepared as they could possibly get. Rowan had even given out the cards left over after their upgrades, giving his men one final boost before the time to march came.

The Mercenary King and Tamara were both present, too, ready to join the Legendary Expeditions.

Rowan found the moniker ridiculous, but he couldn't do much to stifle the mutters of his men and most of the town when it got out that they were planning to finally take the fight to the demons.

"I put my trust in you, in each and every one of you. I trust you to have my back. I trust you to protect your comrades-in-arms. I trust you to give everything to our cause. Because that is the only way for us to triumph."

Rowan's voice boomed out over the gathered crowd. Over a thousand men and women, all ready to follow him into battle.

"I refuse to contemplate the chance of failure. So, when we return, we'll do so as heroes. And those of us who may perish in our quest, know that I will make sure your loved ones are safe and happy. Your families will never want for anything again. Now, march!"

To the hollers of approval and applause, Rowan motioned for the Mercenary King to trigger his cards. In a few minutes, the army led by two heroes ventured forth from Rest's Remorse, intent on slaughtering the four generals of the demon king.

## CHAPTER FOURTEEN

# Civilization

Slipping into a frenzied mood was easy—it was simply a matter of getting carried away by the emotions of a crowd. Retaining that frenzy and keeping a positive, upbeat attitude after hours of marching through the wastes? Now, that was difficult.

The mood of the army slowly settled, leveling out into a quiet indifference induced by the Mercenary King's abilities. In spite of the loss of that initial positivity, Rowan was simply happy to see that gloom hadn't dominated the troops.

Whatever he might say, however hard he might work, it was impossible to guarantee that everyone would be able to return alive.

So, the fact that no one had broken away from the march toward potential death was a relief.

The thought disgusted Rowan. After all, by the same token, the ones most likely to survive were the Epic-tier classes. There were few things, past the Legendary demons themselves, that had a real shot at taking out the two hero parties.

The Mercenary King and Tamara were, of course, in just as good a position. Doubly so considering the fact that they had Rowan's card to fall back on.

Yet as Rowan tapped into his card to see what his [Knights] were feeling, he found that the emotions from the two were diametrically opposed.

While the Mercenary King marched with a sense of dread and bleak anticipation in his chest, Tamara flew overhead with an overwhelming sense of giddiness. She was eager for what was to come—hungry, almost.

The problem was, Rowan couldn't figure out whether the source of her emotions was the thought of getting to kill a Legendary-tier being, or if it came down to her awareness of the scheme brewing on the horizon.

"You really think that the demon who ambushed you is situated close to the spot where we rescued you?" Rowan asked, less for the answer and more for something to take his mind off all the swirling worry.

"Yes. I had a scout under my employ . . . he was brilliant, and the only reason I felt confident trying to quickly locate and take out all the Legendary demons. He said we were close when the ambush happened," Blake replied.

"Isn't there a chance that he was sensing the demon himself, though?" Milena offered from the side, though not in a confrontational tone.

"I'm not sure how his cards worked. He was convinced that we were close to the demon's base. He said something about a ridiculous amount of demonic energy being located ahead, far more than even a truly powerful demon ought to possess," Blake offered.

"So, logic would mean that there might be a base with multiple demons there instead?"

"Exactly." Blake shot Rowan a sunny smile. "All we have to do is track it down and we'll have our first Legendary demon in our sights."

"The Legendary demon that almost took us both out," Rowan cautioned, sensing that Blake was eager to prove himself once more.

Blake's face fell briefly at the reminder, but his optimism came back in force a moment later. "True, but you returned the favor! From what guidance my goddess can offer, it seems like the demon is hurt. He had to invest heavily into the process of trying to corrupt me. So, when that was disrupted, *violently*, he took damage, too."

Cautiously, Rowan cast his senses into his bond with Blake. The other hero wasn't lying, optimism and hope being the predominant emotions he was feeling. Of course, the underlying sense of artificial calm to his emotions betrayed the goddess's influence, too.

"Let's hope that's right," Rowan muttered, casting his eyes on the gloomy jungle ahead.

The foliage around them started showing signs of trauma and combat. The ground went from being soft with leaves underfoot to being bare and pockmarked. Charred remains of half-dissolved plants were strewn about, and the thicker greenery was tangled and mangled. It was impossible not to recognize where they were. This was where Rowan and his party had rescued Blake.

However, the other signs of the conflict had vanished. There was no trace of blood or bone to be found. It was like every last piece of proof that humans and monsters had fought and died there had been erased by some higher power.

Or, more likely, by the hungry jaws of the wastes' inhabitants.

This made it a very convenient spot to set up camp. With the trees and most foliage completely removed, and even somewhat flat ground, the process was easy, too.

As such, Rowan gave out orders for his troops to rest. The only ones who couldn't afford to rest yet were the soldiers assigned to patrols, but they would be switched out regularly to avoid exhaustion.

"How soon do you think the scouts will return?" Rowan posed the question to the Mercenary King as the other man made annotations on a map stretched over a makeshift table. One of the collapsed trees had been cut to size and dragged into the command tent, allowing for a bit more convenience.

"A couple hours at most, lad. The forward troops had to kill a couple of monsters that were acting out of sorts. I wouldn't be surprised if they were some sort of early-warning system for the demons."

"Doesn't that mean we shouldn't be here?" Blake asked immediately, standing up from the spot he'd claimed on the floor. "They could be marching on us right now."

The Mercenary King offered the other hero a kind smile and a shake of his head. "I doubt that. These are at best the outskirts of their claimed territory. They wouldn't count on simple beasts if we were deep enough in their lands."

"These are not their lands," the princess snapped, then winced when all eyes went to her. "We are still within the territories that our kingdom used to own," she added more quietly.

"Be that as it were, does anyone actually know what we might be able to expect to see out there? What do the demons *do* when they take over an area?" Rowan ventured, trying rather blatantly to change the subject.

"Depends on the species," the Treagon offered, looking thoughtful. "Some tend to create burrows and spawning pits. Others just amass, living in herds or prides with or alongside wild animals. Some never really settle down, choosing to haunt the countryside, devouring all they come across."

"So, we can expect anything from an immediate full-scale battle to what amounts to embattlements and traps," Rowan concluded.

"That's accurate, yes, lad," the Mercenary King confirmed, looking troubled. "Be warned, though, there are . . . stories about demons. Some say the subjugation armies come across odd things when they venture into the wastes during a demonic surge. Disturbing things."

"Disturbing how?"

"No one seems keen to discuss that. Couldn't find a single report that made a lick of sense," Lucius admitted, then shrugged his shoulders. "Didn't look too hard, of course. Didn't think I'd ever need that sort of thing. We always played defensive roles in wars and battles."

"That's not going to be an issue, is it?" Olivia asked, perhaps a bit more sharply than necessary.

"No, I don't anticipate it will." The Mercenary King's smile turned downright bloodthirsty. "With how long we were stuck in Rest's Remorse, I suspect my men are eager for combat."

There really wasn't much anyone could contribute to the discussion past that, letting them all fall into a companionable silence.

Things might have been different had Tamara chosen to join them. However, the mage was still with her disciples, hovering high above the tents. There was talk of sending *them* out to scout, but the woman turned down the suggestion quickly, reluctant to expose them to "unnecessary risks."

It was a bit over three hours later, just when a string of unease was starting to underline the mood in the tent, that the scouts finally stumbled into camp.

Dale had led the scouts in their outing, and it was he who approached the main tent to give their findings.

"Welcome back, soldier. At ease. Your report?" Rowan rushed through the greetings, eager to know what had put the slightly dazed look on the man's face. Dale was by no means unflappable, but Rowan swore the man had taken facing down an Epic without batting an eye.

"I—I don't really know how to describe it, my lord," the man spat out, looking pale. "They've definitely dug in. There's, I hesitate to call it a settlement, but . . . they have a solid presence just ahead. A defensible presence."

"Do you mean to tell me they have actual defensive positions? That they're prepared for our army?" the Mercenary King growled, pushing for more information.

"Well . . ."

They settled in, eagerly listening to the man's report.

Rowan's army, by virtue of *being an army*, wasn't capable of traveling stealthily. Sure, their numbers weren't heaven defying, or enough to cover the horizon, or anything like that. But their chances of approaching the demons' base of operations without being spotted were slim.

It was a good thing that Rowan was now in a world where that wasn't a prerequisite for victory.

Frankly, in the context of the Rhys kingdom, Rowan's army was in a very solid position. Having a predominantly Rare-tier army catapulted Rowan leagues ahead of most noble houses, no matter how comparatively small their numbers were.

As such, they advanced proudly and struck down every monster, beast, and whatever else they came across in their march quickly and efficiently. Those that fled before them were allowed to get away. After all, why take the unnecessary risk of letting a party stray too far from the main group?

Yet, in spite of their blunt approach, no army marched out to meet them. No surge of demonic beasts tried to wash over them, either.

They were, in large part, uncontested.

Even the Mercenary King had believed that their approach would involve costly battles, and the contrast to what was happening put him on edge.

When they finally came within sight of their destination, that became the least of Rowan's concerns.

"A part of me genuinely thought the scouts were hallucinating," the Stalwart Hero mumbled, eyeing what was ahead.

The only way to describe it was as an unholy amalgamation of castle bits and massive mansions nestled within a very small town square.

Towers, walls, crenellations, and more were right there alongside ornate windows, beautiful eaves, and several grand doors for ease of access to the various parts of the massive building. It was all done up in tasteful grays, blacks, and midnight blues. Frankly, the whole thing looked like something Picasso would come up with if he were an expired Gothic architect.

And there was not a soul guarding the place.

Even so, it was hard to mistake the estate for a ghost house or an abandoned castle. Vague figures of people swept past the windows in industrious fashion, clearly visible yet difficult to make out.

It reminded Rowan of looking at low-resolution videos back on Earth, where the screen let him see something was there, yet the limitation of the device prevented him from understanding more.

"Well, I suppose none of us expected things to be easy," Rowan commented. "Let's proceed the way we planned."

At his command, a student chosen by Tamara began to mutter into a large crystalline ball they were carrying in one hand, and the collection of mages overhead burst into motion. The force field that bore them spaced out, and the chanting picked up. The light show that followed was something Rowan found inspiring.

In front of each group, a spark quickly became a conflagration, growing in power and intensity. The red of the flames was quickly overtaken by white, then blue, as they pumped more and more mana into the spell.

None, of course, were as impressive as Tamara's spell. While most of the fireballs grew to at most a yard in diameter, hers quickly grew to the size of a small house, and then every time it fluctuated past that, it kept *condensing.*

Rowan could feel the heat of the flames all the way on the ground and wet his lips in nervousness. More than the flames, he was getting a pretty good idea of the excitement roaring within the banished mage's chest.

Then, finally, the projectiles streaked through the skies.

Their passage scorched and warped the air, leaving mirages in their wake. The explosion that followed the impact was almost enough to swipe the front lines of Rowan's army off their feet.

In fact, had the Mercenary King not roared and broken out in a dazzling aura that left Rowan feeling heavier and more rooted to the ground, the hero suspected that's exactly what would have happened.

With the impressive display, Rowan couldn't help the anticipation that bubbled up inside him at the presumed level of destruction the mages had wrought.

As the dust cleared, Rowan faced a near-pristine building.

The only sign of the assault at all was a long, winding crack that stretched over one of the windows, and Rowan was fairly certain that was the impact area of Tamara's own spell.

"That's not good," Milena muttered quietly, and it was all Rowan could do not to curse and agree.

He did curse when the crack in the glass sealed over, then vanished completely.

"We're going to have to go in," he announced bitterly, eyeing the entrance to the mansion.

It wasn't like gaining access seemed difficult. If anything, the grand gate into the mansion was wide-open, providing a generous view into the interior.

The dazzling decorations inside, especially the twisted forms of various statues sprinkled throughout the hall, all glittering in what looked suspiciously similar to gold, almost seemed like they were taunting him.

"What would you have me do, my lord?" the Mercenary King inquired stiffly, eyeing the entrance. "It's going to be difficult to march inside in full force. Still, I request that you let me send a few squads of my men ahead. They're familiar with tight fighting."

Rowan mulled that over for several seconds, but he couldn't come up with any objections. "Very well. They can go right ahead of us, then we'll follow. I want you to understand that we'll be rushing ahead to support them if it seems like they can't handle whatever's in there."

"Thank you for your consideration of my men, my lord."

The Mercenary King barked out orders, and a few squads of men slipped across the divide toward the mansion.

Rowan felt like every step closer to it was making his skin crawl.

There was something deeply unnatural about the sight of the grand structure, simply plopped down right in the middle of the dense jungles. Some of the nearby trees were even reaching out for the mansion, nearly touching its walls.

Far worse was the realization that drawing nearer did not allow him to peek into the structure any better.

The figures flitting past the windows remained frustratingly vague, and space seemed to stretch between them and the grand hall, keeping its interior to what they originally gleaned.

Even when the front-line troops stood just a few yards away from the gates, that didn't change.

"Forward, march!" the Mercenary King yelled, realizing that the entire army had frozen in anticipation.

The front-line soldiers bravely marched forward in lockstep, eight entire parties plunging past the gates and into the demonic domain proper.

And then they vanished.

A ripple of worried chatter swept over the army when no one could catch even a single glimpse of the soldiers who should have been standing just within the hall. For the second time that engagement, Rowan wanted to curse.

"My lord, if we employ a scout and a mage, we can . . ." The Mercenary King broke into a suggestion immediately, but Rowan raised an arm to forestall him.

"No. Thank you, Lucius, but . . . no. We're not just going to feed more people to this thing. We need to go in, sure, but that doesn't mean I'm going to risk reckless losses like this. You and Tamara are here to do your part. Now, it's our turn."

The two hero parties immediately stepped forward in lockstep with Rowan, determination on each and every one of their faces.

Even Blake's harem members looked determined, even if it was obvious that fear had a considerable grip on them.

As if she were summoned by the mention of her name, however, Tamara came floating down.

"Heading inside?" The simple question somehow came out as a sultry taunt as she sent Rowan a smirk. "I'm coming with."

"I, of course, shall also be accompanying you," the Mercenary King proclaimed, giving leave to the [Knights] who were still nominally Rowan's to step forward as well. Rowan even saw a couple of the scouts bravely venture forth, eyes shining with determination.

Unfortunately, they all just made him sigh. "I'd like to remind you that we're not sure this will be all that our enemies have to throw at us. Wanting to help is well and good. However, if all our strongest combatants venture inside, what's stopping the demons from ambushing our army?"

The Mercenary King faltered, but the rest, even Tamara, looked as determined as they were at first.

"There is no shame to doing your part out here," Olivia declared imperiously, clearly picking up on her fiancé's reluctance to take along so many people.

"It's like she says: We need you out here. Your people especially, Dale. I'm counting on you to scout out the vicinity and eliminate any chances of an ambush. Lucius, I'd appreciate it if you could do what you can to bolster the army in preparation of monsters boiling out of this . . . thing. Finally, Tamara, keep trying to bring it down? It can't just regenerate forever."

"Actually, depending on how it was built, it *can*," the mage corrected, her face slipping into one of the rare focused and serious expressions she was capable of. "If the structure taps into the ambient mana or even some kind of local mana well, then yes, it might well be indestructible. I'm better off following you inside."

Rowan tilted his head, closely examining the woman's expression. It was calm, cool, even a little teasing, like it usually was. Using their bond, however, he could feel the swirling mess of desire and envy.

The banished mage *wanted* to get into a fight. To earn experience and Rare cards no doubt, but it was still something that Rowan could rather safely take advantage of.

At least he could still not detect any nefarious scheming from the woman.

"Fine. I guess we could use a mage's wisdom," Rowan conceded, much to the obvious delight of the woman.

"Gather around me!" Blake proclaimed the second they were all done double-checking their equipment. When everyone complied, they erupted into light.

The light felt heavy, somehow. Like it was weighing down Rowan's shoulders. It also felt soft, nourishing, *protective*, like a hug on a particularly cold and gloomy day.

With that, Blake plunged through the gate, and the group faithfully followed.

The second Rowan's leg was over the threshold, the world rippled, stretched, and snapped around him. He couldn't stop himself from stumbling, light nausea sweeping through his system.

"Welcome, one and all, to my master's estate," a voice rasped ahead, and Rowan tensed when he realized that someone had managed to get so close without them immediately spotting them.

When his eyes snapped onto the speaker, the sight made him pause.

The creature wasn't quite like any they'd faced before. Its skin was charcoal black, with a texture that resembled the material as well. Not a single strand of hair could be seen on it, and the only color that stood out against the darkness was the gold of its eyes.

Light smoke wafted from every inch of its skin, too. Enough that it obscured its dimensions and features a little, making the creature look ethereal.

It was also wearing a dashing gray suit with a red shirt and purple tie, like it had stepped out of a wedding or some historical drama piece.

"Who are you, fiend, and what do you want?" Blake demanded harshly, eyes focused on the creature.

Rowan could feel Blake's roiling disgust, distrust, and instinctive desire to hurt the creature. What annoyed the Stalwart Hero was the plastic feeling the emotions had.

"I am but a humble servant to my master," the creature assured them in its raspy voice, a smile that was almost invisible due to its peculiar characteristics still fixed firmly on its face. "He is waiting for you in the audience room."

"Well, I think we should expedite things and . . ."

"Blake, please," Rowan snapped, stepping forward to place a hand on his friend's shoulder. Rowan wasn't exactly about to suggest they trust the creature. However, a single glance around instilled some amount of caution in him.

Servants, some dressed like maids in practical dresses and aprons and some in suits of lower quality than the messenger's own, lined the walls of the place. They all watched them intently, some clearly whispering to each other.

It was, perhaps, the singular most disturbing thing Rowan had ever seen because it meant that the creatures had a true *civilization*.

*No, not creatures*, the Stalwart Hero corrected himself. *Demons.*

Because that's the only thing he could imagine the servants were. They were far too humanoid in appearance, and far too capable of reason. Yet, not a single conversation with the baron couple, Olivia, or any of the other natives so much as hinted that demons could be so organized.

They were almost . . . human.

After all, it wasn't as though the servants were sneering and jeering at the humans like normal demons would. If anything, most looked quite thoroughly bored. Like people, stuck at a job and trying to get through a day.

"Before we commit to anything, I have a question. Where is the previous group that came in before us?" Rowan asked as he stared straight into the demon's eyes, intent on catching him out in a lie.

"They were simply not granted access to this place," the demon answered smoothly and with a smile. "They have been detained until our master concludes his meeting with you."

"I see. May I assume they haven't come to harm?"

The demon shrugged, making Rowan's eyes narrow in consternation. "Are you perhaps ready to follow me now, sirs, madams?"

Blake was shooting Rowan a look somewhere between pleading and disapproval, making the Stalwart Hero's lips twitch into a smile.

"Ah, not quite," Rowan quipped and, before anyone could otherwise react, rammed his glowing spear straight through the demon's stomach.

To the hero's slight shock, the strike slipped smoothly past the demon's skin, and the following explosion rained blood and guts onto the grand staircase and doors that stood behind the demon.

The demon's eyes widened to comical proportions before his body seemed to lose its coherence. He fell apart before their eyes, collapsing into a cloud of rapidly fading smoke.

The attack signaled a shift all around the room. The servants sprang forward, fingers lengthening into claws and jaws unhinging to reveal rows of obsidian-like fangs.

Most were aiming directly for Rowan, screams of rage on their lips.

And then they slammed straight into barriers courtesy of the de Vort, buying everyone precious seconds to react.

Milena and Tamara were the two fastest to respond, spells bursting forth in a variety of colors and with a variety of effects. Almost every spell that Tamara cast was purely offensive, burning, freezing, slicing, or blowing the servants apart. Milena's repertoire, meanwhile, left most of her victims writhing uselessly on the ground. Most of them died shortly, expressions of pain, fear, and anguish fixed on their faces.

Naturally, the others burst into action, too.

Olivia's assault was even more destructive than the other two, bolstered by her ever-increasing mastery of alchemy. Blake's party, meanwhile, focused on support and buffing, the strength welling up within Blake's body proof enough of their competence.

To Rowan's surprise, mopping up the servants didn't take long at all. There were nearly fifty of the demons in the hall with them, yet they all fell quickly under the onslaught of attacks from the humans.

In fact, for all their intelligence and seeming sophistication, Rowan could tell that perhaps only the head butler was at the Epic tier, and at very early levels, too. After all, his ambush was enough to speedily take out the monster all on its own.

When the final enemy fell and quiet descended over the hall, everyone tensed, expecting some kind of retaliation or reinforcements. Instead, everything remained silent and still. Not a single new combatant joining the fray.

"Do you think they're all deeper in? Is anyone even watching us?" Marcus asked, confusion evident in his voice as he looked around.

"They either didn't expect us to do that or they just don't care," Rowan supplied, sighing as he stretched out his shoulders.

The weirdness of the whole situation was freaking the Stalwart Hero out, and the discomfort of killing the polite demons was immense.

In spite of that, he couldn't bring himself to regret his actions.

He didn't know a lot about the demon kind. There was, however, one invariable fact: Demons did not do diplomacy. Demons didn't take hostages. Being near a demon meant a person was either in the process of getting corrupted or dying.

He would show the demons exactly the same amount of mercy and consideration, civilized beings or not. All he had to do was his job.

## CHAPTER FIFTEEN

# War

Should we move on?" Blake phrased it as a question, but his eyes wandered off toward the double doors under the sweeping staircase even as he spoke. Rowan could practically hear the words the goddess of light was whispering in Blake's ears, egging him onward.

Rowan, however, was set on finally doing things right.

"Of course not. We came here with an army, planning to fight an army." Rowan turned away from his friend, eyeing the hall that was decidedly more grim thanks to the recent slaughter staining most of it. "We couldn't do much from the outside, but maybe we can do something now to let the army in?"

"Maybe." It was Milena who spoke, and Rowan finally noticed that her eyes were flitting about the place erratically, taking in every aspect of the hall. "There's . . . something here. I don't really understand it fully, but it's there."

"I feel it, too," Olivia supplied, moving closer to a row of the creepy statues. "There's mana emanating from all the decorations, but the emissions coming from the statues put them all to shame."

"Could breaking them possibly bypass the problem?" de Vort wondered, moving closer to examine one herself. "Maybe these are acting as fulcrums?"

It may have been his own suggestion, but Rowan quickly lost the thread of conversation as it grew more technical. The other two of Blake's fiancées chimed in, offering up their own highly specialized theories about mana.

As he leaned against the railing of the stairs, Rowan felt that it was a blessing, frankly. His mind was still swimming with the image of the demon's face, frozen in time by the spear's power. The full might of his newly added Epic card was astonishing.

The previously impressive butler demon was now mostly a head, a pair of legs, and a smear, and Rowan couldn't stop his eyes from drifting to it.

In spite of his conviction, in spite of *knowing* that demons would never willingly work with humanity without insisting on corruption playing a part in their alliance, it still stung to deal the first blow.

"You okay?" Blake asked quietly, worry plain on his face as he approached, positioning himself so that Rowan was partially shielded from the rest of the room.

Rowan almost made the mistake of lashing out, of making a hurtful quip in the face of his best friend's concern, but he settled on a sad smile. "I'm fine, Blake. Really. I just didn't expect them to try and host us." He gestured around the room vaguely, his smile growing strained.

"Yeah, that was a shock," Marcus said quickly, pulling closer, too, and fully blocking Rowan from the sight of the others. "Never even heard a single story about them trying to be civil."

"Probably an attempt at an ambush," Blake grumbled, but his emotions twisted out of the spiral the goddess seemed to be nudging him toward a moment later. "Listen, this was tough for me, too, but . . . well, if they're that humanlike, then it's obvious: We're at war. And they started it."

"At war . . ." Rowan tasted the words on his tongue, and they were bitter. A war that he had just begun to accept. One that he'd assumed would be against mindless monsters intent on killing and nothing else. But the words still gave him a jolt of energy that he needed to get moving again. "Thank you, both of you."

The sincerity in his voice was obvious, and brought out smiles from both of his friends. Rowan was just about to continue their conversation when the low chanting started.

All three of them immediately gripped their weapons, spinning around toward where the sound was coming from, only for their eyes to fall on the sight of Milena glowing an ominous shade of purple and floating a foot off the ground, legs crossed under her.

The others were gathered around her, either holding ritual implements at certain distances away or walking around the room and sprinkling what appeared to be red powder around the perimeter.

The chanting picked up, and more items and powders were laid around the room, causing unearthly voices to spring forth, and the torches that illuminated the place began to flicker, wink out, and come back an unnatural, bloody red.

"How are we in a creepy demon mansion and *your sister* is the most frightening thing in here?" Blake tried for a joking tone, but his voice did grow a bit too squeaky toward the end.

Even Rowan had to admit that Milena cut an imposing figure, her white fur now marked by rapidly appearing glyphs and sigils; all the while that same creepy glow intensified. Then the wolfkin straightened, stretched midair, and landed one foot almost daintily on the ground.

There was a thump that spread from the point of impact, then crackling lines of purple energy erupted toward every corner of the hall. They covered the floor in moments, climbed the wall, overtook the ceiling, and finally, slowly, facing great resistance, made their way up the statues.

The statues creaked and shook, before they started to *move*. Each of them snapped out of their poses, stumbling, staggering. They were desperately trying to make their way closer to the wolfkin shaman but faltered mere steps after their animation.

One by one, they froze again and collapsed to the floor, scattering in a thousand little pieces. The second the final statue fell, the world twisted in its wake.

The space around Rowan felt like it was compressed, kneaded, and then cut, causing things to burst out of midair.

Things that Rowan recognized.

The bits of what used to be their forward team rained down on the floor, limbs carelessly torn away from bodies, armor crumpled and cut.

Following in their wake was also a very startled group of almost fifty demons, who landed on the floor of the hall in a heap, moaning and struggling to move.

Rowan was in motion before he could even process what he saw or felt. Mechanically, barely delaying the anger that churned in his chest, his glowing spear raised and fell, reaping one demonic life after another.

The others joined him, too, but it couldn't have been called a fight. It was an execution. The demons seemed to be at the upper Rare tier in terms of strength, but they were disoriented, very nearly knocked out by the ritual Milena had cast.

It was only when their grisly work was done that Rowan realized that figures were streaming into the hall from its main entrance.

"Easy there, lad." Hearing Lucius's voice was a relief on its own. The older man scanned the hall, looking for threats that the hero parties hadn't already churned through.

He found none.

An explosion sounded a moment later, actually shaking the entire mansion. The sound of shattering glass and screams accompanied it, but it all brought a smile to Rowan's face. The screams were decidedly inhuman.

"Good to see you again. The hospitality of the demons didn't agree with us," Rowan quipped, spinning his spear to get rid of some of the nervous energy bubbling up inside him.

"Good to be here. I have to say, our Radiant Hero impressed me. I thought he'd have charged after the enemy leader by now instead of making sure we could follow." The Mercenary King's mirth was the only thing that softened the blow of the accusation.

Blake looked suitably chastised, but Rowan just laughed.

With that, unfortunately, it was time to finish regrouping and recommit for another attack. Soldiers continued to stream into the mansion, whose hall now was somehow even bigger. Rowan ignored what they were doing as he eyed the doors ahead of them.

He might have missed it before his training with Olivia to sense mana. Now, the sensation was unmistakable. The demon they'd come to kill was right behind those doors, and for some reason it was content to wait.

"That's our stop." Rowan gestured toward the doors, even as he ventured closer to them. "Want to accompany us in there?"

"Of course, lad," the Mercenary King quipped. "In fact, let me open the way for you. You lot! Get up to the second level, and get ready to storm any rooms you find! We're attacking simultaneously in two minutes!"

The soldiers rushed to obey, lieutenants and officers quickly claiming control over their groups and coordinating the process. Rowan just quirked a brow at Lucius in question.

"They're giving us a chance to strike first. It would be foolish not to take it." The man's comment did resonate.

"And what do you think you're doing without me?" The voice made all their eyes snap up to the second story, only to land on a frustrated-looking Tamara. She glided through the air, her disciples close on her tail.

"I thought you'd be busy—you know—with all the screaming," Rowan admitted, sending the woman a smile. The eagerness and anticipation he kept feeling from their link hadn't diminished in the slightest. If anything, with access to the manor, it had only grown.

"That rabble? Please, we already took care of what opposition we faced. I was just hoping you'd see reason and just exit the building when you took down its protections. We could have reduced it to rubble and fought the demon at our leisure."

Rowan frowned, unable to argue. In spite of that, the voracity coiling in her chest made him hesitate to agree to the plan. There was something there that he didn't really understand or like, but it vanished as quickly as it had appeared.

"Well . . ."

"No, we do this the right way." Blake was the one who cut in, eyes suddenly blazing with divine light. "My goddess demands it."

For the very first time, Rowan felt mildly grateful for the effect the divine had on Blake. If both his instincts and the goddess agreed, then maybe he was right to be cautious.

Tamara opened her mouth, likely to argue, when Lucius interrupted her. "It's time. Let's not argue on the eve of battle." With no hesitation, the large man stepped forward, took a deep breath, and brought one of his feet down on the doors with all the might he could muster.

For an Epic-tier class, strength-focused or not, that meant that the doors nearly exploded as they opened, flying off their hinges and slamming into the walls.

The sight that was revealed actually made Rowan pause in his rush forward.

The throne room beyond the doors was massive, stretching the full length and width of a football field, if not farther.

The floor was sterling silver, polished to such a shine that it may as well have been a mirror, and perfectly reflecting the intricate, sculpted arches of the roof that depicted all manner of creatures, be it beasts or humanoids, draped over each other in slumber.

Balconies lined the walls above the floor and along the sides of the room. Rowan would have admired them, had they not been filled to the brim with all sorts of demons dressed in clothing fancier than he had seen even among the kingdom's nobility. He shivered.

Of course, at the far end of the room, seated on a suitable gilded throne even more ornately carved than the ceiling, was the Legendary demon.

Its throne, in stark contrast to the ceiling, was full of depictions of creatures waking up. The closer to his seat they got, the more aware and animated their expressions became. Each and every one of them was twisted in unnatural rapture. Diamonds and other precious stones stood in for their eyes, giving them a crazed quality with the way light refracted off them.

The demon himself was almost easy to miss, if it weren't for the aura of pure might that emanated from him. It was almost tangible, and it brought a lead-like tang to the air.

Unlike in the dream Rowan and Blake shared, the demon was not a gaseous giant with barely defined features, out to crush them like ants. He was frail, with robes that were practically engulfing his frame.

His face was sunken and gray, like a patient left unattended for too long. His wickedly sharp claws had a dull glow to them, looking like evil Christmas ornaments. Even the obsidian-like tail and horns that gleamed wickedly didn't inspire much fear.

The demon's eyes were the only sign of his might. They shone with an inner gray light, resembling the spokes of an ever-spinning wheel. Rowan could swear that in spite of the distance, in spite of the impossibility of it, he was drawn into those eyes and saw countless souls chained to those same wheels, screaming in anguish, ecstasy, and a thousand other emotions.

Then the doors on the upper level were torn open, and the shouting and screaming that followed broke Rowan out of his reverie. The single moment that seemed to stretch forever was over.

"Well, well, you finally arrive," the demon rasped, taking his time to get out of his seat of power even as ten Epic-tier combatants rushed toward him. "And in such a rude manner."

The demon didn't seem to care about the slaughter of his people. He didn't so much as glance at the upper gallery, where soldiers took to stabbing a little too happily, even for Rowan's taste. He had eyes only for the two heroes in the lead.

A wordless growl tore its way out of Rowan's throat. His spear had progressively grown in its radiance, and now he thrust it forward with the full might of what his card build could support.

The demon swatted negligently at the spear with a single hand, then rocked to the side when the explosion that followed made him stagger and lacerations opened all over said hand. Oily black blood erupted out of the wound, spiraling into the air and then getting sucked toward the spear itself.

Most of it instantly seeped into Rowan's weapon, like it usually did, but some of it sank into his skin, too, sending a jolt of power and energy through him.

The demon glared at the appendage like it had betrayed him, but the reflection was cut off by a screech of agony when Blake burst into a divine glow and slipped his sword right between the demon's ribs.

An explosion of demonic mana threw all of them back, streaming from the demon for several long seconds. Most of his assailants were sent rag-dolling over the floor, but Tamara, floating as she was, was positively launched into the wall right above the double doors.

Rowan could just barely track her. The woman impacted the wall with a loud, wet thunk, started falling, then was catapulted out of the throne room by the continued emission of mana. The emotional feedback Rowan got from her dulled, sending a spike of worry through Rowan.

"THAT GODDESS! THAT DIVINE PARASITE! SHE WILL REGRET EVER WOUNDING ME!" The demon's bellows followed the release of mana, his eyes crazed as he examined his hand and chest.

The demon's robe were now fully torn up around his chest, revealing a gaunt mess of scabs and wounds that were there even before Blake's attack. The wounds looked infected and raw, with a mild golden glow sputtering out of them every couple of seconds.

Rowan saw the opportunity for what it was, bringing all his mana to bear and forcing it out of his core and into the rest of his body as deeply and as thoroughly as he could. He spared what little was left to feed his spear further, but he'd been building another strike from the moment he landed his first one.

With his agility engaged more powerfully than it ever was before, Rowan practically teleported across the space of the throne room. The world seemed to move like molasses around him, the very air of the room pressing back.

Then he was there, and the demon's eyes widened in realization of his speed right before his spear punched forward, aimed right where Blake's previous strike had landed.

The spear's tip further widened the weakened flesh easily, but it bit deeper than Blake's sword did. It scraped right by the ribs, met some small tearing resistance, and finally sank into and through the demon's heart.

Blood erupted around Rowan. More blood than he ever thought any creature of the demon's size could possess.

The blood swept over his spear, and even its gluttonous nature couldn't keep up with the feast that was being provided. It seeped into Rowan's skin, and Rowan felt a jolt of fear when the tendrils of corruption from the foul liquid start questing forward.

Yet, the **Scarlet Envy** did its job flawlessly—the card's effect viciously tore power out of the blood and directed it all into Rowan's own reserves with no regard for the corruption's supposed effects.

Rowan's mana was guttering out just a moment earlier, consumed to the extreme by the rush and blow. Now, his reserves were rapidly refilling, and he sent whatever dregs he recovered spiraling into the card that promised him even more damage against the demon.

The demon's screams echoed out into the throne room with a desperation that was almost enough to knock Rowan out of his concentration, and the monster's hands fell to clasp around the hero's spear, fighting to push it out.

Yet, empowered by the demon's own blood and driven by sudden manic bloodlust, the Stalwart Hero didn't budge an inch.

Another explosion of mana erupted in the room, finally sending Rowan back. However, unlike before, he was barely forced to stumble away, even if the spear finally left the demon's body.

Rowan's head was spinning. The smell of unholy blood nearly overpowered his senses, and odd, hysterical laughter began to echo in his ears. It was grating, full of madness and vitriol and emotions best left unnamed, and he couldn't tell where it was coming from.

"Rowan!"

The word, *his name*, Rowan recognized, and it made him jerk in the direction of the speaker.

A human female was on her knees, left on the floor by the blast, but the way she looked at him irked him. It was a look full of worry, and he didn't like it. He didn't need concern from such—

A blow to his cheek sent the hero smashing into a wall, ears ringing. Through blurry eyes, he spotted the demon teetering on his feet, the wound on his chest torn open to the point of showing all the mangled organs inside it.

The sight wasn't reminiscent of anything inside a human, especially the shriveled, crystalline-looking heart.

The laughter, though, persisted. Rowan so very badly wanted it to stop. Blood, welling from his torn lips and inner cheek made him choke, and the awful laughter cut off for a moment.

Clarity swept over Rowan's battered mind, and suddenly, he understood. He choked back the laughter threatening to bubble up again, groaning as his face knitted itself together.

With steps trembling from too much energy stuffed within his body, he staggered toward the Legendary demon again.

Their foe was no longer paying attention to him, though. Instead, the monster's eyes were fixed on his own chest, disbelief and anger writ large across his features.

Then those eyes snapped up to meet Rowan's, and the pure, unadulterated hatred within them made the hero stagger. Before Rowan could regain his footing, the demon let out an ear-piercing screech. It was nothing like the sound that had come out of the creature before. It wasn't an expression of pain, or fury, or anything that mundane. It was a sound filled with everything that the demon was, everything that the monster encompassed. A wave of madness, of vicious suffering, of fractured awareness and a thousand crippled dreams, flooded everyone—both human and demon alike.

Between one blink and the next, Rowan no longer knew where he was. He didn't know who he was. What he was.

He was a student sitting an exam, eyes briefly shooting toward one of his friends there with him and wondering at the score they'd get.

He was a lonely boy, cuddling up to a cat as he hid from the notice of everyone.

He was a child, sniffling the bitter tears of betrayal that cut their way across his face at the mere thought of a friendship he thought was solid and true.

He was a hero, laying siege to a demon with a handful of true allies and an army full of people he wasn't sure he could trust.

He was a monster, drowned in blood and fear and anger, with a desire to endure total madness just to secure another drop of the liquid.

He was . . .

The scream cut short, and Rowan collapsed to his knees. He was shaking again, but this time the sensation came from the terror gripping him. His mind, a thousand different conflicting shards that had started to drift apart, clicked back into place again, and he heaved a shuddering breath. Rowan used the last of his strength to raise his head and catch sight of the demon, feet dangling in the air.

Before the monster stood Milena, holding a long, wicked-looking spike of crystalline material glittering in the light of the room. A blink drew Rowan's attention to the fact that the weapon had grown out of her staff, and that she'd driven said weapon up through the demon's jaw, holding up the monster like a wetly flapping flag.

Before he could even begin to process what had happened, a status window practically exploded in front of Rowan's face. The font seemed to almost shine, and the letters appeared to wiggle in place slightly with a faint golden glow.

**Congratulations!**
**You have slain [Sybelin, the Earl of Grasping Madness],**
**one of the Four Demonic Pillars!**

A sudden fire erupted inside his chest, and Rowan's mind's eye was drawn to the core of his being where a Heart Card briefly began to glow.

**Calculating . . .**
**Conditions 3/8 fulfilled.**

**Error!**
**Unsealing requirements not met.**

The glow died down, and Rowan slumped when his normal vision was restored, leaving him gasping for air that somehow seemed insufficient to fill his lungs now. Hands gripped him, laying him on his side and quickly fluttering over his bloodied features before they pulled away and the mouth of a potion bottle was forced between his lips. He drank greedily, the jolt of energy finally letting him open his eyes to look up blearily at his extremely worried fiancée.

"Hey there, beautiful," Rowan managed to croak out. Between one blink and the next, the fire in his chest died down, and it became so much easier to function. "Sorry for worrying you."

"You idiot, charging in like that. And what happened back there?" Olivia was asking, but before she could really get going or let him get in a word, she suddenly bent forward, and her lips were on his.

For a glorious couple of minutes, there wasn't much talking to be had. There was only the two of them, and a glorious feeling of being alive and well.

Then Marcus had to clear his throat, and Rowan was thrust back into the arms of reality. He glared up at the beast folk, who was smiling wryly.

"I can't let you just lie there all day," Marcus insisted with a grin, which faded into seriousness with his next question. "What happened back there? Is everything all right? Blake went down at the same time you did."

Rowan quickly looked around, finding the other hero in the middle of the three women he was engaged to. He had a put-upon look on his face, but then again, there was a slight smile tugging on his lips. Rowan rolled his eyes and decided to leave him to it.

"There was a notification from my system."

"Yes, about us killing a Demonic Pillar. I got that, too. Didn't put me on the floor, though."

"No, not that. Something about unsealing . . ." Rowan muttered, absently rubbing his chest. "I have no clue what it was about. Well, I have *guesses*, but . . ." Rowan gestured vaguely around the room. Even if there was no one obviously listening, he was loath to share potentially sensitive information.

"It's fine, we can talk about this later," Marcus assured him, then offered him a hand. "Lots of things to do, anyway."

Over the next several hours, Rowan found out that Marcus was great at understating things.

They had to down potions, regroup, and then immediately start sweeping through the mansion in search of any demonic survivors or loot to be had. They barely even paused to congratulate Milena on her final blow, though Rowan could tell that a lack of celebration didn't bother her.

The wolfkin was too giddy for that. She was more than willing to describe in intricate detail the process of simplifying a ritual into an instant-cast spell, which she'd managed to pull off on the spot to kill the demon.

Apparently, her ability to throw off the demon's madness curse was something less worthy of discussion, and simply chalked up to her "class-related resistances."

By the time they were done pillaging the monstrosity of a castle, Rowan no longer felt like the leader of an army that had just overcome a major obstacle to lasting peace and prosperity. He felt like a wrung-out commander who'd rather not have to look at yet another corpse of someone he'd chosen to lead into battle.

He may not have killed them himself, but every body that was discovered was like a knife right through Rowan's heart. He'd managed to lead his army to victory with practically trivial losses the last time, but his lucky streak simply hadn't held.

Over a hundred and twenty people were dead this time. Some had died in the initial attempt to enter the manor, but most of the losses had occurred when the demon had used his madness-inducing scream to kill them all.

Those that had been lost to the scream were the worst to handle. They weren't exactly dead, but all the mages agreed that their minds, and souls, were completely gone.

Even Blake's [Saintess] confirmed as much, the princess looking unusually severe and pale after giving her verdict.

The only thing the two heroes could do was grant those soldiers the mercy of true rest, and while Rowan had insisted on doing the job himself, he'd also thrown up no fewer than four times. Blake had joined him without a word and refused to leave the room he'd been left in to do the grisly work. Surprisingly, Rowan's best friend held up better than he did.

They didn't even have time for a proper burial. The soldiers were all gathered in the throne room, and a grand pyre was set. As he stared absentmindedly at the flames, his arms wrapped around Olivia, Rowan was interrupted by yet another notification.

**Congratulations!**
**[Marhet, the Countess of Whispering Wounds], one of the Four Demonic Pillars, has been slain!**

This time, Rowan wasn't knocked off his feet when the unsealing process triggered again, the met conditions ticking up by one, before failing again. However, the heat that had sprung up in his chest was there again.

Rowan's eyes met Blake's. Neither hero knew what to say, nor what the sudden notification would mean for them.

## CHAPTER SIXTEEN

# Heroics

The battle, the funeral pyre, and the mansion they'd set aflame were now behind them, figuratively and literally. However, Rowan couldn't help but feel like they'd taken a step forward right into the murk of some kind of ominous swamp.

"It's Kayla, right? It has to be . . ." Rowan repeated for about the tenth time, once again receiving unhappy grumbles from Blake in return. Even though he wasn't the biggest fan of Kayla, either, Rowan didn't understand Blake's issue with Kayla after their arrival in their new reality, but he did have a pretty strong hint now.

Every time the heroine's name was brought up, an unpleasant cocktail of anger and distrust would boil up in Blake. That wouldn't be so bad, but the problematic part was that Rowan could tell that the emotions were not fully his own. Rowan could feel the goddess up in his friend's head, contributing to those emotions. Stoking them. Encouraging them.

And there was nothing he could do about it.

"It's not important." Once more, Blake gave the exact same response, eyes fixated angrily on the horizon. "You know what we need to do. So, let's just do it."

"And where, pray tell, do you want us to head?" Rowan finally snapped, biting his lip to stop from saying anything else. "Which way do you want to go?"

They'd won. There was no denying that. But they'd also taken losses. Plus, it would take time for them to track down the next Legendary demon.

Blake's response to the question was unexpected. The other hero froze, eyes fluttering shut. When they opened, they glowed with a divine radiance and snapped to a particular spot on the horizon.

"That way." There was no uncertainty, no trace of doubt that mere mortals would allow to slip into their voice. Just the plain surety of divine knowledge as Rowan's connection to Blake fed him a fraction of the radiance the other hero's soul was bathed in.

Rowan grimaced. No matter how much he disliked the gods, even he couldn't deny that the secondhand emotions were enough to affect him a little. Just not enough to inspire him to instantly charge into the deeper wastes.

"I get that you're zealous, but we still need to wait until morning. We should be in bed as it is. Or, better yet, back in town to recuperate." Rowan's complaints fell on deaf ears as his best friend navigated past the tents, venturing to the very edge of their camp.

They didn't want to sleep anywhere near the scene of their former battle, so the army had marched until sunset before setting up camp. Thanks to Blake, the route *had* taken them deeper into the wastes, but they were proceeding carefully. Despite that, Rowan could easily tell that Blake's opinion on the matter of their marching speed was going to be contentious come morning.

"Blake, really, can you calm down?" Rowan was forced to grab the other hero's shoulder, finally resigning himself to slightly harsher methods. "Are you going to do the same thing again? Just charge ahead until everyone else dies besides your party?"

The flinch and sudden haunted look in Blake's eyes made Rowan want to wince, but there was no taking the comment back. At least it did its job of jerking him out of whatever the divine insight had done to him.

"It's . . . different?" Blake ventured cautiously, cringing at the look of disbelief Rowan sent him. "It really is?"

"How? How is rushing going to fix *anything*?"

"It's different because my goddess actually wants me to be here now! I'm no longer going against her wishes. She obviously wants me to do this, if she's providing me with guidance. Besides, the girls, I . . ."

"Yes?"

Blake was hesitating, and his face did an *almost* funny cycle between paling and blushing, but he did eventually get the words out. "I don't want to fail them. They need me to do better. Even in this last battle, I didn't perform up to expectations."

"Blake, you wounded that thing badly enough that I could take advantage and almost finish him, and then Milena managed to resist his final efforts and kill him. That's no small part to play. When I first tried, I could barely get past the demon's skin!"

"That's just my goddess's blessing . . ."

"And who was the one who used the blessing?" Rowan was on the verge of snapping again. The only thing that held him back was Blake's sad expression. Thankfully, Blake began to cheer up soon after, a smile stretching across his face. And Rowan would have been even happier if he couldn't feel the whispers of the goddess nudging him to feel that way. But for now, he would take it.

"You know what? You're right! Okay, sure, I get it. I need to be more careful. For . . . for them, I guess," Blake mumbled.

"Finally! Now, how about we finally go get some sleep?" Rowan asked.

"That sounds great! I hope I'll have enough space in my tent left over for that."

This time, when Rowan laughed, the sound was pure relief and amusement. "Your fault, my friend. I have but a single fiancée, so I don't have any issues with tent size."

"No, you have issues with a different kind of size."

Rowan just about face-planted at the innuendo, whirling to face Blake with wide, startled eyes. "Did you just make a . . ."

**Congratulations!**
**[Balkar, the Count of Stoic Pride], one of the Four Demonic Pillars, has been slain!**

The moment of levity evaporated in the face of heat in Rowan's chest. He gasped and clutched the front of his shirt as the heat ramped up past the point of its previous peak.

**Calculating . . .**
**Conditions 5/8 fulfilled.**

**Error!**
**Unsealing requirements not met.**

Once again, the unsealing failed and Rowan was left glaring at the status window, willing it to provide a full and proper explanation of what exactly was happening.

It declined to do so, if its immutability was any indication.

Neither of the heroes got a particularly restful sleep for what remained of the night.

The next morning, it wasn't only Blake and Rowan who looked like they were missing sleep. Each of the Epic-tier classes looked like they'd been put through the wringer.

The hero parties were caught up in the doubtful mood of their nominal leaders.

The Mercenary King was a jumble of nerves, fear, expectation, and guilt.

Tamara was the only one with a relatively stable mood, though the coil of excitement Rowan kept glimpsing was definitely growing to be a worry.

Ironically, in spite of that, most of them looked perfectly fresh and ready for the day, especially since four people had access to Rowan's **Natural Renewal**.

"We need to set out immediately." Blake's version of *good morning* wasn't exactly well received. It was coated with the palpable anxiety that Rowan had hoped he'd smothered yesterday. Once again, his brow furrowed when he felt the goddess's influence.

"What need is there for such a rush, hero?" assured Lucius. "We all got the notification yesterday. There's but a single Legendary demon left, and we're *well* ahead of schedule."

Fortunately or not, while the hero parties were caught up in doubt and suspicion, most of the army was in a celebratory mood, and Lucius was working to emulate them. After all, the notifications had come one after the other, bolstering their conviction and courage.

The man was smiling and a perfect picture of health. Even his clothing and armor were nicely polished and maintained.

If Rowan couldn't sense his actual feelings on the subject, he'd likely have been fooled.

"That's the *exact* reason we need to rush," a buzzkill Blake snapped. "One of those kills may have been Kayla. Both? I refuse to believe that she could have pulled that off. That means there's something out there, plotting something."

"Plotting to help us kill the demon king?" Marcus's voice was calm, but his tone made his implications clear.

"You don't understand, it's . . . !"

"Blake, it's fine," Rowan cut in, feeling the other hero's emotions spike dangerously and artificially. "We'll be okay. Deep breaths."

"But we only got one of them. And the experience . . ." Blake trailed off, flushing at the looks Rowan's party sent him. "I just want us to be ready to fight the demon lord, that's all."

"I understand your concerns. Speaking of, we wanted you to have this." Rowan led the conversation toward a healthier topic, pulling a card out of his pack and presenting it to Blake.

The other hero's expression was full of both shock and wonder as he took it, odd emotions dancing across his features too quickly to identify right after. "Are you sure?"

Rowan could understand his hesitation. Funnily enough, it wasn't even him who suggested this particular course of action last night. His party had come together to evaluate their progress and sort out their loot, and it was Milena who pushed for one of the two drops to go to the other hero party.

According to the woman herself, "It would breed bad feelings if they walked away from the encounter empty-handed." Rowan could see the wisdom of what she'd insisted on as the postures of Blake's party members relaxed, losing a lot of their rigidity.

"We wanted you to have it so you stay safer. Gods know that Rowan spends enough time worrying about you," Milena teased gently, toying with her staff.

Rowan flushed when the attention of everyone focused on him, then coughed. "She's not wrong. But really, the card should be useful."

And it was.

**The Mind Electric (Legendary, Passive)**
**Your mind is your bastion, capable of housing all dreams and nightmares. None shall threaten your sovereignty.**

Rowan had briefly tested it, with Milena's help, and the description really didn't do it justice. After all, it had allowed him to weather the effects of the other card that dropped without even flinching.

**Kiss of Madness (Legendary, Active)**
**The glimpse of eternity in a water droplet, the aria of heavens in the screeching of a storm.**

The description was utterly useless, but in line with what he was starting to associate with higher-tier cards—the more poetic the description, the more profound the effects.

That card had gone to Milena with absolutely no contest or doubt. She'd landed the last blow, and the thing was practically tailor-made for a [Shaman] class. According to the woman herself, it allowed her to cast a curse of madness, either as a spell or a ritual.

The effects of both were ridiculous and threatened to shatter the mind of anyone who so much grazed the curse's area of effect. Rowan couldn't explain it, much like he couldn't explain what had happened to him when the demon used the card. It was like his mind was forced to expand, to take in more and more information all at once, to live through every second of his life and his current reality simultaneously. The worst part of the whole thing was that thinking back on the experience filled him with longing. For just a moment, every part of him was there, expressed and on the surface. He understood every facet of his own being.

But it was a mirror that threatened to shatter and take his mind with it.

For all that **Kiss of Madness** was aggression, **The Mind Electric** was the complete opposite. The card allowed its owner to recognize any curse's effects, categorize them, and then shove them aside in favor of restoring his own will and sense of self.

That was why, when Milena suggested Blake have it, Rowan was fully aboard.

With bated breath and anxiety burning in his chest, Rowan took in the sight of his friend eyeing the card. His face was perfectly blank now, but with their bond, Rowan could tell what he was feeling.

Desire warred with an odd sense of caution.

Gratefulness warred with a profound sense of being undeserving.

On and on, the contrasting feelings warred inside Rowan's best friend, each opposite more artificial than the last.

Then, at last, Blake raised his eyes to meet Rowan's own. Hesitation met nothing but sincerity, and the Stalwart Hero stepped forward, gently pushing Blake's hands that had a death grip on the card until the orange card pressed gently against the hero's chest.

Blake took a shuddering breath as a purple card materialized in front of him and plummeted to the ground, and the Legendary card dissolved into motes of light that went straight into his chest. Immediately, a rush of changes surged through Blake's connection to Rowan. It was like watching a flame lick up against a gasoline puddle, the whole thing turning into an inferno in a matter of seconds.

Each emotion combusted and evaporated before a sense of calm and emptiness surged back down the connection. The inferno stilled, and in its place was a lake, its surface calm like a mirror.

Slowly, owlishly, Blake blinked and looked around, then down at his now-empty hands. For several long seconds, no one spoke.

"Each and every one of you, so dramatic." Rowan swung around when a new voice sounded around them. The voice was smooth and undeniably human, yet when the whole group rounded on the source in a panic, they spotted a plump, shiny black raven giving them the stink eye.

"Kayla?" Rowan's voice was full of disbelief, but there was no denying the familiarity of the voice. Or the fact that it was coming from a raven.

"Correct, 'tis I. The greatest mage to grace this kingdom." The raven mockingly saluted them with a wing, turning its head to the other side in that distinctly birdlike fashion.

"I've had nowhere near enough to drink to deal with this," Rowan sighed, already feeling a headache coming on. His eyes flitted between the bird and his best friend, but Blake was oddly nonresponsive.

Oh, he was there and he was focused. Rowan could tell that much by the flicker in the man's eyes, but he could no longer feel a single emotion coming from him. Not even a hint.

"Like you were ever fun enough to drink this early," the raven scoffed, then fluttered forward and landed right on Rowan's left shoulder, purposefully smacking him in the face with a wing and its tail as it perched itself there.

"Not that I'm unhappy with the visit, but what exactly do you want?" Rowan groused, taking in the reactions of the group.

His own party had mostly glares to spare for the heroine-and-raven, having been there when she admonished Rowan for his lacking prowess after easily killing an Epic they were all about to die at the hands of.

Blake's party, if anything, was even more hostile.

They drew closer to their hero, looking like lionesses about to fight to keep their male out of the clutches of a different pride. Rowan thought that the raven was smirking, somehow.

Blake himself was still nearly emotionless, making Rowan start to regret ever giving him the card.

It was, however, the feelings of the two Rest's Remorse powerhouses that worried him.

The Mercenary King's guilt spiked again, and with it came a sense of resignation.

Meanwhile, the ecstatic glow of Tamara's emotions was more than enough to give Rowan pause. With concentration on his face, he focused on his connection to the woman, but other than happiness and expectation, he got nothing else.

"Well, if this idiot here could finally learn to listen," Kayla started off crassly, pointing a wing at Blake, "I'd like to meet up, and offer up a bit of advice. After all, there's no going back now. It would be a shame if we failed right at the finish line."

"Just tell us what you want, Kayla. I'm not going to play your games. I'm just . . . tired." When he spoke, Blake genuinely sounded like he was hanging on through sheer willpower. Whatever the card's effect had done, it was obvious that the other hero was struggling. Instead of haste or anger, there was just a deep weariness in his expression.

"Can't do it like this. You really think a familiar I'm possessing is a good replacement for an in-person meeting? No. For now, I'd like you to continue heading west. It's deeper into the wastes, yes, but it's where we need to go regardless. You'll find a spot where two rivers meet easily enough. Make camp there."

"And let you do what, ambush us?" Blake snapped, but there was no real heat in his voice.

"You missed a familiar, Blake. If I really wanted to, I could have dropped potions or something on your tents. Or channeled a spell through it if I wanted to go big. Now, please let the adults do the thinking and just follow along like you usually do, okay?"

Kayla's voice was sugary sweet, but her words made Blake go completely pale. Rowan edged a bit closer to his friend, ready to catch him if he passed out. Thankfully, no such thing happened, and without even waiting for a response, the bird took flight, then melted into a mass of shadows overhead.

The shadow drifted over the army camp harmlessly, even if they did provoke a couple shouts of surprise.

The two heroes could only stare, each with complicated emotions of their own.

"Right, well. I'm putting this to a vote. Everyone who wants to actually do as she suggested, hands up." Rowan wasn't about to waste time, but he really wasn't sure whether to hope people voted for or against.

He did decide to put his hand up, however, and a second later, his party followed suit. With great reluctance and great exuberance, respectively, both Lucius and Tamara raised their hands as well.

The real surprise was when a pale-faced princess followed suit, earning looks of angry shock from the other two girls in her party.

"I suppose you two are against," Rowan said. The two girls nodded, shooting more looks of betrayal at the princess. "And you, Blake?" Blake just stared at his friend, making no move to either protest or acquiesce. Rowan winced. "Right, then. Well, I guess we're going."

The mood among the troops was still generally positive as they set out, traipsing through the jungle of the wastes. Supported by the cards of the Mercenary King, that was unlikely to change.

The mood among the leaders of the army, however, could use some improvement.

Three girls were still clustered around Blake like someone would try to steal him, while the man himself was a dazed mess.

Rowan didn't want to ask for the card back. He really didn't. But by the time the sun crested over the horizon and they finally found their way to the destination Kayla had specified, he really was starting to feel tempted. Blake was like a block of ice, impossible to read and melting with weariness.

At least Rowan's own party was ready and functional. They'd slipped a little ahead of the others, and Rowan took the chance to fill them in on everything that was happening and his own fears and suspicions on the subject.

"So, something's coming to a head," Marcus said. It wasn't a question, and the wolfkin's grim expression only accentuated the fact.

"Almost definitely," Rowan confirmed, massaging his forehead. "And Blake's still out of it."

"You're not getting any feelings from him at all? None?" Milena asked to confirm, leafing through a large, old grimoire instead of one of her more recent acquisitions.

"Not a hint. Zero. Zilch. Nada." The string of strange expressions earned him a few odd looks, making him wonder for the first time in a while how his communication ability actually worked.

Milena sighed and closed her book, shrugged, then put it away. "Best I can tell, the card gave Hero Blake blanket immunity to mental effects. You could probably work with him to figure out how to make it possible for you to sense him, but that means you'd need to explain the whole thing to him first."

"Yeah, I don't think I want to do that," Rowan admitted with a wince, looking away. In a very real way, he'd broken Blake's confidence as much as the goddess had.

Maybe more, considering the fact that they'd been friends before landing in a new dimension. It was admittedly for his own good, but still, Rowan was firmly hoping that Blake would never learn about it.

"I'm more worried about your other friend," Olivia said, hugging Rowan's arm a little tighter. "I don't know what she wants, but Lucius's reaction hints that she's involved with the king's plans. And then there's Tamara . . ."

Olivia trailed off, but the look in her eyes was anything but friendly. It seemed Olivia was now ready to carry the torch of her mother's anger.

"I'm not sure whatever Tamara's planning is malicious, per se," Rowan hurried to reassure her, desperate for even a single ally more. "It's more like she's just . . . excited, and yes, I hear myself and know how it sounds. She felt the same when we fought the Legendary, though. Complete with disappointment that followed. Maybe she just wants the experience and cards and knows this is a great opportunity to get them?"

"Why isn't she saying anything, then?" Olivia protested, turning up her nose at the idea that the mage was blameless.

"She wants to swoop in and heroically rescue us, earning our undying gratitude?" Rowan offered, even if the reasoning was rather thin.

Olivia scoffed, and he was forced to admit he agreed. "Anyways, just, please be ready? We don't know what we're walking into."

Their destination was almost impossibly beautiful. Located at the intersection of what appeared to be two major rivers, the surroundings were oddly flat and jungle-free.

The rolling meadows hugged the banks of the rivers, and grass swayed enchantingly in the gentle wind.

There were only a few things that spoiled the beautiful view.

First, no matter how much it added to the scenery, the unfortunate fact of the matter was that both the grass and the rivers were a deep shade of purple. While the rivers were nowhere near as revolting as the one they'd come across closer to the city, Rowan was pretty sure that a single sip of the water contained enough poison to kill the entire army. The river was still filled with filth, corruption, and corpses.

The second thing that marred the view was the corpses themselves, drifting by. Various beasts and monsters dotted the riverbanks, some of them quite fresh, some of them quite not. All of them rather smelly if you got too close.

Otherwise, a pleasant and enticing smell dominated the air, wafting off the purple river water and making Rowan's mouth water.

"Lovely locale, here," Rowan snarked in a vain attempt to distract himself from his building thirst.

Oddly enough, it was the princess that stepped forward with a heavy frown on her face. A corona of light ignited around her and then rolled over the army. It temporarily banished the smell, and with it, the tingles that had sneaked up on Rowan and that he hadn't noticed until they were gone.

"Waiting here is a terrible idea," the princess declared, turning to eye the Stalwart Hero. "The poison in the river dissolves into the air, especially where it's drying on the banks. Inhaling it for just half an hour is enough to be lethal."

Her proclamation wasn't exactly loud, but it was still enough to reach the ears of the closest soldier ranks and then spread out like a ripple.

Rowan sighed, eyeing the river and considering what insisting on meeting there could mean. "We're here already. Any Ideas?"

"I can set up wards," Milena volunteered, eyeing their surroundings. "And that stretch of land between the rivers isn't all that big. We can probably hold it rather easily, especially with the wards added to the mix. Any land troops would be forced to cross through poison to reach us."

"I can help with that, I suppose," the de Vort contributed, watching the wolfkin speculatively. "And good idea on the positioning. We're going to need all the advantages we can get, I suppose, since *someone* decided we needed to be here."

More glares were exchanged with the princess, but Rowan cut them off and got them moving.

Transporting the entirety of their army across the river was a chore, but between the mages and the princess's healing abilities, they managed.

From there, Rowan frankly enjoyed watching the two spell casters work on their warding. The arrangement of symbols carved into the dirt, items buried in it, and ancient chants were all things he found fascinating. He was able to let his mind relax a bit in the monotony of the ritual casting.

When it was done, honest-to-goodness force fields sprang up around them, glowing and opaque, before they faded from view. With the shields in place, the princess performed one final purification ritual and their temporary base was done.

Gone was the sweet, compelling scent, or the way Rowan's surroundings gently rippled at the edges of his vision. It was an odd thought to have, but he almost missed the beauty of it.

That wasn't a thought he could spend much time contemplating, however, because the sound of whistling precluded the sight of a small army of mages cutting through the sky on their way to them.

At their helm stood Kayla, in all her arrogant glory. The heroine looked like someone stepping out of her carriage into the reception hall of a ball, clad in a glamorous dress that shifted through hues of black and violet with every movement of the material.

More tellingly, Kayla's expression wasn't fixed in a smirk. It wasn't the practiced disdain Rowan knew she tested out in the mirror on occasion.

She was stone-faced, focused and intense.

The heroine was on a warpath, and Rowan was only mostly sure her ire wasn't directed at them.

## CHAPTER SEVENTEEN

# Tense Encounters

Stats were a wonderful thing. They rearranged fundamental biology, granted superhuman abilities, resulting in a physique worthy of being preserved in marble.

They allowed people to bend the world to their will, making them hyperaware of supernatural forces that are otherwise intangible. Stats were what helped heroes step beyond the realm of humanity and perform feats typically reserved for myths and legends.

They also made people hyperaware of their surroundings, to the point where the vaunted abilities of detectives like Sherlock Holmes were mere child's play.

Rowan now had *a lot* of stats. Stats he pushed as far as he could to analyze the situation at hand.

Kayla's army was practically . . . vibrating? Their demeanor could charitably be called *focused*. Rowan, without any of that charity, thought they looked paranoid. *How can you lead an army that looks so jittery? What's going on here?*

They glared and squinted at everything they saw. The setting of the meeting, the troops, the barriers they had set up—nothing seemed exempt. More than that, they didn't seem to be really focused on the heroes or their parties. Instead, an outsize portion of their attention landed firmly on the Mercenary King.

There was an astonishing five hundred or so mages. Rowan couldn't understand how Kayla had managed to land her grubby fingers on that many, but here they were. A whole section of fifty was focused solely on Lucius.

The man pretended not to notice or care, but through their bond, Rowan could feel the echo of worry, fear, and shame.

The final thing that Rowan noticed, and that he didn't need his stats for at all, was Tamara's reaction.

Glee, vindication, and a twisted sense of fulfillment swept through the woman at the sight of Kayla. None of Kayla's many mages seemed to pay Tamara any mind, either. A couple of eyes briefly paused on the exiled mage, sparked with something like recognition or approval, and then moved past her.

A bitter smile tugged on Rowan's lips as more than a few hints fell into place. There was something larger at play here. He didn't have the whole picture, but there were enough clues that he wondered if the situation would come back to bite him.

"Kayla!" Rowan shouted up to the woman who was still staring down imperiously at them without a single word. "Would you and your party please come down so we can properly talk?"

For just a moment, Rowan thought he saw the woman's lips twitch. "I suppose that would be for the best," she conceded, then stepped off the platform.

Even knowing that Kayla would never stupidly risk her life, Rowan felt his stomach flutter. The heroine plummeted through the air, the dress somehow perfectly clinging to her form instead of ballooning around her, even if it did flutter.

Just before she was about to impact the ground, her momentum completely disappeared, leaving her to float delicately a foot off the ground. "Lead the way," she said as she gestured.

Rowan grunted and led her toward the main tent they'd set up just for the occasion, with plenty of sound-dampening and antiscrying wards courtesy of the mages in their parties. Rowan idly noted that Kayla didn't let her feet touch the muddy ground until they were inside, where she landed on the carpet.

The others weren't so lucky. Marching boots tracked in mud and purple grass that disappeared a few instants later thanks to special cleaning wards. As it turned out, the intersection of two rivers wasn't the best place in the world to set up camp, even if it was convenient.

"Not going to have your party join you?" Rowan asked in genuine curiosity, only to earn a dismissive snort.

"I don't have one," Kayla claimed with no sign of deception. If anything, she looked downright proud to say that.

"Don't—Wait, how have you been functioning as a hero without a party?" The tone of Rowan's voice might have been a bit too incredulous, but at least the emotion was mirrored by everyone else present.

In fact, it was enough to finally snap Blake out of his silence. "Stop playing games, Kayla. Even you need support." His words were infected with anger, but they lacked most of their usual bite and vitriol. If anything, to Rowan, his best friend looked fragile, like he was desperately trying to pretend that everything was normal. That he was fine.

"Blake." Kayla acknowledged him with the single word and a look, then completely dismissed him on her way to the table they'd set up. Circular, of course, so they wouldn't have to deal with pride, jostling for significance, or other drama. "Not everyone needs a divine mommy to hold their hand. Or a trio of women."

The disdain in Kayla's voice was a dark, bitter thing. Enough so to make Blake wince and shut up, even if anger did flicker over his features for a moment.

Rowan was definitely growing worried. Not just because of Kayla and Blake's uncertain relationship, but because the effect of the card he'd chosen to gift to his best friend might have some kind of unintended consequence. For the first time, Rowan wondered if Blake would be able to deal with the card at all.

Of course, the trio of girls took that as a cue to draw closer to Rowan's friend, holding on to him or standing in front of him defensively, and Blake's tense posture loosened just a smidgen.

"Kayla, you asked us to come here. You stopped us from following the only clue we had in favor of this meeting. If you could stop sniping at us and just tell us what you want, things would be so much easier," Rowan said, taking the reins of the conversation.

Rowan expected the challenge to be met by equal amounts of disdain, but when Kayla turned to look at him, she was just amused.

"You know, Rowan, I almost discounted you. Almost. Even helping you with that puny Epic was, at most, minor entertainment and a long shot. Seeing you now, though . . . well, I didn't think you'd manage to drag this idiot back to a semblance of usefulness, let alone your personal growth."

The first signs of his own temper started to show, if not on Rowan's face, then with the spear he kept by his side at all times. It started to spark with bloodred energy shot through with black strings. "Allow me to repeat myself. Be civil, at least useful, or go away."

Rowan was gritting his teeth by the end of that sentence, so focused on Kayla that his eyes practically looked like they were shining. Or they might actually have been shining, mana slipping out of his control.

"Oh, fine," Kayla scoffed, leaning back in her chair casually. "But first, everyone not engaged to a hero, fucking a hero, or sworn to their service, get out. That means you two." She looked in the direction of Rowan's only two [Knights] who hadn't pledged their allegiance to him.

Kayla's proclamation was met by a brief stunned silence, but to Rowan's eternal surprise, both Tamara and Lucius stood up with no complaint. The Mercenary King's face was frosty, and Tamara looked like a kicked puppy, but they obeyed.

When they were gone, Kayla casually motioned with her hand as an ornate book materialized above her palm, floating in all its ominous glory. A pulse of magic rolled out from the book, phasing through everything in the tent and marking it.

Thousands upon thousands of ridiculously small runes formed up everywhere in a display that took Rowan's breath away. Most of the physical classes in the room immediately tensed and went for their weapons, then paused when the casters didn't seem concerned, just awed.

"There, no chance of anyone spying on us now. So, my master, or former master, I guess, and the Barbie doll's father"—Kayla motioned casually at the princess—"are coming here to kill us."

That particular statement went over about as well as a brick could gently go through a window. Especially when said Barbie doll paled, wobbled on her feet, and collapsed back into Blake's chest. The uproar of noise, questions, and curses did nothing to ruin Kayla's sly smile.

If anything, she looked incredibly smug as two high nobles, the other two members of Blake's party, tore into her for answers. Marcus just stared at her blandly; his sister was freaking out and fumbling with her own grimoire, and Olivia established a death grip on Rowan's arm.

The two male heroes went through a full hard-reboot process themselves, but even then, it didn't seem like they'd taken the news anywhere near as hard as the rest of the room.

Suspicions or not, hearing that the person who was the ultimate authority of the kingdom was gunning for them was a whole new thing.

Rowan closed his eyes to block out the twinkling eyes of the mage hero that were still fixed on his own, took a deep breath, and brought the butt of his spear down on the carpet, hard.

The motion shouldn't have achieved much. However, intent and mana did odd things at the best of times, so the mini explosion that followed did more than enough to quiet the room and draw attention to Rowan.

He didn't even ruin the carpet—as long as the scorched spot didn't count!

"How do you know about this? How long do we have, and why does the king want to sabotage his own heroes so gods-damned badly?" Rowan was growling there at the end, but he didn't overly care.

He'd done his very best to perform the duty they'd *kidnapped* him for, and now he was finding out, pretty decisively if Kayla's expression was anything to go by, that they most definitely *wanted him dead. Before* he could do the thing!

"Okay, let me handle that in order of importance!" Kayla chirped, leaning forward like she was confiding a secret in the middle of a schoolyard instead of giving out state-level secrets. "We have about two or three hours before they get here. It would have taken them days to organize and track us down if my master wasn't involved. As things stand, that's all we're getting now. Second, do you remember the god whose blessing I received? Do you really think that someone blessed by the *goddess of secrets* couldn't figure out when someone's *keeping a secret* that could cost them their life?"

Kayla's voice was, if anything, even more amused. There was a note of danger there, too, but Rowan didn't blame her for feeling highly uncharitable toward people plotting her murder.

"Finally, as to the reason why, that would be power. Lots and lots of power. Oh, and fear of heroes, I guess. There's also that," Kayla said, her smile growing.

"Power and fear," Blake spat. "I suppose I can understand power. Killing a high-tier individual provides plenty of experience, and heroes are supposed to be special. Why in the world would they fear us? Fear *me*? I've done everything they wanted! *Everything!*"

Rowan winced, grateful for the wards once more.

"Well, you did, for a while," the Heroine of Secrets drawled, shooting Blake a lazy wink. "You played a nice little paladin, jumped on every order, and did everything they wanted. Then you argued for Rowan's sake, tried to stay in the capital because your goddess wanted you to, lost your army, and teamed up with Rowan. That's as good as mutiny against the king."

"You're telling me he wants me dead for just having basic free will?" Blake asked emptily, looking through Kayla rather than at her.

"Exactly, now you're getting it! The thing you two don't understand is that *heroes are a big deal.* Now, obviously, they've done everything they could to truncate our power and reduce us to useless puppets that would, hopefully, die in a mutual-destruction move against the demon king, but we're not a good example of what heroes can be."

"Explain." Interestingly, it was Olivia that made the demand, shooting Rowan an alarmed look.

If he didn't know her any better, Rowan would have assumed that his fiancée was scared of him. Instead, he could tell that the panic came from the fact that she was terrified her family had somehow messed up when providing him with support. That they'd somehow ruined his potential.

"Blake's the best example. With that Heart Card of his, and oh, man, am I *jealous*, he could have qualified for a half dozen unique and dangerous classes with minimal effort. Minimal. Effort. The only thing he wasn't supposed to do was select a base starting class. And that's what the king made him do! Then they paraded him around dungeons and power-leveled the holy shit out of him, pardon my pun."

"They were trying to help . . ." the princess protested weakly, but the wretched expression on her face spoke enough on its own.

"Ha! Sure, 'help.' Anyway, that ended with him getting folded the first time he went up against a demon at his own tier. I mean, seriously, Blake? Pathetic. Now, there does seem to be something different about you *now*, and I have it on good authority that you somehow 'fixed' yourself, but no clue what that means yet."

"And that information wouldn't happen to come from a certain mage with a dubiously dangerous build, would it?" Rowan snapped, crossing his arms.

The dazzling grin he got in return was infuriating. "Come on, now, Rowan, don't be a grump. They tried the same shit with me. All the leveling and class picks into the *least* optimal build, and teaching me only a pathetic few spells that mostly relied on parallel casting with a whole contingent of mages to work. Powerful and flashy, but useless without support."

"And I suppose you somehow overcame that on your own?" Marcus was the one who asked, looking like he was immensely enjoying all the drama.

"Oh, I couldn't possibly comment on that!" Kayla laughed. "Anyway, that leaves us with Rowan. While they at least pretended to give us levels and amazingly powerful cards, they didn't even bother with such things for you. They publicly offloaded you on the lowest-ranked noble in the kingdom, and one who had their family ruined just recently. You got practically *no* support, past some advice and training, which didn't even come with hero-unique class paths or secrets!"

Olivia looked vaguely ill, prompting Rowan to draw her closer and glare at Kayla. "I did just fine on my own, thanks."

"And that's the thing! You *did*! Like the first few generations of heroes, you made your own way, got your own cards and experience, and managed to make it all the way up to Epic. Then, you picked the class that could let you level up to Legendary way faster than expected. Oh, they *freaked out* over that!" Kayla was entirely too cheerful for all this. The laughter didn't do much to lift anyone's mood, but Kayla obviously wasn't done once she caught her breath. "If that wasn't enough, you turned around, took over that stupid border city, and actually made it work for you. Before rescuing Blake and earning his loyalty, of course."

"He's my friend. There's no need for loyalty—we were always going to help each other!"

"Were you? Were you, *really*? While you were freaking out over what his goddess and king were doing to him and the way he was acting?" Kayla scoffed, then shook her head in exasperation. "Frankly, you got ridiculously lucky. If it weren't for Blake's little accident, he probably would have fought you at the mere suggestion from his king or goddess. Really, it probably wouldn't have taken much, would it, Blake? Did it feel nice to be brainwashed? Did it feel like you were doing something useful with your life?"

"I—" Blake clearly wanted to protest, but the paleness of his face and thin sheen of sweat all suggested Rowan's best friend was about to have a panic attack.

"That, all compounded along with the general distrust and fear they had of heroes from the start. Turns out, historically, when you kidnap someone and shove them into a war, they don't tend to develop into the most stable of individuals." The saccharine cheeriness of Kayla's voice was revealing a dark undertone.

"We did hear some stories of atrocities heroes of the past committed," Rowan admitted, suddenly uncomfortable with the subject.

"Oh, yes, 'atrocities' is right. The power you need to accumulate to kill a demon king isn't a small thing. Heroes would war, suffer, and then find themselves unable to cope. Most went back to their worlds to chase after normalcy. Some, though, end up so warped they don't want to or don't feel like they can leave. Those *almost always* cause widespread devastation."

"There's not that many stories," the princess protested weakly again. "My father wouldn't only use those to make a decision. You can trust him."

For the first time, Rowan noticed how woodenly she was talking. She didn't exactly have a vacant look in her eyes, but it was like someone, or something, was forcing the words out of her mouth.

"I was wondering, you know," Kayla said conversationally, rounding on the girl. "But now that I see you up close, yep, I'm certain. He really *did* curse his own daughter, didn't he? Huh. Or he had you cursed, I guess. Cursing isn't exactly something a king does personally."

"I am not cursed, and I am not saying any of this against my own will." The princess's voice went even more bland, and Rowan fought down the urge to interrupt what was going on. Blake had no such compunctions as he spun the princess around, taking her in with terrified eyes.

"He cursed you? Is that why you joined my party? Is that why . . . I mean, our . . . That night before we left . . ." Blake was stumbling over his own words, looking more pale by the second.

Thankfully, his fiancée cut him off by diving into his embrace, squeezing her arms around him. "No. No, that's me. That choice was all *me*," she whispered, this time with actual emotion in her voice.

Blake slumped in relief, but he didn't really look any happier.

Rowan struggled to say something that would get their discussion back on track. "So, he was worried we'd get strong and then go off the rails?"

"Not just that, no . . ." Kayla muttered, looking distracted. It took her a minute to tear her eyes away from Blake, and Rowan would swear he saw pain and a flash of regret on Kayla's face before the unbearable smugness made its return.

"What else is there, then?"

"Well, yes, he was worried we'd try to go all social progress on him over slaves, working conditions, treatment of lower classes, and stuff like that. You know, just typical hero stuff. Or that we'd just go insane and become tyrants. But he also wants more power and to secure the future of his kingdom, and if I have it right, that's the bigger thing."

"Can someone finally stop dancing around the issue and finally tell me why killing us is such a big deal?" Rowan snapped, rather angrily.

"Because under the right conditions, with a hero card in hand, you can ascend to godhood."

*And isn't that one hell of a proclamation to make with a ridiculously calm expression?* Rowan thought bitterly.

"Don't look at me like that—it's obvious nothing less would make a king inclined to take stupid risks before the demons are gone. Those things have Legendary cards, you know?"

"I know," Rowan snapped on instinct, then shook his head. "How?"

"Best I can tell, and my theory's been backed up by recent events, we don't have access to our full hero-card effects. You noticed that in addition to the purple glow, our cards have golden rays of light around them?"

Nods came from both heroes, making Kayla grin.

"Well, that's a sign of Divine tier. My best guess is because we were summoned here by gods, they can't prevent a piece of their divinity from sticking to us. What they can do, however, is lock it away behind requirements. Ridiculous requirements. I'm still on four out of eight, even though there's only the final Legendary demon and the demon king himself left to kill."

"Really? I'm only at three out of eight," Blake muttered, confused.

"Well, then it seems like you need to catch up, lover boy."

It was only Rowan's extremely heightened body awareness and control that let him prevent any outward signs of his surprise. Somehow, at five out of eight, he was ahead of his two peers.

Eyes turned toward him, obviously expecting his own progress report. "Four of eight, as well."

The words were delivered flawlessly, but he still caught the shadow of a frown on Kayla's face. He was really starting to hate the whole goddess-of-secrets-blessing thing.

"So, what do you suppose happens when you hit all the requirements?" Milena asked, pure curiosity on her face.

"Well, the way I see it, our Heart Cards probably turn Divine." Kayla shrugged, making a shudder pass through everyone in the tent.

A Divine Heart Card. The ability to pass right through the tiers. All of them. Until, finally, you were made a true god yourself.

The sheer idea boggled Rowan's mind. Although . . .

"Wouldn't that be useless?" De Vort's question cut through the awkward mood, focusing everyone's attention on her. "I mean, what kind of ridiculous stuff would you need to do to get enough experience to hit Divine? Demonic invasions don't happen every day. You'd die of old age long before getting enough experience."

A hiss left Rowan's lips, and several other details finally fell into place. "Unless demons are always around and trying to invade. Unless you let them stick around until you're done grinding. Waiting before you kill the demon king."

Kayla's grin was as good as a declaration that Rowan was right. "That's how I see it, too. Demons have a tendency to grow quickly—ridiculously fast. Research says they're strong from the start, actually. It's only crossing over into our world that cripples them temporarily. The more they hang out here and the more people they kill, the more they get back their original abilities."

"A whole lot of Legendary enemies, served up to whoever wants to take the risk." Blake wrapped up the conversation, looking as disgusted as everyone else.

"Well, that. Or these idiots get our Heart Cards and then muck everything up by getting killed and demons swarm everything until dragons or other Divines wipe them out." Kayla shrugged, looking unconcerned. "It's happened before."

Rowan took a deep, calming breath. What Kayla was saying was fascinating. It was fascinating and terrifying and he didn't want to think about it. However, they had bigger things to worry about.

"Is everyone forgetting that a king is coming to kill us?" Rowan asked in exasperation, and judging by the reaction of everyone but Kayla, they really had forgotten. "What do we do?"

"Well, obviously, I have a few ideas . . ." Kayla's smile had lots of teeth, and for the first time, Rowan felt relieved she'd chosen to reach out.

Rowan was carefully monitoring his bond with Lucius, and the man's anxiety had been climbing ever higher since the meeting started.

At first, it was tinged with hope. However, the longer no one showed up to talk with him, the more the hope died. And then, finally, it winked out in a whirlwind of anguish and resignation.

Just in time for a massive magic circle to light up in the middle of the Mercenary King's section of the camp.

There were shouts, confusion, and even fear raging outside the tent. Interestingly enough, the emotions seemed to be prevalent even among Lucius's own troops, at least from what everyone could see in the scrying glass provided by Kayla.

Then the light of the circle reached a crescendo, and three figures formed out of the light of mana at the center of the ritual.

A grouchy tower master Kayla once answered to.

A warrior in gleaming armor that made Blake draw in a startled breath.

And the king himself, dressed for war and with blood staining parts of his armor.

On a second look, Rowan realized that all three of them showed some signs of combat. Kayla was right, then, when she suggested that the king was likely the one responsible for the death of the final Legendary demon so he could boost the power of his assistants.

That most likely left them with three Legendary-tier humans about to try and kill them all.

The king finished forming out of light, then looked around himself curiously. His eyes alighted on Lucius, but before he could speak, a man confidently stepped forward.

"Greetings, Your Majesty. If it would please you, my lord, Hero Rowan, has invited you to join them at the meeting." Bron looked confident. In control. Rowan assumed that the man was anything but, judging by the near meltdown when he first heard that he would be put in charge of greeting the king.

In spite of that, he'd done an admirable job.

Admirable enough for the king to shoot him an indulgent smile, shake his head in exasperation, and then motion the scout to lead the way.

Things were official. They were about to meet the man set on murdering them.

CHAPTER EIGHTEEN

# The Goal

The king sat in the chair he was offered, wry amusement still dancing in his eyes. This wasn't the man Rowan had met in the throne room, back when he was first summoned to his new and dangerous world.

That man had been stern, focused, the kingdom personified, and cast out of granite.

This man was relaxed, irreverent, and full of easy self-confidence that filled a room and kept it on edge. Not because the person emanating it was obviously dangerous or threatening, but because he demanded attention. Because it felt natural to hang on to his every gesture, just in the hopes of fulfilling whatever need he might indicate.

Likewise, the man before him did not keep his power carefully leashed and ready to uncoil. It was spooling around him, like a well-worn, supremely comfortable cloak.

This was a man unwinding at the end of a long day filled with nothing but stress and anxiety.

Or rather, a king unwinding after he cornered the pesky little heroes that were causing trouble in his domain so he could slaughter them all and open up his path toward divinity.

"I have to say, out of everything I expected, it wasn't this," the man mused, letting his eyes roam over the assembled hero parties. They paused longer on his daughter, pale, shivering, and ready to pass out, but he didn't make any special note of her. "How curious. How did you know I was coming?"

"Please, like you were very subtle about what you were planning to do," Kayla said, dismissing the king.

In spite of that, Rowan felt a very, very faint pulse of fear from the woman. He licked his lips, trying his best to ignore both the newly formed bond and the feedback he was getting.

It did, however, reassure him that Kayla apparently had no way of stonewalling him completely, unlike Blake.

The other hero was still acting off, even if the revelations about the princess and her immediate reassurance that she hadn't been forced into their relationship had done wonders to bring more life to his features.

"I do believe I was, yes. Why, even the man who betrayed me and refused to follow my plans did not share the details of them with his new ward. Isn't that so, Rowan?"

The king's eyes found Rowan, and the hero froze despite his best efforts. There was a vague orange glow in the other man's eyes. A glow that made it feel like he was seeing right through the hero and into the depths of his heart, judging, piercing, searching for personal faults.

"My father? My father knew about this?" Olivia demanded, her voice more outraged than Rowan had ever heard it. Even the sudden attention of the king was not enough to make the alchemist back down. "He would have said something. Done something."

"And he did!" The king laughed, light and airy and frustratingly pleasant. "He took the hero he could, didn't he? As for doing more, no, I don't imagine he *could*. Not with the limits placed on him upon his refusal."

Rowan's mind spun back to all the conversations he'd had with the baron. All the veiled references. All the refusals to pursue certain topics. His face twisted as he realized how much he'd pushed the man for certain answers he simply could not give.

It was only after the group had gleaned or earned information elsewhere that the baron was really willing to discuss things and get involved, and even then, to a very limited extent.

"You cast our family low just because he didn't want to help you kill heroes? You promoted her family because they accepted?" Olivia pointed at the Treagon accusingly, making the girl shrink in on herself, eyes wide and shocked.

"Correct." King Harold sighed, shaking his head. "Your father was my best friend. My loyal duke. The one I knew I could count on to support me. To suddenly be betrayed like that . . . It wasn't easy."

Olivia's face twisted into something dark and ugly, but it surprisingly wasn't she who lashed out.

"Betrayal? Refusing to toy with the fate of the kingdom is not betrayal. The goal of all this—is it really worth risking so many? Sacrificing so many?" Blake growled out, eyes glowing with divine light.

For once, Rowan knew his friend wasn't being influenced. He knew that the anger and the vitriol were genuine. Especially since not a whisper of emotion passed through their link.

"You do not know what you're talking about, boy," the king snapped, straightening for a second as his presence filled the room, threatening to crush everyone. Then, with a sigh, he settled back down and the aggression bled out of him.

"Then enlighten us. Why do all this? Why not just help us and send us away? You could have manipulated us into leaving. *Forced* us into leaving. Don't say you couldn't," Rowan insisted, eyes fixed on the king.

"You are right. I could have. However, where would that leave us? Rebuilding a damaged army, trying to patch up the frontier, rushing to prepare for the future invasion before time runs out . . . No, that is no way to live. No way to guide a kingdom." The king's voice was impassioned.

*He looks crazy—look at that determination. What kind of Heart Card makes a man this deluded?*

"And this will fix it? It will make all that better?" Milena mocked, the beast folk's gaze narrowed and suspicious.

"You have no right to accuse me of anything, northerner." The king's voice went flat as he turned to Milena. "Your people hide away, safe from all major conflicts. When's the last time your armies bled against demons? When were your numbers last decimated?"

"Before or after the most recent conflict with humans?" Milena mused, making the king's face twist in displeasure. "We bleed when our neighbors say we must. Your plight isn't unique. If you weren't fighting demons, you'd be fighting each other. The tribes have seen it. Our history goes back farther than you're making it out to."

When he spoke next, the king's voice was decidedly smug. "Oh, that will stop, too, I assure you. When we grow far enough from the slaughter of demons, we will snuff them out. Who will be left to challenge us then? The other kingdoms? Our so-called neighbors, who refuse to send armies, supplies, or any form of assistance? Those circling to devour the carcass of my kingdom?"

The man paused, taking a deep breath. "No. Things end here. With you. You will die, and the cycle will go with you. With the kind of power we will wield, with that kind of lifespan, heroes won't matter. Other gods won't matter. They're stuck in their heavens, only able to watch! They can't do a thing."

The surety of the man was startling enough to make Rowan almost believe the nonsense he was spouting. If he hadn't seen the way commoners were treated, the way the kingdom was content to sit and let the lower classes suffer, the way the baron was demoted for saying no . . .

Well, he might have believed it.

"And who's going to join you in your ascent, hmm?" Kayla mocked, eyes drifting between the trio. "Three heroes, three cards, three potential chances to earn apotheosis. My master and the head of your knights will become divinities, too?"

The expressions of the people named were something between avarice and caution. Their glances at the king, full of fear and anxiety, were also rather telling. His silence was, too.

The king finally turned to regard the heroine in a way that reminded Rowan of a rather unpleasant-looking animal sizing up prey. Before he could respond, Kayla twisted the knife. "Or are you going to keep them stuck at the Legendary tier and take all the power for yourself?"

"You were amusing." The man sighed, like he was genuinely sorry. "And then you started spouting venom. Truly, I hoped that you would die during your test at the start of our acquaintance. That goddess of yours . . . so very troublesome. More so than the patrons of your friends, even."

"You do know you will be antagonizing the gods, too?" Blake asked conversationally, but the king laughed.

"I do indeed. Nothing for you to worry about, however. It's time for you to die, I'm afraid." The man reached for his sword, and Rowan tensed.

Then the dome of darkness sprang up around them, cutting off the outside world.

It was time to see if their plan would actually work.

Lucius had done as he was ordered.

He'd tagged along with the heroes, an artifact capable of transmitting his location in hand the entire time. He'd triggered the artifact the second he knew that the third hero was planning to join up with the rest, and then again when she finally arrived. Finally, he'd organized the few men he knew he could trust with his life to set up the ritual circle.

All the while hoping, praying to whatever deity was out there and willing to hear him out, that Rowan had caught on. That the hero had used their link to full advantage and accepted his presence in the expedition solely as a means of monitoring and catching the Mercenary King in the act.

Then the summoning started, his emotions reached a crescendo, and the heroes did nothing at all to stop him.

Lucius's hands were shaking at that point, almost to the point of uselessness.

The emotions that built up in his chest were too much.

He'd finally met someone he believed he could trust. Someone he saw as worthy of following one day. A young, earnest hero, looking to make a difference in the world. And his contracts completely prevented him from providing any aid, instead driving him to harm the man.

There was nothing to be done about it. No way to alter the contracts, to step out on his own. He'd knowingly signed away his free will, all to spare the people who followed him from a swift execution for the cheek of him accepting a class like [Mercenary King].

An affront to nobility.

So, as the king patted his shoulder and instructed him to round up the hero's troops and bring them to heel, as Lucius's body started shaking even harder, there was nothing he could do.

He could only shout out orders for his men, grasp hold of his sword, and start heading out of his camp.

"Going somewhere, at this time of day?" Tamara's voice was silky and smooth, and one of the sounds he loathed most in the world.

"Tamara." The name was a mangled snarl, more than making his feelings on the subject clear. Lucius was in no mood for small talk. "I suppose you won't come quietly, will you? And that you somehow know? No matter, this will be the *one* kill I'll actually enjoy today."

Lucius took a deep breath to shed all the stress and tremors, grasped the hilt of his sword as he reached for his shield, pulled it out, and took a stance, right there in the middle of the camp. Or he tried to.

Instead, the Mercenary King watched with wide eyes as the blade slipped past numb fingers that were barely twitching even when he tried to close his fist. "What is this?" was what the large man meant to say, but the sounds that came out of his mouth were garbled white noise.

"Really. Did you think my lady wouldn't know? That a mage of her talent and caliber wouldn't account for you in her plans?" The deranged mage laughed, loud and shrill, as she let her levitation magic drop.

Lucius was locked in place, every muscle quivering in an attempt to do *something* as the woman drew near. She raised her arm slowly with a taunting smile on her face, taking her time and safe in the knowledge that he was helpless.

His soldiers around them were starting to stir, to whisper and protest what was happening, but none of them dared step forward. None of them were, rightly, crazy enough to charge an Epic-tier mage confident enough to stroll through their camp and apparently capable of immobilizing their leader.

"No, you big dumb lump of muscles, my lady is much greater than that. She is the beacon of truth, the gift of our goddess, the purveyor of secrets that slip past any set of lips. She is the one who is going to guide us back to the greatness we deserve and destroy those fools in their towers," Tamara said.

Fanaticism. Plain, rabid fanaticism. Even when control of his body had been snatched from him, Lucius hadn't been afraid. After all, that meant that he couldn't follow orders. Couldn't make things a bit easier for the king.

Now, though, Lucius was afraid.

As figures in cowls stepped out of seemingly nowhere, emerging from all around the main tent, then thrust their hands up into the sky, heralding the appearance of a dark, churning dome, that fear only grew.

He'd heard stories, of course. Stories about cultists that served the goddess of secrets alongside her priests, willing to throw all semblance of true life away to become one of her Secrets. An order with stealth abilities so profound they bordered on divine. Or heretical, depending on who you asked.

The fact that he'd never once associated any of the events in Rest's Remorse with them galled him, especially when all the unexplained things that happened over the years began to float to the top of his mind.

Of course, this also brought along a certain symbol that had recently been retrieved within the city. An eye, rays of sunlight that formed lashes, and a crown hovering at the top.

A symbol and insignia, which, now that he thought about things, bore a striking resemblance to another.

An eye behind a veil, with two hands coming up to cover the eye, yet still leaving enough space to peek through. The symbol of the goddess of secrets.

The Mercenary King tried to gurgle out a question, or perhaps a plea, eyes flicking to the tent and the heroes that he knew were within it, heroes he couldn't even see with the barrier in the way.

"Don't worry, Lucius. We won't hurt you, or your people. The troublemakers are already being dealt with. Nonlethally, of course! So, why don't you take a little nap?"

The Mercenary King couldn't utter a single word as the world narrowed to a single pinprick of light, then winked out completely.

Once again, Rowan was immensely grateful for his enhanced stats. Even with the difference in tiers, they let him process in a fraction of a second all the different reactions of the king as the barrier went up around them.

Amusement, incredulity, then anger. "What is this? This is impossible! The only ones who could—"

The man's tirade was cut short when a dagger whipped past his head. The blade was angled to the right and then swiftly drawn over his throat.

Wet gurgles escaped the king as blood erupted from the wound in unnatural amounts, soaking the table and the entire front of the man's armor.

The tower master and head knight reacted instantly, spell and blade drawn and readied in a fraction of a second.

Neither could do much when the man who attacked their king seemingly phased out of existence.

"Find him!" the king's knight snapped, closing the distance to his king and reaching out to try and steady him somehow. "He can't have—"

The man reappeared, or rather, came into focus, slotting into reality like he'd always been there and Rowan's eyes were simply refusing to process his presence. His dagger whipped forward once again, but before it could do much, a gauntlet gripped his wrist and squeezed.

The assassin gasped in shock or pain, Rowan couldn't tell, before the former won out when he looked down into the angry eyes of the half-kneeling king.

The king wrenched him forward and drove a fist into his stomach, doubling the assassin over and giving the tower master and head knight enough time to strike.

Except a moment later they were blinking in confusion, attacks ready yet incapable of even remembering who their target was. The king seemed to have the same issue, frowning as he loosened the fingers grasping at empty air, then howled in pain as another shower of blood bathed the room, this time from the dagger dug deep into the side of his neck, right into an artery.

The assassin faded away and dodged the strike entirely, but Rowan wasn't feeling particularly good about their situation, because the king was still moving like he'd never been hurt to begin with.

Rowan couldn't even catch sight of his wound healing. One second it was there, spurting blood. The next it was gone, sealed over, and the only sign of it left was the scarlet liquid all over the place.

Another eruption of blood. Another snarl of pain. Mounting panic on the faces of the kingdom's representatives. All these things were details Rowan was extremely grateful his stats let him catch.

So, he couldn't have missed it if he'd tried when vicious desperation entered the eyes of Amanda's father.

"Filthy infiltrators. You think you can slip into *my* kingdom from that bitch's lands? That you can toy with *me*?" The king was snarling, frothy red liquid spilling between his lips from all the wounds he was taking. "I know who brought you here."

The heroes and their retinue had backed off toward the opposite side of the tent, setting up as many barriers and precautions against retaliation as they could. A decent number of the wards were preset, too, boosted by as much mana as they could put into them.

They should have been enough.

However, things were hardly going to plan.

Kayla had strutted in, promised to turn an ambush into a counter, and introduced a Legendary assassin from her goddess's order. One whose skills and poison would be enough to instantly take out the king at the very start of combat.

The rest of the process was supposed to be a simple mop-up of a panicked mage and a distraught knight.

She'd even demanded that Rowan make her his final [Knight], apparently unaware of how the other hero's card worked exactly but knowing that it would provide some kind of security to her.

The same link that now let Rowan know *exactly* how terrified out of her mind the heroine was as she became the sole focus of an enraged, undying king.

Rowan had to admit, he really didn't like it when the shoe was on the other foot.

The king lurched toward Kayla, suddenly having to deal with dozens of wounds that ranged from deadly to crippling as the assassin upped his game. Rowan could even spot sprays of diseased black blood, and whole sections of the king's body that sloughed away, only to be replaced less than a second later with unblemished flesh.

That was to say, the king was making progress, slow and steady, and their assassin was *floundering.*

Freed up by the increased attack speed of the assassin, the tower master and head knight were cutting loose, too. Most of their attacks missed entirely, and some even hit the ruler of their nation, but they didn't seem to care.

Their attention was focused solely on taking out the boogeyman before he could take them out himself.

"Stop the bastard!" It was all Rowan could say to rally the others as he rushed forward, blocking the king's path himself.

The man snarled at the hero, striking out. His arm was hamstrung no less than five times in that one motion, robbing his blow of most of its strength. Even then, when the strike landed on Rowan's spear, it almost drove him to his knees.

Instinctively, even as he stumbled to the side, Rowan lashed out. There were enough holes in the man's armor now that it was harder to find an intact piece of metal, and when the tip of Rowan's spear slipped into the king's skin, Rowan was almost shocked. He had been aiming at the king's heart, and the man hadn't stopped him.

Almost as shocked as the king himself was when the blow to his chest sank deep into his flesh, sending a torrent of blood spinning out of his body and into the hero. He ripped the weapon away, gripping it to stop the weasel from slipping away, then struck.

Rowan couldn't react quickly enough. With the king being dissected by the assassin, his dexterity was enough to let him keep up. However, the second the man's blood washed over his spear and up Rowan's arm, he froze up.

Because the power within it was *intoxicating.*

As Marcus jumped in front of him, taking the blow on his shield, and Blake joined the fray, hacking at the king's arm in an effort to force him to release Rowan, the Stalwart Hero himself could only hear the echo of his card's voice: *more.*

He was ready to oblige.

The battle turned into a whirlwind of chaos, of barely dodged blows and razor-sharp focus. In the middle of that, Rowan and the king looked like they were waging an entirely different battle altogether.

The king was tearing into everyone who dared come close, taking all the punishment that came down on him in return as barely an afterthought and painting the room with more blood than ten elephants should have combined.

Rowan, too, was taking damage. The king was not unskilled enough for the hero to avoid that, but most of the wounds came from taking a blow meant for one of the others or even charging into strikes on purpose just to open up the king to more attacks.

Unlike the king, however, Rowan *wasn't* losing blood.

His card's voracity grew with every wound he inflicted, and as more and more power was sent thrumming through the hero's system, the card's ability to control blood grew.

Ribbons of the stuff were sent splashing out of Rowan's body, only for them to come curling back around, seeping right through his skin again.

And as that happened, Rowan could *feel* the power build. He could *feel* it reaching some kind of threshold, and then . . .

**Perception +1**
**Vitality +1**
**Strength +1**

The notifications started rolling in very slowly, his card yanking the power of the king directly into Rowan's bloodstream.

The man seemed to notice it, too, when his eyes focused briefly on Rowan with burning hate.

With the scream of an animal, the king burst into motion several times faster than before. His sword carved up his enemies faster than the saintess could heal them up, and then he pushed off toward the mages trying to build up their spells.

Straight toward Kayla.

Rowan didn't know why he did what he did next. He didn't know what made him press on the power of his card, making it *burn* through all the power currently stored within his body.

The boost, no matter how wasteful, did let him react.

Rowan practically teleported right in front of the sword set to skewer Kayla, taking the blade right through his heart.

The blow savaged his insides, and even Rowan's regeneration card stuttered briefly before it kicked into gear again.

The blow did not, however, prevent him from retaliating.

Rowan's spear effortlessly punched through the king's chest and right out his back almost at the exact second Rowan took the man's sword, and both fighters froze for just a moment as their eyes locked.

Then the flood of blood burst from the king.

The rule of Rowan's **Scarlet Envy** was simple: The more grievous the damage, the more energy invested into the blow, the more mana fed into the card, the bigger the bleed effect.

And the bleed effect was, on this occasion, *quite* considerable.

The world around Rowan was washed away in the red tide. The power thrumming in the blood, the vivid scarlet color, the smell of copper that was oddly alluring—they all superimposed on each other, captivating the hero and pushing him to drive every dreg of his mana, even as it regenerated, into **Scarlet Envy**.

So he did.

The space around the two became a sphere of churning, roiling blood, where nothing else mattered other than the scarlet liquid.

Rowan's card desired the blood, and he sought to provide.

The king desperately pushed at his own regeneration card, looking to overwhelm the hero's capacity before it was too late.

Rowan couldn't hear, or see, or even perceive anything beyond the blood. Beyond the need to keep it coming, not even the sword that had become encased in his own flesh.

He couldn't see the assassin backing off, then going for the knight first. Couldn't see Kayla, vindictive joy on her face, as she drove the most powerful spell she could manage into her master's back.

He couldn't see the concern on his friends' faces, the panicked shouts, as the expression of sheer power building between the king and the hero drove them back.

He couldn't because he was drowning. Even then, he refused to sink before the king expired first. Mind caught in a daze of focus, the Stalwart Hero stubbornly held on.

## CHAPTER NINETEEN

# Unified Objective

The passing of a legend was a powerful, complicated thing.

The last time, Rowan had been a bit too busy dealing with his own problems to feel anything. This time, Rowan got to feel the full impact even though he was gasping for breath and still reeling from the impacts of his deck.

The second the man's will broke and life drained fully out of the king's body, the world *shuddered.* Something out there was fundamentally altered. Ripped away, forever.

Even with all that the man had cost him, with all that his presence and actions meant for Rowan and his allies, a sense of profound sadness took root in his very soul, made all the worse by the fact that it was *his* hand that had taken the legend's life.

He did not, however, feel even a hint of remorse.

No, the only thing that Rowan could muster was a profound sense of relief when the flow of blood finally stopped sinking into his skin. No longer supported by the voraciousness of his skill, Rowan toppled down on the desiccated corpse, just focusing on trying to breathe.

With the demon, the energy that had come in was torn to shreds, tamed, and then forcefully assimilated. Looking back on the process now, especially with a different point of comparison, Rowan realized that the blood had affected him. He'd very nearly lost his mind, the literal thirst for blood overwhelming him.

With the king, there was no need for such complicated absorption processes. The blood was torn out of the man's body, and its power was shoved right into Rowan's.

Rowan felt bloated. He felt like another drop of blood would send him over some kind of edge he wouldn't recover from.

And then his **Natural Renewal** triggered.

Rowan spasmed, resisting a scream only by the virtue of the fact that his muscles were too stiff to release it. **Scarlet Envy** and **Natural Renewal** were both powerful, essential cards in his deck.

One worked subtly, in the background, always a reliable presence that barely even made itself known. The other was controlling, demanding, and he couldn't miss the impulses it sent at him if he tried.

And now the two were caught in outright war, with his body as the battlefield.

**Scarlet Envy** had earned itself a bounty of blood and power, and it refused to relinquish its prize. **Natural Renewal** saw the power for the poison that it was and fought to purge it through any means necessary.

Both cards reached out at once, laying their claim to the well of power Rowan had sundered from the king's body, and *anything* caught in their game of tug suffered. That anything just so happened to be Rowan's entire soul and body.

And it *was* both—Rowan could feel it.

The physical pain was just one portion of the agony he was suffering. His soul, his deck, pretty much every part of him, was under just as much pressure. Pressure that made it hard for him to think, to focus, to do anything.

Vaguely, Rowan was aware of the voices shouting his name. He might have even felt a hint of the hands gripping him, turning him onto his side. And, vaguely, he heard angry words exchanged about blood and choking and potions and danger.

None of that mattered to him.

Then the words popped up in front of him.

**Error!**

**Safety margins exceeded!**

**Card use exceeds intended parameters!**

**Querying database for past precedence on direct intervention . . .**

**Divine influence detected!**

**Loading solution . . .**

Briefly, Rowan felt relief. Letters formed around the presence of the two cards, and they faltered. Hope sprang forth.

Then Rowan's Heart Card erupted into a halo of purple-golden light, and the pain surged back even more intensely.

**Divine influence detected!**
**Cards limiters failed!**

For a moment, Rowan's world was nothing but pain. The power inside him pulsed, struggling to both worm its way into his body and to surge out of his body as orange-colored vapor.

**System intervention failed!**
**Initiating contact with administrator . . .**
**Attempt failed!**
**Loading procedural guidelines . . .**
**Attempt failed!**
**No procedural guidelines found!**
**I Am SORRY, mORTAL.**

If he could have, Rowan would have whimpered. Right there, plain as day, his death sentence was declared.

They had won; they'd done the impossible. They'd made a plan—well, Kayla made a plan—and Rowan was the one who'd stepped in to save the day. They'd all served their part. They'd exceeded expectations. They'd managed to kill people so far above them that they should have been pancaked a couple of hours ago.

And he was going to die just because his card got too greedy.

That, if anything, was finally enough to snap Rowan out of the pain, the suffering, and the fear. Ascribing emotions to his cards was one thing. Clearly, they carried some level of awareness. Some level of agency, too.

However, it was ultimately he who decided to fully engage the card. He who had clung to every scrap of power he could so he'd hold out until the moment when Harold finally drew his last breath. He wasn't about to foist responsibility for that on anyone, least of all the card that had saved his life.

Of course, with that realization also came the one about what he had to do.

Trying to separate himself from what his entire being was going through was impossible. So, Rowan didn't. He embraced the pain, both of his body and his soul, and he dived right into it.

Right into the conflict that drove his cards to clash and rend his body apart to begin with.

Rowan had never tried such a thing before. Never felt his cards quite as closely as he did at that particular moment. His perception went past the illusion of cards, straight to the bundle of energy that made them up.

Energy trapped, leashed, and bound around the tiniest fragment of soul stuff, just enough of it to be more than a simple object, just enough for the card to continue performing a skill it once knew in life.

Rowan reached out for his two struggling cards, and then, like he would do to children, sternly asked them to play nice, please and thank you.

To the Stalwart Hero's shock, it *worked.*

The two tearing him apart paused, glared at one another, and started working together.

**Error!**
**Card balance achieved!**
**Loading prior solution . . .**

Things jolted, then started flowing together even more smoothly. **Natural Renewal** pushed the energy toward Rowan's soul, and **Scarlet Envy** happily gobbled it up, integrating it there.

The orange energy made Rowan's soul swell as it was concentrated there, but some massive presence, far beyond *anything* Rowan had ever felt, divinity included, reached out and poked the core of his being.

The nudge was slight, but it sent countless ripples over the sphere of Rowan's soul, ripples that made integrating the orange energy ridiculously easy. Rowan wasn't sure how long that continued. He watched, transfixed, until that vast presence gently pulled away.

He did know, however, that he was *tired.* Beyond tired, really.

With one final weary sigh, his whole being basking in a sense of relief, the Stalwart Hero passed out.

Consciousness came back to Rowan in very slow increments.

The first thing that he truly felt was the slow, gentle rocking underneath him and some kind of rough cloth that covered his body. It reminded Rowan of the one time he'd used a hammock, or of stepping onto a boat.

That was enough to send a jolt through his consciousness that fought to bring him back to the surface, but it didn't really help speed things along.

The next thing he became aware of was the steady squelching sound from all around him. That threw him for a loop, but when he finally forced his blurry eyes open, they landed on a pair of boots that were steadily making their way through mud.

Marching. He was in the middle of a marching army.

That was plenty reassuring on its own. If they still had an army that could march, then it was likely that the rest of their plan, past the disastrous beginning of it, had gone well enough.

Rowan tried to call out, but even opening his mouth made him aware of how dry and cracked it felt, sending him into a coughing fit that immediately provoked shouting and calls for help.

Then a familiar pair of hands was there, cupping his face and forcing him to look up. He gazed lovingly into his fiancée's eyes, at least until she proceeded to stuff a potion bottle into his mouth.

Rowan's first instinctive reaction was to gag and try to get away, but the second the sweet liquid touched his tongue, he could think of nothing but getting more of it into his system. He drank deeply, refusing to even come up for air until the entire bottle was gone, then mumbled a request for more.

Olivia obliged him the first time, but bopped his nose when he asked for more still. "That's a *potion*, you dummy." Her voice was relieved, but fragile. "It's meant to help your body replenish missing nutrients and liquids. That one packed an equivalent to eating five feasts and chugging gallons of water, all in a single bottle. And you've already had two."

Rowan grumbled, but grabbed her hand and collapsed onto his back, relieved and breathing easier. The feeling of having a desert in his mouth had fled as well, leaving him feeling fatigued and oddly wrung out, but fine enough.

It was only then that he realized how much his card had spoiled him. Somehow, over the course of just several months, he'd gotten used to the feeling of perfect health. Especially since his acquisition of **Natural Renewal** and the way that card seemed to soothe even the most remote corner of his soul.

The fact that he could even feel as bad as he currently did was vaguely alarming in that sense.

"What happened? Where are we?" Rowan asked softly as he took a second to look around. Other than the vague, withering-jungle look of the wastes, he could not figure out where they'd taken him at all.

It was, however, interesting to note that he was apparently on a stretcher, and that they'd laid him on the ground when he finally started showing signs of being awake.

"Well, after that stunt you pulled with the king, the battle wrapped up rather quickly," Olivia said, shifting slightly so she wasn't kneeling awkwardly next to him. "The other two really weren't much of a threat, not with that Cartian assassin there to assist us."

The woman's expression was still sour, and Rowan was brought back to the moment when Kayla had revealed that she was in contact with the kingdom dedicated to the goddess of secrets. It wasn't pretty, especially the reactions of the nobles in their midst, but then again, that sort of thing was easy to overlook when you had your own king gunning for your head.

"What about the army? Did they manage to stop Lucius from doing whatever that asshole of a king was forcing him into?" The question wasn't as dire as it would have been if there wasn't a sea of soldiers around them, but the fact that they still had an army didn't really tell Rowan how much of said army was left.

"Apparently, their half of the plan went off without a hitch. The poison they slipped to the Mercenary King worked flawlessly, and the dosage was perfect. Actually, he woke up just before you. He's at the head of the army with the rest, helping us march faster and eliminate threats. They should be here soon, actually."

As if that was their cue, the army parted ahead of them, revealing the worried faces of Rowan's friends and allies as they made their way over.

In the lead was Lucius himself, face forlorn and wrinkled with worry. "It is an immense relief that you are finally awake, my lord," the big man whispered, falling to his knees right there in the mud. "You can now impose whatever punishment against me that you please. The only thing I ask is that you spare my troops."

Rowan genuinely didn't know what to say to that for a solid few minutes. The only thing that finally prompted him to speak was the growing tenseness of the kneeling man's shoulders.

"Please stand, Lucius. And I do think I've asked you to call me Rowan before, so you can start *there* with your 'punishment.'" The Stalwart Hero took a deep breath, waiting for Lucius to follow his directions. "Now, as far as I'm concerned, that's the end of that."

"But, my—I mean, Rowan, I—"

A raised hand forestalled further arguments as Rowan slowly struggled to his feet. Olivia protested at first, but she helped him up when she saw that he was serious, and Blake rushed up to do the same, shooting Rowan a relieved smile.

When he was finally up and feeling only slightly woozy, Rowan met the Mercenary King's eyes. "Listen, Lucius, I *know* none of that was your choice. I *know* that you were forced to betray us. You wouldn't have tried to warn us, such as you could, otherwise. So, I refuse to punish a man who was so obviously pained by what others were forcing him to do."

"Well said." Blake beamed, clapping a hand on Rowan's shoulder and earning himself a warning hiss from Olivia.

Lucius himself was silent, but Rowan almost swore that when the big man nodded at him, there were flashes of tears in his eyes.

"Oh, enough with the sappy shit," Kayla crowed, thoroughly ruining the moment with her cocky grin. If he couldn't sense a deep well of envy and discomfort through their link, Rowan would have felt far more upset. "We need to keep going. You do feel good enough for that, right?"

Rowan took a shaky step forward, but when his body cooperated and kept him upright, he nodded. "I'll manage."

"Good. We can talk as we march. We need to wrap this up quickly and take care of the more important problems," Kayla said.

Olivia tensed at the woman's reminder, expression getting guarded. It was enough to make Rowan desperate for context that would make her react like that.

"What actually happened while I was out?"

The more Rowan walked, the more his body shed its sleep, and the better he felt. By the time they made it to the front of the army and called for the march to continue, he felt practically good as new. The only thing that lingered was a vague sense of being stretched a bit too far, deep in his core.

"It's more of what was happening when the king got word of us setting off and launched all his plans at once," Kayla grumbled, her steps growing more aggressive in response to her agitated mood. "There's war. Well, civil war? Or there was supposed to be one."

"I hope you understand that you're making absolutely no sense!" Rowan snapped, the mere idea of what such a thing might mean for the baron making his gut churn.

"Relax, you worrywart. Your precious baron family is just fine. Well, most of them, anyway. I did make some moves to protect your lady love's brother, but you'll understand when I say he wasn't strictly a priority, right?"

Growing frustrated with the woman, Rowan instead turned to Olivia, knowing she'd have grilled Kayla for whatever she was worth at the first sign of trouble coming after her family.

"My brother's stuck in the capital, as you might know. That's where all the danger is. My parents are still in Rest's Remorse, and the king's army was dispatched to first encircle the barony and wait for his orders before either razing it to the ground or extracting my father's surrender. The same thing is happening to all the nobles that refused to follow the king's orders. Surrounded, and waiting for His Royal Majesty to swoop in as a prospective divinity and lay down the new rules," Olivia explained.

"So, they're not in any immediate danger?" Rowan sought to clarify.

"My brother might be. If the king's agents have him. But *she*"—Olivia angrily motioned toward the smug heroine—"assures me that my brother's been in collusion with Cartian agents that have been trying to cause an insurrection for a while, and that they'll protect him. For what good her word is."

"Hey, I'll have you know you're talking to the brand-new duchess of the kingdom of Cartian, Her Holiness the Saintess! My goddess is a big deal over there. They contacted me the first moment I had to myself after being welcomed to this world."

Kayla's words were *dripping* with smugness, and Rowan really didn't like the way satisfaction was radiating off Tamara, who was following a step behind the heroine at all times.

"I see you even have your first loyal follower," Rowan said, eyes set on the exiled mage, who winced but then met his gaze with no remorse.

"Hardly the first. No, that distinction belongs to the deputy tower master of the Rhys kingdom. Turns out, when the whole system is built on the basis of keeping mages under strict management and control, it's easy to undermine an organization. Only the tower master was allowed basic liberties, like, you know, even leveling up to Epic."

Rowan noted, from the corner of his eye, that Blake and his party were looking distinctly uncomfortable. Curiously, the princess looked relatively well. She stood proudly next to Blake and didn't look the slightest bit like someone who'd just watched her father drained into an exsanguinated corpse.

"Guess you're the highest-ranked person around here now. Congratulations." Rowan's voice communicated exactly how indifferent he felt about the topic, but Kayla preened regardless.

At least she did until the princess herself spoke up, sounding just as smug as the heroine. "Actually, she isn't. That honor would go to Blake."

Rowan immediately arched an eyebrow at the other hero, who flushed and looked away.

"Apparently, ah, as Amanda's future husband, I'm second in line to the throne?" Blake asked.

"We'll make you the first." The princess spoke with iron in her voice, eyes flashing dangerously. "My brother may be heir apparent, but he's barely at the Epic tier, and practically nothing in a fight. The kingdom needs a strong ruler to weather what's coming for us. On that subject . . . I'd ask that you check out your rewards from this last battle, please."

The princess was clearly directing her words toward Rowan there at the end, making him furrow his brow in confusion. The rewards, whatever they might be, were party-wide. There was no reason to consult him in particular.

When he shot his party members a questioning look, he was met by wry smiles.

"Look, my friend, we're not going to steal loot that clearly belongs to you. That regeneration card the king had . . . he was going to slaughter all of us, eventually. He wasn't as directly deadly as the assassin, but that guy was already in a bad way with how fragile he was. He had to retreat back to Cartian for treatment post-battle. Whatever you did, it saved all our lives," Marcus explained when no one else did.

Rowan finally dived into his system to check things out. And then promptly froze.

There, just to the right of his class, was a big, fat seventy-eight. Somehow, while he wasn't looking, he'd jumped almost to the very peak of the Epic tier. Two levels were all that separated him from the next level-up and the potential to become a legend himself.

Even as he watched, the experience counter ticked up. It was a negligent amount, just a couple thousand points, which was a drop in the bucket right now, but it was *there.* A quick glance around revealed that every one of his [Knights] was accounted for, and most definitely not in combat.

That left one final option, prompting the Stalwart Hero to dive deep into his deck in search of the **Knight Designation** links.

He didn't think he could have done such a thing before killing the king, but the experience had left Rowan keenly aware of himself and his power. That made it easy to track down all the solid links that made up the connection between himself and his [Knights].

As well as the four weak tethers that connected him to someone else.

*Bron's gambit must have worked,* Rowan thought excitedly, though the emotion dimmed somewhat when he chased those links to their other end.

The hero couldn't explain how he knew, but his instincts, or his card, perhaps, clearly told him that the new second-generation knights did not have the ability to [Knight] others. The explanation came naturally to him: They could only pick cards from Bron's deck, and while he could use it, **Knight Designation** wasn't his.

Rowan moved past the disappointment easily, attention drifting instead to the loot notification blinking in his status window.

The window unfurled, and the two cards that were revealed took Rowan's breath away.

**[Heart] Founding King (Legendary, Passive)**
**You are the parent of a nation, and all shall exalt you for it.**

**Eidolon Body (Legendary, Passive)**
**Your body is the peak of perfection, and it seeks to maintain that balance.**

Rowan's breathing picked up, eyes fully focused on the second card. The reaction of **Natural Renewal** within his deck was visceral. It felt like the epic consciousness of the card was bowing down to its clear superior.

Instantly, Rowan claimed that card, and the rest of his party members denied rolling for it just as quickly.

The Stalwart Hero didn't exactly rip his former lifeline out of his deck, but it was close. The moment he did, a wave of weakness and wariness swept through him. His body, in no uncertain terms, let him know that it was on the verge of breaking.

The only thing that was holding him together was the passive effects of his regeneration card. With it gone, all its work was starting to unravel. Before the Legendary card could react, Rowan gripped it and willed it away into his deck.

And Rowan was whole again.

No, he wasn't whole. He was *better* than whole. Cracking sounds rang out into the jungle around him as his body squirmed, flesh and bones altering themselves, shifting in ways that optimized his build.

Rowan wasn't hideous. Before the fight, he had been in the best shape of his life, complete with a six-pack his self-torture had earned him. He was, however, rough-looking. He was always looming over others, and his squarish frame and features didn't do him any favors. Olivia clearly didn't mind, saying on multiple occasions that she loved him and thought he looked cute.

Now, though, all that was changing.

His features shifted just so, softening in places while sharpening in others. His shoulders were just that tiny bit less door-like and more graceful. His proportions were all still there, yet optimized in a way that, when everything settled, left the surrounding women shooting him appraising glances he'd typically seen directed only toward Blake.

Not that the other hero was in a position to notice. The second Rowan had replaced his old card, change had swept over his [Knights] as well. Not to the extent it did to Rowan, but he could tell that they were *definitely* benefiting from it. Somehow, the system knew that they wanted the new Legendary card to make up for the loss of **Natural Renewal**.

"That was . . . intense." Blake finally breathed out, raising his hands to feel his own face and grimacing lightly.

"And how do you think I feel?" Rowan challenged, only to blink when his voice, too, came out subtly different, more pleasant.

"Boys, boys, you're both pretty," Kayla laughed, but there was an unmistakable smile on her face as she took stock of her own changes.

There was one person who wasn't happy to just sit around and wait, however.

"Is that it?" The princess flushed when all the eyes turned to her. "I mean, I'm sorry, but . . . you didn't get any other cards, maybe?"

Rowan considered her, then finally sighed and summoned the other card. **Founding King** materialized in the air, and the second it did, the princess's eyes were glued to it as she swallowed thickly.

"There's also this one," Rowan said unnecessarily, waving the card just because the way Amanda's whole head tracked the glowing rectangle was amusing. Blake's glare made him stop. "I'm guessing it's important?"

"It's . . . it's the main legacy of the Rhys kingdom. The card that acknowledged its creation. Every royal bloodline has a card like that if they've proven themselves before the system. It's also possible to earn the **Golden-Age King** card, but it's a bit weaker, or at least has a different effect. That one's with my brother."

Rowan stared at the card. Suddenly, just like that, he had something that would let him establish himself as the founder of a royal dynasty.

He didn't like it.

"You want it?" Rowan asked bluntly, offering the card up to Blake, whose eyes bugged out.

"Seriously, mate?" That was the response when the other hero finally managed one. "Just like that?"

Rowan shrugged. "It's a single card. *Maybe* I could give it to my own kid, but then what would I give to the rest of them? I want my kids to have siblings they don't have to go to war with over authority. Your fiancée clearly wants this card, though."

Olivia had flushed a scarlet red, but her eyes softened when Rowan explained his reasoning, doubly confirmed by the way she was snuggling up to him all of a sudden.

"Then . . . thanks." Blake let out a sigh, claimed the card, then passed it off to Amanda. The princess hugged it to her chest, looking like she was about to cry.

A stab of avarice and envy made Rowan's eyes shift over to Kayla, but the heroine just shot him a wink. Then she had to ruin the moment.

"Once again, let me be the voice of reason! We're marching on the seat of our enemies, people. Focus up. I know we won't exactly reach our destination any minute now, but still!"

Rowan rolled his eyes, then paused. "Wait, the seat of our enemies? Where the demon king is? But . . . don't we still have one final Legendary demon left?"

The heroine shrugged, looking unconcerned. "Don't know what to tell you. Everything I've learned, both through mundane and divine means, shows the two are together. Blake's goddess was pointing us in this direction, too. No one knows why, but it seems the demon king is holding this particular general of his close."

Rowan took a deep breath, then let it out as he gripped Olivia's hand.

Apparently, they were marching straight at the demon king now.

"How fun."

Rowan's voice suggested it would be anything but.

## CHAPTER TWENTY

# Pursuit

Their march toward the final battle of the war between humanity and demons was a hurried, wild thing. The Mercenary King hadn't been hurt during the whole debacle with the king, but he was definitely left with something to prove.

As such, the pace he set was at the limit of what his cards could help the army withstand. Rowan and the other Epic tiers had little trouble, of course. But any lower-level Rare tiers were visibly starting to struggle when the march was finally called to a halt some three days after they'd set out.

Oh, they'd had several rests along the way, but even with that accounted for, the soldiers had only gotten around ten hours of sleep against over sixty hours of marching.

"Are they going to be able to fight tomorrow?" Rowan's voice betrayed his worry as he swept his eyes over the troops they passed on their way to the central tent.

"My cards are perfect for this kind of thing, my lord. Don't you worry one whit about what might happen to them. They'll be ready." Lucius's voice was steel, his eyes flinty enough to catch fire.

The man had almost entirely dropped any kind of casualness. It was only at rare occasions that he slipped up now, seemingly set on truly treating Rowan like nothing less than his sworn lord. It was stifling, even if Rowan was aware of all the benefits of having the man in his debt.

"I trust you, of course. I just . . . worry. This is it. This is everything that we've been working toward. If we can just pull this off . . ." Rowan sighed, dropping his head on his chest as he walked.

He couldn't voice all his doubts, all his fears. Perhaps it wasn't perfect, but he'd managed to get through the obstacles he'd faced so far with relatively few losses. The worst he'd fared was the mansion of the Legendary demon, and there was little he could readily do about dimensional shenanigans. Despite that, those losses stayed with him.

Something also told him that the final Legendary demon and the demon king after them wouldn't be quite as simple to dispatch.

So, as he walked past rows and rows of tents, occupied by soldiers who'd willingly placed their lives in his hands and followed him all the way out to the heart of the frontier, Rowan couldn't help but wonder how many of them he'd be able to bring back home.

They were still a day out from encountering their final challenge, at least according to the nebulous senses of Blake and Kayla, and his confidence was already starting to show cracks.

Olivia could clearly tell, too. She'd spent most of their time glued to his side. She was right there at the moment, too, hugging his arm to her chest in a way that Rowan definitely found a little distracting.

He would have been able to appreciate the moment far more if he wasn't wondering if both of them would survive the battles ahead.

When they finally reached the tent, voices were already echoing from inside it. Rowan easily recognized them as Blake and Kayla, though he didn't like the sharp tones he was picking up.

"And I'm telling you, for the thousandth time, that we can't just throw people at the problem while you blow everything up from the sky!" Blake snapped as Rowan pushed open the curtain, the sound suddenly growing much louder.

"I—" Kayla had a feral snarl twisting her features, and Rowan knew there would be deadly venom on her tongue.

"Really?" the Stalwart Hero cut in resolutely, sending both of them disapproving frowns. "I leave you alone for, what? Twenty minutes? Fifteen? And you're already at each other's throats?"

Rowan would have expected Blake's fiancées to be right there with him, but all three were, surprisingly enough, absent. Tamara was there, but the woman was studiously staring at a corner of the tent and pretending like it was the most fascinating thing in the world, so she was no help whatsoever.

"She started it!" That was Blake's stunningly wise response, and Rowan really wanted to face-palm at how whiny the other hero's voice was.

"And I am, as such things go, ending it. Now, can you two actually explain to me what caused this whole mess to begin with?" Rowan was trying to be patient, he really was. However, the sheer tension between the two reminded him of all the times they chose to break up.

They usually showed up a couple of days later, looking loopy and sporting stupid grins. He was fairly certain that would not be happening this time, though.

Whatever fight they'd had before parting in the kingdom's capital, Rowan could tell that something fundamental had been broken in their relationship. He strongly suspected that Blake's issues and his goddess's influence were a strong reason why, but it wasn't like Kayla didn't have plenty of fun hang-ups herself.

"I've been trying to explain to this idiot here that we should have the army storm whatever defenses we discover at our destination. While the foot soldiers do that, I can prepare a Grand Ritual with Tamara's help. There'll be practically nothing left of our enemies if you can buy us enough time to pull that off," Kayla said, as if it were a perfectly reasonable plan.

"And how many soldiers will die during the wait? How many lives would be lost so you can prove that you're the biggest and baddest mage around?" Blake's voice was scathing, and Rowan could see that it made Kayla's blood pressure soar with incredible ease.

"I'm trying to ensure our victory here, you bloody idiot! If you have issues with doing what's necessary for our victory, then you can shove your sword—"

"Kayla!" Rowan took another deep breath, counting to five. Really, it was his fault. He knew they were a hive of issues and just about as willing to set things aside as a honey badger hopped up on poison, and he'd still tried to make them get along.

"Do you see what I've been dealing with, Rowan?" Blake demanded, crossing his arms. "If she could have her way, we wouldn't even have an army by the time things are through."

Rowan was tempted to snap back, but the entire thing was rubbing him wrong. Instead, he looked his best friend in the eye and posed his question. "What's really bothering you here?"

Blake froze like a deer caught in headlights, while Kayla perked up, smelling blood. The smile she sent the other hero was positively vicious. "I think he's just sore I was right, in spite of what he said to me when we parted the last time."

Blake gritted his teeth, but Rowan noted that he didn't exactly deny the accusation.

"Okay, listen. I've known you both for a while now. I have no idea what happened between you. But! Blake, we both know you weren't entirely yourself up until recently. Likewise, Kayla, you've been kind of . . . well, horrible, to say the least. So, I'm going to walk out of this tent and take Tamara and Olivia with me. We're not going to let anyone inside, but we're also not letting you two out until you sort out your shit!"

That said, Rowan angrily marched out of the tent, glaring at the banished mage until she reluctantly and sheepishly followed.

The next hour or so was admittedly awkward, what with hints of shouting making their way to them in spite of Kayla's magicked-up tent doing a marvelous job of dampening sound. However, when the two heroes finally emerged, they did so looking relieved, and even with faint smiles on their faces.

It was much easier to sort out their plans after that.

About a day later, they were finally close enough to the seat of their enemies for the heroes and their parties to sneak ahead of the army for a quick peek.

The first sight of their enemies was admittedly intimidating. They were situated right in the middle of the remains of some ancient, once-glorious city.

Ruins swept up into the sky, grand homes hinting at former greatness, and a fortress that did a solid job of pretending to be a castle jutted out from the center of it all.

It was the only thing that still stood intact.

Some spots on the walls of the glorious structure were still white, hinting at the marble originally used it in its construction. These spots practically shone with inner radiance, like they were trying to shout their divinity to the world.

Such pieces of the fortress were by far in the minority, however, and confined to its outskirts. They seamlessly connected to some kind of dark material that did the exact opposite, swallowing up every trace of light that landed on it.

There was an odd patchwork quality to the transition between the two materials that made up the structure. It was almost like some giant had come across a ruined city and decided to rebuild the most glorious building it knew in the middle of everything.

Except, for lack of identical material, shiny white marble was replaced with black stone.

Rowan couldn't tell how he knew, but he felt that this was a result of countless decades, millennia of conflict that spilled out and destroyed everything in the vicinity, only for some otherworldly force to swoop in and revert the damage imperfectly.

Perhaps, at the start, there was a lot less black in the fortress's construction. How many times did it have to get destroyed to get to that point? How widespread was the destruction? Were they about to contribute to the last few spots of white disappearing?

Of course, while the fortress was breathtaking, far more important were the troops manning it. The same amphibians that Rowan had fought all the way back at Felton's Mill clambered over the walls, patrolled the ramparts, and manned the gates.

The difference was, these particular specimens were far larger and more menacing. Rowan was willing to bet not a single one was under the Rare tier, and each and every one looked ready and dedicated.

Far above these "basic" troops, wraiths cut across the sky. There was a whole cloud of them releasing ghastly wails into the darkened skies, but four stood out even from where Rowan was watching. Those four, the hero knew, were likely to be in the Epic rank, and far more dangerous than their lesser kin.

Finally, there were the troops that were making Rowan's palms sweaty and his armor stick uncomfortably to his back.

There were dozens of featureless knights, just like the one that had almost ended him before Kayla summarily executed it.

Rowan knew there was little reason for him to fear the monsters. He'd advanced far past the hero he used to be back then. However, there was something about them that screamed danger and despair. Something that made them stand out even in comparison to the wraiths overhead.

As he continued to watch the armored silhouettes haunt the walls of the fortress, he realized what was bothering them.

They weren't acting like monsters. They were acting like *people.* His haphazard count put the number of knights at twenty, and every time they crossed each other's paths, the monsters paused, clearly conversing.

Rowan obviously couldn't tell what they were talking about at such a distance, but their motions were animated, almost cheerful.

The knights were also the only monsters with true individuality. The wraiths looked pretty identical to each other, and while the amphibians did have some characteristics that set them apart from one another, Rowan would struggle to pinpoint which was which if he was unlucky enough to be introduced to them.

The knights didn't have this issue.

Each knight's armor was personalized in a way that showed great care and even greater craftsmanship. Their weapons differed wildly, too, from swords to mallets, flails, and even a spear. These weren't just some mindless mob out to conquer another world. These were *people*, sentient and fully in command of their faculties.

Granted, that only made their sins worse.

"Okay, I've seen enough," Rowan whispered hoarsely, mind spinning. "Let's go back."

The others were similarly silent and worried, so their way back to their temporary camp was hushed and fraught with worry.

"There's so many of them." It was the first thing said in their meeting, and de Vort's worry was echoed on the faces of everyone there.

Just the number of amphibian troops was . . . worrying. Rowan would easily put them at two or three thousand from what he was able to gauge. Adding on top of that the hundreds of wraiths, along with a whole contingent of Epic-tier knights?

Yes, they had reason to worry.

"We can do this." Surprisingly, it was the Mercenary King who spoke up, face set in an expression Rowan entirely didn't like. "As Epic tiers, we'll need to seriously push ourselves, but I can empower the army long enough to give us a real fighting chance. I'll just say it now: I can, at most, last half an hour. After that, it's up to the soldiers themselves."

Rowan gnawed at his lower lip furiously, but he had no choice but to eventually nod. "That'll have to do. Can your mages do something about those wraiths, Kayla?"

At that point, Rowan really didn't even want to bother directing a similar question at Tamara. The woman had spent the entirety of their last march right by Kayla's side, pandering to her every whim, and their bond showed she was ecstatic the entire time. It was plainly obvious who was in charge of the mages.

Kayla took a deep, steadying breath, then nodded, an unusually solemn expression on her face. "Yes. We'll take care of it." Rowan could tell from their bond that the heroine was nowhere as calm and certain as she wanted to appear, but the Stalwart Hero certainly wasn't about to pour cold water on their morale.

"Okay, then. Jacqueline, Amanda, can we count on you two to protect the army as well as you can manage? Marcus, I think, can handle protecting all the Epic classes, right?" The beast folk offered up a nod and a grin, which Rowan returned.

The women exchanged a look and then glanced at Blake worriedly, but they eventually confirmed they would do their best.

"Okay, then, I guess the rest of us are on the offense. Unless you'd like to take up a more defensive post, my dear?" Rowan directed the question at Olivia, but she just shot him a look and rolled her eyes.

He couldn't help the smile that tugged at his lips, giving the tense moment just a touch of brevity as he lost himself in her eyes.

Blake clearing his throat snapped them out of it.

"Right, well, is that our whole plan?" the other hero asked, eyes fixed on Rowan.

The Stalwart Hero simply shrugged. "Not much else we can do, I'm afraid," he admitted, once more savaging his lower lip. If it wasn't for his healing, it would be past tender at that point. "We can only hope things go well."

Everyone nodded and gave their assent, and so their final planning session was sealed.

Rowan was convinced that something would go wrong and they'd be discovered before they were ready. In spite of that, no such thing occurred.

The demonic forces seemed completely content to man their fortress and pay attention to nothing else, even if that something was basic scouting of their surroundings. All that meant the humans were free to properly mass up, get in the right formations, and perform their final equipment checks.

Rowan really didn't want to give any grand speeches, and even briefly *hoped* for an early attack on their position, but as the nominal leader of the army, the job did fall to him.

"I can't know your reason for joining this army," the Stalwart Hero began, sweeping his eyes over his troops from one of Kayla's floating mana platforms. "Some of you likely joined for money, some because of levels, and some because you want to make this world safe for your loved ones.

"I'll say this now: Your initial motivation doesn't matter.

"We are here now, all of us, because we managed to pull off what many didn't think we could do. We are here now because we killed a Legendary demon, overcame the scheming of our own allies, and managed to climb higher up the tiers than anyone expected!

"We are here now because in every battle we faced, every challenge we got, we won!

"Now, it is finally time for the last step. It is time for us to excise the presence of demons from our world and reclaim the peace they stole from us. Today, we are going to make sure that all our loved ones can rest easy knowing they're safe! Are you with me?"

The answering roar was so loud that Rowan *knew* the demonic forces had heard it. It also made his blood roar in his veins, to see these people so readily put their lives in his hands. He flexed his legs, jumped, and slammed down in front of the army like a meteor. Raising his spear high, the Stalwart Hero let his voice echo out over his troops.

"Charge!"

The Mercenary King roared, and then the entire army was *moving*. The man's entire body had swelled up with gold and red mana, making every vein squirm and every muscle bulge. The rest of the soldiers seemed to be in a similar state, their stats suddenly pushed to new heights and their courage unnaturally bolstered.

Rowan saw none of this.

The Stalwart Hero put his words to action, literally tearing up the ground with his steps as he streaked toward the fortress.

The fortress's front gate was closed and looked to be made of extremely solid metal that even modern artillery would struggle against.

Rowan didn't care.

As he picked up speed, pushing his body beyond anything he'd ever done before, he also threw his life force, his mana, and every shred of his health into his spearhead. The tip of his spear resembled a small sun when he finally slammed into the gate head-on, before the defenders could even understand, let alone respond to what was happening.

The explosion was deafening as the entire construction exploded. Metal creaked and warped before it shot upward like the payload of a catapult and decimated the entire wall of the fortress. The gate's arch crumbled, too, rocks and dust raining down on the panting form of the Stalwart Hero.

Rowan was in excruciating pain. His opening move made it trivial for his army to stream into the fortress and bypass most of the issues that came with a siege, but it wasn't without a price.

Every muscle in his body was shredded. Every bone was at least cracked. The only reason he was even standing half slumped against his spear was the sheer force of his regenerating mana keeping him upright.

In the time it took to experience all this pain, *his body was already half-way recovered.*

The Legendary card Rowan had earned from the king's demise was stitching his body back together almost as quickly as it had come apart.

The defenders of the fortress had only just started to scramble and sound an alarm as he shook himself off, cracked his neck, and went in search of some demons.

He was distantly aware of the screaming of his troops as they charged after him, and then the snap of bows as the demonic forces finally managed to rally. He needed to find a way to the top of the wall, but he couldn't spot stairs anywhere.

It took Rowan a second to realize the flaw in his thinking. He blinked and shrugged, then leaned on his stats, *every single one of them*. With one bounce that left a small crater in the ground, he slammed halfway up the wall and pushed again, using the momentum to launch himself the rest of the way up.

Then he was on top of the wall, and his spear found the throat of the nearest archer daring to shoot at his troops.

The battle developed into a whirlwind of pain, worry, and death from there on. No matter how many amphibian soldiers Rowan killed, there was always another one popping up to face him. No matter his ferocity and clear relish as he ripped their fellows apart, the enemy soldiers kept coming.

Rowan could respect that.

It made it easier to kill as many of them as he could manage, seeing as they were delivering themselves to him.

The wraiths were a bit trickier. Several times, one of those would manage to sneak up on him in the chaos of battle. Every time, he would experience water suddenly filling his lungs and his body struggled to move.

The amphibians would rush forward, and the Stalwart Hero's blood would flow like a river, making the ramparts slick and tricky to maneuver.

Unfortunately for them, his stats were far beyond theirs, and no matter the damage, his body refused to shut down. An inner explosion of mana would rip apart the card effect and let him deliver swift retribution against the wraith that dared get in his way, and the soldiers were then mopped up quickly.

He didn't care that such stunts left his body shredded from the inside out, because the damage would always fade within a matter of seconds.

It was only when he heard the alarmed shouts of soldiers and Blake's scream of pain that Rowan was snapped out of his bloodlust, suddenly realizing that he was surrounded by a corona of blood that swirled into him from every direction.

A frantic look around let him spot his fellow hero down in the courtyard of the fortress, surrounded by the entire troop of demonic knights. He was fighting valiantly with Lucius, Olivia, and the Treagon by his side, but they were getting pushed back by the overwhelming number of Epic tiers arrayed against him, and Blake was bleeding from his side.

Blake hadn't quite inherited the improvement to Rowan's card. Blake's link registered the change in Rowan's deck, and the [Knight]'s previous regeneration card was replaced by a slightly superior version, but the Epic-tier card that allowed the link to form struggled to properly replicate the effects of a Legendary.

If Rowan didn't do something, Blake *would* eventually get torn apart.

So, it was a rather good thing that the Stalwart Hero could simply take a running start, leap, and then land right on the back of one of the knights, spear first.

The spear caught the Epic demon right in the back of its throat, and the amount of power Rowan infused into his weapon let it shear right through the thing's armor. Seawater splashed upward, drops falling on Rowan's lips as the hero twisted his weapon and blew apart the knight's head.

He could have, with his allies there, approached the battle carefully. He could have fought with grace and poise and tactics.

Instead, Rowan charged into the midst of the demonic knights like a rabid beast. They rallied relatively quickly, aiming most of their attention at the insane hero so willing to throw himself into the middle of danger, but that only sped up their deaths.

Rowan gave even better than he got, dealing lethal damage in exchange for letting them tear his body apart. Their focus on the undying hero also let the rest of Rowan's allies act, potions and weapons flashing forth to reap the lives of the Epic-tier monsters.

One by one, the empty suits of armor fell, failing to do more than slightly slow down the Stalwart Hero. Their doom was particularly sealed by the regular soldiers, who were constantly swarming out of the fortress, seemingly intent on not letting a single person set foot inside.

Each time Rowan was feeling dizzy from loss of mana, life force, and blood, all he had to do was direct his attention to the amphibian soldiers. They fell easily, feeding him their lifeblood and keeping him in the battle.

When the tide of enemies stemmed and then finally faded to nothing, Rowan was a mess.

His armor and clothing were barely rags, clinging to his skin only because they were caked on there by the copious amounts of dried blood, and the hero was desperately panting for breath. He felt like he couldn't get enough oxygen into his lungs.

On the other hand, he also felt oddly electrified and jittery, like his body was only capable of moving in instinctual spasms.

"You absolute idiot . . . have any idea . . . how worried I was?" Olivia's voice was barely a string of wheezes as the exhausted alchemist stumbled over to him, pale and shivering from mana exhaustion. Heedless of the state Rowan was in, she closed her arms around him and pulled him close.

Rowan let out a shuddering breath as some of the tension left his body.

"How . . ." Rowan's voice cracked, forcing him to cough and wheeze before Olivia forced a waterskin into his hand. He drank greedily and finally refocused. "How did our troops do?"

Olivia went to say something, then clicked her mouth shut and shook her head. "Follow me."

Rowan did.

They stumbled their way past the gate, and the Stalwart Hero let out a hiss of pain and regret when he saw the field outside the fortress. He'd done his best, like Lucius had, but there was little he could do when his troops had to charge across a killing field, and that was before the enemy soldiers had streamed out to meet their own in combat once it was obvious that their tactical advantage was lost.

Bodies littered the ground everywhere Rowan looked, both of monsters and of men.

Suddenly, the Stalwart Hero just felt so very, very tired.

"How many?"

"I don't know," Lucious admitted, shaking his head. "We'll do a count later. We need to head deeper into the fortress. The demon king and his final lieutenant must know we're coming by now. We can't delay."

He was right, but Rowan didn't need to like it. With one final reluctant glance, Rowan headed toward the interior of the fortress . . .

. . . only to be immediately intercepted by Kayla.

"You are not going anywhere looking like that," the heroine snapped angrily, with more than a little disgust on her face.

Rowan went to protest, but the look on Olivia's face stopped him dead. He resigned himself to his fate. At the very least, Kayla knew more than a couple cleaning spells, and it wasn't that hard to get a replacement for his armor.

Apparently, the baroness had packed a replacement and sent it with Olivia, explicitly in case "Rowan did something stupid."

The accusation stung, but not as much as the fact that it was apparently warranted.

With that out of the way, however, they were finally ready to venture deeper into the creepy depths of the dark fortress.

At least finding their way through it was easy. There was a massive main corridor that led directly to its depths, and with all their enemies sacrificing themselves in a frenzy rather than letting them approach the fortress, they faced no opposition.

In fact, their progress was smooth sailing, right up until they ran into a pair of imposing doors. The others hesitated, but Rowan had very little to worry about anymore.

He strode forward, and, finding no door handles, placed his hands directly on the doors, only to freeze.

**Offer blood and enter.**

The system message practically forced itself into his head, and the doors refused to budge no matter how much power he brought to bear.

With a sigh, the Stalwart Hero banged his head against the doors.

CHAPTER TWENTY-ONE

# The Bastion

"I really, *really* hate this," Kayla repeated, for what felt like the millionth time.

The doors were, without a shadow of a doubt, still an issue. It didn't matter what they did. It didn't matter how much power they threw at them, heedless of their own reserves.

They didn't budge.

They stood proud and defiant, and offered the exact same message every time someone touched them.

"Can't just magic up a solution every time, I'm afraid," Blake joked, trying to keep both his voice and expression light. It failed, and not just because he kept sending the doors nervous glances.

"I'm still saying just let me do it," Rowan tossed out, feeling the anxiety and anger practically coursing through his veins.

The mere idea that after all they'd done, they would be ground to a halt by *doors* was just about driving him insane.

As were the attempts to get the bloody things—pun fully intended—open.

They'd pushed. They'd *tried* to pull. They had cast spells on them. They had punched them. Kayla had begged. Olivia had tested potions. Marcus had sung at them, and Milena had drawn on them with chalk just to see if they would react.

Nothing.

The three heroes and their parties were left in the middle of enemy territory, in one spectacularly creepy fortress, with wounded and dead troops aplenty, and no way to progress.

Except, of course, doing just what the doors asked.

*Offer blood and enter* wasn't exactly rocket science, at least as far as Rowan was concerned.

"And let you probably almost kill yourself . . ." Olivia's deadpan voice was tired, but Rowan got the sense that was mostly due to his frankly horrible luck. Just luck. Luck that was in no way shape or form indicative of the hero's recklessness.

Rowan winced before forcing himself to look his fiancée in the eye. "Listen, out of all of us, I'm the only one who has an abundance of blood to spare. If there's anyone who can open these doors safely, it's me."

"Unless, of course, their demands aren't based on volume. Unless they demand the life of the person providing the blood. Unless they at least weaken the person trying to pass to the very limit. Unless *every* person who needs to pass has to offer up their blood," Kayla said.

Rowan sighed, thoroughly frustrated by the fact that Kayla seemed keen on pointing out every possible way the doors' demands could go wrong for him, again and again.

"Yes, yes, unless all of that happens. Listen, do you have any better ideas? Well? I'm listening! Yes, everything you just said can happen. But they could also equally not happen. Is sitting here doing nothing, trying things we know won't work, really a better idea than taking a single risk? At this point, isn't it our best bet to just give my blood the old college try?"

"We're not just sitting!" Kayla was getting snappier, and Rowan knew that meant she was getting closer and closer to caving. Well, that or snapping at him, or Blake, or any poor sod who happened to be unlucky enough to be close.

It was a fifty-fifty shot at best.

To be fair to the woman, she really *was* trying. Once Milena's recklessness had proven that the doors didn't particularly object to chalk, the mage hero had taken to covering every inch of them, and most of the hallway, in incredibly detailed runes, glyphs, and symbols Rowan didn't even know the names of.

All of them pulsed with an odd inner light in a myriad of different, shifting patterns. Apparently, the configuration was supposed to help Kayla find weaknesses, analyze the function of the doors, and even potentially force them open.

Unfortunately, over the span of slightly over six hours, none of those things had happened.

If anything, Kayla looked more confused than when they'd started, to the point that her emotions were starting to crack even through the well-set facade that the heroine had learned to put up since their arrival in their new world.

"Really? Because I'm pretty sure that our troops disagree, considering they saw fit to send up sandwiches three hours ago," Rowan countered.

That was the one good thing about the whole scenario. Their troops had the time to sit down and rest, even if the tension among them was palpable.

Things were also still awkward between the different factions that made up the army, especially between the hero-sworn fighters and the mercenaries Lucius was leading. Fighting alongside each other had done a ton to loosen those divides, though they'd yet to crumple.

"Fine!" Kayla finally snapped, spinning away from the doors and stalking toward Rowan. The Stalwart Hero was quick to start backing away in the face of sparks that rose from the woman's skin as her mana became agitated enough to gain physical expression. Kayla cornered him against the wall as she poked his chest, giving him a little zap. "If you're so set on trying to kill yourself in new and inventive ways, just do it!" The heroine motioned at the doors but didn't move an inch. "Go on, have at it!"

Rowan looked imploringly at Olivia, but she just smirked at his plight. With a grumble, he squeezed away from her and ignored disapproving stares from most of his friends and allies as he walked up to the doors.

He briefly examined the doors, eyeing the two spikes that replaced what would traditionally have been their handles.

With one final look back and a shrug, the Stalwart Hero impaled his palms on the spikes.

Instantly, a presence in the doors reached out, grabbed hold of his blood, and yanked it closer. Rowan gasped, feeling a surge of dizziness as the speed of his blood loss almost took him off his feet.

Of course, as he knew it would, his brand-new Legendary card kicked in immediately. Mana surged and energy seeped out of the world and through his body, finding purchase deep inside his bones. New blood welled forth, coursing through his emptying veins.

The doors just pulled harder.

Rowan had just enough time to wonder if he was making the worst and potentially final mistake of his life before he spotted a change in the spikes.

They'd remained a stark bone-white, devouring blood instantly. Now, however, a crimson color was starting to well up from the base of the spikes. It climbed higher slowly, almost reluctantly, but it was climbing.

"It's working," Rowan managed to grit out to the rest of them, then redoubled his focus on his card, nudging it along.

Blood production kicked up a notch, and Rowan found just a hint of relief.

Then, finally, after what felt like a minor eternity, the doors clicked open.

The connection to his blood fell away, the suction stopped, and Rowan pulled his palms away as quickly as he could. He watched the wounds there steadily seal over until not a mark was left.

The spikes were now bloodred, and he really didn't like looking at them.

"Well, that worked!" Rowan chirped, affecting a smile as he turned around.

Olivia groaned, looking like she wished it hadn't, and Kayla nodded along.

"He's going to be even more reckless now," the heroine concluded, shooting Olivia a commiserative look. "My condolences."

Insultingly, everyone seemed to agree with the sentiment.

Rowan just huffed and rolled his eyes. "That's the thanks I get for all my good work."

In spite of the others trying to tease him and imply otherwise, Rowan was not, in fact, tempted to rush ahead to try and quickly finish things.

He knew the value of having an army, or at least an elite unit, as support now. The heroes definitely could not have made it all the way to the central part of the fortress without the support of their armies. And while the effect they had on the battle against the king and his henchmen was limited, the soldiers definitely deserved praise for how they handled themselves against the very first Legendary Blake and Rowan triumphed over.

The battle against Sybelin, the Legendary demon, had been tough enough on its own. Without the soldiers eliminating the threat from the gallery of demons simultaneously? Rowan wasn't so sure it would have gone so well.

As a result, he was perfectly content to watch as their troops assembled.

Compared to how many people made up the army, the final count for those at the Epic tier that would enter with them really wasn't much.

A grand total of five people, not counting the Mercenary King and Tamara.

Senior scout Dale, with his dedication and constant effort to keep everyone safe, and on a freshly charted path.

The [Knight] trio, Fia, Greg, and Desmond, who seemed intent on chasing after their leaders—be it to glory or to inevitable death.

And then, finally, Clarke.

Rowan's thoughts on the boy were complicated.

The final count and reports on those who had managed to both survive the battle and claw their way up to Epic was the first time Rowan had thought about the boy in a long time. It was a small, callous change that the Stalwart Hero was less than thrilled by.

The boy had put his trust in him. He had been the first to volunteer when Rowan's army was in need of new recruits and a thorough reformation. And, in spite of that, Rowan had slowly but surely drifted apart from him. Somehow, along the way, a lot of the people he knew and cared about within his ranks had faded from his mind, become just a background of marching troops.

Now, the boy stood before him, and there was little chance anyone would overlook him again.

The boy was taller, with a much bulkier build. Rowan's eye could spot signs of his training from the calluses and the way his muscles were built around the sword. There was a hardness and determination in the boy's posture.

Plenty of that was commendable. Clarke was an Epic tier now, after all.

However, it was the boy's eyes that Rowan didn't like. He could barely force himself to meet them—eyes that were hard, full of anguish and an unhealthy amount of rage.

A little fact suddenly flitted through Rowan's mind: If a party sticks together, really sticks together for long enough, then it was impossible for a single person to advance to Epic and for the rest to be left behind. Not unless tragedy fell on the other members.

Tragically, Rowan knew that vitriol was not directed at him. No, it seemed squarely aimed at the demons, and what stood behind the final doors set between them and all their goals.

Rowan didn't know how he found himself in that position time and again, but when every piece of equipment was checked, when everything was in order and everyone was ready, all eyes fell on him.

"This is it. Whatever we face on the other side of that door, if we can kill it, we're safe. Everyone we love and care about will be safe." Rowan made the declaration calmly, like it didn't hurt to get the words out, knowing that that particular list was now much shorter for some people. "Shall we?"

Without waiting for a response, Rowan turned and pulled the doors open fully, letting the light of the torches spill into the hallway.

The corridor ahead was long and dark. Unlike the rest of the fortress, not a single torch graced the walls. This wasn't much of an impediment, as Kayla simply waved her hand and conjured a cluster of lights to hover above them, but it did make the group pause as they took everything in.

A dazzling array of murals enveloped every inch of the passage, floor, walls, and ceiling alike.

Rowan stared in awe at the incredible detail. The murals captured the wanton slaughter between humans and demons, seas of faces set in snarls, twisted in pain, or lost to despair. Each and every figure was so lifelike, Rowan swore they couldn't have been lifted from an artist's imagination.

In fact, they probably weren't.

At first, Rowan easily recognized the weapons, armor, and even some of the crests that the humans in the murals wore. The farther from the doors they got, however, the more his recognition faltered.

It wasn't that the weapons were unrecognizable. They were simply growing cruder, rougher, like something that a child might put together based on an idea of armor. There was a whole section of the murals that caught nothing but a tide of demons slaughtering people with barely any weapons.

Then, things changed. The level of technology jumped, far past what even the current kingdoms employed.

Weapons that glowed in mystical colors. Armor that seemed to shift and twist even when depicted in a static image. Feats of magic that would stun the mind.

The gradual decline followed, until everyone was wielding sticks and getting slaughtered once more.

Again and again the patterns repeated, and a sudden realization left Rowan with the sour taste of ash in his mouth.

The murals weren't witness to the technology of humans degrading time after time. The direction of their walk was wrong. They bore witness to humanity rising up, fighting their way to the peak of their world, only to be completely wiped out.

Slowly, other races entered the murals. Beast folk, then elves, then dwarves and more. With each addition, they grew more numerous, until Rowan saw a depiction that reminded him of why those same races were a relative rarity today.

They fought. Tooth and nail, literally and figuratively, and were reduced to pitiful numbers during every cycle.

And according to what Rowan knew, most of those races did not have the virility of humans.

They were literally driven to near extinction, not by human hand, or the hand of the divine, but by a cycle that ground ever onward in this new world of his.

Olivia let out a shuddering breath, her eyes flitting between every depiction of elves, and Rowan realized she'd reached the same conclusion he did. Wordlessly, even heading into battle, Rowan reached out for her hand.

She gripped it, and they continued in silence.

The passage may have seemed endless, and it was certainly much longer than should have fit inside a fortress of this size. Even so, the end arrived eventually.

Rowan, with his stats, was the first to spot the opening ahead of them, but not by much. This hastened their steps, the parade of misery underfoot making them all eager to face anything, even combat.

Even though he was expecting it, Rowan almost froze at the sight of the demon waiting for them.

The creature was shaped like a knight, just like most of its main troops were. Except, where the lesser specimens were almost a parody of water-logged armor, the demon here was clearly a step above them.

The knight's armor was polished to such a sheen that it caught and mirrored all light in dizzying reflections. Unlike the other armor, there were no apparent gaps in its defense.

The demon resembled a statue cast out of some strange, alien metal more than a living thing, especially the way it stood stock-still, hands gripping the hilt of a sword placed tip first on the ground.

As they drew close, Rowan realized there was something off about it.

It reflected light, sure, but it also seemed to absorb part of it, and that part went to illuminating what was *within* the demon. The armor was slightly transparent, and what it offered was a glimpse into the dark, devouring depth of an ocean.

"Visitors!" a voice echoed out just before they stepped foot inside the hall, breaking their stride. "I have so longed for someone to come here. To reach this deep within these unholy walls."

The demon finally moved as it spoke, its head twitching, then its fingers. It was almost like a titan casting off the weight of stone that had encased it during its slumber. Or as if it was throwing off the weight of time it had accumulated.

And the sight was glorious.

As its awareness and mobility returned, the ocean that made up the creature's body lit up. Fish, twisted yet still beautiful, gave off a low incandescence. Corals jutted out of the depths, their crystalline structure making them miniature suns under the waves. Entire stretches of glowing plants reached for some unseen sky.

Rowan felt like some omniscient observer, witnessing the rebirth of a colossal ocean that thrived with life of every shape and size.

"I welcome you with a heavy heart," the demon proclaimed as it switched its sword up and gripped the handle tighter.

Rowan had stood in front of people that had meant him harm before, and every time, their intent was a sharp, cruel thing. Or at the very least merciless and set on the clinical elimination of what got in their way. The demon didn't feel that way. If anything, the aura that blanketed the space, trying to push back the heroes and their entourage, felt distinctly *sad.*

"Who are you? Why would you be happy about our arrival?" Blake ventured, confusion leaking through. Apparently, he felt it, too.

Rowan thought the demon would strike, if it deigned to reply at all.

He was wrong.

"I am but a humble wretch, torn from my home, twisted and forced to serve. Strike me down, heroes, so that I may finally rest. Strike me down, and deny my master his hold over my home," the demon all but pleaded, body shaking even as it settled into an offensive stance.

Somehow, there was only a single question that came to Rowan's mind. "What were you, before all this?"

The knight lacked all features, and yet Rowan felt like it was smiling. "A defender. A leader. A foolish dreamer. My people are gone. My master took me, and then I took them."

A flicker in the darkness of the demon's depth. A single glimpse of a massive castle under the seas, glorious in its alien construction and surrounded by massive, interconnected dwellings. A glimpse of people, strange yet still beautiful, with the features of various underwater races interwoven in their appearance.

And then darkness, choking, grasping, reclaiming the split-second image of a happy past.

But not before the illusion was stripped bare. Not before the current state of the species—decaying, rotting bodies trapped in shells of armor—was revealed.

"Free me, heroes, so I cannot be forced to bring my people back to suffer further."

Blake didn't need further encouragement as he surged forward, sword erupting into holy light.

The knight flinched, but then he blurred forward, and the only thing that kept Blake's head attached to his body was an instinctive attempt to dodge backward. A red line appeared on his neck and then erupted into blood before swiftly clotting again.

Marcus shouted as he made his aura erupt, the protective effects intensifying and growing into a spectral armor that overlaid each of his allies. Jacqueline stepped forward as well, layering shields on themselves again and again as she sought to make the approach much more difficult for the demon.

Rowan ignored the chanting of Kayla and Milena, freely diving into the path of the saintess's beams of light that passed over him harmlessly and even energizing them while making the demon screech in agony.

Patiently, building up his strike as far as he dared, he stalked around the fighting, aiming for the knight's back.

The knight, now that he was moving, felt unstoppable. Each of the creature's movements shook the room, but its unnatural construction let it withstand the quakes.

Blake quickly learned how useless it was trying to match its strength. His sword was almost blown out of his hands when it was parried, paling in front of the demon's monstrous strength. He staggered backward, spared by Marcus's shield bash, which managed to distract the demon from a follow-up strike but failed to make it so much as budge.

The knight wound up for an overhead blow, and Rowan moved in.

He knew that the armor seemed flawless, but he still refused to do something as stupid as aim for the center of the knight's chest. His blow instead fell on the knight's armpit with heavy force.

The ringing explosion staggered *everyone*, and the knight listed, then collapsed onto its side, but the immediate retaliatory strike toward Rowan suggested that the demon wasn't truly affected.

Rowan slid to the side and out of the way, seeking to try and strike a hit against the knight's helmet, but he badly misjudged the dexterity of the demon's blows. Whipping the sword back around with easy grace, the knight drove it straight through Rowan's legs.

With a strangled cry, the hero collapsed to the floor, dyeing it with his blood. The knight immediately raised its foot, ready to bring it down and pulp the hero's skull.

Then the demon spasmed, locking up for just a brief second. That allowed Rowan to tumble aside, bone, muscle, and skin already erupting out of his stumps and forming new limbs.

A cry of rage erupted from deeper within the fortress, and the knight cried out as a red glow enveloped it.

"Hurry . . . heroes . . . I cannot—aaaaaaaaargh!" A screech of fury erupted from the knight, echoing like the ocean's wrath. It was on its feet fast, sword swinging faster than before.

One blow, two, three, all delivered in a blur against anything within reach. Marcus staggered again and again, barely resisting them, and Blake's weapon was finally launched out of his hands with a sickening snap of his fingers and the eruption of blood where the skin between them cracked.

Then the knight was upon him, barriers of force barely redirecting its blows as it sought to end the scrambling hero.

Rowan swung his spear and connected with all his might into the back of the creature's leg. The knight winced but didn't fall, still swinging for Blake. Then Clarke was there, driving his sword into its other leg with a wordless cry of terror and rage.

With this, the knight fell and the ground under it shone with a magic circle as gravity in that area intensified to insane levels. Gravity that the Mercenary King stumbled into, planting his shield on the small of the knight's back and pressing down for all he was worth.

Rowan joined in immediately, biting back a scream when the increased gravity pulled on his flesh, on his muscles, on his *organs*, but he refused to relent. He pinned down the arm that held the knight's sword and ignored the flailing that occasionally nicked him, his regeneration more than up to the task.

It grew increasingly easier when first Blake, then Marcus, joined in.

Rowan risked a brief glance, spotting a pale-faced Tamara, who was trembling with her arms held out in front of her. Olivia flitted between her and Kayla, force-feeding both women her potions. The magic circle seemed to be Tamara's work, her face in full concentration and beads of sweat on her forehead, but Kayla looked much worse off.

The mage heroine was trembling, eyes closed and lips silently moving as two voices echoed out of her, hands bent over a flickering point of light that made Rowan nauseous just to look at it.

Then, like it pained her greatly, Kayla took a step forward, dragging herself closer to the battle. The speck of whatever spell she was casting moved erratically between her hands, rubber banding back and forth like it hated the mere act of motion.

In spite of the strain, Kayla made it all the way up to the gravity field, then stepped into it. Instantly, the heroine folded, screaming as she struggled to keep the spell from coming in contact with the floor.

Blood burst out of her ears, eyes, nose, and even mouth, yet she crawled closer, never once stopping her chant. The knight, seeing her approach, intensified its struggles. Blake was tossed off with such force the hero bounced off a wall and then the floor, but before the knight could do much with its freed hand, Clarke jumped in, pinning it down once more.

Finally, slowly, Kayla pushed her arms the final distance. The spark of light refused to follow, hanging for just a second longer in its previous location, then it surged forward and landed on the knight's helmet.

A thrum rang out, and the world held its breath.

Then everyone staggered as the pieces of armor they were struggling with *crumpled inward.*

The full weight of the world the knight was linked to, the entire force of the ocean he harbored, was brought down crushingly on its own body.

The final echo of a breath was heard from the demon before its armor went dark one final time—for good.

The scream of agony and such potent rage that Rowan felt it in the depth of his soul washed over them as red light erupted from farther inside the fortress, but it could do nothing to stifle the grins that every single fighter sported.

**Congratulations!**
**[Cyraenan, the Earl of Cloying Resentment], one of the Four Demonic Pillars, has been slain!**

***Calculating . . .***
**Conditions 6/8 fulfilled.**
***Error!***
**Unsealing requirements not met.**

CHAPTER TWENTY-TWO

# Unstable

"No, I don't want to" were the exact words that Kayla, the Hero of Secrets, deigned to offer up when Rowan finally decided to prod her with his foot to see if she was alive and urged her to get up. "Mom, just five more minutes, please?"

The heroine had never looked this bedraggled for as long as Rowan and Blake had known her, so neither could quite help smiling.

While the two heroes knew her well enough to ignore the image she was putting on, she *was* doing a rather convincing impression of a poor maiden who had given her all in the conquest of their enemy and left to languish on the ground. Both Clarke and Marcus were giving the woman keen attention, having totally fallen for her acting.

Well, Clarke was blushing furiously and trying to look in any direction other than at her, while Marcus was sneaking glances as he made his way over. "Maybe I could help you up, my lady?"

Rowan choked on a laugh at the sudden, awkward attempt at suavity in his friend's voice, but it was when Kayla demurely offered up her hand that he couldn't keep it in any longer.

Blake joined him a second later, and then all three heroes were laughing as loudly as their lungs could manage, fear and anxiety mixing into a heady cocktail of reckless joy at still being alive. They let out a collective sigh as they came down from their high.

Marcus looked both confused and slightly mortified, but that was quickly solved and morphed into a full-body flush when the heroine in a rumpled and slightly torn dress finally got to her feet and kissed his cheek in passing.

"You got something good, right?" Blake asked as Kayla casually waved her hand, causing a rush of mana to sweep over her and erase all signs of the battle—dirt disappeared, bruises faded, and her clothing mended and readjusted itself.

"Duh? 'Course I did." Kayla's expression was downright smug, but Rowan could hardly blame her.

His own experience bar had jumped right past level seventy-eight and into seventy-nine from the kill Kayla claimed, so he could only imagine how much experience she got. Not to mention the cards.

"One of them I'll be keeping for myself, but . . ." Ponderously, like she really didn't like what she was doing much, the heroine materialized an orange-colored card, then suddenly tossed it at Marcus.

The poor man was so out of it he almost fumbled the catch despite his stats, but then froze when he saw whatever was on the face on the card. "Are you sure . . . ?"

It didn't take more encouragement than a nod from Kayla for Marcus to quickly go through the process of changing his cards, then shuddered as an outline of a full set of plate armor flashed around his body, then faded.

A moment later, he also shared the card description with everyone in his party.

**World Layer (Legendary, Passive)**
**You are inextricably linked to the world of Avalus Atlantis, and it lends you its protection.**

"You got the knight's armor?" Milena whispered in awe, then faked a scrunched-up expression of bitterness. "So not fair. A kiss from a pretty heroine and then a gift on top? When's the wedding?"

Kayla tittered as Marcus blushed again, and the entire group felt just a little more at ease. Just a tiny bit more normal.

It was almost possible to pretend like they weren't all getting the shivers. An immense aura could be felt from the final stretch of hallway, emanating from just around the corner. It was putting them all on constant edge.

They couldn't delay forever, and they knew it.

After realizing that there was nothing else to do, they easily fell in together and set out to meet their final challenge.

Rowan badly wished he could walk alongside Olivia, but he wasn't about to waste his advantages by bringing up the rear or forcing her to expose herself to direct hits by having her up front. As such, it was him and Marcus that walked ahead, Rowan's regeneration and the wolfkin's new defenses being the best bet of surviving the opening salvo.

Except the immediate blow never came, even as they walked past the final murals that showcased a single glowing figure standing tall in the face of a demonic monstrosity. Rowan found the figure oddly familiar, but there was something far more pressing taking up his attention.

The same monstrosity on the mural was right in front of them, seated on a throne of bones and wreathed in a red haze.

**Warning!**
**You have entered an area of Unstable Reality!**

**Warning!**
**You are in the presence of the local Demonic Origin entity!**
**ƧØɱA₦ŦƗƧ, ŦĦE ɱAɌQɄƗƧ ØF EɱⱣŦY ĐɌEAɱƧ,**
**₩ɆⱠȻØɱEƧ YØɄ!**

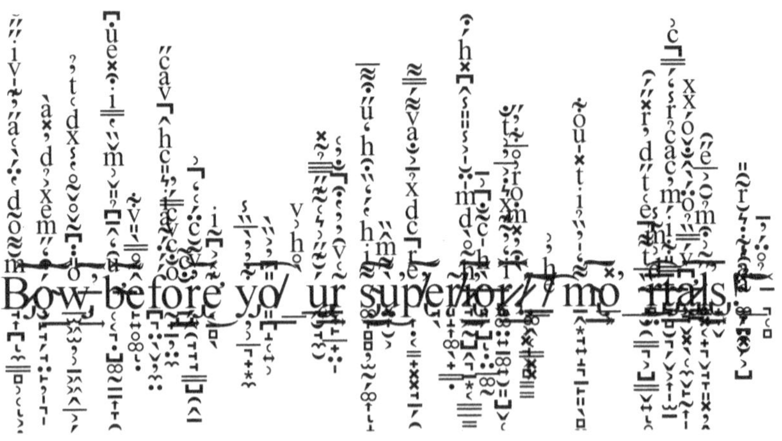


The presence of the demon was overwhelming. It drew the eye, refusing to release the beholder.

In a way, the demon almost looked angelic, in the biblical manner. Its main body was an emaciated humanoid figure, completely covered in bloodred eyes that continued to cry black ichor, staining everything.

Its face was devoid of everything but three sets of eyes, too, and a pair of black feathers jutted out of the back of the demon's skull, curving forward and up like a faux halo, or a pair of horns. Its arms and legs were tipped with wickedly sharp claws that looked metallic, just like its sweeping, galaxy-colored wings did. Those, too, were covered in more eyes, but these were closed in slumber, still weeping, but refusing to dare glance at reality.

Then a tear spread across the demon's face, raw flesh gaping for a second before the hole deepened and a tongue, teeth, and a functional mouth formed. "**You ruin everything, once more. Little mortals, standing in the face of infinity.**"

Its voice stabbed deep into Rowan's conscious, evoking feelings of dread and guilt and self-disgust at his own existence.

The churn of emotions was thankfully enough to let the hero tear his eyes away from the many crimson orbs that dotted the demon's flesh, finally letting him take in the rest of the room.

The space was large, but most of it was taken up by four towering pillars. Said pillars were now cracked and lifeless, the murals of four different demons that once adorned them fading. Rowan easily recognized Cyraenan and Sybelin, which meant that the other two were Legendary demons as well.

Chains twisted around and into the pillars, then extended into the demon king's flesh, piercing deep into his back. Most of the chains were blackened and cracked, though four still bound him to his throne and shone a deep scarlet.

**"You can't leave well enough alone. Can't you see? You can do nothing to stop me. Nothing but delay. Time after time, you force me away, force me to claw my way back here. You would be so much happier in my embrace. Accept me. Accept the ruler of demons, and you will be at peace."**

The speech was interrupted by laughter and jeering.

**"HA! LOOK AT HIM SPEAK! ARE THE BETS CLOSED?"**

**"NOT YET. I'm WILLING TO TAKE YOU UP. TEN THOUSAND SOULS THAT HE FAILS AGAIN?"**

**"THE FOOLISH DREAMER, WEEPING AT HIS WOUNDS!"**

Nausea unlike anything before struck out at Rowan, and it was only his **Eidolon Body** activating that let him avoid emptying his stomach. Some of the others were not that lucky, and the sound of sick splattering made the Stalwart Hero clench his teeth.

His eyes swept over the hall in a hurry, but he regretted it when the twisting lines of space that warped into inhuman faces only made the sensation worse.

**"Silence! Begone, you wretches who mock your own king! I will kill these fools, claim this world's power, and then reclaim my throne!"**

**"THRONE! LIKE HE HAD ONE TO BEGIN WITH."**

**"WHY, A MARQUIS, THROWING HIS WEIGHT AROUND LIKE THIS?"**

**"WATCHING HIM BEG AND WHIMPER IS ALWAYS FUN."**

With a roar of rage and madness, the demon king lurched up off his throne.

**The Marquis of Empty Dreams challenges you!**

**The local Unstable Reality has been sealed!**

The lettering of the demon's title started out as a dark orange, lightened, then faded back to dark before slipping through purple and even down into blue before flickering back to its original color.

The chains that bound the demon to its throne tightened and tugged at its flesh as it moved, causing drops of ichor to splatter into the already-present puddle, but the demon ignored it all and the chains seemed to slowly extend from its efforts.

Rowan took that as his sign to strike.

The tip of his spear exploded against the demon's chest, but it felt more like striking concrete. In spite of that, the Stalwart Hero redoubled his effort with another strike toward the monster's legs. Instead of meeting tough resistance, it easily sliced through.

Overcommitted, Rowan pitched forward and was met by the demon's claws.

For a fraction of a second, they were slicing through him easily and made it several inches into his flesh. Then they became blunt, useless instruments and he was flung against one of the four pillars to the sound of every bone in his body snapping.

Screaming in pain as his body knit itself back together, Rowan watched as the front-line fighters of their party launched themselves forward.

Marcus took the center position, letting the demon rain down blow after blow and not flinching an inch. Each time the demon was about to land a hit, the outline of the knight's armor flashed around Marcus, and he merely grunted.

Clarke had figured out his footing in the mad scramble against the knight earlier, and he was now committed to hit-and-run tactics, weaving in and out of range as he dealt blow after blow. Some left angry gashes that slowly sealed in the demon's flesh, while others bounced off harmlessly.

The Mercenary King, backed up by the trio of Rowan's [Knights], was following the young man's example.

That left Blake, who became a corona of holy energies that pulsed and extended with each of his strikes. The demon seemed entirely incapable of stopping these attacks, to the point where its flesh sizzled and cooked from sheer proximity.

The casters were just as effective, strikes of magic, healing, and protection raining down on the combatants as they strained their mental stats to keep up with and target the right figure in the chaotic melee.

After a few seconds, Rowan managed to shamble over, then take a proper strike as his body returned to its rightful state, spear moving like a meteor in a blaze of black-streaked red energy.

They were winning.

The demon was fighting like an animal, but it could do little to truly punish them. Rowan caught onto its fluctuating strength quickly, and his heart soared as he realized that in spite of all the obstacles, they'd managed to damage the demon king before it could really establish itself and become a true part of their world.

And then reality exploded.

**"Enough!"**

The scream of frustration tore causality apart, and the room wobbled into a horrible spherical mess of matter and energy. On what used to be the far wall, a wide-open gate erupted into being, revealing ethereal chains that wound around the demon. It fought to keep its footing, the chains of the throne grounding it in place somewhat, but Rowan could tell it would eventually lose.

That didn't help them in the moment.

Rowan felt torn into a million different pieces. His left arm was moving so quickly it blurred through the air, while his right was swimming in molasses. His head felt like it was two meters away, and pieces of his torso were in at least twelve different dimensions.

Rowan's mind swam as it broke under the stress of merely processing what he was seeing, and then the demon was moving.

A careless gesture and its claws easily reached Desmond, slicing the knight's body into countless ribbons. Another twitch of leg sent a massive foot crashing down, and turned Fia into a smear. Clarke roared and swung, but the panels of space and time adjusted just so that his arm ceased to exist. Another strike, and Tamara puffed into a cloud of blood as space itself squeezed her.

Marcus screamed, blood erupting out of him as his card fought and failed to contain the kind of damage that had easily slaughtered his companions.

The demon turned and, with every ounce of its strength, brought down one of its wings on Marcus.

The wolfkin cried out at a billion different volumes, and the armor that formed around him actually showed signs of cracks. In spite of that, the beast folk stubbornly reached out to deliver his own hit, and for the first time the demon reeled as all the damage Marcus did manage to absorb was transferred back to it.

For just a moment, the demon's hold on reality slipped.

In the midst of the chaos, in the midst of the slaughter, only a single human stood with a peaceful expression on her face.

Her eyes took everything in, the space and time that fought to restore themselves and the chains that still bound the demon, tugging it in both directions. She saw the demon reach out, seeking to prevent its domain from unraveling so it could finish wiping them all out.

And she made a decision.

"[Bulwark of the End]!" Jacqueline de Vort's voice was determination itself as her mana, her life force, and everything that made up her soul exploded outward and the laws of reality themselves turned their eyes in the woman's direction.

Every soul in the space was caught up in a vision of the woman, standing tall and proud, with a sad smile on her face before the vision fractured, taking a life with it.

The demon's control once more wrapped around the world, but when it brought its fist down punishingly on Marcus to finish the fight, it was met by a thin, protective field.

The field looked spun out of the thinnest glass imaginable. But it held against the demon's attack.

Roaring in pain as the full force of its attack landed on its own flesh, the demon chose a new target. It clawed out at Blake, but its claws bent and began to crack. Feathers of alien metal shattered when they swept out at Olivia. A beam of destructive red force was released in a moment of despair, but it washed over the casters without so much as ruffling their clothes.

Rowan gasped in relief the moment the protective field settled on him, and even with all the space-time craziness going on, he felt firmly rooted to reality. As the demon pointlessly rampaged, the hero struck.

Rowan didn't aim for the creature itself. Blake had beaten him to it and was screaming as he laid into the enemy, sword and fist flashing. But he was barely doing any damage, and it was healing faster than the pace at which Blake could create those tiny wounds.

Instead, Rowan's spear aimed for the throne, right where one of the chains sprang up out of it. With an explosion that shook the space around them and sent time and space into yet another wonky spiral, the chain snapped off alongside a whole section of the throne.

The demon was tugged toward the gate violently, and certainly noticed. It turned its hate-filled eyes on Rowan, and the hero was suddenly the focus of a whirlwind of blows that sent the demon's own blood and flesh flying around when it failed to reach him.

The others, however, noticed what Rowan was doing.

With a rage that Rowan didn't think the man capable of, the grim-faced Mercenary King tore into the throne.

Another chain snapped, another lurch of the demon closer to the gate.

It spun, panic and fear finally showing on its face as it tried to strike at every soul in the room at once. It couldn't damage them yet, but it was keeping them stuck in place and the protective film that covered them was growing dimmer and losing its slight shine even as the demon's own ability to resist the forces of reality was slipping.

It was then that Blake's rage reached a crescendo, and the hero ignited even brighter, pushing his way closer to the throne. With a rageful scream, one of the last two chains was severed along with most of the throne.

The demon sailed through the air, incapable of resisting anymore, before the twisted world stuttered and abruptly turned back to normal. The demon slammed into the now-empty stretch of wall, its singular chain glowing weakly, cracks showing throughout. With furious eyes, it raised its head.

"Empty . . . dreams," it rasped, and crimson light erupted.

Kayla huffed, carefully maintaining a practiced expression of disappointed indifference. Her eyes swept over the hall and the nobility gathered there, before once more falling on the terrified face of the man who had failed her.

"Repeat what you just told me."

"M-my queen . . . We did our best! I swear to you! The capital of the Rhys kingdom will fall within the week! I apologize for the delays, but I swear—"

The man was cut off when one of Kayla's sworn knights stepped forward and landed a blow on the back of his head, making him collapse like a puppet. To the pin-drop silence of the room, he was dragged out of the hall, his fate plain to all.

"I do not allow for failure. You will either obey . . . or you will serve me in other ways," the Hero Queen declared, settling down on her throne with a smirk.

Blake abruptly came to, eyes blinking wide as he took in the room around him. Confusion warred within his mind, flashes of murals and blood spinning away in his thoughts even as he took in the calm beige tones of his room within the castle.

"Blake? What's wrong?" Amanda mumbled quietly, making his face flush when the woman rose up out of bed, leaning on her arm and rubbing her eyes sleepily. "How early is it? I've *told* you we're not doing anything until noon."

Blake really wanted to look away from the expanse of soft flesh before him, but it was rapidly emptying his head of any lingering nightmares, so he was practically *forced* to look!

Mirabella's soft giggle sounded from Amanda's other side, and the woman plopped her chin down on the princess's shoulder, shooting Blake a conspiratorial smile. "Told you we can't keep him in bed until noon."

"True, though we did try," Jacqueline drawled as she wrapped an arm around Blake's back, and the hero froze.

*Rage. His entire world was rage.*

"Blake, what's wrong?" the woman behind him asked, worry slipping into her voice.

The hero turned slowly, reluctantly, until his eyes finally landed on her face.

**Your fragmented portfolio of [Freedom] is reacting!**
**Your fragmented portfolio of [Radiance] is reacting!**

Blake's world was rage. And he wasn't about to let any illusion lull him away from reality.

The Hero of Light screamed, and the world around him cracked.

Rowan blinked and waved away an annoying fly that would just not stop buzzing around his face. The night was clammy and hot, and he was just thankful that the mosquitoes were not out in force yet.

"Can you please stop playing with the insects and walk a little faster? They're waiting for us, and it should really not take this long for us to walk to the store," Olivia complained, swinging their hands and doing her best to make him walk faster.

"And what if I'm just enjoying a stroll with my girlfriend, hmm?" Rowan quipped right back, resisting the smile that threatened to take over his face.

Olivia sighed, but did snuggle up closer to him. The new angle gave him a view right down the front of her loose shirt, and she caught him in the act and giggled mischievously.

"You know what? You were right. I wouldn't want to leave Emma waiting with those five idiots. Who knows how far they're going to push her sanity."

Something about the mention of that name made Rowan flinch, then look around. When he met Olivia's eyes again, the fear faded. He'd stress over exams or whatever it was later. He had his lovely girlfriend right there next to him, and not even his best friend's complicated romance was enough to distract him.

And then Rowan's world was washed away in a tide of rage.

Olivia's voice didn't matter. The pain of hitting the pavement didn't matter. The only thing that dominated his thoughts was the pure rage slamming into his soul through the link with his best friend.

*A link?* Rowan's thoughts screeched to a halt as memories came flooding in.

The world around him shattered, dominated by an animalistic scream.

Rowan jerked upright, his head still swimming in pain unlike anything he'd ever experienced before. Through blurry eyes, he could spot the bodies of his friends scattered around him, their eyes closed in slumber.

All but one of his friends, that was.

Blake's howls of rage and agony were echoing through the chamber as the sounds of combat spread, and Rowan finally forced himself to stumble to his feet, looking toward where the commotion was.

Light was gushing out from under Blake's skin, scorching everything around him as he threw himself against the demon king again and again. Rowan was practically watching in real time as the strikes grew stronger, more refined, more *vicious*.

The demon was on the back foot, barely managing to keep a step ahead of the hero, placing limbs in the path of his sword just to prevent Blake from reaching vital organs.

Even then, the spray of its black blood was stemming, exhaustion was weighing down its limbs, and fear was the chief emotion that dominated its unnatural features.

**"No! No! Not again! I will not be forced to give up once more! I'll—!"**

With the scream of a wounded animal, Blake's sword flickered and cut straight through the demon's jaw. The lower half of its face and a flapping tongue landed wetly a few feet away, silencing the demon's tirade and turning its speech into wordless cries of horror.

Blake didn't stop attacking, but his focus shifted.

Inch by inch, limb by limb, he brutalized the being who declared itself the demon king, until it was reduced to a whimpering mass of flesh in front of the crazed hero. Even then, a single chain linked it to the throne.

The chain looked ready to snap from the many cracks that spread throughout it, but the demon clung to its lifeline stubbornly, refusing to fade from the mortal plane.

Blake stood now, sword gripped in his hands so hard it was creaking, his breathing ragged and eyes still wild.

Slowly, like he would approach a highly dangerous animal, Rowan stepped forward.

"Finish it, Blake. Just cut the chain, or stab it in its heart, or cut off its head. Finish this," Rowan implored quietly, daring to lay a hand on the other hero's shoulder.

Blake shuddered and made a sound somewhere between a sob and a laugh. "I don't want to. I want it to suffer."

"How long? Until it bleeds out? You do see that it doesn't even have blood leaving what's left of its body anymore. Or are we going to wait until it somehow regenerates?" Rowan kept his voice calm, conversational.

Even then, Blake practically growled as he spun to face his friend. "It killed her! This thing killed her! I promised I'd protect them, and—"

Rowan hugged his best friend, making the other hero freeze. For a long moment, the Stalwart Hero was convinced he'd just get stabbed. Then Blake dropped his sword and clung to Rowan as sobs racked his body.

"You didn't fail, Blake. Jacqueline de Vort made her own choice. For you and Amanda and Mirabella. For all of us. Just because she chose to protect you doesn't mean you failed her."

Blake sobbed harder, but Rowan didn't care about the snot and tears dripping down his shirt. He did stiffen when a new set of arms wrapped around them, only for a startled glance to reveal the pained face of Kayla.

Rowan didn't know how long the three of them stood there like that, shivering and pretending like tears weren't streaming down their cheeks, but when they broke apart, they refused to look at each other, as if by an agreement, until they'd wiped their faces clean.

"Well, you gonna stab it then, or should I?" Kayla asked, affecting that same cocky tone she always used. It sounded weak and hollow at the moment, but Blake still sent her a fond smile.

Slowly, like he was performing a ceremony, Blake picked up the sword he'd dropped. With determined steps, he drew up to the demon king, and with his eyes locked on one of the few pairs of crimson orbs left on the creature's face, he brought the blade down.

A whisper, a cursed promise, touched the minds of the heroes. "You accomplish . . . nothing . . . a dream . . . cannot die . . . I will . . . return . . ."

The final chain shattered, and Rowan's world tilted sideways.

**Congratulations!**
**[Somantis, the Marquis of Empty Dreams], the source of Demonic Corruption, has been slain!**

***Calculating . . .***
**Conditions 8/8 fulfilled.**
**Unsealing requirements met.**

CHAPTER TWENTY-THREE

# Blame

When Rowan came to, his world was nothing but golden radiance. The concepts of up and down, of left and right, of space and time, simply did not exist. All that there was, was himself and the Divine Void around him.

Then, footsteps.

Reality realigned itself, and the Stalwart Hero was standing once more. He was also suddenly granted a body again, as evidenced by the fact that looking around at the space of pure infinity with no angles or breaks anywhere in sight was giving him a headache.

"I do apologize. Is this better?" A voice rose up from the void, making it twist and bunch until Rowan was standing in a cozy, humble room.

It was some kind of cottage, with a beautiful view of a forest just outside, a crackling hearth, and a table set for two.

One of the chairs was taken up by a man of large stature, his hair a wild mane and beard flawlessly trimmed close to his skin. He was dressed humbly, but every shift in his stance made the tunic he was wearing strain against the muscles it was trying to cover.

No matter how disarming the man looked, as Rowan stared into a pair of pale blue orbs, he knew exactly who he was talking to. "Aristaeus."

The god gave the hero a lopsided smile. "Rowan. You really should sit down—you've had a rough go of it."

Rowan could feel his regeneration card burning in his chest, but he did feel worn-out. With great reluctance, the hero collapsed into the chair, eyeing the god who, what seemed like an eternity ago, had laid claim to him. "So, what is this, exactly?"

"Well, I guess some would say this is a reward for all that you have done. The defining moment of your journey, where your divine patron descends to offer you their favor. Really, though, this is just where the system-mandated process of giving a hero what he deserves is going to happen."

Rowan sighed, already feeling even more drained by the interaction. "Okay. Fine. Then just hand over whatever it is that you've got for me so I can go back."

"Ah, but first, I have to ask: Would you like to go back home, hero of mine? You do have that right now."

**Your divine patron, Aristaeus, offers you a way back home!**
**Are you going to accept?**
**Y/N**

With a roll of his eyes, Rowan hit no. "Really?"

Aristaeus grinned merrily and shrugged his shoulders. "Sorry, but it is a requirement. You count as a divine summon. As your summoner, I must offer you a chance to be returned to your world of origin after you've fulfilled your end of the contract."

"My end of the contract, you say. Like you ever asked for my opinion. Like you didn't just kidnap us and tell us what we had to do." Rowan didn't even bother keeping the bitterness out of his voice. If the god was going to smite him, it would probably have happened a while ago.

Aristaeus just laughed. "Hold still now."

His hand shot out faster than Rowan could blink, plunging right into the hero's chest.

Only shock kept Rowan from disobeying the command, but he felt his body lock in place anyway when the god gently extracted a glowing purple-gold card from his chest. Unlike the last time he'd seen his Heart Card, Rowan noted that the gold was by far the more predominant color. Golden cracks were all over the card, and Rowan could glimpse something underneath them.

"I really do dislike the way we cripple hero cards before we send you down. Not my choice, of course. I'm just a minor divinity. Still, it's not right," the god muttered quietly, reaching out with his other hand.

He grabbed for the card, but his hand closed around a glowing chain instead. The chain was chock-full of divine mana, glowing like a miniature sun. The god tightened his grip, and the thing shattered. More cracks spread over Rowan's Heart Card. One by one, the god revealed and snapped eight glowing chains, and Rowan could do nothing but watch as the god worked.

When the last divine construct was crushed, the golden glow of Rowan's card erupted, sending shards of its previous purple face flying everywhere. In the previous card's place, a card that looked like it was cast out of solid gold remained.

Aristaeus flicked it at Rowan, and the second it slipped into the hero's chest, he drew in a ragged breath, doubling over.

"I'm apologizing a lot, but I really am sorry for how unpleasant that was. Still, considering the fact that I just tore out a core part of your soul, fiddled with it, and then replaced it, what could you expect?"

"C-core part of my soul?" Rowan wheezed, rubbing at his chest. It wasn't his flesh that was feeling achy, but the gesture still made him feel a tiny bit better.

"What do you think Heart Cards are? When people access their system fully for the first time, it plucks a piece of their soul's core, does diagnostics, and then crafts a personalized card for them. Now, people can reject their own Heart Card in favor of another. Or even go without. That's not deathly, since the system takes only a tiny amount of their soul."

"Then why don't people replace their Heart Cards more often once they've chosen? On that subject, why do people get different card tiers? Why doesn't everyone start at Common?"

Rowan knew he should be freaking out at least a little. His calmness, stirred only the slightest bit by whatever emotion the god evoked, was unnatural. At the very least, he should have been desperate to go back to Olivia. But he wasn't, and since he was there already, a part of him demanded answers.

Aristaeus sighed and laid his arms on the table, giving the hero a pitying look. "I get it. The system really isn't fair, is it? The sad truth is, not all souls are of equal quality. Some can handle higher tiers of power naturally, and others need to perform incredible feats for the system to recognize and decide to grant them some of its power so they could advance."

Rowan's mind spun at the implications, but he pushed right on. "You still haven't told me why Heart Cards can't be replaced. Also, how come nobility consistently get better-grade cards? And how do heroes never get lower tiers?"

"Sheesh, so many questions. Still, I guess you deserve your answers. Let's start from the top, shall we?

"Hero cards are never low in tier because the summoning itself imbues your souls with incredible power. Even if the summoning didn't look for people with strong souls to begin with, which it does, heroes would still turn out Epic. Incidentally, the stronger the soul of the summoned, the less power is consumed. That's why three or even four heroes pop out on occasion. Those are clusters of people with incredibly powerful souls.

"As for the nobility . . . well, the basic answer is often right, and that's the case here. Strong parents give birth to strong children. The soul of a parent imparts a piece of its power to their child at the moment of conception. When you've been hoarding power for generations, the advantages tend to pile up.

"Finally, Heart Card replacement is extremely difficult under most circumstances because the second you accept a Heart Card, it becomes a piece of your soul's core. Doesn't matter who it came from, it's grafted right into your being. Obviously, if the card isn't yours, that can have some . . . consequences."

Rowan didn't like the sound of that.

On second thought, he *really* didn't like the sound of that, especially considering the fact that he had just handed off a Legendary-tier Heart Card to Blake. "What kind of consequences?"

The god rubbed his beard. "Well, you're grafting a piece of someone else into the core of your being. Obviously, you'd be a tiny bit influenced by that. Some very subtle attitude shifts. Small new preferences and tastes. You might suddenly like some food you used to hate, or vice versa, that kind of thing."

"And it's impossible to avoid this?" Rowan was suddenly feeling sick.

"Sure, it's possible. Don't accept Heart Cards from strangers and just stick to your own!" Aristaeus guffawed, then sighed when he saw the look on Rowan's face. "Oh, fine. No, you can't avoid it. I should also note that the higher the tier of the Heart Card, the bigger the impact. It's not possession or rebirth or anything, but it's there. It's why, for example, all royal bloodlines are known for certain character traits."

Rowan slumped and looked away. He was going to have to confront his best friend on the subject, but there was really little he could do. If the happy couple decided to hand off a Legendary card to their kid, who was he to stop them? Really, should he be trying to stop them at all? It was a powerful card.

Power came at a price.

Looking back, wasn't Rowan doing the exact same thing to himself? Perhaps he wasn't permanently welding pieces of someone else to his soul, but he'd definitely shoved different cards into his deck readily enough.

Even as he sat there, the immense power of his **Eidolon Body** thrummed through his being, filling him with cocky pride, **Scarlet Envy** cried out for him to try and skewer the god sitting across from him, and **Gluttonous Banquet** tried to get him to devour everything in the room.

Granted, the emotional numbness made it even easier than usual to deal with those issues, but they were definitely there. In comparison, the rest of his cards must have originated from calmer individuals, because they were almost inert by comparison.

"You know, you still haven't checked out your card," Aristaeus pointed out smugly, making Rowan squint his eyes at him.

He knew.

He was just putting it off, suddenly and inexplicably worried about taking a peek. After all, one's Heart Card was apparently supposed to suit them perfectly, and while he loved his **Keen Spear**, Rowan wondered at the changes it would undertake now that it was restored to what it was meant to be.

He couldn't delay forever, though.

**[Heart] Divine Spear Insight (Divine, Passive)**
**With a spear in hand, the world reveals itself before you.**

Rowan took a sharp breath as the details of the card fell into place. The description was vague, a mere teaser of the card's potential, but he *knew.*

The card would make him a terror with a spear in hand. His mastery over his emotions would grow. Spear combat would become a triviality, and even the slightest nick of his spear would reveal every detail of his opponents to him.

There it was, the ultimate ability to peek at the system status of anyone he fought, simply granted to him by his shiny new card.

He looked up at Aristaeus, bitterness broiling within him. "I really could have used this sooner."

"I know." For just a moment, the god looked genuinely more miserable than Rowan felt. "Do you have a clue what it's like to watch? To see them throw heroes into the fray, all the while hobbling their potential to survive?"

"Then why watch? Why are gods even playing these games?"

"Because they're afraid, Rowan." The admission floored the hero. "They don't want new gods jostling for influence and power. They don't want to wane and be forgotten, only to get killed by some uppity upstart. I'm the youngest of the gods, and I'm still so very, very old."

The Stalwart Hero looked at the god across from him then, taking him in fully. This being of perfection, of ultimate power. Yet, in spite of his status, worry lines were obvious on his face, and Rowan couldn't help but feel that he looked tired.

It was also the moment recognition finally sparked within him.

"The mural. The very first mural. You were the one who fought the demon king first," Rowan whispered, awe bleeding into his voice.

If anything, Aristaeus looked even more tired. "Correct. I was there, at the start of the cycle. Rather, I am the beginning of the cycle. Me and that wretch of a delusional demon."

"Explain."

Aristaeus sighed and drove a hand through his hair roughly. "How do you think all this started, Rowan? How do you think the first invasion happened?"

"The demons discovered this world, ripped a path to it, and invaded?" The question was tenuous, almost pleading. Something told Rowan he would really dislike whatever answer he got.

"I'm afraid not. You see, once upon a time, summoning a person, a thinking, reasoning being, from beyond our world was considered impossible. Legendary summoners, arcanists, and magic researchers all tried to do it, and they all failed. Travel between worlds is not a gentle process.

"This persisted, until one Carreen Zola stepped onto the scene. He was a man so beloved by gods that they granted him the ability to wield a secondary class. At the peak of his power, he was both an [Archpriest] and an [Arcanist] of worldwide renown. And then he begged the gods for assistance with the ritual.

"With him performing a ritual and the gods powering and controlling it, they reached out, plucked a soul, and brought it to this world. In doing so, the dimensional veil protecting this world was devastated, a hole was punched right through it. What do you think came through that hole?"

Rowan's voice was a stunned whisper. "The demon king."

Aristaeus scoffed. "A demon whose mind was so twisted it proclaimed itself a king of its kind, sure. And the gods? Well, they weren't exactly expecting such a thing. They'd long withdrawn their direct presence from the world as a way to stop their incessant warring from blighting their reality beyond repair. That left them with only one solution."

"You."

Aristaeus's smile was bitter. "Me. They slapped their blessings on me, wished me luck, and threw me at the demons. In spite of all that followed, even though the greatest mortal civilizations were damaged almost beyond repair, I won. And when I did, I ascended. They didn't expect that, either."

There was still something that bothered Rowan about the story. "If that's true, if they know why and how the demons are invading this world, why haven't they tried to fix it? Why haven't *you*?"

"Me? Because I can't. When I ascended, I made the mistake of putting my trust in the older gods. They claimed that I needed to join them, to isolate myself in a divine kingdom, for the good of all. Then they bound me with all the agreements and accords they themselves were under already."

"They didn't even let you try to fix the problem first?" If there was more than a little disbelief in Rowan's voice, he didn't think he could be blamed for it.

"They didn't because it's not necessary. The dimensional veil is part of every world, and worlds are living, breathing things. It's the same as you suffering a minor cut. It hurts, it bleeds, but it scabs and seals over."

"If that's true, then why is the cycle still happening?" Rowan demanded.

The god shot him a pitying look and shook his head. "Think, Rowan, and then you tell me why."

He went to argue, but the weight of the truth slammed down on his shoulders. "Hero summoning. The demons come back because heroes are still being summoned."

"Correct. It's hard to tell from a mortal point of view, since the temples always send out warnings and oracles ahead of time, but corruptions only ever start to appear *after* the heroes are summoned." Aristaeus's proclamation also added to the weight that was now pressing down on the hero, threatening to drown him.

"But . . . how . . . why . . . They don't want more gods! You said it yourself! Why would they . . . !"

"Because demons and devastation and the appearance of heroes all paint gods in a positive light. They are the protectors, the ones who summon champions who fight in their names, and this drives worship. Demons also drag otherworldly souls into our reality when they invade, and when they are slaughtered, our world is enriched. The world gods are intrinsically linked to, empowering them further."

"It's just a massive farming method, then? Summon heroes, let the demons in, then kick back and harvest the bounty?"

"Yes."

For a long, long while, neither the hero nor the god spoke. Rowan's eyes were fixed blankly on the table, without even the ability to really perceive it anymore. Aristaeus eventually sighed and stood so he could land a hand on the hero's shoulder.

"It's not your fault."

"It kind of feels like it is," Rowan said.

The god smiled wryly, and Rowan saw pure anguish in his eyes. There they were, the very first and last heroes, united in their misery. "I know. I suggest you check out your status, though."

Having no better idea, Rowan did.

**Congratulations!**
**Class evolution requirements met.**
**System evaluation in progress . . .**
**Class generated!**

**[Spear Saint]**
**You are the spear of your people, and you bear their hopes, dreams, and burdens.**
**This class grants you the ability to tap into your spark of divine potential, enhancing every aspect of your being and setting you on the path of apotheosis.**
**Warning: This class will trigger a racial change from [Human] to [Demigod].**

**Additional beneficial effects:**
**An ascendant boost to the effectiveness of all your stats.**

**The ability to feel the devotion of your people and, through their belief, harvest power.**
**All spear-related cards gain an ascendant boost to their effectiveness.**
**As a demigod, your lifespan is limitless.**

**Class penalties:**
**Your name is upon their lips.**
**Attached card: Spear of Devotion (Legendary, Passive)**

**Congratulations!**
**You have earned a portfolio of [Spears]!**
**You have earned a portfolio of [Hope]!**

**[Class] Spear of Devotion (Legendary, Passive)**
**You draw on the devotion of your people so that their faith may empower your blows.**

"A demigod?" Somehow, that was all that Rowan could manage.

The god laughed, and the sound was so full of vindication Rowan shrank in on himself. "Oh, that's perfect. Can you *imagine* what those old idiots are going to think when they find out about your class?"

"That I'm better off dead?"

"That, yes. Oh, I can also picture the terror on their faces." Aristaeus looked wistful as he spoke. "I was hoping for something like this when you picked your last class. It gave you a nice base to build up to demigod status—that and your city. It's going to be tremendously important for you to take full advantage of it."

"Because I can 'harvest power' from 'my people'?" Rowan asked.

"Experience. You can harvest *experience.* Every time they feel grateful, every time they hope or pray for your well-being, you will be able to harvest experience. Emotions are powerful things, Rowan. Now, you can tap into them, too."

"I didn't choose this," the hero protested, because the idea of cultivating devotion as a commodity he could exchange for progress did not appeal to him.

"You didn't. No one gets to choose, not when they become a Legendary or a Divine. This is no longer about picking your path. It's about following who and what your choices forged you into."

Rowan let himself fall until his head hit the smooth wood of the table. He might have protested the morality of treating people like cattle, but he was more than aware of the fact that the comparison wasn't quite fair.

He just had additional incentive to treat them well now.

No, it was the other implication of his new status that worried him far more. His brand-new limitless lifespan. He was immortal.

Olivia wasn't.

As if reading his mind, Aristaeus spoke up again. "You know, you need to pay more attention to your reading comprehension. Your status told you that you can harvest experience from people. No one ever said anything about having to use that experience yourself."

Rowan tilted his head just enough to the side that he could shoot the god a glare. "So, I can share my experience with my party? Get them up to, what, Legendary before they hit the ceiling? Unless my fiancée is going to turn into a demigod, too, I really don't see how this is going to fix any of my new problems."

Aristaeus's smile grew. "I'm afraid not. However, I wouldn't be worried about her if I were you. After all, your beloved *is* an [Alchemist]." Rowan shot up in his seat, a question already on his lips. Before he could speak, however, the god beat him to it. "Well, I'm afraid that's all the time we have. Until we meet again, Rowan."

Rowan cursed, the cackling laughter of a god following him as everything around him dissolved back into the void, and then it rose up to swallow him.

Rowan blinked his eyes, and swayed.

He was already tipping over when his body finally decided to cooperate and his stats kicked in, firming up his footing.

"Stop and answer, you . . . !" Blake's voice rang out, drawing Rowan's attention to the other hero where he stood, spinning on the spot and looking around like a man possessed.

"Blake?" Kayla asked hesitantly, hand to her head as she looked around. "Wait, am I back to the exact moment when the vision started?"

It certainly seemed that way to Rowan. Everyone else was still passed out on the floor, and the body of the so-called demon king was only starting to dissolve and flake away as black-tinged mana.

That realization finally forced Rowan into motion as he raced over to Olivia, tenderly checking her over for any signs of wounds. He let out a long breath of relief when he realized she had none. For all appearances, she'd simply decided to take a nap on the floor.

Scooping her up, he turned to the other two heroes, only to find them studying a massive gate that had materialized on the far wall at some point.

"Why is that back?" Rowan asked as he cautiously walked closer, shifting his hold on Olivia so her head was cradled against his shoulder.

"Probably so the demon king can slip its soul back to where it came from," Kayla groused, glaring ineffectually at the gate. "We can't pass through. I tried."

"Of course you did." Rowan sighed tiredly as he ventured a little closer himself, eyeing the gate.

"No, really. If you try, you'll just get a system message."

"She's right." At the look Rowan sent him, Blake flushed and looked away. "What? I . . . might have wanted to try and make sure that thing couldn't come back."

"And potentially leave everyone who cares about you behind, Blake?" Rowan chided, but his curiosity was piqued.

Slowly, cautiously, and making doubly sure that no part of Olivia could even brush up against the gate, Rowan pushed his left hand forward. It met an invisible shield long before he could even start crossing the gate's threshold.

**ERROR!**<br>**THE GATES OF HELL ARE CLOSED TO YOU.**<br>**APPROACH AS A HUMBLE SUPPLICANT?**<br>**Y/N**

Rowan clicked the "no" button faster than he had ever done anything in his life. The only thing that eclipsed the sense of dread the message inspired was the contemplative look on Kayla's face.

"Kayla, no."

The heroine shot him a smug smile, opened her mouth, then reconsidered. "Okay, fine. I'm not about to say, 'Kayla yes' and then make the worst mistake of my life, but I want you to know it was close and entirely your fault!"

Rowan rolled his eyes and elected to ignore her, turning to watch Blake collect his fiancées instead. The pained expression on the man's face sent Rowan's stomach churning and made him pull Olivia closer against his chest.

That was apparently enough to rouse her from whatever she was experiencing, and Rowan felt a smile of his own growing when she practically blinded him with the grin she gave him. "Morning, love," the adorable alchemist murmured, snaking her arm around his neck and pulling him down for a kiss.

Rowan didn't exactly fight her, and when they finally parted so they could breathe, he gently pressed his forehead against hers. "Are you ready to go home?"

The question left him with all the weight of his exhaustion, the fear that had raged in him, and the anguish at all they'd lost.

Her small smile still made it all worth it. "Yes."

CHAPTER TWENTY-FOUR

# Settling In

When the group of demon-king slayers finally stumbled out of the fortress, they were met with resounding applause, hollers, and congratulations. The army transformed into a roiling mass of faces, all looking to have a moment with the heroes of the hour.

Rowan just felt tired.

Even with their ecstatic mood taken into account, the soldiers looked like a sorry lot. Most were dirty. All had tear tracks running down their faces. They were celebrating like people on death row given one final opportunity to run wild.

In the midst of all that, with the wild difference between their state and their emotions, Rowan found himself numb to all that had happened. His fellow demon-king slayers seemed to share his sentiment.

The brief moment of their own elation over their survival had swiftly given way to profound sorrow when they were forced to clean up the battlefield.

They, and the rest of the army, refused to leave the bodies of their allies to rot in there, but with how thorough the demon king's destruction was, scraping their dead off the floors and walls would be closer in nature to hazmat cleanup than something that could be described as *collecting their remains.*

They ultimately decided not to even make the attempt. Working together, Kayla and Olivia were able to produce a flame that burned so hot it started to warp the ridiculously tough murals of the demonic lair.

By the time they were done, not even ashes were left, and Rowan was struck by a profound sense of loss.

He hadn't known any of the fallen particularly well. However, just the tragedy of Fia and Desmond's young age was enough to weigh down Rowan's conscience. It was funny, in a way, but now that she was gone, he would miss Tamara.

Blake, of course, had it far worse than him. The other hero moved through the crowds blank-faced and completely zoned out, focused only on gripping his two fiancées as close to him as he could. Even the twins were sticking unusually close together, and Rowan noticed the way they would occasionally glance at the other, like they were checking if the other was still there.

The Mercenary King, at least, still had his soldiers. They welcomed him with open arms, and the man was soon contributing to the local noise pollution with the best of them.

That left Kayla as the odd one out.

The heroine swept her eyes over the gathered crowds, evaluated the conduct of her mages, and then found herself standing all alone, with no one to grip close or fuss over.

Food was brought out, emptying almost the entirety of their supplies that were meant to support them on their way back, and the mercenaries managed to offer up a decent stock of spirits. Rowan didn't stop the chaos from spreading, nor did he try to rein the soldiers in.

There was, of course, a secondary reason why the celebration was so awkward for Rowan.

Every time a soldier would approach him to earnestly express their thanks, every time one of them gave a muttered prayer that contained mention of his name, Rowan could feel a trickle of something well up in his soul.

It was just pooling there at the moment, but it practically felt eager to the Stalwart Hero's mystical senses.

He could tell just how easy it would be to use it, to transform it into something else—into *experience.*

It was these odd feelings that drove him to slip out of his and Olivia's bed later that night when everyone else had gone to sleep. With the world eerily quiet, there was no one and nothing stopping Rowan from claiming a seat right next to one of the guttering bonfires that had blazed so brightly such a short time ago.

"Somehow, I thought I'd find you here." Rowan turned his head toward Blake, who stood there, pale and lightly shivering. "Want me to get this thing going again?"

"Nah, I'll be fine," Blake assured him, plopping down right next to Rowan.

"Ugh, boys. I'm not interrupting a touching moment, am I?" Kayla's voice quipped from the other side of Rowan, and then she was sitting next to him, too.

Ruefully, the Stalwart Hero shook his head, then collapsed backward so he could have a proper view of the stunning night sky. With the bonfire all out and not a tree in sight for miles, it was the most enchanting scene Rowan had seen in a while.

"Couldn't sleep, either?" Rowan pointlessly asked, keeping his eyes trained skyward.

"None of us could, apparently. I mean, it's not every day that you come face-to-face with a god who's obligated to answer your questions."

Kayla's comment made Rowan furrow his brow and tilt his head to face her. "Obligated? Honestly, Aristaeus looked downright happy to be having a chat."

"Lucky you. I'm stuck with the goddess of secrets, remember? Pulling those out of her is like pulling teeth. Worse, really. At least force helps there," Kayla grumbled, but Rowan knew she'd likely have it no other way.

"Sarina was . . . Well, it's passed," Blake conceded, and all three friends fell silent.

"Did your gods . . . did they talk about the cycle, at all?" Rowan finally whispered his question, unsure how to broach the subject.

"Of course she did—I made sure to ask about it. Really, I can totally believe that it would be the Divines themselves who kicked off this shit party everyone's had to deal with since. And, of course, they're trying to keep people from ascending by messing with the system."

"Wait, what?" Rowan was sitting up now, alarm obvious on his face.

"What, what? Don't tell me you haven't noticed all the inconsistencies and then asked for clarification?" Kayla taunted with her signature smirk of superiority.

"Kayla, not the time. I want to know about this, too," Blake joined in.

"Traitor," Rowan hissed. "You're implying that she could keep taunting me if you didn't want answers as badly!"

"Do you want me to explain or not?" the heroine snapped, and the two guys finally decided to shut up.

She gave it a few moments longer knowing they were prone to breaking out into bickering quickly, then finally launched into an explanation.

"You know how people say the system constantly grows? That's because it *does*. It's testing things, evolving, checking to see what works. Most changes roll out automatically, but some require direct admin access to confirm. Gods can act as very low-level admins, so they've been vetoing a whole host of upgrades meant to take the system further and make it more convenient."

"Like what?" Rowan demanded, outrage easily slipping into his voice.

"Like the ability to upgrade your Heart Card, or crafter-based tier-progression systems that don't necessitate a world where everyone ventures out of civilization to kill something if they don't have a Heart Card of sufficient quality."

"They're saying no to that? That's just . . . barbaric!" Rowan growled, but he couldn't find it in himself to doubt the claims. Frankly, that sounded exactly like something a bored Divine creature set on keeping their position would do.

"It's something, all right. Just be grateful they can't completely cut off all the ways to progress through tiers and levels, or we'd be in real trouble."

"You know . . . it's kind of ironic, and makes me want to smash my head against the wall, but I really can't blame the king for what he did with all the information laid out like that," Rowan admitted.

"You're kidding, right? Right?" Kayla looked less than amused.

"I mean, if his plan did work, he could have prevented future summons and fixed the problem permanently."

"That's a pretty big if. I'll tell you right now, he couldn't have managed with what the gods do to hero cards so that they're neutered versions of the real thing," Kayla insisted, and Rowan quickly latched on to the subject.

"I'm assuming, then, that you got all the details on the requirements that had to be met in order to unseal our hero cards? And did you meet all of them yourselves?" Rowan asked.

An odd expression swept over Kayla's face before she collected herself and shot Rowan a smirk. "You know, you're asking for a lot right there, asking us to trust you with such personal details like the state of our Heart Card."

Blake rolled his eyes, but Kayla's joking tone prevented any danger of an argument breaking out. "No on the details, but I did get my Heart Card unsealed, too," Blake said.

"Mine's Divine as well, and you two are no fun to tease anymore. Anyway, yes, I got the details from my goddess. Apparently, past the murder of all the demonic leaders, you need to kill one of the legends yourself, to be present when the demon lord dies, and receive the approval of at least three different gods."

Rowan latched on to that last requirement, disbelief coloring his face. "Wait, how did any of us manage to get enough gods to sign off on us unsealing our Heart Cards? Isn't that the sort of thing that they'd work as hard as they could to prevent?"

"I had the same question," Kayla admitted. "Apparently, you're to blame."

"Me?" Rowan almost looked affronted.

"You. Apparently, my goddess absolutely loved it when you managed to somehow provoke citywide panic among people scheming against you and decided to officially endorse you. Without telling anyone, of course. I think she thought no one else would be foolish enough to do it."

"And the last god that had to sign off on me getting a shot at divinity?"

"That would be *his* goddess." Kayla motioned at Blake, who looked more surprised than Rowan. "When you saved his life, she reluctantly did it as a gesture of goodwill toward Aristaeus. She didn't know she'd be the third to do so."

Rowan took a moment to process that before grinning smugly. "Checks out. Divine reluctance to coordinate, right there. Okay, that was me—what about you two?"

"Well, when that happened, all the gods received a notification about it. Then our goddesses got upset and leaned on Aristaeus to reciprocate. Once he did, it was simple for the two to find a subordinate god of theirs to approve of their chosen."

"So . . . we're in the position to possibly ascend, just because the gods decided to get prissy that their own toy wasn't as successful as the others?" Blake sounded so done with gods that Rowan felt immense satisfaction.

It wasn't all that long ago that his best friend was the perfect picture of devotion. No matter what the future held for them, Rowan would never regret handing off that mental defense card to Blake.

"Pretty much, yes," Kayla confirmed, and all three of them fell into a comfortable silence.

Their stories weren't done. There would be much to do. Much to plan around, and even scheme, to protect the people they cared about or pursue personal ambitions. The chances of them clashing in the future were also nonnegligible.

In spite of all that, in that moment, they were almost better off than before their summoning. The dysfunctional, broken pieces of their friendship had been dragged to the surface and at least somewhat resolved.

And they could still call each other friend.

"I want a promise from both of you," Rowan suddenly declared, keeping his eyes fixed on the stars. "No matter what happens, no matter what we become, let's at least *try* to avoid becoming enemies and killing each other. I promise, here and now, that unless you directly threaten the people I love, I'll . . . well, not necessarily support you, but I'll be your friend."

Rowan appreciated the fact that neither of them rushed to agree. He could tell they were seriously considering his request, and all the implications it had.

"I promise." Blake was the first to make the declaration, voice solemn.

Kayla took a bit longer, expression shifting between emotions too complex to easily name, but she eventually sighed and nodded her head. "Fine. I promise, too. Really, how hard can it be for us to avoid killing each other?"

"Pretty hard, I'll reckon," Rowan said with a grin. "Thank you, though. Funny how things worked out. If you asked me when we first got here, I'd have thought we'd all jump at the chance to go back home."

Nobody said anything in response to that, and their thoughtful faces didn't give away much about how they were feeling. Still, when he stood up and went to rejoin Olivia in their bed, Rowan was content with the way things had turned out.

The next morning, Rowan woke up early and found himself in the unenviable position of forcing his army back into action thanks to the bleak realities of their situation. For one, the remnants of a battlefield that had claimed upward of six hundred lives didn't make for a very good place to rest.

The soldiers had done their best to retrieve bodies and sort out the belongings of the dead while the hero parties sought access to the inner reaches of the fortress and fought the last two demonic leaders, but that still left plenty to be done.

In the end, they resorted to a similar way of honoring the dead to what the heroes had employed. Massive pyres were constructed, and the air was thick with the nauseating smell of cooking meat before Kayla took pity on everyone and cast some sort of spell to protect their noses.

The heroine slipped away shortly after, without a word of parting.

Kayla didn't hate the other heroes. In fact, the disdain she'd started to nurture toward them had been broken down, and last night had cleared the air between them fully.

Still, it was a basic fact of reality that she wouldn't be able to spend much time with them, be it now or in the future.

Her troops were at least not too badly damaged, with only a quarter of their number falling in combat. This meant that most of her long-term plans were still intact, and her eyes narrowed dangerously as she guided the mages toward the Cartian kingdom.

Blake wasn't in as much of a hurry to leave, and surprisingly, his two noble ladies didn't press for it, either. This time, none of Rowan's party members protested their presence.

In Olivia's own words, "I've kind of grown fond of them. Yes, even the Treagon."

Rowan supposed that there was definitely some truth in that you couldn't risk your life alongside someone without growing to respect them at least little.

When all the work was done and it was finally time to set out, Rowan found himself standing in front of his troops one more time. His eyes scanned their faces, the odd duality of happiness and grief shining through.

One thing united them all: They were ready to go back home.

"I know how difficult what I asked of you was. We ventured here, with no support from the wider kingdom, with a fraction of the numbers we should have had. In spite of that, even with the king himself trying to stop us, we've prevailed.

"The demons are routed, their leaders dead, and our lands safe! Their corruption wanes as we speak, and the land they tainted can now be cleansed. I promise you, one and all, that is what we shall do. Rest's Remorse will recover, and then it will *grow.*

"No matter what the future has in store for us, you and yours will never find yourself wanting for anything again. You have my promise as your lord and as the man who fought alongside you."

Rowan bowed, and the cheers he was met with were deafening.

He meant every word.

Maybe he couldn't ensure universal peace. The kingdom was likely in chaos at that very moment with the king missing. But he would do everything he possibly could to prevent his people from getting swept up in it all.

Rest's Remorse was already out on the frontier. It wasn't a place any kingdom would be in a hurry to claim, not with the demons slain and their corruption no longer driving the levels of monsters ever higher.

Likewise, Olivia had assured him that her alchemy would let her perform minor miracles when it came to cleansing and enriching the land around their city. For the first time in countless generations, industry and agriculture would witness a resurgence in the area.

Hopefully, that would give all of Rowan's citizens stable livelihoods and employment. Still, that was something for the future.

For the time, they focused on a mad rush home. No one wanted to spend any additional time out on the frontier, and the Mercenary King put his all into getting them back as quickly as possible.

They still saw combat.

The source of demonic corruption might have been destroyed, but the many creatures already affected by it weren't. Some ran when confronted by the overwhelming number of humans marching past their territory, but just as many challenged them freely.

Some of these remnants were actually powerful enough to reach the Epic tier.

Those Rowan enthusiastically hunted down himself. He didn't need the experience anymore, but he wanted his party to be as high a level as he could help them get to, and Epics would likely become harder to come by in the future.

Of course, the steady buildup of power in his chest brought on by his new class was reassuring on that front, even if he still needed to experiment with it.

Monsters or not, they were still traveling faster than when making their push into the wastes. They didn't need to worry about preserving their strength or ambushes by the Legendary demons. All in all, it took a mere five days to make their way from the core of the wastes back to Rest's Remorse.

The first sight of the city was a balm on Rowan's soul. There was no hostile army surrounding it, and no monsters anywhere in sight. The city walls, now completely rebuilt, towered higher than ever and practically gleamed in the light of day.

Banners were hung from the same walls, and wreaths of flowers decorated them. There was a festive atmosphere to the city, and they hadn't even stepped foot inside yet.

They were spotted well before they reached the gates by guards patrolling the battlements. This meant that, by the time they were walking past the entrance to Rowan's city, people were already lining the streets.

Rowan doubted that the whole thing was spontaneous, but the true hero's welcome they received, complete with flower petals raining down on them and people cheering their names, was touching.

More than a few soldiers broke down crying, or even broke ranks to clasp their arms possessively around their loved ones.

Rowan didn't mind.

In fact, he immediately proclaimed that while those who wanted to accompany them all the way to the mayor's manor were free to do so, the soldiers were officially free to reunite with their families. He felt more than a little honored when the vast majority of the army chose to stay.

They found Kayden and Camilla, along with the manor's staff, waiting for them in front of the building. The baroness did not wait for them to close the distance, instead surging forward to envelop her daughter in a hug. Rowan was touched when she dragged him into the same hug a moment later, gripping them both like she was afraid they would vanish.

"With everything we heard . . . and what was happening . . . Welcome home, both of you. Welcome home," Camilla whispered tearfully, only holding them tighter.

Rowan missed the wistful way Blake was watching the interaction, but the hero's fiancées didn't. He got plenty of hugs himself, even as they were practically dragged into the house. Kayden watched them go with a smile and a brief hug, staying behind to declare to the army that they were free and to invite them to a feast prepared in their honor.

As the cheering soldiers headed off to the training grounds where tables were being dragged out, the baron's family congregated in the dining room, where a feast of their own waited. Blake, too, was invited to the more private setting, provoking embarrassed mutters of thanks, especially when the baroness hugged him, too, and thanked him for helping protect her family.

No one spoke while they ate. The food, after all the travel rations, the fighting, and the stress that was finally draining out of their bodies, tasted divine. When they were finally done, however, Rowan couldn't put off his questions anymore.

He opened his mouth, but a thousand different things to ask surged up, and he could only settle on "What happened?"

The baron sighed and leaned back in his chair, but his expression was more wistful than upset. "Shortly after the first announcement of a Legendary demon falling, we got news that an army was laying siege to all the border fortresses between our territory and the rest of the kingdom. One army even ventured deep into our lands, laying siege on our home itself. When they found out we weren't there, they sent out a messenger demanding our immediate return and surrender."

"They didn't push all the way out to Rest's Remorse itself?"

"No." The baroness seemed amused by the suggestion. "The king certainly has plenty of soldiers under his command. However, trying something like *that* would still stretch his armies thin. No, they just sat there and pressured us to comply."

"It was looking like we might just have to do that, too. Especially when a messenger came, declaring that if we did, our daughter would be spared when the heroes were executed for their rebellion against the kingdom." The baron's voice was incredibly bitter.

The news made both Rowan and Blake bristle. The only thing that prevented a more visceral reaction was the fact that the problem was already dealt with.

"They're not laying siege on your lands anymore, right?" Rowan hurried to ask, wondering if the kingdom had any clue about the death of their monarch.

"No, they're not. That was brought to a swift conclusion when the death of the king came out," the baron confessed, making Rowan frown and shoot the princess a questioning look.

The woman looked confused, but then blushed as a look of realization crossed her face. "I'm sorry, I forgot you wouldn't know. When a king or other important officials are instated, they link to special artifacts. When they die, those artifacts immediately send out an alert to the linked watcher on duty."

"So, people knew about it the second we killed the king?" Rowan's words made the baron give him a startled look, and the baroness smile smugly.

"I did tell you it was them," the woman declared, looking pleased.

Her husband looked conflicted. "I don't know how you managed that, but . . . I'm just happy you survived." There was plenty he wasn't saying, and Rowan could see that.

Then again, the hero had heard plenty about what the relationship between the king and the baron used to be like before it soured. In a way, Rowan imagined that it would be like him hearing about Blake's demise.

"For what it's worth, I'm sorry it had to come to that," Rowan offered.

"No, no, he . . . he wanted to protect our kingdom, but the way he decided to do it . . ."

"Um, on the subject, what *is* happening in the capital? If you happen to know?" It was the princess who asked the question, and though she tried to look relaxed, the anxiety in her voice was impossible to miss.

"It's not good, I'm afraid," the baroness confessed, giving the woman a look of pity. "Your brother and sister have erupted into all-out hostilities. The crown prince is the designated heir, but no one knows what happened to the king's Heart Card, and the elder princess has supporters of her own."

"I . . . see." Blake's princess looked anything but pleased.

Rowan didn't know whether the princess harbored a desire to claim the throne for herself, but the trio would have their work cut out for them. After all, Blake had outright expressed their intentions to return to the capital posthaste. It was all Rowan could do to convince them to rest for a day.

Blake's party excused themselves shortly after, leaving the baron's family alone. It was with a small, happy smile that Rowan reflected on the fact that he was part of that family now.

"Your friends will be heading off to the capital, won't they?" the baroness asked, clearly picking up on the trio's tension. "Will you be heading out with them?"

"No." And Rowan meant it, too. He wasn't going to abandon Blake entirely, but he was neither willing to immediately jump into another conflict nor happy about all the potential politicking.

"What, then, will you two be getting up to?"

"Well . . ." Olivia drawled as she laid her head against Rowan's shoulder. "With the kingdom in chaos, it will take a while for anyone to come bother us, unless we get involved voluntarily. And, well, I've always wanted at least three children. We do need to get started on those."

Rowan flushed scarlet, much to the amusement of his in-laws. Olivia did drive a very good point home, though.

For the first time since his arrival in his world, there was nothing truly hanging over the hero's head. No quest to save the world. No ticking timer that was pushing him onward before the demon lord could grow beyond any mortal's ability to handle.

He had the time to enjoy his new life, and to properly settle in.

He wasn't going to waste it.

# Side Story

## The First Hero Summoner

It had long been theorized by [Scholars] that there are infinite parallel universes and realities. Those theories eventually led to the development of the summoning rituals, with [Scholar] Vindictis Estarial discovering the formula of the **Spirit Summoning**, otherwise known as the **Familiar Contract**.

Ever since then, the question of whether other humanoids could also become the targets of summonings has been explored from many angles without any progress, thus being mostly ignored and treated as little more than a passing curiosity. That was, until the blessed dual-class [Arcanist/Archpriest][1] Carreen Zola tried a completely different and new approach.

He theorized that mana had inherent tiers of power defined by its concentration and an additional undefined element. The example he brought forward was the rarity tiers in the cards, and especially the Heart Cards everyone received upon reaching the age of majority.[2] He explained that what the system called "rarity" was, in fact, more than just an indicator of how difficult it was to acquire one. It was also a descriptor of the type of

[1] While dual classes are rare, they are not unheard-of. The system and the gods reward effort and faith, respectively. If one manages to prove themselves with noteworthy achievements to their name, the system will eventually grant them a powerful boon that is aligned with their desires. For a full list of all known system boons, please reference *A History of the System* (203 PD), by [Historian] Orpha Zolla. Divine boons are granted in the forms of blessings to the ones favored by the gods. Due to it being costly to do, they are only usually provided to exceptional believers or the [Archpriest] of their pantheon. With some variations, they seem to mostly be a mirror of system-granted boons, albeit touched with the "flavor" of the deity or pantheon that granted them. For more information, please refer to *The Gods and Their Miracles* (46 PD), by [Bishop] Inga Orpheus.

[2] The age of majority as defined by the system is fourteen cycles by the Taylan calendar.[6]

mana those cards used and were made of. Other [Scholars], while initially opposed to the idea, could not counterargue that the mana fluctuations upon the formations of cards or Heart Cards varied by tier and even color, with the following reference table being created:

**Rarity—Color**

- Common → White
- Uncommon → Green
- Rare → Azure
- Epic → Magenta
- Legendary → Orange (the color of divine mana)

For about two decades, this was the agreed-upon system, although Carreen Zola still felt that there was something missing. He had witnessed a blessing once in his youth and knew that the color of Divine mana was not the same as that of Legendary cards, as much as kings and other Legendary card holders disagreed. Due to endangering the monarch's claims of demigodhood, he ended up being chased from the kingdom he resided in, eventually finding shelter in the Church of Sarina and the Pantheon of the Effervescent Sun.[3]

Even though Zola changed his class to [Deacon], he didn't stop researching the nature of mana and trying to create a summoning ritual for intelligent life. As he made more and more discoveries in the field of mana, the higher-stationed clergy started taking note of him, with even one of the Seven showing passing interest in his work. Eventually, his work[4] earned him the Legendary version of the class card [Arcanist], it being one of the few documented examples of the world bestowing Legendary cards outside of combat.

---

[3] The Pantheon of the Effervescent Sun is composed of seven high gods and dozens of lower gods. The Seven are: 1) Sarina, Goddess of the Everlasting Light, 2) Petrut, God of Unwavering Strength, 3) Lindiwe, Goddess of Love and Beauty, 4) Issac, God of the Sun, 5) Ta'oma, God of Death, 6) Ivka, Goddess of Victory, and 7) Nestori, God of the Hearth. The full descriptions of each god as well as a list and descriptions of all the lower gods can be found in *The Gods and Their Miracles* (46 PD), by [Bishop] Inga Orpheus.

[4] The full list of Carreen Zola's discoveries and accomplishments can be found on page 300 of this book, or in the appendix under the chapter titled "Discoveries and Research (Parts 1–7)". Additional information can be found in the book *The Life and Works of Carreen Zola* (168 PD), by [Historian] Elisabet Aistulf.

During that time, he had already advanced his class and station to [Bishop] and chose to continue pursuing his existing class instead of performing the class-change ceremony and leaving the church. Impressed by his dedication to his gods and religion, the gods eventually chose him as their [Archpriest] at the age of sixty-seven and bestowed upon him the [Blessing of the Second Class], one of the rarer and more expensive gifts they could give. Of note here is that he requested the gods grant him the boon while he stood in a measuring and recording array.

He then used that data to not only disprove the then-prevalent notions that Legendary mana was Divine mana, but also added a new color to the existing table, thus resulting in the following:

**Rarity—Color**

- Common → White
- Uncommon → Green
- Rare → Azure
- Epic → Magenta
- Legendary → Orange
- Divine → Gold

In notes he never published but that were found locked in a hidden safe decades after his time had passed, he noted that divinity itself just seemed to be a tier of mana, instead of some unreachable concept, and that, in theory, if one managed to level and tier up their cards enough to reach the peak of Legendary tier, they would only need a Divine catalyst in order to condense their own divinity and domain—a catalyst that existed in every Divine being, and later was also found to exist within summoned heroes under certain conditions and power level.[5] But this is the topic of a different book.

Continuing from his ascension to the seat of power of the Pantheon of Seven, [Archpriest] Zola turned to the gods for help with the last phase of

[5] Information on the history of the discovery of Divine catalysts within the bodies of heroes, and the subsequent Great Cataclysm, can be found in *The Sins of Esteria's People* by [Divine Inquisitor] Alphius Yudes.

[6] The Taylan calendar was named after its creator, the [Astrologist] Alexis Taylan, who spent most of his life looking at the night sky and the celestial cycles. According to it, a cycle is three hundred days, divided into ten groupings of thirty days. A season spans roughly a third of a cycle, for a total of three seasons. Most of the world has adopted a similar calendar system, if by different names in some regions.

his experiment. His previous attempts to form a stable, if one-way, passage between worlds using Legendary mana had not been a full failure, but their results were gory and left the subjects of such transportation unable to stay in the world of the living. He had experimented with fishing for and transporting just the soul, but even then, Legendary mana created a tunnel that was too unstable and shredded the soul whole. By the time the soul reached the summoner, all that was left of a person was a word, or maybe if they were lucky, an image.

Zola assumed that he needed a higher tier of mana and control in order to properly stabilize the dimensional tunnel and bring through the unharmed souls of recently deceased individuals. He prayed to the goddess Sarina, asking for her to possess him and to try and complete the ritual together. This was the date of the first success, and the arrival of the first otherworlder on Esteria.

It was also the date of the arrival of the first demon king through the weakened veil of our world.

# About the Author

A. T. Valentine is the author of the Legend of the Spear Saint series, originally released on Royal Road. He strives to write the best possible books across a variety of genres. Valentine resides in Potomac, Maryland.

www.ingramcontent.com/pod-product-compliance
Lightning Source LLC
LaVergne TN
LVHW091254150826
845673LV00006B/1417
*9798895393994*